UNTETHERED

Also by KayLynn Flanders

Shielded

UNTETHERED

KayLynn Flanders

DELACORTE PRESS

Text copyright © 2021 by KayLynn Flanders
Jacket art copyright © 2021 by Alex Dos Diaz

All rights reserved. Published in the United States by Delacorte Press, an imprint of Random House Children's Books, a division of Penguin Random House LLC, New York.

Delacorte Press is a registered trademark and the colophon is a trademark of Penguin Random House LLC.

Visit us on the Web! GetUnderlined.com

Educators and librarians, for a variety of teaching tools, visit us at RHTeachersLibrarians.com

Library of Congress Cataloging-in-Publication Data is available upon request.
ISBN 978-0-593-11857-3 (trade) — ISBN 978-0-593-11858-0 (lib. bdg.) — ISBN 978-0-593-11859-7 (ebook)

The text of this book is set in 11-point Sabon MT Pro.
Interior design by Cathy Bobak

Printed in the United States of America
10 9 8 7 6 5 4 3 2 1
First Edition

To my children:
You make the world brighter.

✦ ✦ ✦

CHAPTER ONE

Ren

The flowers on my father's tomb had withered and died two months ago. And though it was my duty to replace the flowers, to remember my father's life, those dried husks remained.

The white entrance to the castle's crypt arched over my head, beckoning me in as it did at least once a day since I returned to Hálendi.

I clenched a cluster of the season's last blooms in my fist, their fragile stems already broken.

This was my duty. Whether or not I accepted my father's death, or wished I'd never left for North Watch to protect the border, or taken the Medallion from him when he'd offered it, this was my duty. To care for his tomb. To honor his life.

Black ash stained the stone walls above the dimly lit sconces on either side of the archway—the perpetual flames standing guard to the tombs of the kings. They'd started carving my section of the crypt the day after my coronation.

Down here, the crash of light and sound from the dining hall were a distant memory, though my stomach still swirled with cider. After a full month of parties and dinners to celebrate the commencement of my reign—festivities the kingdom couldn't really afford—one would think I knew my limits. Yet here I stood, swaying.

I took a few deep breaths, hoping the cool air would clear my head. The Medallion rested against my chest, right over my heart. It had warmed during dinner, a tingling sense of foreboding that was gone before dessert had been served.

The Medallion had been like that ever since I'd left Turia. Warm, then cool. Warning, then nothing. It had been nudging me for the past two weeks, but toward what, I couldn't decipher. It was a key to the Black Library, but my father hadn't told me about that. He'd said the Medallion would guide me, help me detect deceit. He was supposed to teach me more, but . . . we'd run out of time. The last advice he'd given me was to trust it. But how could I if I didn't understand it?

My stomach lurched again, like it couldn't decide if it should eject its contents. The Medallion warmed again. If it was *poison* coursing through my system and not cider, deep breathing wouldn't exactly help. But my magic would protect me.

It was time to pay my respects.

Orange petals shook to the perpetually cold ground, and a puff of breath escaped as I relaxed my grip on the flowers and stepped into the crypt.

I'd slipped away from my ever-vigilant guard and left the party because I couldn't pretend to laugh and charm anymore. I was too tired to carry my father's kingdom tonight.

The rough ceiling arched from one stone column to the next, and with each step I took past the kings of old, their stone coffins tucked away in the shadows, the columns trapped more light behind me until everything was more shadow than flame.

My parents lay side by side now, and would evermore. Both entombed in coffins of the whitest stone, casting an unearthly glow in the dim, wavering light.

The little stool I'd hidden behind my mother's tomb fourteen years ago remained untouched in its alcove. The jumble of emotions inside me pushed for release, but I couldn't sit and chat. Not tonight.

Although I'd been training to become king my whole life, I couldn't seem to manage anything. I'd thought it would be easy to step into my father's role and lead our people. But his assassination and Leland's betrayal had left the council in shambles. Leland's war with Turia fractured the peaceful relations we'd maintained with them for centuries. We'd signed treaties, but the damage would take much longer to heal.

Jenna had had to remain in Turia—her wedding to Enzo a promise of peace. I clutched the poor flowers tighter. She could handle herself there, but I wished she were here next to me. Wished my sister could help me with *this* burden.

Two months since burying Father. One since my coronation. Yet nothing was secure—not the council, not the kingdom. My stomach heaved. Not even my own castle, apparently.

I stood silently in front of my parents' tombs. I couldn't ask *why* or *how* or what to do next. Not again. Not when the answer was unending silence.

While I had brought countless bundles of flowers to the crypt, I hadn't laid a single petal of my own on his tomb. It had been two months of unanswered questions and broken flowers tossed away.

Tonight, instead of pleading for guidance, my gaze slid from my father's tomb to my mother's. She used to ruffle my hair whenever I'd run by her, and I still remembered the bright sound of her laugh. If I'd been there when she passed, she wouldn't—

Gravel crunched behind me. One step, then two.

The fresh air hadn't cleared my head as well as I'd thought, because as I spun, I didn't quite dodge the knife slashing toward me. It tore through my dress jacket and tunic, then through my skin.

I slammed my forearm into my assailant's arm as a burning trail blossomed across my stomach. Someone else reached around my neck from behind, choking my airway. I leaned back into him and brought both legs up, kicking the knifer as hard as I could in the chest. He grunted and rolled away. My lungs screamed for air.

I tucked my leg up and slipped a knife out of my boot, then jammed it into the thigh of whoever had been stupid enough to attack me in the land of the dead.

This was the closest I'd ever be to my parents now, and at least here, in this place, I wouldn't let them down.

The arm around my neck fell away. I yanked my dagger from his thigh, then forced my elbow into his gut. I had time for one gulping breath before the knifer's blade slashed at me again. I jumped back, tripping over the man who'd tried to choke me. My backside hit unyielding stone and a spasm shot up my spine. I rolled to my feet and deflected his next attack, slicing my blade through his forearm, then shoving my elbow into his face. He spun into a kick. But my knife was there first, slashing through his calf muscle before he could connect.

He fell to the ground, his scream rattling in my aching head. I kicked his weapon, and it spun into the shadows. My chest heaved and dark splatters of blood marred my once-fine jacket. Both attackers wore the gray uniform of the king's guards—*my* guards.

I pressed my hand against my sputtering heart—the Medallion had fallen out from its hiding spot. I tucked it back under my tunic, hoping neither of my attackers had seen it.

"Arrest him!" a high-pitched voice yelled, adding to the banging in my head.

Lady Isarr stood under the crypt's arch, one long fingernail pointed directly at me. A whole troop of people crowded around her, pushing their way in, with gasps from the wide-eyed courtiers, shock and anger from the guards she'd conveniently brought along.

Well, this complicated things a bit. My opposition was moving openly.

"Do not screech at your king, Lady Isarr. My head is already pounding, and I need to think," I said, rubbing my temple.

"What have you done, Your Majesty?" Isarr breathed out, oil dripping from her words like I'd never heard before. "You've murdered them!" she accused, spreading her arms to indicate the two groaning men sprawled at my feet. The men who clearly weren't dead. But who'd clearly wanted *me* dead.

The Medallion warmed against my chest, but I didn't need its help to sense her lie.

My dagger hung limp at my side, dripping blood into the cracks in the stone. The guards Isarr had brought in her entourage rushed to their fallen comrades.

"May I ask, Lady Isarr, why you and your associates are visiting the crypt at this hour?" I asked as I wiped my blade on my trousers. I'd known most of these people my entire life, yet they would charge me with murder?

Her hand flew to her chest. "We heard yelling and came at once!"

My eyebrows shot up and I stared down her entourage. "You heard yelling through all this rock?" I shook my head. "Try again."

Some in the crowd shifted. Others watched Isarr, to see how she would respond. The man on her immediate left and the woman on her right—her best friend and her known lover—didn't flinch. Loyal to Isarr, then.

She'd been relentless at the dinner parties over the course of the month, always pursuing me, always on the hunt. I thought I'd known her, her type. A harmless title chaser. Yet something in her countenance had changed. As though a mask I hadn't known she was wearing had fallen off. The worst part wasn't seeing her true nature. It was that I hadn't realized she'd been wearing a mask in the first place.

I studied her and those she'd surrounded herself with. Pieces clicked into place—snippets of conversations I'd overheard in the halls, looks, messages. She'd done well, filling her witness pool with some who were loyal to me, as well as those who would support her.

Isarr tilted her chin, looking down her long nose at me. "You *killed* those men," she said, her words snaking toward me.

I nudged the guards surrounding the man who'd tried to choke me to the side and slowly knelt, one knee digging into the unforgiving rock. A tremor racked my hand as I covered his wound, which bled more than it should have. "Not yet, I haven't."

A wave of unease moved through the crowd. There— a darted glance, shuffling feet. More were involved than just Isarr. But how many? I didn't sheath my knife.

"Your Majesty," one guard started, leaning toward me like he thought I would hurt the injured man. Well, hurt him more than the knife I'd stuck in his thigh.

"If you want him to live, stand back," I snapped.

The guard swallowed, but retreated. I turned my focus inward, on the man's wound. My skin prickled at the risk of diverting all my attention into the healing magic that flowed from my hands. But I needed him alive—for questioning, and to prove my innocence. And because Hálendi didn't need more death.

My surroundings faded to a dull murmur. My focus narrowed to his skin knitting together, the veins reconnecting. Energy flowed out of me and into this man who'd tried to take my life.

My vision spun as I pulled my hand away, and the watchful crowd came back into my peripheral vision. I pushed against my knee, forcing myself to stand tall, shoulders back.

Another guard, a silver knot on his uniform, inspected the other would-be assassin, who lay on the ground, still groaning, clutching his calf as others tried to wrap it. Isarr had brought a captain. One recently instated since I'd had to clean out the ranks loyal to General Leland. He shifted his feet, his eyes darting everywhere, one hand on the hilt of his sword. "Sire, according to law—"

"Am I not allowed to defend myself from assassins?" I cut in before he could commit treason and accuse me of murder. I'd give him *one* chance to show his loyalty.

The captain swallowed so hard I could see the bob in his neck. Hesitant. Not part of the plot, then.

Isarr clucked her tongue. "But how to prove it was defense? They are wearing *your* uniform, Your Majesty. Why would your own guards attack you?" She smiled as though she'd proved her point.

And she had, in a way. Proved that the list of those I could trust had dwindled far indeed. Ever since my closest friend, Cris, had drawn his sword and attacked me in the tent on the Turian front line, my friends and allies had fallen away in betrayal one by one. My stomach clenched and swirled until I thought I'd be sick. Who would be next?

They wanted proof of self-defense? Fine. I gritted my teeth and unbuttoned my dress jacket, then hooked a finger under my blood-soaked tunic, lifting it slowly. A red slash—not deep anymore, but long—slanted along my stomach from ribs to hip. Blood still dripped from it onto my trousers.

Gasps rang out so loud that the urge to laugh bubbled up. Everyone already thought me a murderer, though; I wouldn't add *crazy* to the list. I wished again that Jenna were here—not only did I need her support, I desperately wanted someone to laugh with. To talk to. One single person I could trust not to shove a knife in my back. Or stomach, as the case may be.

"As I said, am I not allowed to defend myself? Now, what is your excuse for interrupting my mourning?"

Isarr's reaction was slight: a lift of her chin, flashing eyes that had once lured me into a dark hallway for a kiss.

I kept my growl back, but only just. "Unless, perhaps, you orchestrated the assassination attempt? And conveniently brought your *friends* as witnesses?"

The courtiers behind her began to whisper, and more than a few stepped back, no doubt remembering in a new light whatever Isarr and her companions had said to lure them here. Distancing themselves from the guilty.

Isarr's narrowed gaze focused on the man clutching his calf. "If either of them die," she said, nodding to the attackers still on the ground, "you'll have to stand trial before the council." Her lips pulled up into the barest hint of triumph.

I smirked, and though it wasn't wise to taunt her, I couldn't help it. "Haven't you heard, or did you just forget, Isarr," I said, intentionally leaving off her title, "I'm a *healer*."

My cursed hands wouldn't stop shaking as I brushed my fingers over the assassin's calf. His cries immediately quieted even as my reserve drained. I lifted his trouser, and instead of a knife wound, there was only a line of pink skin. He could keep the cut on his forearm.

Silence dropped heavy over us, weighing as much as the castle over our heads.

The courtiers and guards bragged of Hálendi's magic. I wore the white streak in my hair prominently. But *seeing* magic was another matter altogether. And now that I'd revealed how strong my magic actually was—beyond healing a scrape or an illness—the next assassin would no doubt account for it.

Glaciers, I was an ice-headed idiot. I could blame it on whatever my cider had been tainted with, but I was also tired. Tired of secrets and betrayal and deception. And I wanted these men to spill the names of every courtier who'd funded this little endeavor.

"I wonder what sort of tales they have to tell the council," I said, tilting my head and pushing up to stand, my hands covered in blood, red and brown smears that would take ages to scrub away. "You want to accuse me of anything?" I asked the guard who had knifed me. He shook his head so hard his hair fell into his face, but he never took his eyes off his newly healed leg.

I turned to the captain. "I trust you can handle arresting these men, Isarr, and"—I pointed to the man and woman at her side—"those two?"

He nodded once, touching his fist to his shoulder.

No one said anything as the guards took hold of Isarr and her friends. Her simpering, lust-filled facade was completely gone now. Only rage remained. Rage that she'd been caught.

How many more in the castle watched and waited for their chance to dethrone me? How many more would bow to me as their king, only to light my boots on fire?

Guards moved to lift the assassins into the hall, and courtiers moved to get a closer look at their healed wounds. So many people. Shuffling feet and crunching gravel and whispers.

I wiped my forehead with my mostly clean sleeve and jerked my arm back to my side. "And, Captain, get everyone out of here!" I said, my voice rising to a shout at the end. Another wave of dizziness passed over me. "This is a crypt, not a gallery!"

My parents' tombs rested still and ever silent behind me. Watching all of it. Everything. All around me, broken stems and mangled orange petals lay scattered and crushed into the dusty floor.

Space. I needed space.

Bodies pressed against me as I pushed toward the exit. Dresses and shoulders too close. And *why* in all the glaciers was it so blasted warm down here?

My guard, Kaldur, pushed his way against the crowd.

I blinked and his hand gripped my elbow. "Your Majesty?"

I'd snuck away because I didn't need protection. And I didn't—I needed a witness. But if I ever wanted to keep the sliver of freedom I still had, he couldn't see my trembling hands.

"Kaldur, it's barely fall," I said, my lips twisted into some semblance of a smile as my stomach heaved and swirled. "Tell the castle steward we don't need fireplaces lit at dinner just yet. I've been abominably warm all evening."

Kaldur clenched his jaw and took several calming breaths before answering. "Sire, you really should allow me to accompany you when you decide to visit the crypt."

I didn't have a witty response to that, because he was right. I should have. I thought I'd be safe here, that the hallowed ground would be respected. But just like so many other things, other people, I was wrong.

I allowed Kaldur to escort me back to my chambers, more

to assuage his fears than mine. My enemies would regroup after tonight. I cursed myself again for showing my hand.

Kaldur checked everywhere, even behind the long blue drapes and under my bed, before taking position beside my door.

"You are not standing there all night," I said with a frown.

He straightened. "Yes, I am."

My chest tightened and my breaths came faster. *Wait, hold it in a bit longer.*

I stalked over to him. "No, you're not." I took his arm and shoved him out the door, then locked it behind him. He took up position outside, grumbling curses I couldn't decipher.

I rested my back against the door. Kaldur could grumble all he wanted, but he wasn't staying in here while I was asleep. No one was.

For good measure, I slid a side table in front of the door and perched a vase on its edge. A warning before the next knife came for me.

They'd been so close. Had I turned a half second later . . .

My stomach squeezed. I stumbled to my bathing chamber and retched into an empty bucket. I wiped my mouth on my sleeve and braced my hands on the edge of the bucket. The servants would have to remove the mess tomorrow—no one was coming into this room tonight.

There had definitely been something in my cider. But the question remained: Was it part of Isarr's play against me? Or were others plotting to kill me?

I left the foul-smelling bathing chamber, yanked off my dress jacket, and fell into the chair next to the empty fireplace. The jacket had been embroidered with painstaking detail, and the buttons carefully sewn in two neat rows down the front. Now it was torn and smeared with blood and dust, with three buttons missing. I tossed it in the corner, then used an almost-clean patch of my tunic to wipe away the red caked on my torso, then tossed it as well. The last of the skin on my stomach knit together as I watched, leaving only a tiny pale scar.

I traced my finger along it, hating and loving my magic. My body healed itself without a thought, yet two people I loved dearly lay in the crypt beneath my feet. My magic hadn't prevented my best friend from betraying me. I shoved away any thought of Cris, lacing my fingers together until they stopped shaking.

I tilted my head back against the chair, exhaustion from healing the two men and myself finally claiming me.

A searing heat flashed against my chest, hotter than I'd ever felt. I snatched the Medallion away from my skin, expecting to see a brand mark where it had rested. But my skin remained unmarred. I ran my finger over the tiny notches and bumps on the Medallion's back, over the intricate runes carved into its front.

Had my father known a mage was coming after him? Coming after the key to the Black Library? Is that why he'd given me the Medallion before I'd left for North Watch?

Foreboding trickled along my skin. The Medallion remained hot.

"Oh, sure, *now* you warn me," I muttered into the empty room.

CHAPTER TWO

Chiara

I shook out one of my nicest dresses—nice enough to wear to a Riigan royal wedding—and lined up the embroidered seams so it wouldn't wrinkle in my trunk alongside the rest of the clothes I'd need while away for the four weeks leading to the nuptials.

I didn't want to go to Riiga. The only two Riigans I'd been personally acquainted with had both attacked me, so I wasn't eager to surround myself with potential enemies. But going anywhere was an improvement on being kept within the palace for another month. These walls had ghosts now. Enough memories to keep me out of my favorite garden, and to make me take the long way to my room.

The truth was, the entire palace had been drowning in silence ever since Ren returned to his kingdom three months ago.

It might have been the strain between the nobility and council after Lord Hallen's betrayal, when Jenna discovered he'd been working with the mages. Or the fathers, brothers, and sons we lost to Hálendi's soldiers and traitorous general. Even Riiga remained a looming threat after its ambassador, Koranth, had taken the palace hostage and then disappeared with a black shade blade.

Ren had done his duty—he'd found his sister and stopped the war between our kingdom and his. He'd even stayed two extra weeks in Turia, but his return to Hálendi had been inevitable.

Now, tensions simmered in every corner, waiting to boil over. Would the mages attack again? Would Hálendi's council abide by the treaty?

So while maybe it wasn't Ren's absence in particular that left the palace in shadows, the shadows were undeniable.

But I was finally getting out. Away from the ghosts and silence—*if,* that is, I could convince my father that I could be of service in Riiga.

I'd stayed up last night packing but decided last minute that I needed a more elaborate dress, so I had to repack to make room for the addition. Now I was late.

I shoved the lid closed and latched it, then dug my fingers under the handle on one side, but I couldn't reach the other handle even though it was my smallest trunk. I huffed, blowing a stray hair that had fallen out of the twist at the back of my neck. I used both hands on one side, lifting and dragging the trunk out of my closet and to the door of my rooms.

Navigating the door was trickier, but after a bumped elbow,

I managed. My fingers slipped and the trunk landed with a thud, barely missing my foot. I set my hands on my hips and kicked the offending luggage.

"Excuse me, Princess Chiara," a quiet voice said. "Did you need help with that?"

A boy stared, wide-eyed, from two paces down the hall. Based on his livery, he worked in the kitchens. From the size of his arms, I wasn't sure he'd do much better than I was.

But I nodded with all the grace my tutors had drilled into me. Might as well let him try.

He leveraged his arms around the awkward trunk, hefted it onto one hip, and started lugging it down the hall. The tiniest sigh escaped me. Even this scrawny boy from the kitchens could accomplish the simple task.

I followed him, swallowing back my stomach every time it jumped up. I'd tried to speak with my father about this, about letting me accompany him to Riiga to attend King Janiis's wedding, but he'd been in constant meetings, and I'd never been able to catch him alone.

If he let me accompany him, there was a chance, however slim, that I could *do* something instead of sitting quietly out of the way. Do something to ease the tensions between the Plateaus' kingdoms. To fight the mages who had almost destroyed my home.

The back of my neck prickled as the memory of Koranth's arms coming around me, using me as a shield between him and Jenna, threatened to resurface.

My father had to let me come. He'd always seen what I needed, seen me.

When we got to the long stairway, I almost offered to help the boy carry my trunk—I didn't want him falling on my account—but he would only have refused. Everyone always refused when I offered to help.

Instead, I followed sedately, every step as graceful as my dancing tutor demanded. "Take it to the courtyard, please," I said, my voice dropping to a whisper. The boy looked at me a beat too long, then readjusted the trunk on his hip, and led the way.

As the doors opened, a cacophony of shouts and laughter slammed into me. The loudest the palace had been in months. I paused on the threshold, taking in the movement, the excitement and anxiousness bubbling over the courtyard's expanse.

Riiga's borders into the capital city of Vera would be open for four weeks. My father would have to negotiate some kind of alliance between the kingdoms before the borders were closed again after the wedding. Even though Riiga had attempted to invade our southern border only months ago, *all* the kingdoms would have to work together—Jenna had defeated Graymere, but there were still two mages unaccounted for.

A nondescript carriage waited in the middle of the chaos. Horses stamped and nickered, puffs of dust rising up with every step. Servants and soldiers ran from horse to horse, from pack to pack, readying everything for the journey.

Despite the anticipation that soaked the yard, I'd frozen on the first step.

A thunk next to my feet startled me into jumping a half step back. My trunk. Several heads turned my way, masks of confusion and, worse, pity, as they surveyed my traveling cloak. The boy dipped his head, keeping his eyes on the ground, then ran back into the palace.

I swallowed, hiding my hands in the folds of my cloak. Then I stepped down the three stairs, careful not to trip, and approached my father. He spoke with an advisor who was thrusting papers into his hands. On the top paper, a large rectangle like a serving tray filled with a checkerboard of small squares had been drawn, with straight lines going up from their corners.

"They offered to show the apparatus. The farmers all support it—" The advisor broke off when she noticed me.

"Good morning," I said. My father tipped his head, and the advisor scurried off to bother someone else. The grooves on my father's forehead had deepened since I'd last seen him. Was there more gray at his temples?

My hands, the traitors, started shaking when my father's gaze turned my way. He let out a breath and the skin by his eyes crinkled as he smiled down at me. "I was hoping you'd come to say goodbye."

I straightened my already straight shoulders. "Of course, I wouldn't miss it." I tapped one finger against my leg. "But I want to come with you. To Vera," I added, then internally kicked myself for stating the obvious. I'd hoped that asking him in front of everyone might get him to say yes, and pushed ahead. "King Janiis invited the whole family to the capital."

I didn't trust any Riigans, and while I knew full well I couldn't protect my father from a physical threat—I had no magic or fighting skills—I *could* be an extra set of eyes, an extra layer of protection at King Janiis's court.

His mouth opened and shut, no sound coming out. It had been months since we'd spent time together like we used to, before the mages attacked, before there was a wedding to plan for Enzo and Jenna that would help convince our people of Hálendi's support and true intentions toward Turia. But surely my father knew, surely he would see the value of bringing me to Riiga's court.

Those closest to us quieted—their stares burned into me more than the sun's meager fall rays.

"I'm packed and ready to go," I said in a quieter voice when he didn't respond.

His small sigh, one of defeat, raised my hopes. But then he shook his head. "I'm sorry, Chiara, but I cannot allow you to accompany me."

Someone behind me coughed. The courtyard had gone almost completely silent. There was no shouting to cover my humiliation now, no chaos to prevent everyone from seeing my hot cheeks.

"But—" I started.

"No," he said again. He took me by the elbow, guiding me farther from the crowd to the steps leading back to the palace, back to where my pitiful trunk lay forgotten by the door. "It is a risk to go at all. One I would not expose you to."

"If it's such a risk, you shouldn't go either." I folded my arms, my fists so tight my fingernails bit into my palms. "I don't trust Riiga. No runners have returned with any information on the mages' location. No one has found Koranth." Half of the courtyard was openly staring at us, and my stomach churned with a breakfast I now regretted.

My father edged between me and the crowd, and it must have been a signal, because the shouting started up again, everyone going about their business.

"Janiis would see it as a slight if I did not attend his wedding myself. This invitation is a gift, a chance to strengthen our alliance with Riiga," he said.

I heard what he didn't say, felt the threat he didn't mention. We'd need everyone—including Riiga—in a fight against magic.

"And if you can't form an alliance with them?" I asked. Koranth had resisted any policy that didn't elevate Riiga's power over Turia, and Lord Sennor—I clenched my teeth, unwilling to relive the memories from the maze garden.

Father folded the papers from the advisor and tapped them against his hand. "Then I'll have done my best." He sighed and nodded to his guard, who'd come to tell him they were ready to leave. "You'll have your mother, Mari, Enzo, and Jenna to keep you company."

I dug the toe of my shoe into the dirt. As if all I needed was *company*. "I could be an asset in Riiga. I can move freely through any social circle, and hear things—"

"I'm sorry, Chiara," he said. "But my answer is no. Your place is here in Turiana." He reached for my hand, but I shied away, almost tripping up a step.

I pressed my lips together, afraid I'd say something I would later regret. I didn't bid him farewell or safe journey or any of the other platitudes our kingdom was famous for. Instead, I turned away, my skirts brushing the steps. I left my trunk where it lay. I thought I heard a faint *goodbye* before I pushed the doors closed.

My eyes stung and my ribs pressed against my lungs and heart like a cage that grew tighter with every passing day I stayed in the palace. Smiling, laughing, wearing whichever dress my maids told me to wear, attending the dinners and functions my mother asked me to attend, dancing with the boys my father approved of.

Quiet. Unseen. My father, who'd always noticed me when no one else did, had completely missed the point. I wasn't lonely; I was restless. Powerless.

I wiped my nose on the back of my hand and set my jaw. *Make it back to your room,* then *you can fall apart.*

When I turned the first corner, I almost ran into Jenna.

"What happened?" she asked, eyes flashing, hand on her sword. Her braid curved over her shoulder, and the gold band of betrothal winked from her wrist. It was the first time in a long time I'd seen her without Enzo by her side. I didn't begrudge them their happiness—I was happy for them and to be getting Jenna as another sister. But things were just . . . different now.

It took two tries for me to speak. "Nothing" was all I could get out. I looked past her shoulder. It was bad enough my humiliation would be spread all over the palace by nightfall. I wouldn't be a whimpering mess in the hall as well.

"Try again," she said, slightly out of breath. "Something happened, something strong enough for me to feel it all the way in the library."

I sighed. The tethers. Magic from her Hálendian bloodline that allowed her to feel what those closest to her were feeling. When she'd told me she was starting to develop a tether with Enzo, Mari, my parents, and me, I thought it sounded wonderful. But now that she was prying into feelings I'd rather cry out alone, it felt less so.

I pursed my lips and shrugged. "I asked if I could go with my father."

"Ah," she said with a nod. "And he said no."

"He said no—in front of the entire courtyard."

She squeezed one eye shut and winced. "Sounds like you need to hit something."

I choked out a sound between a laugh and sob. "Practice ring?"

Her eyes flashed and she rubbed her hands together. "Practice ring."

Maybe her reading my emotions wasn't so bad.

✦ ✦ ✦

I was nowhere near as steady with a staff as Jenna was, but focusing on something that required all my concentration was exactly the distraction I needed.

"Keep your feet apart, balanced," she said, and waited for my swing.

I twisted as I swung to get more force behind the move, like Jenna had taught me. My staff hit hers with a satisfying *crack*.

"Good. Again," she said, holding her staff out parallel to

the ground with both hands. She was always like this. Focused. Ready. Powerful.

I swung again. And again and again. Until I wasn't thinking about my form or where my feet or hands were supposed to go or what I would do next. Until Jenna's staff was the palace walls, my father's rejection, the kingdom's expectations, Koranth's grasping hands, Sennor's leer.

I swung again, and Jenna's staff wasn't there. My staff careened through the air, into the ground, and I toppled forward, barely catching myself from hitting face-first. My chest heaved; I sat in the dust, not caring about the dirt on my borrowed trousers or the sweat streaking down the sides of my face or the splinter in my palm.

Jenna, who'd jumped out of the way of my furious attack, tossed her staff next to mine and sat nearby, stretching her arms. "I owe you for getting me out of that meeting. Your mother has the softest heart of anyone I've ever met, but she is very determined when it comes to weddings."

Jenna gave a small sigh, and her smile was only a little forced. Even though we'd signed treaties, her and Enzo's wedding, planned for the spring, was the final seal that would unite our kingdoms. It was a symbol of the peace Hálendi had promised—meaning every detail had to be perfect.

I wiped sweat from my temple. "We're even, then. I didn't realize how cathartic hitting something could be."

Her lips tipped into a true smile. "There's not much else you can do in the winter back home. And winter is *long* in Hálendi."

I laughed with her. She'd complained of the heat in Turia all summer, but now that fall had arrived and leaves were changing and the temperature dropping, she had a spring in her step. Would she be disappointed when the snow only reached her ankles?

Jenna shifted to one side and reached into her pocket, her features relaxing as she pulled out a small book and brushed her fingers across the cover. "I was cleaning out my room and found this. I want you to have it."

I tilted my head and tentatively reached for the gift. "A novel?" I asked. She had held it so carefully, like it contained all the treasures and secrets in the world. *Flora and Fauna of the Wild* was stamped on the leather cover; most of the foil lettering had flecked off. When I flipped it open, the pages were blank. "It's . . . there's nothing here."

Jenna clutched her hands in her lap, and did she shiver? "The ink got washed away in the Wild, but it helped me remember my purpose when . . . when I forgot. It helped me figure out who I wanted to be. I thought you might like to have it."

I studied the gift anew. She never talked about her time in the Wild. Never. "Thank you." I wasn't sure how a small, blank book would help me figure out my purpose, but she'd noticed me, when it felt like no one else had.

"Princess?" a voice called from the edge of the practice ring we sat in.

We both turned and responded, "Yes?" then laughed at each other.

The young girl's gaze darted away from mine. "Princess Jennesara, you've been summoned to the queen's sitting room."

Jenna cleared her throat and stood. "I'd better get back."

I forced a smile. *She* was needed. "Of course. Thank you again for this." I held up the book, and Jenna pressed her fist to her shoulder and followed the girl back toward the palace.

I flipped through the pages again. Blank.

We faced so many perils—as a kingdom, as a Plateau. I was just one girl with good posture who could barely heft a sword. I couldn't even get my father to agree to let me travel with him. What could I possibly do against a mage?

Brownlok

"This plan is unwise," Brownlok said for the second time, and yet again, Redalia wouldn't listen.

"It's necessary, Brownlok; you know this." Redalia dug her nails into her scalp and twisted her red hair up, angling her head one way, then the other, staring into the water of the broken fountain in the palace's gardens to see her reflection.

Most everything in this kingdom showed some form of decay, and though Redalia had managed more progress than Brownlok had expected, he wasn't sure even she could salvage something here.

She smirked at the bow slung across his back. "It's been a while since I've seen you with a bow."

Brownlok ignored her jab and paced, his dark cloak out of place among the last of the bright blooms. The breeze from the ocean rustled the branches of the trees on the palace grounds, but the sunlight couldn't penetrate the shadow they'd met in. "The plan is flawed."

Redalia went perfectly still, the breeze ruffling the lace at her sleeves. Her eyes moved slowly from her reflection to him.

Brownlok continued, treading carefully. "Graymere didn't hold all my loyalty," he said softly, willing her to listen for once. "He never did. I didn't leave everything for—"

Redalia scoffed and shook her hair back over her shoulders, letting it fall to her waist. "Graymere's remaining power within Koranth and me is all that is keeping you alive right now. You will follow his plan. We both will."

Brownlok paced deeper into the shadows. "We are missing something. The artifact I found in Turia cannot be everything."

Redalia stroked the dagger at her waist. "These are simpleminded creatures. Perhaps it *is* everything."

"In the book, there was a page cut and Kais—"

Redalia was at his throat so fast, nails digging into his skin, that he couldn't finish, couldn't do anything but hold her wrist and hope she didn't snap his neck.

He'd forgotten. A stupid mistake.

"Do. Not. Speak. His. Name," she hissed, tightening her hold with every word.

Brownlok stared her down, unmoving, black spots filling his vision. His bow would be useless against her if she decided to kill him. But she needed him. And she knew it.

"Fool," she muttered, and released him. Brownlok tried not to gulp in air, but he couldn't help his body's reflex. "Before I gutted him, Janiis's advisor said the library was in the Wastelands to the west."

Brownlok shook his head. "That's not enough to go on." He didn't say that she should know that, that she should share her plans with him, that he wouldn't betray her like Kais had. Because no matter how much she needed him, he'd end up with her golden dagger in his stomach before he could finish. "You still have your artifact. We could build our own empire on the Continent."

"The Continent is broken and will fall easily." Redalia drew her dagger from its gilded sheath. She pressed the blade into the tip of her finger until a drop of blood formed, then sucked it clean. Her eyes flashed red in the shadows, the tendons of her neck creating stark hollows. She leaned closer and wiped the next droplet of blood onto Brownlok's cheek. "Koranth's plan will work. And then the game will really begin."

CHAPTER THREE

Ren

Icy water engulfed my head, freezing and burning all at once. I gripped the sides of the bucket that held water for cleaning my hands in my bathing chamber. I stayed under until my lungs ached and the dream faded.

The woman in red had haunted me again. The same dream from the night my father died.

I lifted my head and shook out my hair, then rested my elbows on the sides of the bucket. The muscles in my neck screamed at me for falling asleep sitting up, and everything hurt. It had been months since I'd used so much magic in one day. But it didn't matter how tired I was, how sore—I had a kingdom to put back in order.

I stripped down—except the Medallion—and climbed into the now-cold bath that had been drawn last night before I'd come to my room. I scrubbed at the blood still caked on my hands and torso until the water turned brown. By the time I was dressed, with two more knives hidden at my waist and my cleaned dagger in my boot, the door to my chambers rattled against the lock, followed by a timid knock.

"Fresh water, Your Majesty?" a small voice called out.

I pushed my fingers through my hair, exposing the white streak—the mark of my lineage and my magic—and straightened my spine despite the aches and twinges. My father had set aside his personal concerns to rule his kingdom, and I would do the same.

Dawn glimmered through the thin slit window in my room as I passed through, shoving the papers from the stand by my bed into the drawer, careful of the topmost note that had been burned.

It was a stack of notes I'd found in Leland's belongings. I'd picked out his handwriting, but there were multiple correspondents. Which meant there were more within the kingdom who believed like Leland had, that we should use our strength to expand Hálendi's borders.

I pulled down the blankets on my bed before I went to the door, mussing them up and punching down the pillows. Servants talked, and I didn't want rumors or questions about why I'd slept on the sofa. It was bad enough I hadn't moved into the king's chambers. That room would remain my father's for a long while yet.

I quietly moved the table back and unlatched the door.

A small boy stood with a bucket of fresh hot water. Kaldur stood behind him, dark circles under his eyes.

"What are you doing?" he asked, hands moving to his hips.

I tipped my head to the boy, and he darted around me to complete his chores. "There is too much to be done to spend a day languishing in bed," I said, starting down the hall.

Kaldur fell into step beside me. "Sire, your injury—" He cleared his throat. "Take the day to rest. No one expects you to attend to your duties today."

Kaldur was all about protocol, and while it was usually good—and predictable—I didn't miss a step. "Which is exactly why I must continue as before. I won't give anyone else a chance to plot against me. Not in my own council room." I shoved my hands in my pockets and changed the subject. "Did you have a nice night in the hall?"

Kaldur scowled at me, then at every servant we passed. "You should hang me along with those traitors."

I stopped fast, and he retraced his steps back to me. The servants dusting the slot windows scurried away. "Why would I do that?"

He lowered his voice. "I should have been there. Should have protected you. If I'd performed my duties—"

"I underestimated my opposition. It won't happen again." My neck was abominably sore. I kept my hands in my pockets to keep from rubbing it. "Besides, if you were hanged, there'd be one less man in the castle I could trust."

Kaldur stood straight, chest up, shoulders taut, staring at some invisible speck over my shoulder. "I let you down, sire, but it won't happen again. From now on, where you go, I go."

I wouldn't always be as lucky as I'd been in the crypt, but I wouldn't agree to another shadow. There were already too many of those chasing me.

I pressed a hand to my shoulder, accepting his pledge for what it was. Loyalty. "Thank you."

He breathed out a sigh and touched his fist to his shoulder.

Three soldiers marched down the hall, and we were silent until they passed. There had been more patrols, more guards, ever since my father had been killed. But it wasn't comforting anymore—not when the assassins last night had worn the same uniforms.

A throat cleared behind me—a small girl from the kitchens stood against the wall opposite us, carrying a rattling tray.

"Pardon, Your Majesty," she said, eyes fixed on my boots. "But would you like your tray in your room still? Or . . ." She trailed off and the tray rattled even more.

I held in a sigh. Everyone spoke and acted with such deference now. I missed the ease that used to come so readily. No one wanted a king who teased and laughed. Still, the girl had shown courage to address me at all, so I waved her closer.

She took tiny steps, approaching me as she would a lion. Her hair hung in two braids down her back like that of most young Hálendian girls, but something about her was familiar.

"Do I know you?" I asked.

She froze, then nodded. "You healed my whole family, Majesty. When the fevers spread. You came to our house, and you healed us."

I snapped my fingers. "That's it. How is your family?"

Two years ago, a sickness had ravaged the mining towns. I'd begged my father to let me help until he relented. His council had turned it into a campaign to flaunt the future king, but I hadn't cared—I rarely got to use my magic to actually help people, then or now. I was always kept from the people. Separate.

"They're well, sire," she whispered, though she'd lifted her chin. The tray steadied.

"Good," I said. Despite being proud that an heir had been born with magic, most Hálendians didn't want to *see* the magic. I understood the sentiment—a regular weapon couldn't defend against magic, against the unknown. But the three weeks I spent using my magic, testing its boundaries and weaknesses, had been the most exhausting and informative three weeks of my life.

"Well, I hope the scones are warm, at least," I said as I wrapped my fingers around the pastry on the tray she held out.

"Y-yes, sire," she stuttered. She was likely the one who left the tray next to my bed when I bothered to sleep in it. I paused, pastry halfway to my mouth. Why had she approached me when I was clearly leaving, when she had to know I wouldn't want the tray in my room?

"Tell me," I asked in a quiet voice, "do you have a key to my room?"

She shook her head, wide-eyed.

I took the wooden cup of cider from the tray that still rattled a bit, and swirled its contents. Her eyes followed the movement. "Then what do you do with the tray if my door is locked?" I took a bite of the scone, and the flaky softness almost distracted me from my inquiry. Almost.

She swallowed, still staring at the cup. "I return the tray to the kitchens, and the castle steward takes it—he has a key. Or I find Master Kaldur—he has a key, too."

Kaldur nodded, brows furrowed as he watched us converse. I licked the crumbs from my fingers and winked when she widened her eyes at my lack of manners. "Makes sense. Tell me, oh bringer of delicious pastries, do you know if anyone else has a key to my chambers?"

She shook her head, then paused. "There is one lady who has been awfully friendly with the steward lately, though," she finished in a whisper so quiet I knew this girl understood how fast news could travel in an empty hallway. She took the cup out of my hand and returned it to the tray. "And I'd be careful with your drinks, Your Majesty. I . . . I didn't pull this cider myself, and it might be fine, but, well, the steward was in Cook's way this morning, making a fuss about things."

A knot unloosened in my stomach. I believed her. Which meant Cook hadn't been involved in the attempted poisoning last night. "Thank you," I said, pressing my fist to my shoulder. She opened her mouth like she was about to say more, but something over my shoulder snapped her jaw shut. She curtsied, then scurried off.

So the castle steward was in Isarr's pocket as well. I tapped my fingers against my leg. "Know anyone who could fill in as steward in a pinch?" I asked Kaldur.

Kaldur scratched at the stubble on his jaw, staring after the girl with a frown. "I'll handle it, Your Majesty."

I finished off the scone as we walked the cool halls, then rubbed my hands together to get rid of the crumbs. The doors to the council chambers were closed when we reached them. I wasn't late, which meant they'd started without me.

What would the council discuss when they didn't think I'd be in attendance?

I tilted my head, the bones in my neck popping, then opened the door with a *whoosh*. No matter that I was nineteen years old, had seen battle at North Watch, and lost both parents, I always felt like a child when I entered this room.

Murmurs skittered around the long table in the middle, and the five slot windows let in the cool morning light. "Your Majesty." One of the council members stood, hands on the table. "Surely you should be resting!"

I made my way to my seat, the one directly next to my father's wide, padded chair. "I appreciate your concern." The fireplace behind me crackled, a full four logs strong. "In the future, do not begin council meetings until I am present."

No one responded; no one met my stare. I sat quickly, scooting closer to the table. Were they trying to make me so uncomfortably warm I'd acquiesce to their demands sooner?

Kaldur shut the door and stood next to it, though he usually stood outside. Jenna's old tutor, Edda, sat to my right. Jenna had trusted her, and I hoped she was still trustworthy, because I'd given her the top position on the council. Waves of discontent had pounded through the castle at that, but I hadn't regretted it yet.

"I am relieved to see you recovered, Your Majesty," she murmured. I nodded my thanks. At least someone was happy to see me.

Everyone else shuffled their papers and wouldn't look at me. I cleared my throat. "What is on the schedule to discuss today?"

The man across from me tapped his pen against the table. "Your Majesty, with the events of last night, you really should consid—"

"I will worry about my health, Councilor. You worry about yours," I said, and the muttering finally stopped.

A throat cleared down the table. "About the assassins, Your Majesty, what is being done?"

I picked up my pen and brought the first blank page in front of me from the stack I'd requested always be refilled after meetings. "Kaldur will oversee the inquiries."

The mysterious notes in my room called to me. Had Isarr been one of Leland's contacts in the castle? The assassins would talk, but could I trust their information?

The councilor frowned and someone not in my line of sight grumbled. When I turned to see who it was, everyone was silent. Perhaps I'd have to move to my father's chair soon so I could have a better view of the table.

We'd met daily in the month since the coronation, and most of those meetings involved me removing men and women from the room and stripping them of their title for their involvement in the attempted invasion of Turia. Now wasn't the time to turn against our allies. Not with two power-hungry mages on the Plateau seeking revenge.

Edda continued the meeting, calling for concerns, and the council members took off like wolves after their prey. The men and women spoke to me and around me. Edda handled most questions. She was the only one at the table who seemed to have common sense.

I wrote down the main concerns, scribbling notes so I could

ponder them later. One councilman had said I should employ a scribe for such work, but I wanted *my* thoughts, not a scribe's, so I continued even though my hand always ached by the end.

Villages along our northern border, near the Ice Deserts, were still recuperating from the destruction the mages had caused—herds destroyed in the north, mines collapsed in the west. The port city of Osta we'd promised to allow Turia to use free of import charges for the next ten years was not yet equipped to handle the extra traffic. And there were ships harassing those coming into port. The ships didn't fly Riiga's colors, but they could only be Riigan.

Hálendi had existed for centuries, yet I felt like I was starting from nothing.

"Sire, I believe we need to discuss the issue of an heir," said the councilor at the end of the table, chin in the air. "And possible marriage candidates."

My eyebrows shot up and ink blotted on the page. "We will address that later. Next topic, please."

"But, Your Majesty, with the question of your heir unanswered, it leaves room for uncertainty and . . ."

And assassination attempts, I finished for him in my head. The thought of uniting myself to someone in marriage, someone who could roll over in bed and shove a knife into my heart without me even waking . . .

"Next. Topic. Please." I relaxed my grip on my pen when I realized I was holding it like a weapon.

"Fine. You've sent a refusal—a *polite* refusal—to King Janiis already?"

Ah, glaciers. I'd forgotten. "Yes, of course," I answered. I jotted a note to send the missive today. Janiis was unhinged if he thought I'd leave my kingdom just for his wedding. I couldn't leave affairs as they were, especially since I wouldn't be able to return before the pass closed for the winter. Especially not if I wanted to have my kingdom ready for when I *would* have to leave—for Jenna's wedding in the spring.

As if I'd summoned the topic, a councilor at the end of the table leaned forward. "I think we should insist that Princess Jennesara return home for a time." Finally, something we could agree on. If she were here— "I feel it unwise to allow the princess to wed the crown prince of Turia. Her magic is powerful; we should keep that power within Hálendian bloodlines."

The Medallion at my chest went cold. It had never been cold like this before, but I didn't care what it was trying to communicate. I pressed the pen's tip into the paper until a giant blot stained the page. Better the page ruined than that councilor's face.

"I agree," another councilman spoke up. Edda leaned closer, her hand brushing against my arm. A casual motion, but grounding enough to help me act the part of king.

"First of all," I announced in a deadly-calm voice, "you will not speak of the princess as some expendable piece in your game of politics." I looked around the table, and even the fire had stopped crackling. "*You* sent her away. She is fulfilling her duty to her kingdom and doing more to repair our relationship with Turia than any of you. So I suggest you leave her out of your machinations."

And she's happy, I added silently. She'd managed to find

people who accepted her as she was; who loved her. I knew how rare that was, and I would fight anyone who threatened that.

I cleared my throat and sat back. "Anything else?"

The meeting flowed on, more complaints of low crop yield, more issues at the borders. We'd been sorting through a massive list of needs from the western towns for an hour when the Medallion—still uncomfortably cold—warmed.

You must leave, it seemed to whisper. *You must help.*

My brow furrowed, and I traced over the lines I had just written about sheep's wool. Help? Help with the sheep? No, that didn't feel right.

"Your Majesty?" the councilor directly across the table from me asked, probably not for the first time.

"Yes, what is it?" I stared at my notes. An entire line was filled with *I must leave.* I dropped my pen.

The councilor pursed his lips. "I *said,* we need to address the terms of the treaty with Turia."

I shook my head, taking my pen up again. Edda glanced at my notes. She frowned before I could cover the last lines I'd written.

"We've already discussed this," I said. "*We* attacked *them.* The terms hold. We will need our alliance with Turia in the coming days."

"Because of the *mages,*" another councilor spoke up, three seats down from the other. A murmur flittered along the table.

I went perfectly still. They lifted me above everyone else, kept me separate, held me to a higher standard as king, yet also deemed it acceptable to ignore and belittle what I said?

"Yes," I snapped, pressing my pen into the paper around the word *leave*. "There are threats on the Plateau you do not understand." I swallowed, and the Medallion seemed to grow heavier, the thoughts in my head louder.

Everything I'd read about the ancient artifact suggested it was more than what my father had taught me. It supposedly connected to the land's magic, which made sense considering it had originally belonged to the first king of Hálendi, Kais, who had been a land mage. But interpreting it wasn't something extensively covered in the texts.

Help. How was I supposed to help when I didn't know where or how or who? And were these my own thoughts? Or was the Medallion finally communica— "Leave," I whispered, the word falling out before I could catch it.

"What was that?" Edda asked, leaning closer, scanning me as if she'd see some sign of illness.

I licked my lips. "I must leave." A thrill shot through me at finally understanding something. The castle? No, farther. *South.* A tremor passed through my hand. *Turia.*

A frisson of fear laced through my aching head. Why would the land warn me about Turia? Could it be Jenna again? The Medallion had been the only thing pushing me forward when news of her "death" had reached me.

Edda tilted her head. "Leave the meeting?"

"No." I tapped the paper and leaned back. "Never mind."

It didn't matter what the Medallion wanted me to do— I couldn't abandon Hálendi in its current state. The kingdom was on the verge of collapse, both economically and politically. And if I left now it would look like I was running—from the problems, from my duty, from the assassins in the crypt. It would only make my enemies bolder, would only leave Hálendi adrift to be taken by whoever snatched enough power.

Edda cleared her throat with one last side glance at me. "Let's continue on, then. What are your proposals to fortify Osta to handle the extra load Turia will bring?"

South, the Medallion whispered again, though not in words. I shook off the feeling.

By the time the meeting ended, an endless loop of complaints and demands circled through my head until my eyes throbbed. Always something more demanded of me. Always a greater weight to carry.

I'd have to hope the Medallion calmed, because if I left now, I wasn't sure I'd have a throne to come back to.

CHAPTER FOUR

Ren

"Your Majesty?" Edda murmured. I refrained from startling, but only just. I thought she'd left with the other councilors.

I rubbed my temple and forced a light expression. I was king. The king could shoulder the burdens of his kingdom. "Yes, oh wise tutor?" I asked, and nodded to Kaldur, who stepped into the hall, leaving us alone.

Edda's lips pinched to one side, but she chuckled. "Tell me what you meant when you said you needed to leave." She folded her arms and sat back.

I leaned my elbow on the armrest, my head in my palm, studying her. She never held back—Jenna had good taste in tutors. "It's nothing. I can't leave now."

She put her hand on my arm, and it was surprisingly warm,

like I'd forgotten what it was to have contact with someone else. Well, someone not trying to kill me.

"Atháren, you assigned me to this position to assist you, but I cannot help if I do not have all the facts. Why do you feel you should leave? Because of the attack?" She leaned back and stared right through me, like I was a boy in trouble and not the king of a warrior nation.

I couldn't sit still under her gaze. I pushed away from the table and paced. She was right—I'd placed her on the council because I trusted her, or at least trusted Jenna's trust in her.

She wanted the facts? I rubbed my hands on my trousers. "My father gave me the Medallion of Sight before he died," I started. Edda sucked in a breath, but didn't interrupt. I'd let everyone assume the artifact had been stolen from my father. "He told me it would keep my mind free of deception, but it's more than that. I found out it connects to land magic, but beyond that, I'm unsure how to decipher its meaning."

Edda leaned forward, clasping her hands on the table in a move I was sure she'd used to teach Jenna for years. "Connects to the land?" I nodded and she gazed into the distance. "Long ago when I traveled to Turia's library to study, I read that magic began awakening in the Plateau when Kais enchanted the border of the Ice Deserts. And ever since, the land has been striving to regain its balance."

"Balance?" I asked. "Like the Wild that keeps everyone out, and the Ice Deserts that keep everyone in?"

She nodded. "But it's more than that. For all the evil, there is good to combat it. The mages came, but so did Kais. Balance isn't always about good and evil, though, or about what would benefit *you*—or Hálendi, for that matter."

I shook my head. "So . . . the Medallion isn't helping me?"

Edda chuckled. "Like a wildfire, for example. By outward appearance, it's bad, correct? Loss of life and home for plants and animals, which turns to scarcity for us as well. But fire also nourishes the soil and encourages new growth that revitalizes the land, creating homes for wildlife for years to come."

"Balance," I repeated. The Medallion had been warning me of deception with the poisoned cider. Warning of the assassins. Because Hálendi was part of the balance of the Plateau. And now it urged me south with increasing intensity. Back to Turia.

What was upsetting the land's balance there? And what would my departure bring to the Plateau, unless it was meant to let my kingdom fall into chaos?

"The Medallion has been . . . nudging me for weeks now. I haven't always understood its warnings, and I thought it was about the assassination attempt, but today"—I took a deep breath and shrugged—"well, you saw my notes."

"The Medallion is telling you to leave?"

I resumed pacing. "Except I can't leave now. Everything would collapse."

Edda started laughing, a sound I'd never heard from her before, one that stopped me in my tracks and pulled a smile from me as well. "Oh, Atháren, I forget how young you are. No matter how you might wish it, a kingdom does not rise or fall on the shoulders of the king alone."

I shoved my hands into my pockets, all levity gone. "It feels like it does."

She patted the chair next to her and I sat, stretching my legs in front of me. "I'm sure it does. But all kings have opposition. All kings rely on those they trust."

"But who can I trust? I found a stack of letters in Leland's belongings. Proof that there were more than just Leland who disagreed with my father's policies, with Hálendi's long-standing duty." I clenched my fists in my pockets. "And now there are people trying to kill me within my own castle."

"Why did you place me as your advisor, Your Majesty?"

I stared at a spot of dust on my boot. "Because you smell better than the other advisors."

She snorted a laugh, then wiped her hand over her mouth, controlling her expression. "Try again."

I sighed and tipped my head against the back of the chair. "Because I trust you."

"Good," Edda said, scooting her chair closer and pulling a scrap of paper toward her. She wrote her name. "Who else?"

Kaldur. Cook. The girl from the kitchens. There was a handful of other nobility and advisors who I knew had backed my father and the line of kings resolutely and would back me as well. Another handful who supported me, but I wasn't sure how easily their loyalty could be bought—like that of the steward.

The list, when Edda had finished, was longer than I expected, though not nearly long enough.

"You see, sire? You have more on your side than you thought. Now, tell me again what the Medallion is telling you."

I tapped the wood table, the pads of my fingers catching on the rough surface. "That I need to leave. South. To Turia.

That's the only clear direction I understand. I don't know specifically where or why."

Edda tilted her head and clasped her hands on the table. "What do *you* think, Your Majesty? Regardless of what the Medallion says or does not say."

I pressed my lips together and stared at the table. "I . . . I don't know."

She frowned. "Your father used the Medallion as a tool. To assist him. Not to rule for him."

I touched my chest, a move I'd seen my father make countless times. She was wrong, though. How could I be letting the Medallion lead for me if I couldn't understand it fully? If I wasn't as strong as my father?

"Do you know what it means if the Medallion turns cold?" I finally forced myself to ask.

"I do not." Edda traced a stray line on the page, turning it into a swirling line. "Maybe it's for the best if you leave," she finally said after a too-long silence.

I couldn't speak for a moment, like the wind had been knocked out of me. "I might not make it back before the pass closes. What if everything crumbles because I'm gone?"

She cocked her head. "If the Medallion is telling you to leave, maybe everything will crumble if you stay. We made this list of people you trust, people who will keep your throne safe in your absence. And if you're away, your enemies won't be trying to assassinate you. Maybe they won't be so subtle about their dissent."

The corner of my mouth lifted. It was an interesting way to weed out the unloyal, but perhaps it would work.

Edda folded the paper in half and slid it toward me. "If the Medallion were warning you something bad was happening to Jennesara?"

I brushed my thumb against the paper. "I'd already be gone." It felt different from last time, when it had urged me into Turia after Jenna instead of back home when my father had been killed.

But now I'd worry about Jenna, too. Wonderful.

"The Medallion wouldn't guide you to Turia if it weren't important," Edda said, her voice quiet and firm.

She made a good point, yet the sense of duty my father instilled in me from childhood rebelled at the thought of running away. And there was the smallest worm of doubt wriggling in the back of my mind—if Edda wasn't trustworthy, there was a good chance I might not have a throne to come back to. I'd need a contingency plan. Luckily, the council had given me the perfect idea.

The Medallion pulsed. If I did go, it would have to be now. I couldn't wait any longer.

I could learn more about the Medallion in Turia—how its magic worked, and maybe find out more of its purpose as a key to the Black Library. Leaving my kingdom as it was would be like ripping my soul out. But maybe it would be better for Hálendi if I left.

◆ ◆ ◆

Edda and I stayed in the council room for hours. We decided she would tell the council I was attending King Janiis's wedding after all. That I'd received word King Marko would attend, and didn't want Hálendi to be left out of any political maneuvering. I had heard no such thing about Marko, though there was a chance it was true, as the pile of unopened correspondence on the desk in my father's study grew every week. I flipped through the letters only briefly, looking for anything from Jenna.

"Just don't actually *go* to Riiga," Edda said, raising an eyebrow at me.

I laughed. "I can safely promise that."

So I would go to Turiana to consult with Jenna and King Marko. Perhaps there were pieces I was missing, reasons the Medallion flared against my chest that I wasn't yet aware of.

I also left orders for the assassins and Isarr, to allow the council final ruling over them. Edda thrust a paper in front of me from the bottom of her hefty stack, a document filled with official writing.

"Are you certain?" she asked.

I went to the door and asked Kaldur to join us. "I'm certain." I filled in the blanks, my pen moving easily over the page. This was a decision I felt good about, for once. I signed the paper with a flourish fit for a king and set my pen alongside it.

Edda signed as witness, then I held the pen out to Kaldur. He glanced at the paper, brows furrowing deeply, but signed without comment. My contingency plan was as good as I could make it. I hoped no one would ever have to see this document.

"Ready?" Edda asked, shoulders dropping from fatigue.

"Ready or not, it's time."

Kaldur followed me silently down to the crypt. I hoped it

wouldn't be my last goodbye as king, but I wouldn't leave without saying farewell.

A tiny bouquet of white flowers sat atop my father's tomb, and I halted, staring at it. Kaldur, who'd been checking behind every pillar and tomb, cleared his throat.

"While you were in the council room with Edda, I asked for these to be placed. It was my fault yours got trampled last night," he said, scuffing his boot against the ground.

An emotion I couldn't name squeezed my chest, tight but not uncomfortable. "Thank you. Would you . . . would you continue laying flowers? My father deserves to be remembered, but I can't . . ."

Kaldur touched his fist to his shoulder and bowed. "It would be my honor, Your Majesty." He took his position at the entrance of the crypt.

I hooked my foot around the stool in the alcove's corner and sat, my elbows on my knees. I didn't say anything. Couldn't.

It was a huge risk to leave. One I hoped my father would have approved of.

✦ ✦ ✦

That night, when the castle had long since retired, I moved the table away from my door and eased out with my bags over my shoulder. Kaldur snored lightly, chin dropped to his chest as he sat in the hall.

I slipped a note onto his lap. Other than the apology for the herbs I'd slipped into his drink, the note read *Go see the Tutor.* Edda would explain.

She had probably assumed I would take Kaldur with me, but I needed him here. And, a tiny part of me whispered, I needed to be myself on the road. To remember, if I could, who *Ren* was.

Darkened hallways had never bothered me; now every shadow jumped and stretched unnaturally.

I ducked under the low archway leading into the kitchens. Cook was still there despite the late hour, along with a row of young girls and boys kneading dough for tomorrow and washing the endless stack of pots in a tub in the corner.

Cook startled when I bent and kissed her cheek, turning to me with wide eyes and swinging her spoon.

"Now, Prince, you know you can't have any of this," she scolded, drops of sauce flicking from the spoon. "It's too late for a snack. You'll be up all night."

I reached around her and snatched a cold roll from the table. "It's *king* now, actually."

I'd meant it as a joke, but my voice hitched on *king*. My shoulders fell; her eyes dimmed in grief. I pulled her aside, away from the others working beside her. "I need supplies. For a journey."

Her eyebrows shot up. "I haven't received any requests for something like that from the steward. How am I supposed to prepare for these things when I don't know how many are going or how long or where or—"

"One," I interrupted with a quick glance around to see who was listening. "One is going. Twelve days."

Her jaw snapped shut. She put her fists to her sides and a cloud of fine brown flour puffed off her apron. "Majesty, I don't think it's safe—"

My fingers tightened around the strap digging into my shoulder. It was a risk coming here. Any of the kitchen staffers could talk. But if I went with permission of the council—unlikely as that permission would be—I'd expend all my focus protecting myself from my own guards.

"Please," I whispered, despising the note of begging in my voice. If she wouldn't give me food, I'd have to buy some in the city. And while I had a little money to bring with me, it wouldn't be enough for the whole journey. Apparently, being king meant others held the purse strings for me. Something I'd change, once I returned home.

Cook nodded, her chins swaying. She set out a large square cloth, and she and the girl who'd brought the tray to my room started piling it with food I could travel with—breads, cheese, dried meat and fruit, nuts, even a few potatoes. Cook bent under the table and pulled a waterskin with instructions for the girl to fill it.

"Majesty, I don't pretend to know what's happening up top, but we hear things in the kitchen—"

I pulled air in slowly through my nose, but it didn't help the crushing weight against my chest.

"And I just . . ." She trailed off with a worried frown. "Just, be safe, Your Majesty."

She bowed with her fist to her shoulder, then pulled me into a hug. She squeezed me tight and sniffled into my chest.

I'd be covered in flour, but I didn't care. My eyes fell shut and I squeezed her right back.

"Thank you," I whispered into her wispy hair.

I made my way across the cold, dark field to the stables. The door creaked as I entered, but nothing inside moved. I brushed my hand against the rough wall, counting the doors until my horse's stall.

"Your Majesty?" The voice was so quiet I barely heard it, yet it was made loud by the silence.

I squinted, hand on my sword. "Who goes there?"

A latch lifted and the shuttered window opened, letting light from the sliver of moon in. A boy stood before me. I swallowed. Aleinn's brother.

"I couldn't sleep. Thought I'd go for a ride," I said. When I'd returned from Turia, I'd awarded Aleinn's family enough money from the treasury that they'd never have to work again. It wasn't enough to cover the price their daughter had paid, dying in my sister's place, but I wanted them to know I saw what she had done. I'd assumed her brother would return home since he no longer needed to work, yet here he stood, blocking my path.

"You shouldn't ride at night," he said, voice a little stronger now. "Horse could step wrong in the dark, lose a shoe."

"I'll be careful." I moved to brush past him. He stepped to the side with me.

His throat bobbed, the moon casting just enough light for me to see the movement. "Will your guard carry your things, Your Majesty?" he asked with a nod to my pack.

I twisted the strap on my shoulder. "No one must know I've left. I believe I can trust you not to spread news of my departure?"

I'd expected him to grumble or put up opposition, but he

nodded and said, "I'll fetch your saddle," then slipped into the shadows, toward the tack room.

My horse, Nótt, must have heard my voice, because he was awake when I opened his stall. He pushed his nose into my chest, knocking me back a step until I rubbed his soft head. "Hey, boy. Are you up for a long ride?"

He shook his head and bumped his nose into me again. I laughed and pulled an apple from my pocket. He ate it in one bite.

"How about now?" I asked, and this time he nodded. I rubbed him down, reveling in the contact, in his strength under my hands and his heat next to me. I smiled to myself in the dark. My horse. I'd forgotten to add Nótt to Edda's list of those I trusted.

The boy finally returned with the tack, and we worked in the dark, cinching the saddle and attaching the bridle. When I moved to mount, he put his hand on my arm.

"Sire, I'm coming with you."

He'd tried to sound brave, but I heard the waver in his voice. I shrugged out from under his hand. "No, you're not." I took Nótt's reins and led him toward the door of the stables. But there, in the moonlight, another, smaller horse was already saddled.

The boy stepped in front of me. "You cannot go alone." He looked down, and the next words were quiet, but they hit me hardest. "And if you're going south, I want to see my sister's grave."

I closed my eyes and puffed out a breath. When Leland had

returned, the sole survivor of the Gray Mage's massacre, he'd roused an army against Turia, which had been blamed for the attack. As the army marched toward Turia's border, they'd come across the site of the ambush and buried everyone along the side of the road. They'd said the ground had opened to allow it, that the graves had almost dug themselves.

"All right, let's go," I said, and turned my horse. The boy was right—there were still mages loose on the Plateau, and he could be my runner if needed. No one would have to see me or know I'd passed through their land.

He scrambled onto his horse, and we plodded to the gate— I'd had Edda leave instructions for the guards to keep it open. Eventually, I'd have to address how easily we breached security, but tonight, I was glad for it.

Out here, the air smelled of spiced cider and golden leaves. Icy winds from the north chased behind us, pushing us through the city and into the rolling hills south. Moonlight bathed the grasses in silver light patched with shadows from the clouds.

"Will you remind me of your name?" I asked. I'd forgotten, though I'd been told it more than once. Exhaustion dulled my mind—I couldn't remember the last time I'd slept well.

"Adri, Your Majesty," he said.

I shook my head. "As we're trying to keep my identity secret, you'll have to call me Ren."

Adri shifted in his saddle, then nodded. "Ren," he whispered, trying the name out.

Something loosened in me at hearing my name and not my title. "It takes twelve days to get to Turiana," I said, pressing my knees to urge Nótt a little faster. "Think we can make it in ten?"

The boy chuckled, his grip loosening on the reins. "If any-one can, sire—Ren—it'd be us."

I whooped in the night, and we raced south. With every hoofbeat, every minute we traveled, the Medallion's heat eased against my skin.

Jenna would be there when I arrived. She'd always kept me centered, made sure I was on the right path. And she was the only person on the Plateau I trusted completely.

She would know what to do.

CHAPTER FIVE

Chiara

Petitioner's hour was almost complete, and though it usually lasted longer, the restrictions on who could enter the palace had kept it close to an actual hour. The sun's golden light shone through the throne room's tall windows, splashing everything with an ethereal glow.

My feet didn't care for the glow—they ached from standing near the wall so long. In the shadows, avoiding the whispers that *still* followed me even though it had been over a week since my father left.

I probably deserved the whispers: my father had left for Riiga, and I hadn't said goodbye.

My mother sat on the dais with Enzo, and my father's advisors on chairs below the dais in front of them. Today, Jenna sat on the dais as well, a reminder that she would keep the peace between our kingdoms.

Those of the kingdom's nobility who'd been trusted to attend mingled and chatted throughout the long room, keeping quiet enough to hear the petitioners. Even with the palace under construction and the mages' whereabouts unknown, they looked for gossip.

I'd never particularly wanted to sit on the dais with my mother and father and brother—I'd rather get out and *do* the help than listen to complaints. Today, I wished a tiny bit that I could sit up there. Even if no one wanted or heeded my advice, it'd be better than trying to avoid the pitying looks.

The letter from Riiga I'd received this morning in my room hadn't helped, either. I'd thought the message was from my father and torn it open eagerly.

I'm sorry for what happened in the garden during my visit—
The words marched through my mind again. I'd read the first line, then skipped to the end. When I saw Sennor's name instead of my father's, my stomach turned to stone and I crumpled the note and tossed it unread into the back of my desk drawer.

My mother had come directly after, telling me I'd hidden away long enough. She said it with a hug, so it stung less, but I'd still rather be anywhere but here.

I kept my shoulders back, chin up, hands lightly clasped in front of me, serene smile firmly in place. Eventually, everyone would go back to ignoring me.

I wished the boy in front of me would. He'd been whispering

about the worms he was experimenting with in his family's gardens for at least ten minutes in a misguided attempt to woo me. But he was keeping me from standing alone, so I listened patiently about the worms, holding back a shiver. Best of all, he wasn't handsome in the least. I'd had my fill of handsome, arrogant men.

A hand gripped my arm, tugging me to the side, and then an arm looped through mine. I stiffened, remembering a different hand, a different place, but shook the thought away and cursed the letter in my desk for dredging up unwanted memories.

This grip, though still unwanted, belonged to Cynthia Hallen. Her nose was stuck into the air so high I could see up her nostrils. It had been that way ever since my brother rejected her.

"*Miss* Hallen, how nice of you to make the trip to the palace," I said, proud that my voice didn't drip with sarcasm or betray my unease.

Cynthia's lips pursed into a smile—grimace?—and she bowed her head to the boy in front of us. "You'll excuse us?"

The boy, mouth hanging open midsentence, nodded, turned on his heel, and immediately found some other girl to share his exploits with. I almost wished he had refused and kept me here. Worms were better company than Cynthia.

She didn't speak as she led me arm in arm along the side of the throne room. Her nails dug through my blouse and into my skin, and though I understood her purpose almost immediately, I waited until we'd gone the length of the room to stop her.

I extricated my arm from hers. "Using my standing to scrape up a little higher? Isn't that low, even for you?" I asked quietly. We stood near enough the door that a slight draft from the hallway carried in wafts scented with burning wood and freshly turned earth.

Cynthia's pleasant expression didn't slip. "Took you long enough to figure that out," she whispered. Others in attendance took notice of us, but not many. Not enough to boost her standing.

For once, it was nice to be the invisible princess, because at least Cynthia couldn't use me like she used everyone else. Like she'd tried to before Enzo had chosen Jenna.

She brushed her perfectly curled black hair over her shoulder. "I wanted to make a statement before I left, and I think I've done just that. I'd thank you, but it's not like you did anything."

Dozens of responses flitted through my head, each more cutting than the last. I ground my teeth and dug the toe of my slipper into the marble floor—a habit I'd developed once I realized my tutors couldn't see it under my long court skirts and correct it. "You're leaving? How delightful."

Her eyes narrowed at the double meaning and she tilted her chin up. "Yes, I'm going to Riiga for King Janiis's wedding. It will be quite the party, I'm told."

She'd been invited? I wouldn't trust the daughter of a traitor, no matter how much land she'd inherited. Why had Janiis invited *her*?

I was grateful for the hours of practice with my tutors, because my expression didn't slip, didn't betray me. All I could think of to say was "Oh?"

Cynthia's amber eyes glowed. "I heard about the courtyard incident. Pity your father didn't allow you to come. Think of the fun we could have had."

Her words dripped with disdain and my neck heated up. I *wanted* to tell Cynthia she was only going because she was such an outcast in Turian society, she'd have to find a Riigan to marry, if one would have her. Or that she was leaving so late because she couldn't afford to stay longer.

I *wanted* to say my father had good reasons for not allowing me to accompany him to Riiga, even if I didn't know what those reasons were.

"You were asking about me?" I said instead. "How nice."

Her upper lip curled and she rolled her eyes—a punishable offense in my tutors' eyes. "This is why your father refused to let you come, you know," she said with a careless shrug, though she aimed her words with deadly accuracy. "Any hint of conflict, and you bow before it." She waved her fingers at someone she recognized across the room, then leaned in. "What a waste of a princess," she murmured, then smiled as though we were the best of friends, dropped the barest of curtsies for the benefit of those watching our exchange, and floated away.

I counted the white knuckles on my hands, which still gripped each other. Once. Twice. Studied the view out the window without seeing it as I blinked away unshed tears. Cynthia's words were always laced with barbs. I could usually brush them away, but today she'd hit her mark.

Because I was afraid she was right. No one noticed me. No one outside of my family really even cared. I was a waste of a princess. I swallowed hard.

If I could go back and stand up to her, lash out at her, would I?

I smoothed the front of my gown. No. I didn't think I would.

Maybe I *was* weak.

The call was put out for any other petitioners, and the last came forward. It was another farmer speaking in favor of the pulley system that Janiis wanted to build, pleading for the king to give the land to construct it. Mother noted it and thanked him, and then the event was over. Finally.

My mother, Enzo, and Jenna stood and spoke with each other while the advisors congregated, waiting for them to come off the dais. By the vaguely panicked look on Jenna's face, I'd wager it was something about the wedding. No hope they'd come down anytime soon, then.

A long table filled with a light repast for anyone in attendance was set up near the back of the room. I made my way over to it, my mind repeating the conversation with Cynthia again and again, coming up with scathing responses and putting her in her place. Words I'd never manage to say but that made me feel better anyway. It didn't matter what I said, though. She was getting out, and I was stuck here. With all the reminders of the mages' attacks, the dungeon escape, the maze garden.

Mari stood next to a tall stool, a plate resting atop it loaded with foods of all varieties—most of them were Enzo's favorites or delicacies from Hálendi that Jenna had spoken of fondly.

"Are there any apple tarts?" I asked Mari, craning my neck as I searched the table. She shook her head, cheeks full. Of course my favorites wouldn't be here. I tugged on one of her curls and reached for a crystal glass of lemon water. "Don't choke on all that, or Mother won't let you come again."

Mari swallowed everything in one great gulp, and grinned up at me. "I'm glad I get to eat without hiding under the table now. The food on the edge is never as delicious as the food in the middle."

I choked on my drink. "That's how you swiped food? You hid under the table?"

Mari shrugged. "No one checks once the cloths are in place."

We both stared at the gold cloth that draped to the floor. I reached out with the toe of my slipper and lifted the cloth's edge. Both Mari and I peered beneath the table, then looked at each other and giggled when we saw there was nothing there.

A heavy arm draped over my shoulder, and another went over Mari's. Mari elbowed whoever was behind us straight off, and a grunt sounded as he retreated from her blow and hid behind me. His warm hands rested on my shoulders. Not heavy, not holding tight.

"Save me from your sister, Chiara!" said a deep, laughing voice I hadn't expected to hear again until spring.

I spun, trying to keep my jaw from dropping. "Atháren?" My skin went hot, from my neck all the way to the roots of my hair. I curtsied deep enough for a sovereign, grateful I didn't show the blush like Hálendians. "I mean, Your Majesty."

I hadn't bungled a title in *years*. Ren was *definitely* too handsome. The kind of handsome you had to prepare yourself at least a day in advance to resist.

Ren's mouth tilted up in a delicious grin, and he shrugged, his golden hair glowing in the setting sun. "I haven't been away long enough for you to forget my name, have I? Call me Ren. We're practically family, after all."

The air left my lungs like I'd been punched right in the stomach. Mari launched herself at him with a laugh, and he caught her and swung her around once, her squeals carrying over the conversations around us.

Mud flaked from his boots, and he smelled like the outdoors. Had he been so eager to see his sister that he hadn't even changed?

Grandmother Yesilia stood behind him with the smile reserved for her grandchildren. She poked them both. "Don't cause a scene. At least not before I've sampled the food." I raised my eyebrows at her, and she shrugged—she was allowed to shrug, now that she was older than the tutors, she always said. "He wandered into the healing chambers to see where his sister was. I didn't trust him not to get lost, so I brought him here."

We all chuckled, but Ren's eyes scanned over my shoulder, then stopped. If I hadn't been watching him so closely, I would have missed the change that came over him when he found his sister in the crowd. His shoulders relaxed, his smile went from flattering to natural, and his deep blue eyes lit up. Tiny changes I'd never noticed before, though he stayed only a few weeks after the treaty had been signed.

"All right," Ren said quietly right next to me. "Let's see how long before my anonymity is spoiled." On the dais, Jenna's brows furrowed, and she tipped her head, though I got the feeling she wasn't listening to my mother's latest worries about the wedding feast.

Heads began to turn our way. Jenna whirled around and gasped, and conversations ceased. All eyes turned to Ren, and whispered shock rippled outward.

I could only see his profile, but even with the attention of the entire throne room on him, he *smirked*. Like it didn't bother him one bit that everyone stared, many disapprovingly.

Jenna, her face shining with delight, jumped off the dais, dodged the remaining advisors caging her in, and ran into Ren's arms. She couldn't see it, but when Ren ducked his head to her shoulder as he hugged her, he squeezed his eyes shut, like this was the first moment he thought he'd survive to see another sunrise.

"What are you doing here?" she said, her voice carrying. Around the siblings, worried looks and hushed plans were already spreading. Speculation as to why the Hálendian king would visit unannounced.

"My sister doesn't write often enough," Ren said, lifting his shoulder and speaking to the crowd. "Who could I address this petition to so she actually sends a letter every now and then?" Many laughed, but not enough to ease the coiling tension.

"Come on." Mari took my hand and our grandmother's and pulled us toward the gathering in the center of the room, where my mother and Enzo greeted Ren.

"A lack of letters is not enough to warrant a kingly visit," Jenna said to Ren with a frown. I smoothed the front of my dress as my stomach dropped. She was right.

"Can't a brother visit his favorite sister?" Ren asked, subtly scanning the crowd. A dark look flickered over his expression before he recovered. He put a hand over his heart, exaggerating the motion. "It's lonely all the way up in Hálendi."

If my tutors had ever allowed me to snort, I would have. I very much doubted Ren lacked company of any sort.

My mother started in on new arrangements for meals and

schedules. Most of us had stopped listening, gauging by the glazed look in everyone's eyes. Except Ren's. His roved over every corner of the room, only pausing for brief moments before continuing on.

"We have guards posted, you know," I said quietly.

"Guards?" he responded absently.

I lifted a shoulder. "You're watching the shadows like they might attack."

He looked at me, then. Really looked. Not flirting; assessing. I'd hit on something. A wriggle of doubt started. He wasn't here because he missed his sister.

Then his carefree smile was back. "Habit, I guess."

Lie. I tilted my head, but let the matter drop.

"Your Majesty," Cynthia's grating voice cut in. She dipped into a deep curtsy that Ren only caught the last of because he'd been watching me. He couldn't have missed it when I flinched at the sound of her voice. "Are you traveling to Riiga as well?" She looked up at him through her lashes. "Perhaps we could travel together. Economy, and all that."

My eyebrows rose—how brazen could she be? Cynthia was a rare beauty in our kingdom, enough so that she'd somehow convinced my father she'd had nothing to do with her family's betrayal and begged for a chance to redeem herself. But so far, she'd only tried to snatch power and standing by any means possible. I seemed to be the only one who noticed.

Ren pasted on his most flattering smile—the same one he'd used on me. "I do apologize, my lady," he said with a flourish. "I hadn't planned on continuing south. However, I'm happy to have at least arrived before your departure."

I left the conversation despite the years of etiquette I'd mastered. Just turned and walked away, searching for food or air or something to quell the caged feeling tightening inside me. Watching Cynthia flirt with Ren was not something I wanted to witness. Watching him flirt back was worse.

I stumbled into a noblewoman and mumbled an apology, then changed course from the food table. Out. I needed to get away from everyone and everything.

The open doors beckoned me toward the hall, but then Luc was there, appearing as if in a strange dream. He had been in my father's guard. He should be in Riiga, but he stood in the doorway, boots dirty. Sword at his side. Deep circles under his eyes and scruff shadowing his jaw.

I'd never seen anyone look so grim in my life.

My heart froze in my chest, then took off, trying to escape out of my throat. It wouldn't slow no matter how many deep breaths I took.

Luc made his way through the crowd, sending me a dark look—even for him. Not many took note of him, just wrinkled their noses at the muddy path he left on the polished floors. He made it all the way to my mother, who followed him through the small door behind the dais with Jenna, Enzo, Yesilia, and Mari trailing them.

I couldn't make my feet move. Did I want to know what news Luc brought?

Then Ren was next to me, taking my elbow and gently leading me through the closest door. I wasn't sure how I'd known it was him, why I didn't jump, why his touch didn't make me nervous. It should have.

"Come on," he whispered with a resigned sort of dread. What had happened to the carefree boy who'd laughed and joked with us once the treaty was signed? Who'd claimed he traveled for over a week because his sister hadn't written enough letters. Why was he searching the shadows? Why had he shown up unannounced, and what did that have to do with Luc's arrival? "We'll want to hear this, too."

My head jerked back and forth. I couldn't hide my shaking hands.

Ren sighed, a bone-weary sound that came from six feet beneath him. "Not hearing it won't change the news."

We slipped into the cool air of the hallway. Chills raced up my arms and along my neck.

"Over here," I said, and led him to the room around the corner that fed onto the dais. The door stood open. We slipped inside and shut it behind us.

Luc stood by the fireplace, poking at the charred wood like it had offended him.

"What is it? What's happened?" Mother asked from his side. Grandmother Yesilia stood in a corner, a hand to her forehead, eyes closed.

Jenna clung to Enzo's arm like it would keep her from collapsing. Mari slipped her hand into our mother's, helping her to a chair when Luc didn't answer right away. Enzo stood like a pillar—as if he knew his strength would have to hold up the entire room. Perhaps the entire kingdom. I stood utterly still.

Luc swallowed, then swallowed again. "It's King Marko," he said, his voice rougher than I'd ever heard. "He . . . he never arrived in Riiga."

Koranth

"Get Brownlok in line," Koranth growled, pacing along the sand. Time slipped away fast now, but they were *so close.* He dragged his fingers through his hair. Several strands came away. Gray, not brown. The roar of the waves crashing against rocks, and the dark clouds blowing in promised a cold night. But he didn't feel it. Didn't feel anything anymore.

Nothing except the pull toward the Black Library and his silver sword.

"Brownlok's loyalty has been mine all along," Redalia said, her red hair whipping in the wind as her fingers brushed her lips. "He will follow the plan."

Koranth caressed the black blade at his side as he nodded. "The pieces are set; the roads are watched. The Black Library will be ours within the month."

Redalia cleared her throat. Only a slight sound, but Koranth scowled nonetheless. Her cloak whipped against her legs, snapping and pulling. "Brownlok said he searched Turia's palace from top to bottom. He didn't find a map, only a key. We need a map. A location. Something."

Koranth tugged his cloak back over his shoulder where the wind had blown it off. "I've done my part. All that's left is to extract the information from our guest."

"And if he doesn't have it?"

Koranth shrugged. "I don't care how you get it. Just find the map."

Redalia's eyes narrowed and it took a moment for her to speak. "I'm a little busy at the moment as you know. I'll send Brownlok."

"Get it done," Koranth growled. "Soon." He shook off the hair clutched in his fist, and the strands spiraled up into the sky.

Redalia tapped her gold blade once, twice. But she nodded and turned away, disappearing into the night. Koranth sighed and pulled his sword from its sheath, holding it carefully, pressing the flat edge of the black blade against his cheek and inhaling its power. Soon. Soon he'd have the Black Library and its power. And then he'd have his revenge.

CHAPTER SIX

Ren

I was too late. Curses circled my mind as Luc's pronouncement blasted through the room. I couldn't have failed. Couldn't be too late. My lungs tightened until I thought my chest would collapse.

A hand wrapped around my forearm, squeezing. My gaze shot to the hand, then to its owner. Chiara. All color had left her cheeks, and I wasn't sure whether she was holding me up, or whether I was holding her.

"I knew I shouldn't have allowed him to go," the queen muttered over and over again from her chair, a small sob breaking from her throat.

Enzo hadn't moved. "Do we know it wasn't a detour, or a visit to a nearby village that delayed him?"

Jenna cursed—a word I wasn't familiar with, though it sounded Turian. "I *knew* something would go wrong."

Luc paced in front of the fire. "I followed orders to take four men and ride ahead through Rialzo, at the top of the cliffs, and down into Riiga to assure the king's path to the palace in Vera was clear. Marko should have followed the next day. He didn't," he said to Enzo. "My men and I raced back up the cliff, but couldn't find anyone from the rest of the party—not in Rialzo, or any of the surrounding villages or land. No trace." He shook his head slowly. "I've been riding almost nonstop to get here."

"The tethers," Jenna murmured. She'd gone pale and gripped Enzo's arm. She closed her eyes, then shook her head. "I can't tell. Marko is so far away, and the connection isn't very strong. But he's not dead." She pressed one hand against her stomach and looked vaguely sick. She wouldn't meet my eyes. "I would have felt that."

Chiara's grip relaxed at the news. My eyebrows shot up. Jenna was developing a tether with Marko? Did she have a tether with everyone else here? And why did my stomach twist at that thought?

"What's being done to find him?" I asked when I'd found my voice.

Luc squeezed his hand around the hilt of his sword. "I was only with four men. I've left them looking for him, two by two, and I told them to keep the search discreet. Riiga must be behind this. On the way to Vera, we encountered rumors of something big happening in connection with the king's wedding."

"Something bigger than a royal wedding?" I asked. Something big enough that the Medallion would urge me south?

Luc rubbed his eyes. "I didn't think anything of it—until the king went missing." He turned to Enzo. "*Diri,* if the *something big* has anything to do with all of the Riigans I saw in the southern villages, we could be looking at another attempted attack."

Enzo frowned. "We handled them easily three months ago. Why would they try such a thing again? And why wouldn't the advisors we placed on their council have mentioned any of these rumors?"

"If Riiga had an army on your border three months ago, why did Marko accept the invitation?" I growled. I knew I wasn't helping the situation, but I should have come sooner, should have . . . done . . . something.

Enzo folded his arms. "The advisors on Riiga's council recommended the king pay his respects at the wedding as a way to heal the breach between the kingdoms. All of them. Seals intact."

So either they were all traitors, or there were a few more missing people we didn't know about yet.

"I'm telling you," Luc said, "Riiga is behind this."

"So withhold your exports—deny them food and fresh water," I said. "Slowly at first. A hint at what could happen if Marko isn't released. If that doesn't work, war. You said yourself you handled the conflict easily three months ago."

Enzo's hand covered his mouth, then moved to his hip. "Invading Riiga is nearly impossible. There'd be a bottleneck of troops at the path down the cliffs, and their fleet is far superior to ours if we tried an invasion by sea."

My head jerked back. "Why haven't you addressed these issues before? Riiga has been a threat for years."

Enzo glared at me. "It hasn't been necessary. The bottleneck works both ways, protecting *us* from a large-scale attack as well."

Jenna edged a half step in front of Enzo. "We need to stay calm. Work together."

Guilt rolled in my gut like a rock. I should have come sooner.

Enzo slipped his hand into hers. "The messengers we sent to find the mages haven't returned. If there aren't any traces of what happened to my father, there could be magic involved."

Jenna's cheeks turned a shade paler, which I hadn't thought possible. She grasped the hilt of the sword tucked into the folds of her skirt with a white-knuckle grip. "No," she said hoarsely, then swallowed. "Mages are brutal. There would be rumors. Stories. Bodies." Her voice dropped to a whisper on the last word, and she leaned into Enzo.

I swallowed and stared at the ground. Ever since our mother died, I'd been the one Jenna turned to—any problem, any hurt, it was my shoulder she leaned on, my job to cheer her up.

"No bodies," Luc said, collapsing into a chair near the fire. "No rumors."

I sighed and tilted my head to the side, working out a kink from making the twelve-day journey from Hálendi in ten. At least it wasn't mages.

Enzo kissed the side of Jenna's head, and she started pacing like she always did when she had a problem to think through. She truly didn't need me anymore.

Jenna tugged her dress out of the way of a chair. "The mages were summoned from the Ice Deserts. It wasn't Leland, though he was working with Graymere. It could be someone in Hálendi." She looked to me and I nodded to confirm my agreement. I'd have to write to Edda—perhaps Isarr or the assassins could be persuaded to reveal information about that, if they had any.

The finger of a cool breeze snuck down the back of my collar. The stone arches of the crypt rose at the edges of my vision. I shook my head hard.

"Or it could be someone in Riiga. It could be anyone," Enzo said.

"Does it matter?" Chiara asked her brother. At some point, she'd removed her hand from my arm and sat in a chair facing the others. "You and Jenna are betrothed. Use that alliance to bring in the soldiers and supplies we need from Hálendi." She was fraying at the edges, her composure cracking, and I didn't want to say what I had to. But everyone in this room needed to understand the state of alarm on the Plateau.

"If you did declare war against Riiga, would your people fight alongside Hálendians?" I asked. "I got the impression on my journey to Turiana that no one trusted me." Evidenced by the innkeepers with no rooms for me to stay in and bakers who refused to let me buy their offerings.

"They would," Chiara said with a frown, but Queen Cora had put her head in her hand.

I rubbed my hand along my jaw and sighed. "Also, I'm not sure how much of Hálendi's forces could be spared."

Silence dropped over the room like a bucket of ice water. Accusing stares hit me from every corner. Yesilia's gaze burned a hole into my forehead, like she was trying to see into my mind.

"Why not?" Mari finally spoke up from where she stood by the silent Cora. "I thought we were friends now."

A breathless chuckle escaped before I could lock it back. "We are, Mari. We are friends." I sat in the chair next to Chiara's. It was as hard and uncomfortable as it looked, and my backside still ached from ten days in a saddle. Didn't Turians believe in cushions? "Hálendi is . . . ill prepared for conflict at the moment."

Jenna narrowed her eyes. "Explain."

I swallowed, knowing she could feel the rising panic that tightened my throat. Although if there were other tethers, maybe she wouldn't feel mine as much.

Deep breath in, out. Steady. "I cut the council in half. There's no general leading the army—I installed a council of five captains instead. I'm only sure three of those are loyal to me. Mostly loyal, anyway, as I couldn't get the three without the other two." My voice dropped off as I rambled.

It didn't matter how much I rationalized my choices—the entire Plateau would suffer, maybe even fall, because I couldn't manage to transition the monarchy despite having spent my entire life training for it.

"Why didn't you write? Why didn't you tell me how bad things have gotten?" Jenna asked quietly.

I pressed my lips together. It wasn't as though she'd written to me. She was here in her new role with her new family. She didn't need me or my troubles.

The Medallion cooled against my skin, pulling me out of my thoughts.

The very capable, though distressed, queen of Turia sat on

my right. The future king and queen of Turia stood before me. Yesilia's gaze only held pity. It was *my* kingdom that was in shambles. *I* was the weak ruler in the room.

"We need to focus on King Marko," I said, infusing as much confidence into my words as I could. "We must retrieve him before the wedding and whatever Riiga is planning."

Jenna's stare promised we'd talk later.

"So we keep looking. Send more men—" Enzo started.

"But not too many," I interrupted, and Chiara's glare burned into my side.

"What do you mean?" she asked with a frown. "We should send every available person to look for him!"

Enzo caught on and muttered something under his breath.

I shook my head slowly. "So far, no one knows he's missing. Marko is the key to stability on the Plateau. He has the strength to keep the Turian nobility in line, a chance to talk sense into Riiga, to call on Hálendi for aid with enough power to get the council's head out of its own problems." I stopped. Licked my lips. "If he's . . . if *two* kingdoms have young, untested leaders—no offense meant, Enzo—the *entire* Plateau could fall into chaos with the slightest nudge from any enemy."

Enzo groaned and slumped onto a sofa. "The kingdom—the Plateau—will panic if they find out."

Chiara's eyes snapped and she held her jaw tight. "So we do nothing? Sit here while something awful happens to our father?"

"No. We have to find him," I said. I touched my chest, feeling for the Medallion, wishing it had guidance, answers, anything. Wishing I'd come sooner.

Enzo's head jerked up. "What about Cynthia Hallen?"

Chiara's nose wrinkled. "What about her?" she muttered low enough that I was probably the only one who heard.

If Cynthia had been the girl throwing herself at me earlier, I agreed with Chiara's assessment. "Can we trust her?" I asked.

"Father saw something in her, enough to not banish her with the rest of her family. She's been allowed a trial period to prove she's loyal. If she passes, she'll inherit her father's lands. And she's leaving soon for Riiga," Enzo said. "With an *official invitation* to the wedding."

Jenna rubbed her hands together, catching on to his idea. "We can use her to get our people into Riiga to search without raising any alarm."

Luc nodded. "That could work. She's vain enough to need a large entourage, and she has a lot at stake to prove her loyalty."

Enzo nodded to him. "Get it done. I want to know the exact location my father disappeared, and possible routes to anywhere a king and his entourage could be hidden."

Mari, who'd been silent, helped the queen stand, with Yesilia on the other side.

"We'll find him, Mother. I promise," Enzo said. And despite all the possible ways for his plan to go sideways, even I believed the conviction in his voice.

Cora gave a watery smile. "I know you will, carino." She left, still holding tight to Mari and Yesilia.

"What if we ask Janiis?" Chiara said in the silence that filled the space the queen had occupied. "See if he denies it or takes responsibility?"

I leaned my elbows on my knees. "We can't ask him outright—can't alert him that anything's amiss. But what if we *did* send him a letter saying Marko's been delayed at the cliffs, and asking whether he knows anything about it?"

The others nodded slowly, and Enzo rubbed his hands together. "It's a start, anyway. I'll pen the letter myself. Send it with a messenger within the hour."

Luc, Enzo, and Jenna continued planning—where to place men, roles, timing. Chiara watched them, staring without seeing. What was playing in her memory to make her look so lost? Finally, she slowly eased out of the chair with the perfect posture and bearing of a princess. But she radiated sadness in a way that tore at something deep in me.

Jenna didn't need me, but making sure Chiara was okay was one thing I *could* do.

I grabbed her hand before she could slip out of the room. A warmth I hadn't expected shot up my arm, and I released her, staring at her hand with furrowed brows.

She tucked it into the folds of her dress. "Did you need something, Ren?"

My mind was wiped blank. I'd forgotten what I was going to say. Was it the warmth from her hand? The relentless journey here? The way her dark hair moved around her shoulders?

"I just . . ." I swallowed and stood, hoping that would jolt my brain enough to put together a coherent sentence. *Say* something, *you ice head.* "It will be okay." I winced as soon as the words left my mouth.

Her eyes brightened with unshed tears and I wanted to throw myself into the dungeon. "I hope so," she whispered, though her voice remained steady.

Someone walking by in the hall burst into laughter. I startled, nudging Chiara behind me, my hand going to my sword. I'd forgotten everything but Chiara for one precarious moment. A luxury I couldn't afford.

My chest tightened and I started to sweat, though my skin felt clammy.

Oh no. Not here.

Jenna's eyes darted to me. "What's wrong, Ren?"

My jaw flexed. What *wasn't* wrong was a better question. "Did you really ask me that?" I said, brushing her question aside, trying to steady my breathing. "Did you hear everything we've been talking about?"

She glared at me. "You flinch at every loud sound. You aren't supposed to be here—"

I inched away from Chiara. Did she realize I'd repositioned myself to protect her? I hoped not. "I was serious about you not writing often enough," I said with a shrug, eyeing the door to freedom.

"But that's not the reason you came," Chiara said quietly. "You knew something was wrong."

I swallowed, and every eye landed on me. The tight feeling in my chest returned. I rubbed the Medallion. "Something . . . felt off. Like I needed to leave Hálendi. But I don't know more than any of you. Less, probably."

I didn't know why, but Chiara's eyes were the ones I felt heaviest on me. Like she saw right through me. My breaths got shorter, and I couldn't—I needed—

"E-excuse me," I said, then turned and slipped out the door.

CHAPTER SEVEN

Ren

I took off at a jog, darting through hallways that all looked the same, trying to find my room. I turned corner after corner. Tried one stairway, only to have it lead me in a circle.

I grabbed a boy carrying a bucket. "You," I said, my raspy voice unrecognizable, "where is my room?"

The boy looked up at me with wide eyes and shook his head. He backed away a step. I advanced. I wanted to ask nicely, explain I was lost, but nothing came out.

And then a shadow moved in the corner of my eye. A weapon coming at me.

I brought my arm down hard, blocking the blow, and spun with my elbow aimed at my attacker's gut. But they dodged my blow and hooked a leg in front of mine, trying to flip me.

I shifted my weight and took them down instead, drawing my sword and bringing it to their throat.

"Whoa!" my sister's voice yelled. "It's me, Ren! What is wrong with you?"

The edges of my vision lined with pillars, darkness, tombs of the kings.

"Ren!" she said again.

I shook my head. Focused.

Jenna lay beneath me. Not an assassin.

"*Cavolo,*" a tiny voice whispered. The boy was pressed up against the wall watching us, his bucket clutched tight to his chest.

I sheathed my sword and held my hand out to him, palm up. "I'm sorry," I murmured between gasping breaths. "I—" Jenna grunted and shoved me off her, then helped me stand. "I was trying to find my room. I need . . . I need to . . . to find my room."

"It's okay," she murmured, slipping her arm around my waist and nodding to the boy, who ran off.

I let her lead me through the palace. I didn't recognize any of the turns, any of the hallways, but then we were at the room the steward had taken me to when I'd arrived.

We stumbled inside and I immediately locked the door, then shoved a chair in front of it for good measure. I stumbled to the basin with clean water and dunked my head. With all sounds muffled, my thoughts settled, and I stayed under until my lungs burned. Jenna grabbed my collar and yanked me out again, splashing water over both of us.

"You show up in the throne room with no notice, no guards, in *traveling* clothes. Your tether is . . . a mess. What. Is going. On." She brushed the water from her hands and the front of her skirt. "The seamstresses will kill you if they see what you've done to this dress, by the way."

"They can join the club," I muttered, and yanked at the buttons of my tunic. It was too blasted hot in here. I pulled the whole thing off and tossed it on a chair. I shook out my wet hair, flinging water everywhere. I should have changed before finding Jenna, but I'd been so anxious to see her again. To get answers about the Medallion's warning.

Jenna sucked in a sharp breath. She stared at my stomach. Right where—I cursed, spinning so my back was to her.

"Who did that to you?" she asked, and yanked me around to inspect the long scar across my torso. I couldn't read anything in her voice—it was flat. Emotionless. Sometimes I wished I had her gift of the tethers, because I had no clue what she was feeling.

I reached around her and pulled out a wrinkled tunic from my bag, then threw it on.

She folded her arms. "I felt something a while ago, but I didn't know what it was. How—"

"It's not your problem," I said, maybe too harshly, because she recoiled. I sighed. "I only meant you have enough problems here. We need to figure out what to do about Marko." Just as soon as my hands stopped shaking.

Jenna went to the sofa and sat. "We were trying to. But then you ran out like you were being chased by wolves." She patted the cushion on her right and raised an eyebrow.

I fell onto the sofa, next to her.

Oh, glaciers. Everyone had seen me run from the room. The boy in the hall saw me attack my sister. I ran my fingers through my hair until it stuck up everywhere. "Two of my guards cornered me in the crypt." I swallowed down the contents of my churning stomach. "I got lucky."

Jenna's face might as well have been made of stone, but she flickered in and out of sight, almost like she'd lost control of her magic for a moment. I couldn't help the small smile forming on my lips—her magic was *incredible*.

"You don't get to smile about this," she said in a deadly voice. "Who was responsible?"

I wiped my expression clean, my constant companion, dread, settling in the pit of my stomach again. "Isarr. The other attempts weren't close to successful."

She growled. "Other attempts?" She took a minute to compose herself, and I wished again that she could be with me in Hálendi. "And the attack, the panic, is staying with you?" she finally asked.

I licked my lips. She knew what this felt like. I wasn't sure how, but she knew. A tiny part of me relaxed. "Yes."

She stared at the floor. "It gets easier," she whispered. "The memories won't hit you out of nowhere."

I leaned my head back against the sofa. "Do the nightmares go away?"

She tucked her legs up onto the seat and rested her head on my shoulder. "I don't know."

✦ ✦ ✦

I woke with a gasp and sat up in bed. But it wasn't my bed.

"What is it?" Jenna asked from the sofa. She'd sprung up, sword in hand, spinning around unsteadily. "What happened?" she slurred.

I pressed my palms into my eyes. "How . . . what happened?"

She sheathed her blade and sat down with a yawn. "You fell asleep. You said you didn't sleep well anymore, so I stayed. If you ask me, you could use a month's worth of sleep. You look awful. Worse than when you showed up in a throne room in your travel gear." She grinned and pulled out the tie from her braid, running her hand through her hair.

"You aren't going to let that one go, are you?" I asked.

She chuckled. "Nope."

She was free here. Happy. In a way she never had been back home. I should have been happy for her—the chances of finding this kind of life were slim with a kingdom riding on your shoulders. But all I felt was lonely.

Jenna paused, brows furrowed, and I tucked those emotions away. I'd gotten good at that over the years.

"So you fired half the council, huh?" she asked.

I pulled my knees up and rested my arms on them. "You should have seen their faces."

She smirked. "Lenor?"

"Gone."

"Good. I never liked him."

"He didn't like me much, either. But at least he was vocal about it. Maybe I should have kept him. At least I knew where his loyalty lay."

Jenna shook her head and arched her back. "Everyone loves you, Ren. What's going on up there?"

I didn't know if she meant up in Hálendi or up in my head, so I shrugged. She patted the cushion next to her. I grumbled about getting out of bed, but the truth was I hadn't slept so well in months.

"I received the invitation to Janiis's wedding almost as soon as I got back to Hálendi after we'd signed the treaty," I said. "The council rejected it outright, saying they didn't trust the Riigans. With the pass closing, I agreed; it was the one item of business we came together on. But they were looking at *me*, saying they didn't trust *me*. Then little things started happening. Cider that had been tainted—"

"But you can heal—"

"*I* know that, and *you* know that, but I'm glad *they* didn't. So I sent out feelers, trying to figure out who was angry about the treaty's terms. I made sure not to move forward with dismissals without proof, but the more changes I made, the less everyone trusted me." I sighed and Jenna waited for me to continue. "Then the Medallion started changing. Warming against me. Then, the day after"—I gestured to my stomach, unwilling to say the words in case it brought the memories back—"I don't know how to explain it, but it was almost like the Medallion was in my mind. Urging me to leave. So I did."

Her eyebrows shot up. "Just like that? Alone? Ren, you don't have an heir."

I stood and paced between the bed and the empty fireplace. "I didn't come alone." I paused, then muttered, "I brought Aleinn's brother with me."

"A stablehand?" Jenna almost shouted. "That's not the right company! There are mages who want you dead! You hold one of the keys to the Black Library—"

"I'm aware of that," I said, kicking at the rug. "Edda counseled me to go. We set everything up nice and tidy."

Jenna lowered her head and rubbed her face with shaking hands. "I can't believe you went through the Wild with only Adri."

I sat next to her again. Would she want my help? I wasn't sure, but I put one hand on her shoulder.

Jenna calmed, but more worry uncurled within me.

"Shouldn't the messengers have returned?" I asked. "How hard is it to find two really old mages? The Plateau isn't that big."

Jenna frowned and rubbed a finger along the embroidery of her skirt. "There's a lot of inhabitable land in the Wild and to the west, where no one goes. Or the Ice Deserts. What if they went back?"

I shook my head. "Why would they retreat? They have a key—they're closer than they've ever been. And if someone killed my friend, I'd—" I stopped cold. "You're not using your wedding to draw them out, are you?"

Jenna held out her hands. "I don't know what the mages are planning, but the sooner Enzo and I are married, the stronger both kingdoms become. The bigger the threat to the mages. And Riiga." She pursed her lips and sat back. I waited for her to spill whatever she wasn't telling me. She folded her arms and huffed. "I tried to convince them to have the wedding sooner, to lure the mages here before they could regroup. Enzo didn't like using me as bait."

I tilted my head and looked up. "Well, actually, that's not a bad—"

She threw a cushion at my head and we laughed. "Stop it. You know I tried to convince Marko and Enzo that it was a perfect scenario. Neither of them would listen, and Cora insisted she needed more time to plan. Though Enzo *might* be persuaded to change his mind."

I burst out laughing, a sound that surprised me as much as Jenna. "I'm sorry," I said, waving my hands to fend off another pillow attack. "Enzo's getting antsy, is he?"

Jenna rolled her eyes but blushed bright red to the roots of her hair. "Shut up." But she was smiling, too.

I lounged against the back of the sofa, my lungs getting lighter the more I laughed. She tried to keep back her smile. "I'm sorry. I'm done," I said, then took a deep breath. "Marko is gone for now—though I'm sorry to be the one to say it," I added when Jenna's shoulders dropped. "So do we use you as bait? Do we use the Medallion and go after the Mages' Library even though we don't have the Turian key? Or know where it is . . ."

She adjusted her skirt and tucked her feet up onto the cushion. "What do you know of the Medallion? Could it get us to the library?"

I pulled the Medallion from beneath my shirt and held it flat in my palm, as though that would enable me to understand it better. "It's connected to the land's magic. Edda told me that ever since Kais came and enchanted the Ice Deserts, the land has been striving to regain its balance. But that balance wasn't always *helpful* to me or to Hálendi."

Jenna frowned. "That makes sense. I've been studying as well." I snorted, because of course she had. She continued like she hadn't heard me. "I wanted to know the difference between the mage's artifacts and mine. Turns out, all artifacts must be crafted by a land mage and be free of any imperfection. The mage chooses the material, and the land mage crafts it in such a way that the artifact resonates with what it's made from."

I stared at the ceiling. "Resonate? Like . . . like it catches the sound of the magic and carries it between the artifact and the mage?"

"Exactly. But the difference between our artifacts and theirs is that theirs required a sacrifice—one with a lot of blood—to crack their magic reserves open and create a direct connection between *their* magic and the artifact."

I tilted my head back. Jenna and I had magic. We had artifacts. We were exactly like the mages, unless you understood what Jenna had learned. How could we help people—especially Turians—trust us?

"Did you find anything more on the Medallion being a key to the Black Library?" I asked.

She shook her head and slouched back. The seamstresses really might kill me after they saw what a mess her dress had become. "I've searched, but nothing yet."

"And the Black Library itself? Should we go after it?" I'd forgotten how good it felt to *do* something. Coming here—as impulsive as it'd been—reminded me.

"Marko urged us to wait. He said going after the library blind, without knowing where the mages are and without all the pieces, would only expose us and endanger Turia. And Hálendi."

My eyes darted away from hers. She'd added Hálendi as an afterthought. How had everything changed in the course of a few months? Leading troops at North Watch was supposed to be my chance to prove myself. Instead, I'd been hurled off a cliff.

"Hey," Jenna said softly. "I'm sorry. I didn't mean—"

I gently shrugged her hand from my shoulder. "Don't read my emotions right now, Jen. I'm tired and I don't have the energy to filter or process or even understand what I'm feeling. So unless you're going to illuminate my feelings for me, don't. Please," I added softly. If Jenna pitied me, if she thought I couldn't do this, I wasn't sure I'd ever recover.

She clasped her hands in her lap. "Ren, what's happened to you? You are the most confident person I've ever known."

"You lived most of your life within the walls of one castle, so that's not saying much." I snorted, and she laughed, nudging my shoulder.

"I'm saying you used to trust yourself."

I rested my elbow on my knee, my temple settling against my palm. A thousand responses went through my head, all the times the Medallion flashed hot and cold, the dismissive glances from courtiers and councilors alike. "I'm trying."

Jenna nodded and stood, moving the chair away from the door while casting me a pointed look. "Get ready, then come eat. You'll feel better with some food in you."

I laughed as she left, glad that at least one person on this cursed Plateau knew me. I leaned back against the sofa when the door clicked shut, my laughter fading into silence.

Whoever had ambushed Marko was either very smart, or very stupid. We'd have to play this game carefully to keep the fragile balance of the Plateau intact.

CHAPTER EIGHT

Chiara

A cool breeze ruffled the dry leaves above me, rustling them like bones. The autumn rains would hit the capital soon. The earth was being prepared for winter. Clipped back. Turned over.

Shadows danced in patches over the bench I sat on, Jenna's unopened book by my side. Still blank. I'd meant to start filling the pages, but every time I held a pen over them, I couldn't write.

I watched the main gate instead. The people coming and going. The busyness distracted me from the solemnity indoors. How quiet everyone was, even the servants. They didn't know what had happened, only that something was drastically wrong.

It had been three days. Three days since Luc spoke the words that haunted my every footstep.

Cynthia would leave with reinforcements today. And I could do nothing.

I'd once longed for free time, hours to spend how I wished. But now, most of my tutors had been temporarily dismissed, so my days stretched endlessly. Trapped in a place with too many reminders.

I didn't know why Enzo and Ren insisted on the secrecy. I mean, I understood it, the idea behind it. But I also understood that news—especially bad news—always spread, no matter how hard you tried to conceal it. Would the Plateau really descend into chaos like Ren thought?

The roofs of the city's taller buildings peeked over the top of the wall. The only home I'd ever known felt cold today despite the sunshine. My father was missing, and they were dispatching guards with a traitor's daughter?

I knew why Enzo couldn't go—he was next in line if the worst happened. My mother was too gentle for a mission like this, too distraught; Mari too young. Jenna . . . I didn't think Enzo would let her go on her own. Ren was king of his own country with his own troubles.

Everyone was too *something* to go.

Everyone except me.

"Good afternoon, Princess," a falsely sweet voice added to the jarring din at the gate.

How did she always find me when I didn't want to be found? I sighed and turned. It wasn't just Cynthia, though. Her arm was looped through Ren's. Because of course she'd find a way to flaunt him in front of me.

"Cynthia." I didn't have the energy today for platitudes, to play her games. I avoided Ren's gaze altogether.

"Princess Chiara, you look pale. Is anything the matter?" she asked. Her concern was a thinly veiled attempt to get more gossip. Which I wouldn't be indulging. How much had she been told about the men she would get into Riiga? I hoped not a lot—she'd turn traitor the moment someone offered her something shiny.

Ren stayed silent, his arm rigid in Cynthia's.

"What could be wrong on a beautiful day like today?" I addressed them both, but my mind stayed latched on the gate. I didn't care if Ren saw the puffiness around my eyes from crying all night—only at night, when no one could see. But I didn't have the patience for him to turn his charm on me. Not now.

Cynthia glared at me and released her grip on Ren's arm. "Maybe you need better entertainment." She snatched my book from the bench.

I lunged for it, but Cynthia danced back, holding it out of reach as a page fluttered to the ground. My hands clenched into fists.

"Reading about pirates again?" She giggled, no doubt remembering how she'd held that over me for weeks.

Her voice rang out over the gardens, drawing the eye of a few gardeners. Ren's lips tipped up and he looked at me with something even worse than the flirtatious grin he gave everyone—he looked at me like he looked at Mari.

Cynthia's laugh faded. She studied the book's cover, then flipped it open.

I stood and held out my hand. "Return my book, please."

Cynthia frowned. "It's blank."

I glared at her. "I am aware of that, yes."

Faster than I thought possible, Ren snatched the book from her. He snapped it closed, fumbling it when he saw the cover. But he recovered and stepped away from Cynthia, handing it to me. "I love a good adventure," he said with a wink.

"I'm sure you do," I murmured as I picked up the fallen page. My cheeks heated and I sucked in a breath. I hadn't meant to say the words out loud. But Ren wasn't angry; he choked out a surprised laugh, one even louder than Cynthia's.

I pursed my lips against the smile trying to form at the sound of his laugh and tucked the loose page inside the cover. I'd have to see if Master Romo could help me repair the book.

When Ren had recovered, he turned to Cynthia. "I believe your party is leaving soon, is it not? You'd be remiss not to check that the servants have stowed everything properly for your journey."

She opened and closed her mouth like a fish. I almost laughed. There wasn't a good way to agree with him *and* stay. I'd wanted her to leave two days ago. Enzo had assured me they'd use the time well, preparing the men and supplies to give them the best chance to find our father.

But at least Cynthia was *doing* something. I was stuck here. Useless.

"You are quite right, Your Majesty," she acquiesced with a deep curtsy—deep enough to show off the neckline of her dress. I rolled my eyes, which Ren caught. He snorted. Cynthia jerked her head up, her cheeks slightly pink, and glared at me. "Until next time."

She didn't bid me farewell, but she had missed her mark if she thought I'd be upset because of it.

When she was out of hearing, Ren settled himself on the bench. "That girl is a leech."

The corner of my lips threatened to curve up. He was a better judge of character than I gave him credit for. I took a step back, not sure whether I should return to my place on the bench or leave him be. For the two days he'd been here, he always had a noble or council member following him. Did he want to be left alone? But then he tipped his head to the space on the bench beside him.

I turned the book so the cover lay against my stomach and took my time settling my skirts, making sure to stay at the very edge of the bench so we didn't touch. Not that I didn't *want* to sit right next to him, but every time he flirted with someone, I couldn't help but wonder what he was hiding. I wasn't going to be part of any game—I'd had enough of that. Though if he kept looking at me like a sister and referring to me as "family," I guess I wouldn't have to worry much about flirting anyway.

"Any change?" I asked when he didn't break the silence.

"No. Luc is already gone. His men will leave with Cynthia within the hour. The letter your brother sent might get to Vera tonight if the messengers don't encounter any delays."

At the gate, a group of merchants laughed, their wagons empty, their business complete. Returning to a world much wider than the walls of the palace. A world my father was lost in.

"Will Enzo tell the council?"

Ren shook his head slowly. "He said Lord Hallen's betrayal is too new to trust them with this."

Why, then, would they trust Hallen's daughter? Was I the only one who saw this flaw in their plan?

I waited to see if he would tell me more, explain his bleak look when he mentioned councils and betrayals. He didn't. Instead, he said after a long pause, "How are you?"

I stared at my skirt, tracing a seam. It was one of the skirts I'd packed for Riiga. "I wanted to go with my father." Ren didn't move. From what Jenna had said about him, it didn't surprise me that he was a good listener. "I was packed and ready. Asked to accompany him." I swallowed hard. "He refused. I backed down." I always backed down. I clasped my hands and stared straight ahead. "I can't help but wonder—if I'd gone, could I have made a difference?"

Ren sighed deep and long, but I cut him off. "I know I'm not like you or Jenna. But maybe I would have noticed something amiss. Been able to raise a warning."

I couldn't look at Ren, but from the corner of my eye, I saw him rubbing his leg. "I . . ." He hesitated, then switched whatever he'd been about to say. "Whoever did this orchestrated it perfectly."

I'd been dismissed again, and a tiny part of me folded in on itself. I'd expected different from him. More.

A long silence stretched between us. "So that's it?" I said quietly. "The king of Turia is missing and we keep it a secret?"

"It's not as simple as—"

"Yes, it is. He's my father. We need to find him. If it was

your—" I broke off at Ren's sharp inhale. Cavolo, I'd forgotten. I squeezed my eyes shut and rubbed them, then shifted to face him. "I'm sorry," I said quietly. "I shouldn't have said that."

Ren put his hands on his knees and pushed himself to stand. His face, so expressive and alive when flirting with Cynthia, was now gray and closed off. "I should go. I've business to attend to."

His boots crunched on the gravel as he walked away, hands deep in his pockets, head bent. I hadn't meant to add more weight to the burdens he already carried. I sighed and stared up at the patches of blue through the leaves turning from green to gold. I didn't want to lose my father like Jenna and Ren had lost theirs. I wouldn't.

My father had been the rock of our family, of our kingdom. He shouldered our problems, our tears.

My problems. My tears.

I furiously wiped my cheeks and settled the book on my lap again. I'd thought to write notes or memories in it, but something about the book—the reverence Jenna had shown when she gave it to me—left me unsure I had anything worth recording.

I pulled the page that had fallen from where I'd tucked it, silently cursing Cynthia for mishandling my gift. But the page was yellow and brittle—much older than the rest of the book. And it wasn't blank.

I carefully unfolded the page, holding its edges. Two lines— a circle within a circle. The space between had been shaded by an expert hand. In tiny, looping script at the bottom, a single word: *Turia.*

Jenna had told me about this, about what the mages sought when they'd stormed the palace and forced us to hide in the secret compartment behind the drawing room fireplace. This was a picture of a key to the Black Library, where all the learning and artifacts of the ancient mages had been banished to keep magic from spreading once again.

Jenna had pulled this page from a book about Graymere—I didn't think she'd ever admitted that to Master Romo, and I wouldn't be the one to tell him what she'd done. Had she meant to give this to me? Or just forgotten it was tucked within the book?

I sighed and began to refold the page, but faint words written on the back of the illustration smudged under my fingers:

Three keys to find the library black:
one in snow, the heart of attack.
Another within the heart,
and surrounding it, too,
a ring of flax, of brown and blue.

And then, in script I could barely make out, the words *vineyards that touch the sky.*

The library black? Koranth's black eyes flashed in my memory. A tiny fire lit within me. I scanned the words again. *Three keys? Vineyards that touch the sky?* This was more than a simple poem. It seemed like . . . a clue.

✦ ✦ ✦

My back ached from the past three days of sitting on hard chairs and leaning over the wooden table by the library's largest window. I usually opted for the cushions in the window seat, but for my research, I needed a table, somewhere to spread out.

Master Romo had left a tray at lunchtime, but it lay mostly untouched. He was probably the only one who realized I'd been here so long. Dark emotions filled the corners of every room in the palace; the very air tightened around me the longer we waited with no word.

Even here, in the library, the mages had left their mark. New curtains and furniture, half-empty shelves as the scribes mended what Brownlok had destroyed. And yet with my work spread out around me, the weight in the palace wasn't so crushing.

Enzo and Jenna stayed busy with wedding plans—their union more important than ever. Ren, I assumed, was dealing with his own kingdom's troubles.

My mother wouldn't leave her chambers. She'd been sitting in the same chair, unmoving, without hope. We'd said she had a slight illness—nothing rest wouldn't cure but enough to keep rumors from starting.

My schedule was a fraction of what it once was, and I begged off the rest of my studies, saying I didn't feel well. My tutor assumed I must have caught something from my mother. Only my guard tracked where I went, watching in the background—she was new, but loyal to me.

Something about the poem—the clue—stayed with me, running through my mind. Three keys, two kingdoms, vineyards that touch the sky.

The vineyards bit didn't seem connected with the other part, yet it had been included. The script was different, shakier, than that of the poem. Like it had been added later, or by someone else.

Whatever this poem was, it was important. One thing my father taught me was that when negotiating, it's always better to have the upper hand, to have what the other person wants. I could be mistaken, but Koranth—Janiis's ambassador—had helped the mages before. If this clue was valuable to the mages, maybe it would be valuable to Janiis. Maybe he'd be willing to trade it—or at least a piece of it—for my father.

I cracked open another book, looking for any hint of keys or flax or vineyards or magic. Something to prove that this clue had value. Enough value to save my father.

"Here you are," Yesilia whispered right next to my ear, making me jump so high my tailbone hurt when I landed back in the chair.

"Grandmother," I scolded as I laughed. "Don't scare me like that."

She chuckled and pulled over a chair from another table so she could sit with me. She held a tray—was it dinnertime already?

"What has you holed up in here for so long?" She leaned closer, squinting at the tiny script in the books laid out before me. Her silver hair was up in her usual bun, held back by a blue scarf today.

Would she help me? Or report me to Mother for skipping lessons? It was hard to tell with her sometimes. Her view of what was *good* varied.

I scooted the books closer to me. "Just some research."

Her eyebrows raised. "Your tutor said you were sick. Said you were taking a respite from classes."

I pressed my lips together and lifted a shoulder. "I'm sick of lessons. And I *am* taking a respite from classes. This is . . . unrelated."

"Good." Yesilia chuckled and nudged the books out of the way so the tray was in front of me. My shoulders relaxed. She wouldn't make me stop reading. "Eat this, then we'll talk."

Once I started eating, I found I was ravenous. "Any news?" I asked, twirling the noodles with basil and a hint of lemon around the tines of my fork. Keeping myself tucked away in the library had its advantages, and one of them was staying completely away from palace gossip.

Yesilia shook her head. "Not until you've finished."

Once she decided, she never budged, no matter how I cajoled, so I shoveled the food into my mouth faster, even going so far as to slurp. Grandmother winked at me. We'd had slurping competitions when I was younger, seeing who could make the loudest, longest sound.

When I pushed the empty tray to the corner of the table, Yesilia rested her hands on her stomach. I began to regret eating so much. "News?" I asked again, quieter now.

Yesilia sighed. "Janiis answered the message your brother sent. He said he wasn't aware of any delays, but that whoever had caused it must be a fool to impede the *great* Marko."

I wrinkled my nose. "Janiis is as slippery as they come."

"Agreed."

"Do the others think he's behind it?"

Yesilia tilted her head so she could better stare me down. "You would know if you hadn't locked yourself away in here."

I sighed and tapped my fingers against the poem. "I need to *do* something. Everyone else has pressing demands on their time. I don't."

Instead of insisting otherwise, like anyone else would, my grandmother nodded. "They see your potential, but don't know how to use it, child. Tell me what you're working on."

A coil inside me loosened the tiniest bit.

I slid the poem in front of her, and she picked it up, holding it closer to the candle Romo had brought earlier. Her eyebrows rose higher the longer she read. She set the page back on the table and faced me, all hint of mirth gone from her eyes. "Where did you get this?"

I folded my hands in my lap. "It's from Jenna." I explained about the book, the page I'd found in it. "I don't know if she remembers it was there, but the poem was on the back. I thought . . . I thought perhaps it might be important." I left off the part about trading the poem for Father. I wasn't even sure what it meant. Didn't want to raise a fuss if I was wrong.

Yesilia's gaze snapped back to the poem, her aged finger tracing the lines. "I recognize this line."

Vineyards that touch the sky.

I leaned forward and gripped the table. "I've been searching everywhere for a similar reference, but haven't found anything!"

Her head bobbed and she traced the lines again. "Our ancestors lived along the cliffs, long before Riiga was formed, long before our people moved inland. They used every inch of the land, every resource they had. They even developed a method of farming on the cliffs. I saw it when I was much younger, and there were indeed vineyards that seemed to grow straight into the sky." She slowly pushed back her chair and stood. "I think I can show you. Wait here."

She went into the shadows between the shelves and I turned back to the poem. I pulled another book, this one on the mages of old, toward me. I flipped to where I'd seen a line about how the Mages' Library was hidden at the edge of the world. Riiga. The cliffs.

"Look," Yesilia said, settling a large book on top of the other ones. Across the spread of pages, an illustration, faded and smudged, showed the cliffs, with terraces cut into the face, and rows and rows of vineyards climbing into the sky.

"This is amazing," I whispered. I turned to the preceding page and squinted at the tiny script, my tired eyes watering as I deciphered the location and uses of the terraced vineyards. When I turned to the page following the illustration, my gaze fell on an inscription in familiar looping script in the wide margin.

The final key, not a key at all: behind the falling
door, that gives life, but takes it more.
Need blood.

A shiver went through me at the mention of blood. "Three," I muttered. Grandmother leaned closer to peer over my shoulder. "Three!" I placed the illustration of the Turian ring on top of the book. " 'One in snow, the heart of attack'—a Hálendian key. And this"—I traced the ring, noting a small triangle along one edge—"is the Turian key."

"But there's another," Grandmother said, a sparkle entering her eyes for the first time since Luc had announced my father—her son—was missing.

"And it's hidden behind a falling door." I didn't know what that meant, or the blood part, but it was a start. "The third key." The mages had one. I hoped Hálendi still had theirs—maybe I could ask Jenna.

Grandmother rubbed her leg like she always did when it ached or when she was thinking. "*Something* is hidden there."

I straightened my shoulders and stopped fidgeting. Called on every deportment lesson I'd ever had. Anyone else would brush me off, but maybe not her.

"Grandmother, what if we could use this to trade for Father's life? Give the clue, or part of it, to Janiis?"

She sighed and sat back, taking her time to think it through. "Perhaps."

The weight inside me lifted so fast I almost rose out of my chair. "You really think so?" I whispered, barely daring to utter the words.

She tapped the ragged corner. "But even more valuable would be whatever this clue leads to. Maybe we—"

"I want to go!" I blurted out. Yesilia looked at me, studied me like my father always did, and I missed him with a sharp ache. "Everyone else has duties to attend to. Riiga will grant me passage down the cliffs the same as Cynthia. Luc said himself that Turia needs its king before Janiis's wedding."

My grandmother shook her head slowly. "It's too dangerous for you to go alone."

I'd never been this impulsive in my life. I stayed where I was supposed to, did what was expected of me. But for my father? For him I'd scour every inch of the Plateau. Even Riiga.

"Please, Grandmother, I'll—"

She tapped her fingers against the table. "I'm coming with you."

My mouth froze half-open, the words on my tongue dissipating into the air. "You'd go with me?" I asked, disbelieving. "But, your duties. You're the best healer in the palace—"

"There are other healers, and more sickness in the wide world." Her sharp eyes cut to me. "Nobody messes with my boy."

A sound escaped my throat, a whoop that echoed through the library. My guard shifted at the door. I covered my mouth with both hands, holding back the laugh. We were doing this. Finding a way to save my father. "I don't think we should tell the others," I warned. Would she tell them anyway? It was the responsible thing to do, but Enzo would stop us before we'd even begun.

Yesilia rose slowly. "I agree. We leave tomorrow before dawn."

I gathered everything on the table, tucking the poem into Jenna's book and then the book into my pocket. No one here would miss us. The mages wouldn't care about us, a grandmother and her granddaughter traveling south. And if we didn't end up finding anything, no one would be the wiser.

"Can you evade your guard?" she asked softly.

I grinned. "I've learned a few tricks from Mari over the years."

Yesilia rubbed her bony hands together and cackled. "It's about time I had an adventure."

I smiled and slipped her hand into the crook of my elbow. "It's about time we both did."

CHAPTER NINE

Ren

The letter from home caught flame in the morning's remaining embers and burned to ash in the grate. Jenna would have told me to keep it, but I didn't care. I'd been in Turiana a week, and news that Isarr had pled her case convincingly and that the two assassins I'd healed weren't talking wasn't much motivation to go home.

Edda reported that the council wasn't taking my departure well. I couldn't do anything about that; she would tell them about the provision we'd signed when she deemed it necessary.

Had I made the wrong choice to come? Marko wasn't here to advise me; I'd been too late for that. Jenna was busy with wedding preparations—enough to ensure I wouldn't marry for a *long* while yet, not if it required *that* many details.

And yet, to be as happy as Jenna was with Enzo . . . But I'd have to wade through a thousand Isarrs to find such happiness.

I growled and poked at the fire with the long stick next to the hearth. But poking the fire wasn't enough. I grabbed my sword and buckled it on, jammed my feet into my boots, and stomped outside.

The door to the palace's practice ring groaned in protest as I shouldered it open. Scuffling feet sounded from within— someone had beat me to the ring.

"Fancy seeing you here, Your Majesty." My sister executed a deep court bow, more mocking than anything.

I ignored the prickle in my chest at the reminder of my new title and laughed at Jenna, the only person I knew who trained more than I did. "Shouldn't you be doing something princessy?"

She rolled her eyes and tossed a staff at me. "I needed to move. Besides, this is the only time I have to myself now."

I understood the feeling. We stretched and started slow, building to our favorite fight. Swinging, moving, dancing around each other as our staffs thunked together in the silence.

"Why did you come alone?" Jenna asked between breaths. "I mean, besides Adri."

I shrugged and swung my staff down hard. She blocked the strike and stepped away, waiting for an answer. "There aren't many I can trust."

She nodded, accepting what I'd said. She stepped into the fight again. "Tell me."

A single, mirthless laugh escaped me as we circled each other. She swung at me, and our staffs banged together. "The council second-guesses every word I say. Most of them support

Leland's views and are trying to push me to break our agreement with Turia. They want me to bring you back and end your betrothal to Enzo."

She stumbled. "What?"

"They want your magic to strengthen Hálendi." I made sure to roll my eyes hard enough to start a headache so she'd know how I felt about that one, in case the tethers weren't clear.

A long pause followed. Too long. "Any word on Cris? Has anyone found him?"

I swallowed the bile that always came with his name and swung harder at my sister. "If he enjoys his health, he'd better never be found."

My jaw clenched at the memory of Cris in the tent after the mages' attack. How he'd drawn his sword on me. Of Leland's dagger sunk to the hilt in Enzo's side.

I'd been weak from healing Jenna, and I'd known I didn't have enough magic to heal Enzo from such a deep wound. But she'd begged me to try. So I'd placed my hands on him and let my magic work. Even though I knew I didn't have enough, knew there was a very good chance I'd die in his place.

But then I felt the tether that Jenna had lived with her entire life. A brief, bright glimpse of our connection. Jenna's magic had flowed through it into me, healing Enzo, and saving us both. I didn't think she realized how close I'd come to giving too much.

"The Medallion guided you here," Jenna said, circling me, trying to find a weak spot. "Has there been any change since you've come?"

Under my tunic, the Medallion shifted against my chest. "I

don't know. Nothing feels right anymore. It started getting hot again yesterday. But nothing's changed, so I don't know what the warning meant. There's not exactly a guide that goes with it."

Jenna rolled her shoulders back and tightened her grip on her staff, no doubt feeling my tension through her tethers. "You'll figure it out, Ren." She swung at my knees, then stumbled back one step. I flicked my staff up against hers. It flew out of her hands and landed heavily in the dust as she stumbled back again.

My brow furrowed. "What's wrong? I haven't beaten you with a staff in years." I picked up her staff and set them both against the wall.

She was breathing heavily, her hand at her stomach. "Enzo's worried."

"The tethers?" I asked. She nodded. So it *was* with more than just Marko. "I thought the bond was to protect family . . ." I drifted off and shoveled the hurt away before she could sense it. Enzo would be her new family. They all would. "Can you do that?"

"There's no guide." She shrugged. "But I am."

My hands twitched at my side. I clenched my fingers into fists to keep them from trembling. We were in so far over our heads. How could we manage to win against two ancient mages with centuries of knowledge?

Jenna went to a closet I hadn't seen in the shadowed corner and pulled out two wooden practice swords. "You beat me one round. Let's see if you can do it again."

"You just want to avoid choosing which tapestries to display for the wedding," I said to keep things light. She didn't need to feel worse because I couldn't get my emotions under control.

"You're right." She shrugged and held up her sword, but the tip wobbled. Was she keeping her troubles from me? She never used to. "Maybe I should have taken you up on your offer to run away to the countryside."

It had been only a few months since I'd joked about that, but three lifetimes had passed. If only I could go back and make good on the offer.

✦ ✦ ✦

Jenna must have needed that release because she annihilated me. Afterward, I'd bathed and attended a meeting with Enzo. But the council had only wanted me to briefly consult about the state of our port in Osta, and then I'd been summarily excused. Not that I minded. I'd been holed up in a study ever since with a stack of notes on what I'd need to address when I returned to Hálendi.

I'd have to return soon. The entire trip had been pointless— I'd been too late to help Marko, which had to be what the Medallion urged me here for. Jenna didn't need me any longer. In fact, my presence was probably making things worse for her—Turia didn't want another Hálendian in the palace.

But I didn't want to return yet. Especially not as a failure.

I was about to dump the entire stack of paper into the grate when Mari burst into the room. "Ren!"

I folded my hands over the papers and leaned across the

desk. "To what do I owe the pleasure of your company, Miss Mari? Have you finally come to steal a dance with me? Because I accept." I pulled one of her crazy curls and watched it bounce back into place.

But instead of laughing at my teasing, Mari bit her lip and rubbed her arm.

"What is it?" I asked, my heart dropping at her seriousness. "Your mother?" Cora's health had become more fragile the longer we went without any word—she still hadn't left her chambers and wasn't eating much.

Mari shook her head and her curls slapped her face. "It's Chiara."

I scooted away from the desk and waved her closer. "What's wrong with Chiara?" My stomach tied itself into knots. She'd been crying the last time I saw her a couple of days ago—not actual tears, but the effects of it had been all over her face.

"She . . . she's not here. I can't find her, and I can find anyone!"

I blinked twice. "What do you mean, she's not here?"

Mari tucked her elbows in tight. "I mean, she's not anywhere. I've searched and searched."

"Has anyone seen her? Maybe she just—"

"Her maids haven't seen her in two days."

On my chest, the Medallion lay dormant. "Did she just get up early? What about her tutors?"

"No!" Mari took my face in her small hands. Tears began running down her cheeks. "She's. Not. Here."

I pulled her into a hug as my mind raced through possibilities. "Find Yesilia. Ask her to help you search Chiara's room.

Look for a note. See if her traveling cloak is still in her closet. But don't tell anyone what you're doing."

"I'm good at keeping secrets." Mari sniffed and wiped her tears on her sleeve. "What are you going to do?"

"I'm going to find Jenna."

✦ ✦ ✦

"Hasn't anyone seen Chiara?" I asked as I paced the king's study off the council room. Enzo drummed his fingers on the desk he sat at.

"Maybe she went to visit the orphanage," Jenna said, tugging on her braid where she sat across from Enzo. "She does that when she's worried about something."

"Do you have a tether with her, too?" I asked, nudging a chair out of my way.

"It's . . . distant." She rubbed her hands against her sides. "It's usually faint, anyway, but . . . I hadn't realized . . . with all the meetings . . ."

Enzo put his head in his hands.

Mari burst into the room with enough force to slam the door against the wall behind it. "I can't find Yesilia, either. Her healers said she'd told them she was visiting a friend in the city for a few days. I told you, they're gone." She waved a folded paper in front of her. "This was under Chiara's jewel case."

Enzo's chair scraped against the stone floor. He bolted to Mari and snatched the letter from her, his eyes scanning the words.

"Out loud, Enzo," Jenna whispered.

"*Mother, Enzo, Mari, and Jenna,*"

Something inside me twanged at being left out.

"*I knew you wouldn't approve, so I didn't ask. Enzo,
you have a duty to Turia to honor. Jenna, Enzo
needs you, our family and kingdom need you, now
more than ever. Mari, you are Mother's bright spot,
her hope. But I can do something. So I'm leaving. I'm
going to find our father and bring him home. Don't
worry, Yesilia is with me, and we'll be careful and
safe. Love to you all . . .*"

Enzo's voice faded into nothing. Jenna reached up and
slipped her hand into his, easing him into a chair next to her.
She held on tight—for him, for her, for us all.

Mari looked lost in the corner, her brows furrowed in sor-
row or anger, maybe in disappointment at being left behind.

"When?" I asked into the heavy room. "How?"

"I haven't seen Chiara for at least two days," Jenna said
quietly. "I'd heard she'd been spending her time in the library. I
thought she was finding a way to handle . . ."

"Mari?" I asked.

Mari shook her head, a tear escaping into the curls at her
neck. "We haven't had family dinners lately. Not since—not
with . . . everything."

"They've been gone for *two days* and nobody noticed?" My
brittle jaw ached, like my teeth would shatter at any moment.
Chiara wasn't my responsibility—I already had the burden of

one kingdom to bear. But her bright smile assaulted my mind. The world would destroy her in a heartbeat.

Yesilia. At least she had Yesilia. I squeezed my eyes shut. Not that Yesilia could offer much protection.

But Chiara was also right. No one here could go after her.

Enzo banged his fist against the desk. "What was she thinking? She knows I'll just send every guard—"

"No," Jenna whispered, rubbing her forehead. "It's the same as Marko—if word gets out that Chiara is wandering the kingdom with only her grandmother for protection, you'll mark her as a target. She's safer if no one knows."

Enzo dropped his head into his hands. I didn't need Jenna's tethers to feel his frustration, the hopelessness that was slowly breaking him apart. I'd felt the same, when everyone said that Jenna was dead.

"Should we tell Mother?" Mari asked.

Enzo and Jenna stared at each other, and finally Enzo shook his head. "She's got enough to worry about," he said. "We'll find someone we trust to go—"

"I can go." The words were out of my mouth before I had even finished the thought.

Jenna's head snapped up. "You can't risk it."

Enzo wiped his hand down his face. "I can't ask you to go, Ren. You have your own set of troubles."

I stood a little taller and pulled a lost-looking Mari to my side. "You aren't asking me to go, I'm offering. No, demanding." Mari sniffled. She leaned into me and I wrapped my arm around her shoulders.

Jenna jumped out of her chair and began pacing. "Hálendi

is too fragile—you don't even have an heir. Anything could go wrong, and then what would our people do?"

I squeezed Mari's shoulder before addressing my very angry sister. "I am aware of the state of affairs in Hálendi. I've made arrangements that will keep things stable. My troubles will wait." I hoped. "I don't know why the Medallion led me here. But I was too late for Marko. I won't be too late for Chiara."

A gentle warmth shivered into me from the Medallion. Was it relief at not having to return home? Or did the land want me to go after Chiara?

"I'm coming with you." Jenna folded her arms. Enzo didn't speak. He wouldn't stop her.

"No, you're not," I said before she could argue. I sent a pointed glance at Enzo then Mari. "You're needed here." I wasn't.

Jenna pulled her shoulders back and glared at me. "I can't let you go alone. I was the one who defeated Graymere. *My* magic and artifacts—"

"You're not the only one with magic," I said quietly. "You had the adventure last time. It's my turn."

She was still for so long, I wasn't sure whether or not I'd won the argument. "Take my ring," she finally said, twisting her lips to the side and swallowing hard.

My lips lifted into a half smile. "If only it were that simple. I have the Medallion. I'll be fine." A spike of heat shot into me. What that heat meant, I had no idea.

"You are *not* going alone." Jenna held tight to Enzo's hand, like he was the only thing grounding her. He probably was. "I can't lose you again."

I shook my head and backed away. "When I find Chiara and Yesilia, I won't be alone. And besides, you didn't lose me the first time, so you can't technically lose me *again*."

Enzo stood and edged in front of Jenna, probably to prevent her from slapping me. But the levity, the joking, was all I could do—I couldn't stand here and let my sister risk everything she'd ever wanted. Couldn't let her feel my true feelings through the tethers.

"I'll check with the stables," Enzo said, interrupting the staring match between Jenna and me. "They can't have gone far without transportation."

Mari sniffed and wiped her nose on the back of her arm. "I'll ask Cook if she gave them food. And get some for you, too."

I pressed my fist to my shoulder and jogged out before Jenna could protest further. I wasn't sure I could turn down her offer to come with me again.

I didn't get lost on the way to my room this time. I rolled up my clothes, lamenting how hot I'd be and how many nights I'd have to sleep outside if the innkeepers didn't trust a Hálendian. I rifled through the messages by my bed and scribbled a note to Edda to continue on—I'd return when I could.

A short knock sounded, then the door swung open. I spun, my hand on my sword, but it was only Enzo, Jenna, and Mari piling into my room.

"Here, you'll need this," Enzo said, and thrust a pile of Turian clothing and a coin pouch toward me. I took the bundle and passed him the sealed note to send to Edda in exchange.

"And these," Mari added, tossing an ugly brown cap onto the pile along with a wrapped parcel of food.

"They took the carriage to the orphanage," Enzo said. "It returned empty—Yesilia claimed she wanted to walk back to the palace."

"Where is the orphanage?"

"West side of Turiana." He pulled out a paper—a map that had been folded in quarters. "There's the orphanage"—he pointed to its general vicinity, then to three routes that had been drawn in—"these are the possible routes they took south. But all paths lead to Rialzo; it's the only way to get down the cliffs and into Riiga." He paused. "It's a rough city, Ren. I can't—"

"I'll find them before they get that far." I spread out the map and grabbed a pen. "Show me where your father disappeared, too. I'll see if the Medallion senses anything while I'm there."

Jenna swallowed and put her finger on Riiga's capital city, Vera. "You must return before Janiis's wedding and whatever he's planning."

I nodded. We were already separated enough as a Plateau; Janiis was positioning himself a little too well for my comfort. "Seven days," I said, mostly to myself. Seven days to find them and return.

Jenna handed me a tiny jar of what looked like horse excrement. I wrinkled my nose. "I'm not eating that."

She rolled her eyes. "It's for your hair. So it won't be so blindingly foreign. You need to be careful, especially now."

Because I was king? Because I carried the Medallion? Because Turians didn't like Hálendians? I sniffed the jar's contents and coughed. "I think I'd rather be reckless."

"Cris could be out there," Jenna continued, ignoring my sarcasm. "And the mages."

Right. Mages. And Cris. "And whoever summoned the mages, and most of Riiga." I sighed and gathered a set of clothes. "I am well aware."

I ducked into my bathing chamber to change before she could thrust something else awful into my hands, and came out a few moments later, tugging at the vest Enzo had found for me. Jenna helped me rub the foul-smelling concoction into my hair, and Mari tugged the cap down tight.

I wrinkled my nose as I tilted my now-brunette head in the mirror. "This looks awful."

Jenna threw herself into my arms, almost tipping us both over. I hugged her tight. I needed to get ahold of my worry, of the weight crushing me inside. I couldn't leave Jenna feeling my weight, adding to her worry. "I'll be careful, I promise. And if I find Marko while I'm out there, I'll bring him home, too."

"You do that." Jenna half laughed, half sobbed. "Are you sure you won't take anyone with you?"

I nodded, but I wasn't as sure as I had been about my decision to travel alone. I swallowed and touched my chest where the Medallion rested. "I'll be okay."

Jenna's eyes narrowed. Glaciers, I hated that she could read my emotions sometimes. So I covered my neck with my hands. "How do you people stand so much wind down your collar?" I asked to mask my heavier thoughts.

The material was fine enough on the Turian tunic, straight trousers, and tall boots, but I felt uncomfortable in the clothing, and anyone looking at me could tell. At least I wouldn't be so unbearably hot. Well, not *as* unbearably hot.

"That's what a coat is for," Mari piped up. "Our way is better."

I snorted and ruffled her wild curls. "For this heat, you're probably right, Mari."

Enzo shook my hand, and Jenna took me by the shoulders. "Trust yourself, Ren. Trust yourself and listen to whatever the Medallion is trying to tell you."

I kissed her cheek, then swung Mari around in a hug. I took my small bag with a change of clothes and food that Mari had pinched from the kitchens, with the coin purse at the bottom.

I paused at the door and studied them. They were already a family, whether the vows had been said or not. I stepped through the doorway into the hall. "I'll bring her home."

Marko

When the door opened, Marko didn't flinch. Janiis entered, stooping through the low doorway, the bright flare of candlelight behind him hiding his expression. Two cloaked figures followed him and stood in a corner of the room, the candle's light barely licking against them.

Unease tightened Marko's already thin frame. Hunger and thirst burned in him, consuming his thoughts and body, yet those shadowy figures in the corner were like a bolt down his spine. *They* were the ones to watch.

"Old friend," Janiis started, his oily voice bouncing off the damp walls. "Give us what we need, and you will be moved to more comfortable accommodations."

Marko's tongue stuck in his mouth, too dry to speak.

Janiis ground his teeth and puffed out his chest. As though that could intimidate anyone into obeying him. "You know what we seek. Do you have it?"

Marko shook his head slowly, every muscle protesting the movement.

"Do you know where they can be found?" One cloaked figure spoke from the corner, the dulcet tones of her voice sending a shiver across Marko's skin.

It was harder to shake his head this time, but Marko managed it.

The other figure stepped away from the wall, boots crunching against the bones of whatever rodent had died in the corner. Long, fine-boned fingers emerged from the cloak and pulled back the hood, revealing the former ambassador—Koranth. Alive. With black eyes. Marko's heart thumped against his ribs and everything spun around him. But he didn't move. Wouldn't.

Koranth pulled a tiny vial of amber liquid from beneath his cloak and held it up in the candlelight.

Janiis shifted so slightly that Marko almost didn't catch it. If Janiis was worried, Marko should be terrified. Yet all he felt was hunger.

"We seek a map, King," the woman said. "A map to the Black Library. And a key. I'll ask one more time. Do you know where they are?"

Marko bit his tongue with the effort to keep silent. Words banged against his clenched teeth, fighting to be free, to end the silence and darkness of his cell.

"You continue to resist? Very well," Koranth said. He uncorked the vial and stepped closer. "I was saving it for someone else, but—"

"Wait," Janiis said, head tilted to the side, a confused expression marring his face. "What . . . I don't think we should—"

But then his mouth snapped shut. A dazed look washed over him. Like his will had been wiped from his mind.

Whatever the vial contained, Marko would not bend. Could not.

Koranth pinched Marko's face, nails digging into his cheeks as he forced his mouth to open. A few drops of the amber liquid splashed onto Marko's tongue, and though he knew whatever that vial contained would be very, very bad, he couldn't help but swallow the sweet liquid. It coated his burning throat, eased his pain.

"Where is the map?" Koranth's voice echoed in Marko's brain as though he'd spoken directly into his skull.

He couldn't keep his teeth clenched any longer. "I do not know," he heard his voice say, though he hadn't given the words permission to leave his mouth.

Koranth growled. "Where is the key?"

Slow burning began at the base of his neck, and Marko squeezed his eyes shut.

"Where is the key?"

He shook his head again and again, but the pain wouldn't leave. "I don't know!" he cried out. So many answers ran through his mind—that he didn't know where Brownlok was with his piece. Didn't know where Atháren was with the other. But Koranth hadn't asked either of those things, so they stayed locked away.

The pain burned slowly higher and higher, up into his skull. Like the sun had reached inside and scraped it clean. An ear-shattering scream pierced the cell, bouncing against the walls and back. It was him, Marko realized from far, far away. He was screaming. His life flashed before his mind's eye, scene after scene, choice after choice. His wife. His children. His people. As the burning reached the top of his head, silence once again returned, leaving only a blank expanse in front of him. Behind him.

Everything.

Gone.

CHAPTER TEN

Chiara

I'd never been jealous of my own grandmother before, but no one questioned her decisions. Not when we'd borrowed a carriage to leave the palace, not when we arrived at the orphanage in Turiana and switched clothing for more serviceable garb, not when she told the driver to return to the palace without us.

Then she'd found us a ride south.

We'd walked only a short way from the orphanage when Grandmother stopped. She approached a man with a large hay cart, its wagon box still half full as the sun was setting.

"Could we ride with you a ways?" she asked the man. He'd been about to say no, but my grandmother, the devious old duck, rounded her shoulders so she stooped more than usual and leaned a little heavier on me.

The man grunted his agreement, and we had a comfortable

ride through the night under the stars and moon. The farther we traveled from the palace and its burdens, the lighter I felt.

We didn't head straight south, as I'd assumed we would. Instead, we took a southeastern road. I asked Grandmother why she hadn't wanted to stay in the carriage, and she said, "A hay cart is harder to track than a palace carriage."

So although we weren't getting to Riiga as fast as possible, I didn't have to check over my shoulder quite so often. Out here, the caged feeling went away.

When the mage had trapped me in the palace with Jenna and Mari, my father was prepared to attack his own home with as many men as he could find. I would do the same for him.

We'd been traveling for two days, walking and hitching rides, and no one had paid a girl and her grandmother any mind. We were not a threat. Not important.

The village we now approached, Cozzare, was larger than any of the others. Everything looked . . . sturdy. Wooden planks lined the cobblestone roads for walking, every window's shutters were in good repair, and the rooftops were some of the best mended I'd seen yet.

We'd been walking most of the day, since the farmer who gave us a ride had turned off toward his village, and Yesilia leaned heavily on me. "You'll have to find us dinner, *carina*," she said. "I might have overworked these old bones today."

"Of course, Grandmother," I replied, though I had no idea how to find quality food for a good price. We'd need both to make my coin purse stretch all the way to Riiga.

Tents and carts overflowing with bright fruit, dirt-covered

vegetables, and colorful fabric crowded the main road through Cozzare. I helped Yesilia sit as we observed the teeming throng, getting an idea of where people clustered and who people avoided. It was something Yesilia had taught me: how to fit in, how to act like a local. My stomach cramped with hunger—we hadn't eaten anything since the early morning, when we left a tiny inn.

"Miss! Miss!" a young man with a dark vest called. He'd been pulling his cart out of the square when he spotted us. "I have fine food here for your dinner! And at such a price!" He held up a handful of beets, stalks still attached. He held the bunch out to me, ignoring Yesilia. "Only four silvers for this bushel, miss."

The beets' color was good. The boy's dark hair and eyes had probably sold a fair share of his produce. But he was leaving with vegetables still to sell, and he wouldn't look at Yesilia. "No, thank you."

He lowered his deep voice and put a hand on my arm. "I see you drive a hard deal, miss. For you, I could lower the price."

I stepped away and shook my head. I helped Yesilia stand, and we moved on, the boy scowling at us.

"He'd have taken every coin in your purse," Yesilia whispered. "How did you know not to trust him?" She studied the market as we walked.

I lifted a shoulder. "He didn't seem honest."

She chuckled and shook her head. "You've got a good instinct."

"Excuse me, miss," another voice called out to us. Older,

softer. "Would you like to buy this lovely scarf? It'll keep your grandmother's hair back nicely in the wind."

A woman stood in the shadow of the town's chandler displaying a scrap of emerald silk. Her table was small and piled high with silks and wools. She had to have seen our dusty hems and boots, our windswept hair. Yet she didn't look at us like strangers to swindle.

I wanted food, not a scarf, but something about the woman transfixed me.

"How much?" I dug into the pouch at my side that held the savings from the past few months of my shopping allowance.

Her gap-toothed smile widened. "Just one, miss."

"You are mistaken, ma'am. This piece of finery is surely worth more." I pulled out two coins and dropped them into her palm. "Tell me, where would you buy food for a long journey? That cart at the end?" I nodded toward a busy cart whose wares were depleting fast.

Instead of answering, the woman pulled a crate from under her table and started folding the scarves into it. "A storm is brewing, miss. You two have somewhere to stay?"

"We've only just arrived," I said with a nervous glance at Yesilia. Had I been wrong to admit that? Yesilia stared down the woman but didn't comment. She must be more tired than I realized.

The woman clicked her tongue. "Both inns are full up for the night—my sister runs the nicer one. But if you like, you can stay with me." She set the crate of folded scarves on the ground as a gust of wind snaked down the worn road. "Can't have you two staying out in this weather tonight. I've a daughter about your age, and you can both sleep in her old room—she's recently married, you see, and I've been low on the company side."

She bent over, still packing up. Yesilia shrugged, so I said, "Thank you. We can't pay much, but—"

"Nonsense. It'll be nice having visitors." She nodded to the cart next to the one I'd pointed to. "If you'll buy us a bushel of his mixed vegetables—tell him Dora sent you—I'll make us all dinner."

Yesilia agreed to her terms, so I hurried over to the cart. The seller handed me a bundle—bigger and better than what he was selling to those surrounding me. I paid and made it back just as Dora finished packing up her wares.

"Thank you," I told her. "I'm Chiara, and this is my grand-mother, Yesilia."

Dora paused at hearing Yesilia's name, then shook both our hands. Should I have come up with different names? No one had bothered to ask them before. But this far from Turiana, I didn't think we would have any issues, especially with our borrowed clothes caked in dust and grime.

"Pleasure to meet you both. Watch this for me while I put the table in?" She picked up the table and took it into the shop, which smelled like scented wax and tallow.

"You think we can trust her?" Yesilia whispered. Not doubting, just curious. Like she wanted my opinion.

I took the scarf and wrapped it around her head, tying a knot on the side and slipping it under her white hair. "Yes, I think we can."

Dora returned and placed a small parcel on top of the crate, hefted the load, and gestured for us to follow her.

"We didn't mean to make you close up early," I said, Yesilia's arm draped through mine. A chill wind lifted my cloak and distant thunder sounded.

"Nonsense. Everyone will be packing up soon—if not, they'll find themselves with a soggy load."

The clouds still looked distant to me, but we followed Dora obediently as she turned off the main road and into an alley.

"Is a little rain so bad?" I asked. It rained a lot during autumn at the palace, but nothing that would warrant Dora's hurried steps. Yesilia's limp was getting worse. I bit my lip—we still had a long way until Riiga, and then we'd have to make it down the cliffs.

"A little rain? Hah!" Dora harrumphed. "This is where clouds collide." She gestured north, away from the clouds I'd been watching all day.

My brow furrowed, but I looked behind me—something I hadn't done since leaving the capital city—and saw another assault of black clouds racing our way. My eyes widened and Yesilia's sparkled.

"I haven't seen a rain like this in ages," she said, delighted.

We kept to side roads to avoid the crowds pressing to find shelter. Eventually, we ended up back on the main road, but at the edge of the village this time.

An inn, three stories tall with a stable in the back, had cheery orange flowers in all its window boxes. Dora turned right, and tucked on the other side of the stable, a tiny house peeked out from the surrounding trees.

I wished Yesilia and I could borrow a horse and ride tomorrow, but it would cost too much, and she would probably fare worse in a saddle than on her feet. I had at least two blisters on each foot. I wasn't sure I'd be able to get my boots back on once I took them off.

"So many horses for such a small village," I commented. "Where did they all come from?"

"We're the midpoint between the port of Almare and Rialzo—the crossroads to change horses if you're in a hurry to get to Riiga. Come now." Dora guided us into her home, and set her crate just inside the door.

My room at the palace was bigger than this entire house, yet I loved the small space. Every detail was clean and cared for and served a purpose.

I set the bundle of vegetables on the well-oiled wood table. Dora bustled in next to me, helping Yesilia into a small rocking chair in a corner by the window.

"Come, child," Dora said to me. "I'll show you how to make a stew that will woo any man's heart."

I washed my hands in the basin, more concerned about wooing my own stomach, while Dora stoked the coals in the fireplace. She showed me how to clean and chop the vegetables, which spices to dump in and which to sprinkle. By the time the concoction was bubbling, my stomach was growling in response.

Yesilia had dozed in the chair, but came to sit with us at the table when the food was ready. Dora placed a bowl in front of me, and I dug in, moaning as the warm, salty broth slid down my throat. She chuckled and set a chunk of bread next to my bowl. Even Yesilia dug into the food like she hadn't seen a meal in months. I tore off a small piece of bread and tapped it against the bowl. My grandmother was spry, but we still had so far to go.

"What brings you two to Cozzare?" Dora asked, ladling a bowl for herself and sitting next to us.

My ravenous appetite melted away and I stirred my spoon in circles. It had been ten days since Luc had brought his terrible news. Days of my father suffering who knows what.

"We're going to meet family," I said. Part of my family, anyway.

Now that we were at the midpoint approaching Rialzo, we'd have to be careful and avoid anyone on the trail. Enzo was sure to have sent someone after us.

If, that is, anyone had even noticed I was missing.

I shook off the thought. It didn't matter. The words of the poem echoed in my head, and I patted the pocket of my skirt where Jenna's book rested. All we needed was to figure out what the clue led to and we'd have the key to my father's freedom.

A crash against the small window startled me and I dropped the rest of my bread into my stew. "What—" I looked at the window, expecting shards of glass to cover the counter below it.

"The rains are here," Dora said in a low voice.

And they were. Drops of water pounded with more force than I'd ever seen against the pane, against the entire house. Lightning flashed in the dark sky, thunder booming right after. I shuddered at the thought of sleeping out in this weather.

Yesilia sat back, her hands clasped over her stomach. "The scarf was worth it," she muttered so only I could hear.

I reached across the table and took Dora's hand in mine. "Thank you for offering us shelter. I had no idea."

She chuckled and patted my hand. "I know you had no idea, carina. That's why I offered."

✦ ✦ ✦

I slept well for the first time in months. The little room hidden behind the fireplace had just enough space for a bed that fit Grandmother and me. The rains continued the next morning, but not with the crashing force of the day before.

"Wonderful, you're up," Dora said as Yesilia and I emerged into the main part of the house after fixing our hair as best we could. "Come to the inn and meet my sister. She's busier than a bee in springtime, but her breakfast is something of a specialty."

My stomach growled on cue, and my cheeks heated. We held our cloaks over our heads and dashed into the yard. Boards had been placed to form a walkway between Dora's door and the inn, so our boots didn't catch even a spot of mud.

We went through a back door that led right into the kitchen. Dora waved to a girl about my age working at the long table in the middle of the room. Her shoulders drooped with weariness, but her knife flew over the vegetables around her. She dumped the pile into one of the large pots on the wide stove and smiled at Dora. It was barely a smile, and it dimmed when she noticed us.

"Taking in more strays?" a woman slightly younger than Dora scolded, hands on her hips.

Dora kissed her cheek. "Good morning to you, too." She turned to us. "Lessia, meet Yesilia and Chiara. They needed a bit of shelter from the rains, and you know as well as I that your inn was full to the brim last night."

Yesilia held out her hand and shook the innkeeper's. "We needed a fair portion more than a bit of shelter," she said with a chuckle. "It's nice to meet you."

I held out my hand in greeting as well, and then Lessia shooed us all to the long table where the girl chopped vegetables.

"Sit here, and I'll bring you breakfast." Lessia went to the fire and pulled a large lid off a black pan, then scooped out a flaky pastry. From a different pot, she dished out a sloppy mess of oatmeal for each of us. She set the trays on the table, topped the oats with berries and a shaker full of dark spices—ones I'd never had on oatmeal—then bustled up a set of stairs and out of the kitchen.

"Never stops," Dora muttered.

I took a bite of the pastry and had to sit back at the flavors bursting on my tongue. Apricot marmalade oozed out of the center onto my fingers. And the oats—I hadn't known oats could taste like *this*.

"Dora, what—"

Horrendous coughing started in a room off the kitchen, loud and deep and rattling. The girl peeling potatoes froze and her hands trembled.

Yesilia brushed crumbs off her dress. "A body shouldn't make such noises," she said.

Dora worried her bottom lip between her teeth. "It's

Aleksa's sister," she said quietly with a nod to the girl, who was peeling much slower now. "Found them both on the street three days ago. I talked Lessia into keeping them here, but the sister is fiercely ill." Her voice dropped even further until I could barely hear it over the coughing. "I'm not sure if . . ."

Aleksa's knife froze again. "She will make it." Aleksa spoke softly but firmly. Her accent . . . I finally marked her dark hair and fair skin. She was too dark to be Hálendian, too fair to be Turian. Did Enzo know there were Riigans this far north?

I expected Yesilia to question the girl about why she was here, but she only said, "I'm a decent healer. Let me look to your sister and I'll see if I can put her to rights."

But . . . my father. We needed to continue on. The rains would let up soon, and even if they didn't, surely we could find some way to make progress.

The girl's knife clattered to the table and she shot a panicked glance to Dora. "I don't have anything to pay you with," she whispered, staring down at the peelings.

"Did I ask for money?" Yesilia said, raising a brow. "The potatoes will keep. Come show me your sister and tell me what happened."

Aleksa wiped her hands on her apron and led us to the room off the kitchen. I took the last bite of my pastry and followed. Yesilia was talented—maybe we wouldn't have to stay long.

There were only two candles in the room, but illness dampened what little light they gave. The window was cracked open, letting cool, fresh air into the room. A bundle covered in blankets on the bed groaned and rattled with cough.

Yesilia pulled the covers back, revealing a small girl near Mari's age with flushed cheeks. She had lighter hair than Aleksa, the same fair skin. Her chest sank with each cough.

This was no simple illness.

"How long has she been like this?" Yesilia asked, pressing her fingers against the girl's throat and stomach, then feeling her forehead and feet.

Aleksa stared at her sister, then shook herself. "The cough started two weeks ago," she said, twisting her apron in her hands. "We worked for the baker in town." Dora spat over her shoulder at the mention and I jumped. "When Ilma got worse, he tossed us into the street. Said it was cheaper than buying medicine or burying her," she finished, her voice barely a whisper, like if she spoke softly enough we wouldn't hear her accent.

Yesilia grumbled under her breath, but I couldn't stay quiet. "Why would he do such an awful thing?"

Aleksa stared at me. "We're Riigan, that's why."

Like Koranth. Sennor. Like the men who'd probably attacked my father.

I expected the usual anger to swell when anyone mentioned Riiga. But a different burning started in my chest. These sisters had nothing to do with mages or ambassadors or my father. "You shouldn't be treated like that."

Aleksa folded her arms and glared at me. "Most of your people don't agree."

Yesilia clicked her tongue. "Are we arguing, or are we helping your sister?"

All the fight in Aleksa immediately dropped away. "What can I do?"

Yesilia wrote a list of herbs on a scrap of paper Dora brought her. "Get these from the herbary. And hot water for tea and cold water for rags."

Aleksa scurried out, with Dora not far behind, consulting on where the herbs could be found.

"Can you help her?" I asked, desperate to do something, to prove that we weren't all like the baker. Trying—and not quite succeeding—to push away the need to continue south.

"Rub her feet," Yesilia said. I sat and pressed my palms against the bottoms of the girl's feet in quick strokes to make the blood flow better. "I'm tired from traveling, but I will try to help."

Yesilia sat near the head of the bed and placed her hands on Ilma's shoulders. She closed her eyes and breathed deep. I'd seen her do this with patients—I only hoped she didn't overtax herself.

When the others came back in, we switched out the bedding, then Dora ordered Aleksa, Yesilia, and me to change into borrowed dresses. She sent Aleksa and me to wash them while she and Yesilia worked.

We didn't have time for this. For the rain, washing, healing, any of it. I needed to find my father. Needed to get to Riiga before whoever Enzo sent after us caught up.

But Yesilia also needed rest, so I followed Aleksa out.

The roof of the inn extended over a patch of dirt where three huge basins sat. A system of long, hollowed-out logs along the edge of the roof funneled water back under the porch and into the basins.

I trailed my fingers along the contraption, held together

with strips of leather and nails. I'd read about this manner of gathering rainwater, but I'd never seen it. I wished with a sharp pang I could tell my father about it. I *would,* and soon. I hoped.

Aleksa ignored me and dumped the bundle of blankets into one of the basins, then plunged her hands into the water, soap and all. Perhaps having clean clothes would be worth the time spent here.

I stood at the next basin and clumsily tried to follow her movements. I pulled out one piece at a time and rubbed the soap against the fabric, sloshing water down the front of my clean, dry dress.

Wind from the storm caught the wet fabric against my legs, and I shivered as I tried to scrub the dirt and dust out of my and Yesilia's things. Then there was so much soap on everything I had a hard time rinsing it off. My front got another helping of water splashed everywhere, and my feet began to freeze as a stiff wind pummeled the side of the inn.

"What are you doing?" Aleksa asked, breaking the silence between us.

I was twisting the water out of my skirt. It was long, so as I twisted from the top, the hem, which I'd already wrung out, hung in the water.

"Um," I said, frozen hands still trying to get as much water out as I could. "Washing?"

Aleksa shook her head and grumbled under her breath, then left her basin to come help me. "Like this," she said. She dunked my skirt again, shaking it under the water until all the soap was gone, then twisted it as she pulled it out of the basin, pressing the fabric against the wood to get even more water out and hanging the drier part outside the basin as she moved up the skirt.

"Oh," I said sheepishly. "That does make more sense, doesn't it?"

She shook her head and went back to the bedclothes.

"How long have you been in Turia?" I asked quietly. I really wanted to ask *why* she was in Turia, but I didn't think she'd answer that question.

Aleksa chewed on her bottom lip and kept her eyes down, focused on scrubbing. I thought maybe she'd decided not to answer, when she said quietly, "Two months."

Two months. So she wouldn't have any information about my father. If Aleksa didn't want to talk, I wouldn't force her to. I needed to focus all my energy on figuring out washing.

When I went back inside with my dripping, slightly sudsy bundle, Lessia took one look at me and started laughing. "You look like a drowned cat!" She handed me wooden clothespins to hang the laundry, then took a basket of folded blankets through the doorway leading to the dining room. Someone was sitting at a table just outside the door, a man who struck me as familiar, though I couldn't pinpoint why before the door swung shut. I moved my soggy pile of clothes to my hip and went to the door, nudging it open, but whoever it was had gone.

"What is it?" Aleksa asked, pinning up the blankets in front of the fire on rope strung along the rafters.

I shook my head and clumsily followed her lead. "I thought I saw someone I know."

Aleksa went back to her work. Perhaps I needed a good night's sleep. Because I'd thought I'd seen someone with white-blond hair in the dining room. Enzo wouldn't have sent Ren after us—he had his own kingdom full of trouble.

Aleksa glared at my crooked clothing, then came over and straightened it. "If you hang it crooked, it'll dry crooked."

"Oh," I whispered, trying to mimic her movements, but she worked so fast it was hard to imitate. I scooted a little closer to the fire. We'd come so far. I couldn't let anyone take us back to the palace.

"Can I ask you something?" I asked hesitantly.

She didn't answer, just continued hanging the blankets.

I cleared my throat. "Do you think my grandmother could make the journey to Rialzo and down the cliffs?"

Aleksa dropped a pin and stared at me. "Do not tell me you're going to Riiga."

I pursed my lips. If she didn't want me to tell her that, I wouldn't.

Aleksa let out a deep sigh and glanced at the room where Yesilia tended to Ilma. "No," she said quietly. "I don't think so. I got out of Rialzo as fast as I could. You've the same chance of being swindled there as getting wet standing in a field during a rainstorm."

I shivered and crossed my arms.

Her lips twisted as she studied me. "The passage down the cliff is a steep path built into the rock face. A full day of switching back and forth. It's incredibly difficult to do on foot, and incredibly expensive to hire a cart."

"Are there guards? Or can anyone descend?" My father had said they opened the border for the wedding, but . . . wait. The border had been closed two months ago.

Aleksa furrowed her brows and looked at me like I should know all this already. "Aye, there are guards. Last I heard, the bribe to cross was six golds—three at the bottom, three at the top."

"Six golds!" I said, then lowered my voice. "How did you find such a sum?"

"Do not go there. Especially not now," she muttered. She headed toward her sister's room without answering my question. How had she gotten here, and *why* had she been so desperate to leave her homeland?

I followed her into the room. Already Ilma rested easier. Her cheeks weren't so flushed, and she didn't cough so deep or so often. But Yesilia . . . She sat low in her chair, skin pale, breath labored.

"Grandmother." I knelt by her side. "You need to rest."

She nodded feebly. "Aye, child. I do. I'm not sure I can continue traveling."

"We can continue when the rain stops," I said, taking her hand in mine.

"No, child. I'd thought to finish this journey with you, but my time for climbing cliffs has passed. And Ilma needs to see more summers."

I swallowed.

"Don't go to Riiga," Aleksa said, squeezing her sister's hand. "It's madness. A prison."

Prison? It was her kingdom, her people. How could it be a prison? Though the palace had started feeling more like a prison than a home lately.

"We have to." I rubbed Yesilia's age-spotted hand. "*I* have to."

"Surely you can find what you seek elsewhere?"

I shook my head.

"I am sorry," Yesilia said, closing her eyes.

I held her hand tighter. "It's okay, Grandmother. I'll continue on my own." I wasn't sure how, but I'd find a way.

"Dora tells me there are more Riigans here who need help," she said. "I will write to your brother, alert him to what is happening. He can send a carriage for my return."

I swallowed hard. The easier path was staying with her and returning home. The fire in the grate popped and the words of the poem whispered to me from my pocket.

I wasn't sure I could do any of it—navigate Rialzo, make it down the cliffs, follow the clue to the map. But for my father, I would never stop trying.

"Why are you going?" Aleksa asked, staring at her sister's hand.

She wouldn't look at me, wouldn't trust me. "Personal business."

She shook her head. "Riiga is too dangerous to risk for *business*. You may not return."

A shiver raised gooseflesh on my arms. "Why not?"

Aleksa didn't respond, just held her sister's hand tight.

Trusting a Riigan went against what I'd been told my entire life. But it wasn't about trusting a Riigan. It was about trusting Aleksa. Who cared for her sister as fiercely as I cared for Mari.

"My father went to Riiga and never returned. I must find him."

Aleksa closed her eyes and pressed her free hand against them. "It's too dangerous."

I shook my head. "I must. He's my father. I'd do anything for my family."

Aleksa was silent for some time, then heaved a sigh. "If your grandmother will help my sister, I will help you get into Riiga. No more."

I pressed the toe of my boot into the floor. "How can I trust—"

"I don't know what you know about Riigans," she interrupted, standing so fast her chair scraped the rough wood floor. "But we pay our debts."

I looked to Yesilia. Her eyes were still closed. She patted my hand. "It's your choice."

Aleksa was hostile and didn't trust me, and I wasn't fully certain I trusted her. But I needed her. "We can leave at first light."

Aleksa touched her shoulder and shook my hand in agreement, then sat and murmured to her sister, brushing her hair from her face and ignoring the rest of us.

Yesilia would help Ilma and be safe here until Enzo sent a carriage. And I would find a way to save my father.

CHAPTER ELEVEN

Ren

A young woman and her grandmother should not be this hard to track.

It was easy enough to find the orphanage in Turiana, but from there, it was as though they'd disappeared. The headmistress told me about their exchanging clothes, apologizing that she had already sold off the fine fabrics.

I didn't care about their silks—I was tired of crisscrossing the kingdom looking for Chiara and Yesilia.

And now I was stuck under a grove of trees while more hail and rain than I'd ever seen thundered down around me and my horse. Nótt was well trained and warm, so we weren't bad off, but Chiara and Yesilia were out there somewhere. Had they found shelter before the rains came?

I'd searched all of the cities closest to Turiana, but no one had seen a girl and her grandmother. Three routes led to Rialzo. Chiara would take the fastest way to Riiga; she'd follow her father's route. So I'd continued along the main road, getting suspicious looks and eating mildly edible food from inns, taken the wrong fork, and ended up in a town farther east than I'd intended.

Every time I'd tried to access the Medallion's magic, it remained distant and cool. I fleetingly considered banging it on a rock—maybe it needed to *reconnect* with the land to be helpful.

The rain didn't let up. The cap didn't protect my hair, and most of the dye had washed clean. After shivering through the night and most of the next day, I was pretty sure there wasn't any part of me left dry. Where were my high collars and fur-lined boots when I needed them?

I set out south again once the sun returned like it had never left, beating onto me, turning my neck red and soaking my back in sweat. If my body didn't heal itself so quickly, I had no doubt I would have been laid up with fevers for at least a week. As it was, every movement took effort, and I fell asleep in the saddle twice.

Deep mud covered the ground. If Chiara and Yesilia had been stuck out in the storm, they'd be in dire need of help. My grip on the reins tightened and I pushed my horse a little faster.

There were streams aplenty here, with acres of rolling, empty fields edged with short hedges or tall, skinny trees I'd never seen before. Wooden houses sat tucked away from the road among patches of wide trees, their broad leaves more gold than green now.

Someone had to be helping Chiara and Yesilia. There was

no way they could have made it this far south on their own, nor was it possible for their trail to disappear so completely.

Or—and this was a possibility I tried not to think about—something had happened to them.

The food from the palace had run out, and no one in the last village would sell to me—the price of being a roaming Hálendian. My stomach ached with hunger. I found a few berry bushes that hadn't been picked clean, and I detoured into a nearby field for a brief lunch when I spotted some fallen fruit in the long grass under a wild apple tree.

By dinner, I regretted my food choice, as my stomach cramped in a different way. After I'd tossed my accounts by the wayside, my throat burned and my head pounded, draining my magic little by little, and I cursed every unhelpful Turian to an icy grave.

But I kept going. The way Mari had clung to me, the trust Enzo and Jenna had shown in letting me go after Chiara and Yesilia, weighed heavy.

The Medallion lay dormant against my skin—I wasn't sure whether it was because I was on the right path or the wrong one—but doing something, as miserable as the trek was, was better than doing nothing.

I rested my horse for a spell, then continued on as the sun set behind the hills. I had fallen asleep in the saddle when I woke suddenly. Nótt stopped so fast I almost fell off him.

A gentle white fog had settled into the valleys of the fields, swirling over the furrows and ditches. A patch of trees that grew closer to the road shaded it from the dim light of the stars. The moon wasn't out tonight. Everything was silent, except for my breathing.

But *something* had awoken me. With a jolt, I realized the Medallion was warm. Hot, even.

The scrape of a sword being drawn broke the silence. My senses snapped alert. I pulled my own sword and kicked Nótt into a gallop without waiting for the shadows from the trees to materialize into men. A breathy whistling was the only warning before something slammed into my arm, pushing me out of the saddle and into the grass at the side of the road.

My horse reared back from the man trying to mount it, the ground trembling with his hoofbeats as I bit back a curse and lay still. Fire throbbed near my shoulder where the shaft of an arrow protruded, its head buried deep in the fleshy part of my arm.

At least it wasn't my sword arm. Well, my stronger sword arm.

A twig cracked to my right and I rolled, swinging hard at the man's legs. My blade sliced into him and he fell with a cry. I lunged to my feet, stumbling once because of the shaft still in me. I swung at every blade I saw, frantically beating them away through a haze of anger and pain.

But the men kept coming. I had taken down three when I missed a block. The blade nicked my thigh. I grunted and spun, sinking my sword into the man's gut. Another sword knocked into the arrow shaft in my arm. I stumbled as stars, far brighter than those in the sky, danced in my vision. Another man stepped in front of me. I barely had time to raise my sword before something hard slammed into my head from behind. I groaned and fell forward. Everything blurred and blackened, but I didn't lose consciousness. The tingling of my magic fought the nick in my thigh, the fog in my mind, the fire in my arm.

My chest heaved as I tried to suck in air to keep me awake around the magic pulling me into unconsciousness.

A pair of muddy boots stopped by my face. Short boots, so not Turian. Not sturdy enough to be Hálendian. Riigan? I couldn't tell in the dark.

"Kill him," a voice rasped in an accent I'd never heard before. Not Riigan or Turian. What in all the glaciers were mercenaries from the Continent doing this deep into Turia? Hadn't Marko kicked them all out months ago?

Mercenaries or no, I was not about to die on some desolate road. I launched my blade up into the man in front of me, pushed myself off the ground, and lunged after him, pulling my sword free and spinning to meet the man behind me. But there were still six men. Six angry men, one holding my horse. Blood dripped onto my hand from the wound in my shoulder.

Maybe I should have let Jenna accompany me. She'd never forgive me if I died.

A man in the back cried out, then fell. The two next to him turned their swords into the night. Both fell with a thud before they finished the turn.

"Show yourself!" one of the men called. The man holding my horse leapt atop him and galloped into the night, unwilling to be the next target.

I cursed and inched backward, sword still raised.

The man who had yelled fell next. I saw the silhouette of

an arrow protruding from his chest. I stepped back, into the line of trees. The bowman remained hidden. The shaft in my arm knocked against a branch. I bit my cheek to keep from crying out.

The remaining two men looked at each other, then turned to run, but fell before they'd taken two steps, arrows in their backs.

I swallowed as silence pressed in once again. Energy pulsed in my arm, but the wound couldn't heal as long as the arrow was lodged in it.

A tall cloaked figure dropped from the branches of a tree on the opposite side of the road and stalked toward me, bow lax at his side.

"Come out." His voice was solid and sure in the misty night.

I left the protection of the foliage, careful not to bump my arm, and tightened my grip on my hilt to keep it from slipping under the blood and sweat on my hand. "Who are you?" I asked, stopping at the edge of the road. The man paused and slung his bow over his shoulder.

"You looked like you needed help."

My arm shook under the weight of my sword. "Your arrow in my arm didn't *help* very much."

He didn't back down, didn't approach. "It's not my arrow."

I studied what I could see of the shaft. It was short and thick, with rough feathers at the end. The arrow in the back of the man at my feet was long with sleek fletching.

I grunted and lowered my sword, wincing as I sheathed it. "In that case, thank you."

The man took a step forward. "I've a camp not far. Can you make it?"

My horse was long gone. We were alone. The Medallion warmed against me, a whisper of caution echoing in my mind, but nothing more. I grunted and followed the man into the trees. My steps dragged as we trudged into a clearing, every step causing a jolt in my arm.

The man crouched by the remains of a fire, and flames leapt into the air. The flickering light illuminated his youthful features. He might have been even younger than me, but his eyes were ancient, older than they had any right to be, and he had dark smudges beneath them and hollows at his cheeks.

I slumped onto the ground across from him. My hand wrapped around the arrow's shaft and I sucked in a breath. I hoped I didn't pass out.

"Wait," the man said, and knelt in front of me. I exhaled. I wasn't sure I could make myself pull it out anyway. "Here." He leaned me back and braced his knee against my chest, then drew a long dagger from his belt.

Curses ran through my head as he lowered the dagger. *Caution,* the Medallion had warned. I hadn't listened, and now this man would gut me.

It didn't matter what choice I made, I was always wrong.

I squeezed my eyes shut, but his knife didn't slice open my belly or my neck or any other important part. Instead, he widened the wound the arrow stuck out from.

"Breathe," he commanded, and I breathed loudly in and out. Fire erupted in my arm, every nerve screaming as he pulled the arrowhead out, but I breathed with him. In, out. He pressed my hand against the wound as blood bubbled up. "Let me find something—"

"I'll be fine." I gritted my teeth and sat up, keeping my hand over the wound. I stretched my back and neck, pouring in extra magic to heal it faster. My skin stitched together, slowing the flow of blood; the muscle below took longer.

The man studied me. I pulled off my cap and ran my fingers through my sweaty hair, remembering too late the dye had mostly come out. I slammed the cap back on, but the man had to have noticed.

"Why did you help me?"

The man clasped his hands in his lap. "Do I need a reason to help?"

"Yes, I think you do."

"I just wanted to even the odds a little." He smirked, glancing at my shoulder and cap. "But I'm glad I did."

I narrowed my eyes. "Who are you?"

He watched me across the flickering flames, the shadows deep around him. "Erron."

His name sounded unfamiliar on his tongue. I didn't offer my name in return; he didn't ask.

"You have a gift." His eyes flicked to my shoulder. "There are many here who do."

I shifted, every sense sharpening, the chill in the air settling around me despite the fire.

Erron leaned away from the fire as if he were too hot despite the cool night. "I've heard some of the most powerful mages of old had this gift of healing."

I studied him again. His brown eyes were so deep they looked black, and his skin ageless. Alarm slithered through me. Surely the Medallion would have given a bigger warning if this was a *mage*. "The mages of old had destructive powers. Healing is a gift that can't be twisted by their evil."

Erron laughed, a mirthless chuckle that faded into the night. "Anything can be twisted."

My hand drifted toward my sword. "You seem to know a lot about these . . . gifts." I wouldn't call it magic until he did.

He shrugged and stood, brushing leaves and dirt from his cloak. "I think you'll find the friend you're looking for if you take the road east at the next fork." He whistled once and a huge brown gelding emerged from the shadows. He mounted and turned north. "And I wouldn't take the main path at Rialzo down into Riiga."

I gripped the sword at my waist and pulled my tired body to stand. "How did you know—"

"There's a better path to the east, one that has been forgotten. Look for twin pines and twin peaks."

"Who are you?"

His eyes darkened as he looked to the south. "It's not your concern." He kicked his heels into his horse and galloped into the night.

I leaned against a tree and rubbed my hands over my face, stubble scratching my palms. Twin pines and twin peaks? What was he talking about? How had he known so much about mages, about who I was and where I was going?

A nearby stream gurgled in the silence. Even the fire had gone out with Erron's departure. *You'll find the friend you're looking for* . . . Could I trust him? Could I risk *not* trusting him? If there was a chance Chiara had taken a different route to Riiga, I needed to know.

The Medallion warmed, a comforting heat, but my thoughts warred against each other—she would have taken the fastest route to her father. Wouldn't she? Yet I hadn't sensed a lie in anything Erron said.

I found the stream and dipped my hands into it, drinking from my cupped palms and splashing the cool water over my face and hair. The chill invigorated me, masking the ache in my muscles, the emptiness where my store of magic usually was.

Chiara *would* have taken the fastest route south. I splashed my hands into the water and muttered a curse. *Yesilia* wouldn't have. She'd know the main road was easier to track.

I'd take the eastern route, then. After I'd gotten some sleep. I hoped there weren't more mercenaries close by, because I didn't have the strength to take another step.

I needed to find Chiara and Yesilia. Soon.

CHAPTER TWELVE

Chiara

The road south yawned in front of us, lined with fields and tall grass, gentle hills rolling into the distance, tall trees marking property borders. The clouds still hung low, but only a light drizzle fell, coating everything in tiny beads of clear water.

Aleksa and I had left before first light, with food from Lessia and a hug from Dora, who told us to keep our eyes on the clouds.

Yesilia had squeezed me tight. "It's a sad day when you realize your days of adventuring have passed." Then she'd leaned close, and whispered, "You'll figure out the clue."

Ilma hadn't awoken when Aleksa left, but she seemed to be breathing easier than yesterday.

As we left town, walking on the side of the muddy road, my

shoulders itched like we were being watched. When I turned, no one was there.

After we'd walked more than an hour, Aleksa finally broke the silence. "Why are you going to Riiga? The truth, please," she added.

"I'm looking for my father," I said, tucking my hands inside my cloak. Both the hem on my cloak and my dress were heavy with mud again. "Why did you come to Turia?" If she was asking questions, so could I.

"I told you—to escape a prison."

I tilted my head. "Are you a criminal?"

She snorted. "No." We continued on, and I thought she'd given up questioning me, but then she said, "What kind of business did your father have in Riiga?"

There was no one on the road today—everything was still too wet to travel easily. "A wedding in Vera. He never arrived." It was as close to the truth as I could get.

Aleksa skidded to a stop. "You don't know if he's in Riiga?" she asked with a worried frown.

I sighed, the familiar anxiety coiling inside me. "He disappeared either right before crossing into Riiga, or right after."

Aleksa rubbed her forehead and started walking again. I lifted my hems and hurried to keep up. "If you can find him, *if* he's alive, how do you plan on getting him back? You don't seem the type to wield a sword."

I kicked a rock into the grass. She was right, there wasn't much I could do. I pulled the book out of my pocket. "I found a poem—a clue, I think—that leads to something . . .

to something valuable," I finished. Tales of mages would have sounded far-fetched to me if I hadn't experienced one firsthand. "I was hoping to find whatever the clue leads to, then trade it for my father's life."

"That could work. *If* you find it. And *if* you find whoever took your father. *And* if whoever took him cares about your treasure." Aleksa stared at the path beneath our feet, the beaten-down grass and mud that squished with every step. "But whoever took him won't deal fairly. What will you do if they take your treasure and don't give up your father?"

I closed my eyes and tilted my head back. I hadn't considered that.

Aleksa kicked a downed branch out of the path with a grunt. "The world isn't a nice, safe place, Chiara. I don't know what life you've lived to think anything is fair, but it isn't. And the sooner you realize that, the better off you'll be."

I swallowed and tucked my cold fingers back into my pockets. She was right. If Janiis refused to trade, I'd have nothing to protect myself or the poem's reward or anything.

"Can you tell me more about what's happening in Riiga? What I will face when I arrive?"

She didn't answer for a long time.

"Ilma will get better," I said quietly instead of asking again. "Yesilia is the best healer in the kingdom."

We walked five more steps, and Aleksa let out a deep, low sigh. "I'm not used to sharing my burdens with others." I waited, hoping she'd trust me a little. I needed her—if not her help in Riiga, then her knowledge. "Riiga is . . . in a dangerous position. The king's been cruel since his wife died eighteen years ago, but something changed in the palace. Something worse than even him." She squeezed her eyes shut and shook her head back and forth. "There's never enough food, barely enough water. You work in the king's vineyards or you starve. Two months ago, they started killing anyone found on the street at night."

"What?" I asked, loud enough that a bird startled out of a nearby tree. I lowered my voice. "The king didn't stop them?"

She shrugged. "It's the king's men who do it. He's passed laws that no one can be outdoors past curfew, that everyone must work in his camps. Only it's not just the vineyards now. He's mining at the cliffs. When the soldiers came to drag me and Ilma and our little brother to work, our mother told us to run to the neighbor's and hide."

She twisted her threadbare dress between her fingers, tighter and tighter. "There were soldiers there, too. One grabbed my brother. I tried to . . ." She swallowed. "I tried to get him back, but the soldier tossed him into a wagon with bars all around it. My mother was already in it. She screamed at us to run. So we ran." Her hands swiped at her cheeks in hard cuts. "I heard my brother was conscripted into the army. He's only fourteen. I should have stayed. Should have gone with them. But I thought maybe I could find someone to help."

A cold fury started in my gut. I wanted to rage against them all—how could Janiis do something like this to his own people? How could his men follow such awful orders? And how could my father not know? We had advisors on Janiis's council—how could this have gone on so long without detection?

"No one in Riiga would help you?" I whispered. The Riigans

I'd met were cunning and opportunistic, but surely they'd help one of their own.

Aleksa sniffed and straightened her shoulders. "I got plenty of help," she said in a hard voice. "Friends who took us in at night so we wouldn't be arrested or killed. Who kept us away from the soldiers and camps. They helped us get into Turia. But I got hungry. Needed money for food, needed work for money. We adapted. Learned enough to make money and slowly continue north. Then Ilma got sick."

I relaxed my fists and took a deep breath. I couldn't do anything *now*, but once I figured out the poem and found my father, we could do . . . something. Find a way to remove Janiis from the throne. *Something.*

"Where did the guards take your mother?" I asked.

Aleksa shook her head. "I've never seen it, but others said King Janiis is cutting away at the cliffs. His men round up wagons full of people, force them to work for days, then let them go home to rest. But so many never return. I don't know if my . . . if she . . ."

"And your father?" I asked quietly.

She stared at the ground. "He passed away last year."

Why did life have to be so hard? "Thank you for helping me," I whispered, stepping around a wide puddle.

Aleksa cleared her throat and scratched under her scarf. "I only said I'd get you into Riiga. Once we're down the cliff, you're on your own. I'll return to Ilma and continue to Turiana."

"Turiana?"

She brushed away a stick that had caught on her boot. "I'm going to see the king. Plead for help."

I tilted my head—she claimed to be no one, yet she would plead her kingdom's case before Turia's king? I wanted to tell her she'd speak with him sooner by accompanying me, but I couldn't reveal he was missing. Not now, when I might be close to recovering him.

I hoped Ilma reported the same to Yesilia—Enzo needed to understand that our towns weren't being invaded by Riigans, the Riigans were *fleeing* their homes. If I'd been in Aleksa's situation, I would have done the same.

I'd once thought all Riigans were like Koranth and Sennor—power hungry, ambitious, selfish. But I was coming to find out how wrong I'd been.

My foot slipped and I tumbled forward, throwing my hand out to catch my fall. Mud squished up over my wrist. I grunted and stood, trying unsuccessfully to wipe the muck away. "Thank you for showing me the way. I'll take whatever help I can get."

Aleksa's brows furrowed and she studied me, then shook her head and didn't say more. We walked in silence, the peaceful countryside penetrating the haze of awkwardness surrounding us.

My legs ached from pulling my feet out of the mud, but we still ate as we walked. Janiis's wedding was in four days—we'd lost too much time in Cozzare.

"Why is no one traveling north?" Aleksa asked, breaking the silence.

I shrugged, too tired and muddy to care. The sun set behind us, casting its last rays of orange and purple over us.

One of Aleksa's feet stuck in the mud, and she twisted it up with a slurp. "Cozzare was always bustling with people coming up from the south."

She was right. We hadn't seen *anyone*. But what could have stopped the travelers? The rain had been bad, but surely it wouldn't stop people used to it? "Should we camp off the road?"

Aleksa nodded. "And take turns keeping watch."

We followed a stream along the road until it cut through the edge of a field, turned over and ready for winter, and into a small wooded area that hadn't been cultivated for farming like most of the surrounding land.

By the time we reached the bosco, the sun had set. We huddled under a broad-leafed tree that still had most of its leaves, and tried to sleep.

I missed my bed, missed my family. Missed Yesilia's wisdom and spark. Missed having a full stomach. Being clean. And the closer we got to Riiga, the more nervous I became. Aleksa would get me down the cliff somehow, but then what? How would I figure out the clue on my own? And then how would I find my father and rescue him?

The first tinges of doubt seeped into me like the fog wrapping around us, a cold blanket that settled over my skin. Perhaps I shouldn't have come. But if not me, who? No, I was the best hope my father had. The thought didn't give me much comfort.

◆ ◆ ◆

I slept only a few hours before Aleksa woke me. "I'm falling asleep," she whispered. "Can you take a turn?"

I nodded and lay back down, then jerked up when I realized I'd fallen asleep again. I put my cold hands against my neck and patted my cheeks to stay awake. I thought about my family. About my father. How brave and how reckless he'd been to go to Riiga. He'd been counting on his position to protect him. And if it hadn't protected him, there was nothing to protect me, either.

Clouds passed overhead, leaving pockets of stars winking through. Branches rustled in the night, but no walls stood between me and the world anymore. No glass. No barriers. And while it was freeing, I'd also never felt so exposed. So vulnerable. Out here, anything could happen.

A stick cracked. I tensed, my heart beating loud in the silence. I strained to see something—anything—I could use as a weapon. I grabbed Aleksa's walking stick. My mind flipped through different options of what could be out there, each scarier than the last, until the spit had dried in my mouth and the ridges of the stick bit into my hands.

I eased off the ground, wincing as dry leaves tumbled from my cloak. Another crunch, closer this time. I could wake Aleksa, but if whatever was out there didn't know we were here, she might startle awake and make noise. Instead, I leaned into the tree behind me, hoping I could surprise whatever was approaching.

Soft footsteps padded closer, quiet but distinct. Two feet—not an animal. Long stride, so probably a man. A thief, to make such little noise.

I widened my grip on the makeshift staff. The steps came closer, pausing just behind the thick tree at my back. Now or never.

I inhaled deeply and spun around the tree, twisting my torso to put more force into the swing like Jenna had taught me. I brought the stick down hard, but the thief caught it and pulled even harder. I stumbled forward. He spun me around, his hard chest at my back.

Panic bubbled up at his tight grip. Jenna's training took over, and I cried out for Aleksa, then lunged to the side, trying to get enough leverage to flip him. He moved with me, and we both rolled backward. He was faster and pinned me, but Aleksa swung at him with what sounded like a branch, its *crack* exploding in the night.

"*Jöklar,*" he cursed, tumbling off me. Glaciers?

"Run!" Aleksa grabbed my arm and started dragging me.

The voice. It couldn't be. Not him. Not this far south. The man propped himself up on his elbows.

"Ren?" I whispered.

He launched up, without the staff, and wrapped his arms around me, hugging me tight, then holding me at arm's length. "What were you thinking? Do you know how worried your family is?"

"I . . . Ren?" I couldn't believe he was here. "They sent *you* to find me?"

"I sent myself." He rubbed his chest.

"Who are you?" Aleksa interrupted. She held a knife in front of her.

I put my hand out. "It's okay. He's . . ." I trailed off. The king of Hálendi? My soon-to-be sister-in-law's brother? The man I'd had a major crush on until he flirted with me like he did everyone else?

"I'm Ren," he said, rubbing his head. "Who are you?"

"Aleksa," she whispered, inching behind me.

I held my breath right along with her. Ren didn't show any surprise at the Riigan name.

He groaned. "Good move, Aleksa. Stunned me enough you both might have gotten away."

Something in me loosened when he didn't dismiss her or berate her for being Riigan. She'd started to trust me; I didn't want that work to go to waste.

"Where did you learn to fight like that?" he asked me.

He was still so close. So warm. I stepped back, next to Aleksa. "Jenna."

He chuckled, the warm sound intimate in the darkness. "Just so you know, your tell is your deep breath before you make a move."

"What?" I said, huffing an indignant laugh.

"Right before you swung at me, you took a deep breath. I heard it. That's how I knew you were about to try and take my head off."

I shrugged and held my hand out for the staff. "Someone was sneaking up on us in the middle of the night. What was I supposed to do?"

I couldn't see his expression, but I felt a change in the air when he spoke. "You were supposed to stay home. You have no idea how much danger—"

"I know exactly how much danger is out here," I shot back. "Just because I'm young—"

"And inexperienced. And unarmed. And—"

"—doesn't mean I don't understand the risk."

"Your brother and I had everything well in hand—"

"You absolutely did not. Your plan was to do nothing and hope it was the right choice."

Ren pulled the cap from his head and his hair glinted in the night as he paced between the trees. "Why sneak out? Why risk everything, and make your family worry more?"

I put my hands on my hips. "Because he's my father, Ren." He stopped his frenzied pacing. "I didn't say goodbye," I whispered. My lips pressed together, but the words were already out. "I had a chance to hug him before he left. To wish him safe travels. But I didn't." I sniffed. "No one else could go, but I could." I shrugged. "No one would miss me."

His head dropped. "Chiara—"

"How long did it take anyone to notice I was gone?" Ren hesitated just long enough for me to know I'd hit my mark. "How many days?"

His shoulders dropped. "Two."

Aleksa sucked in a breath. I'd almost forgotten she was here.

My throat tightened, but I forced the words out. "He's my father, Ren. If I can find him, it's worth any risk. Any danger."

He heaved a sigh and rubbed one hand over his face. "You shouldn't have gone alone."

"Yesilia was with me—"

"Wrong person."

"Aleksa—"

"Still the wrong person. Sorry," he added with a nod to her.

"How did you find us?" Aleksa asked.

Even in the darkness, I could see his stance tighten, and his hand moved to his sword, though I wasn't sure he realized what he'd done. "I found Yesilia in Cozzare; she told me what road you'd taken—"

"Did you see my sister?" Aleksa blurted out. "Is she . . . How is she?"

Ren arched his back, and I finally took in how slumped his shoulders were, how he leaned on a tree for support. "She's better."

Aleksa froze. "Better?" She set her hands on her hips. "Do not lie to me."

I closed my eyes. Ren had healed her. Had used his magic to pull the sickness out.

"Yesilia is very talented," he said softly.

Aleksa studied him, then me. "Yesilia didn't know we'd be in this bosco."

Ren hesitated. "I was trying to catch up, but was too tired to continue and thought to rest here."

But he touched his chest when he said it. Had his magic helped him? Or the Medallion? I wasn't sure how it worked, what its limits were. I wasn't even sure if he still had it—I'd overheard Jenna talking about it, but I'd never seen Ren wearing it.

"Ren, are *you* okay?" I asked. "You look halfway to death."

He chuckled ruefully. "More like three-quarters. I've been rained on, cheated, ambushed—"

"You came alone?" I interrupted. "You're—" *The king,* I almost said, but bit my tongue in time.

He shrugged. "I was the expendable one." His voice was low, missing all of its usual cadence and charm. Flat. "You need to go home."

"No," I said, and widened my stance. "We're almost to Riiga."

"Chiara—" he started, widening his own stance.

"We can talk in the morning," Aleksa said, interrupting the brewing fight. She was right, though. We needed sleep.

Ren sank to the ground, deflated, and rested his head in his hands like he couldn't hold it up any longer. "We're returning to Turiana in the morning."

A tiny spark of hope had ignited when I realized Ren was here, that I wouldn't have to venture into Riiga alone. But seeing him crumple to the ground like that, like he'd only kept himself together until this very moment, extinguished that hope.

I glanced over at Aleksa, willing her to understand, to agree with me.

Aleksa gave the barest of nods, then glared at Ren.

I would *not* be returning home tomorrow. Not when we were this close.

CHAPTER THIRTEEN

Ren

Chiara and Aleksa were gone when I woke up. I spent an hour behind them on the road, cursing their light feet and my exhaustion. At least they were easy to track. And I didn't have any luggage to drag along. No change of clothes or coin purse, either. I sighed—I hoped the belongings the mercenaries had ridden off with weren't important to whoever Enzo had borrowed them from.

The girls maintained their distance ahead of me on the road. They knew I was following them, but they kept going anyway. I couldn't understand why—I mean, I knew Chiara wanted to help her father. I understood that more than she could imagine. But she had to know the dangers of Rialzo. Of Riiga. Did she think she could waltz in and demand her father's return?

"Give me one good reason not to throw you over my shoulder

and take you home," I said when I was close enough that they'd hear. Maybe not what Yesilia had in mind when she asked me to listen to Chiara's plan when I sat with her in Cozzarre, but I hadn't eaten nearly enough food for this.

Chiara kept trudging forward, ignoring me.

"They'll catch you, and then do you know what will happen? They'll torture you, Chiara. One scream from you, and your father will give them anything they ask."

She tugged her skirt higher out of the mud as she walked. "They won't catch me."

She said it with enough certainty to make me pause. I was tired of talking to her back, so after a deep breath, I jogged the distance between us and gently took her arm, turning her to face me. "What do you know that En . . . your brother doesn't?" I asked, wary of how keenly Aleksa watched us. No matter if Chiara trusted her enough to travel with; I'd only reveal what I had to.

Chiara folded her arms and stared up at me. "I know how to get into Riiga without getting caught. Without going through Rialzo."

My eyebrows shot up and my chin tilted down. "You do?"

She fidgeted and swallowed. "Well, I don't, but Aleksa does."

Aleksa's hands went to her hips. "I said I'd get you into Riiga. I didn't say anything—"

Chiara shook her head. "You came to Turia two months ago—when the border was closed. When there was no passage granted through Rialzo."

Aleksa's mouth snapped shut. She mimicked Chiara's pose, with arms folded across her chest. But I remembered what the man—Erron—had said. "Twin pines," I muttered.

Aleksa's head snapped toward me. "What did you say?"

Maybe there *was* another way into Riiga. "And when you get into Riiga without getting caught?" I asked. "How do you plan to find him?"

Chiara tilted her head, like she was weighing her words. Weighing *me*. "How about the same way you found us in a patch of trees off the road in the middle of the night?"

She raised her eyebrow at me, and I almost—*almost*—laughed. She'd been masquerading as an obedient, quiet princess, when in fact she had been collecting information like a crow collects pretty things.

I folded my arms across my chest as well. "Okay, so you get into Riiga. *We* find your father. How do you plan to rescue him?"

She tipped one shoulder up and started walking again. "I have something Janiis wants."

Aleksa and I glared at each other, then hurried after her. "Janiis?" Aleksa asked. She pulled Chiara to a stop again. "Whatever you have, you need to keep it. You cannot give him anything he wants."

Chiara pulled away from Aleksa's grip. "You said you'd get me into Riiga if your sister was healed. She is. Now, we go to Riiga."

Aleksa shook her head back and forth so hard *my* neck hurt. "I have only *his* word on this?" she said, throwing her thumb toward me. "No. You cannot do this. When you negotiate with Janiis, you always lose."

"I agree with Aleksa," I said. "We should turn back. Your brother will—"

"I'm going. With or without your help," Chiara gritted out, and started along the path again.

Aleksa and I heaved a sigh together. She glared at me, then called out, "Wait. You want to know why I warn you away from Riiga? I will tell you."

Chiara stopped and faced us.

"It started when Janiis took on a new advisor. Everything deteriorated, like Vera was a mountain of sand against the tide. There is more than the curfew and labor camps and forcing the oldest boy in every family into the army. There are dangerous mines that collapse when a storm brings the tide too high—"

"What are they mining?" I interrupted. Riiga was known for vineyards and wine. Trading.

Aleksa brushed my question away with her hand. "I do not know, only that the blacksmiths are working all the time now. And it gets worse."

A songbird trilled as it swooped over the rocky field surrounding us, a lone bird in the vast expanse.

She swallowed hard. "There are those who opposed Janiis and his new advisor. But they either mysteriously disappeared or became Janiis's most vocal supporters—overnight, with no reason. *All* of them. You would do better to accompany me to Turiana and address our concerns to King Marko. He is a good man. He will help us."

My jaw clenched tighter the longer Aleksa spoke. If what she said was true, the Plateau wouldn't withstand the threat of the mages. "How has no one heard of this before?"

"Soldiers at the base of the cliffs arrest anyone who tries to leave," she said.

I took off my cap and scrubbed my hand through my hair. "Glaciers."

My head pounded. No, wait. The pounding wasn't in my head. I squinted into the rising sun. The Medallion flashed hot against my chest as the pounding grew louder.

"Quick," I hissed, jamming my cap back on. "We need to hide."

I pulled them off the road, toward a patch of scrubby bushes. Tucked behind the bushes, a gulley ran alongside the road—once full of runoff, now nothing more than a trickling stream.

I landed on the loose rocks at the bottom of the gulley and turned to help Chiara and Aleksa as the pounding continued, but they were already jumping down. Chiara landed hard and fell against me. My arms went around her, but Aleksa crashed into us, and we sprawled on the muddy rocks.

The hilt of my sword dug into my side, forcing out my breath. The Medallion had settled, but not completely.

Chiara froze next to me. "What—"

"Someone's coming," I whispered.

We remained still, my arm tucked around her waist, as horses—at least five from the way the ground trembled—galloped by. Without stopping. I untangled myself from Chiara and Aleksa—and my sword—and crouched low to see over the edge of the gulley. Who had the Medallion warned against?

"That's Nótt!" I whisper-shouted. I had a hand on an exposed root, ready to pull myself up, when Chiara tugged me back down.

"Who's Nótt?" she asked, my sleeve bunched in her fist.

"My horse." I peeked over the ledge as the riders disappeared around a bend. "It means *nightfall*. I wanted to name him Crowberry, but Jenna wouldn't let me name him after food." I snapped my mouth shut so I'd stop rambling. We'd almost been caught; that had been too close.

"How did they get your horse?" she asked, releasing my sleeve and adjusting the strap of her bag on her shoulder.

I rubbed the back of my neck, then realized I was covered in mud. I tried shaking it off my hands, but it stuck to everything. "I was ambushed two nights ago."

"By whom?" she asked.

I scraped my hand against a rock to get the mud off. "Mercenaries from the Continent, I think."

Aleksa gasped, but not from what I'd said. She tried to stand, but fell when she set her foot down.

"Where does it hurt?" Chiara asked, kneeling next to her.

Aleksa pursed her lips until they were purple slits against pale skin. "Ankle," she choked out.

Chiara eased off Aleksa's shoe and brushed the mud away from her skin to feel the bone.

Aleksa groaned and tucked her chin against her chest, breathing hard. "It twisted when I landed."

Chiara looked up at me with her huge hazel eyes. She tilted her head at Aleksa's ankle.

I closed my eyes. I didn't mind helping Aleksa. I *didn't* think I should reveal my identity.

"Ren," Chiara said quietly. Had she learned that look from her mother? Because it seemed like a look Cora would give.

I heaved a sigh and checked one more time that the riders had passed, then knelt in the mud next to the two girls. Aleksa leaned away from me, her elbows tight to her sides like she'd scramble away if she could.

"May I?" I asked. She glanced at Chiara, then nodded. I rested my hands on either side of Aleksa's ankle, feeling for broken bones. "Hold still." I closed my eyes and dug into the center of myself, where the rushing magic swirled, eager to be released. I hadn't fully recovered from healing Ilma, but there was enough for this.

My hands didn't change temperature, though Jenna said she felt heat when I healed her. Aleksa didn't move, didn't make a sound. The rushing continued, and I felt Aleksa's ankle mending itself back together, then pushing my magic away once it had returned to its complete state.

I sat back in the cold mud, taking slow breaths to hide how little energy I had left. Aleksa stared at me.

"*You* healed my sister." It wasn't a question, so I didn't respond. She stood with Chiara's help and tested her ankle. "Who are you people?" she asked, brows furrowed so deep they nearly met in the middle.

I used the exposed root to pull myself out of the gulley, then reached down for Chiara. She stared at my hand before taking it. Was it the mud? The magic? I'd *never* seen a girl hesitate to take my hand.

I braced one foot against the root, then heaved her up. Easily. How could she think she would be able to stand against Janiis?

Then we both reached for Aleksa, helped her up, and sat next to the short bush. I rubbed my forehead. The sun had risen above the trees and beat against us, and my empty stomach cramped.

Aleksa stared at me, shaking her head.

"Out with it," I said, too tired to deal with this back-and-forth. Sitting on the roadside arguing wasn't helping Turia or Hálendi.

"*You* cannot go to Riiga," she said. She'd pieced together my identity, then.

"He has to. We both do," Chiara said. Faint lines deepened around her eyes and mouth, and she looked as tired as I felt. "My father—the man we seek—is the king of Turia."

Aleksa sighed, then closed her eyes and tilted her face to the sky. "As you said, glaciers."

I studied the road, the tracks the riders had made as they kicked up mud on the way to Cozzare. Three of the horses were shod differently from any I'd ever seen. Mercenaries. One horse was from somewhere on the Plateau, and one was *my* horse. I faced the path to Rialzo, hoping the Medallion would warn or whisper or *anything*. Nothing. I turned back toward Cozzare slowly, dreading that I'd have to tell Chiara we shouldn't go after her father. Dreading finding a way to keep her from continuing on alone.

But the Medallion remained silent.

My brows furrowed and I turned toward Rialzo again, but this time, the Medallion warmed when I faced east, into the countryside. "What's out there?" I asked, pointing to the rolling, rocky hills that almost looked like Hálendi.

Chiara shook her head. "Nothing, as far as I know."

Aleksa stared at me so long I shifted my feet. Rested my hand on the pommel of my sword.

"I will take you to Riiga through the twin pines," Aleksa

announced, standing and scraping what mud she could off her skirt with a rock.

She left the road, leaping over the gulley. Heading the same direction the Medallion had indicated.

Chiara grinned at me and ran after Aleksa. She almost slipped back into the gulley when she jumped but found her balance at the last moment—her dancing instructors had taught her well.

I stared back toward Cozzare one more time. Yesilia could take care of herself. The provision I'd signed with Edda before leaving would hold. Hálendi would be taken care of should anything happen to me.

◆ ◆ ◆

The sun blazed from the east, with no trees to offer shade, no path to ease the trek as we climbed over boulders and around scrubby bushes.

A bird sang somewhere nearby. Empty countryside stretched as far as we could see. The chain of the Medallion rubbed against my neck as we crossed the uneven terrain.

"What do you plan to trade?" I asked Chiara when the silence became too much for me. I needed something to distract me from the fact I'd specifically told Edda I would *not* go to Riiga. That if Marko had been a target, *I* would be as well.

That although I'd left Hálendi in capable hands, I still wanted to return and have a chance to do what my father had wanted me to do.

"I found a clue to something important. A treasure," Chiara said, with a long look at me.

"And you want to trade the treasure for your father," I said. If that wasn't the vaguest plan I'd ever heard, I'd eat rocks for dinner.

She shook her head and jumped onto a boulder, landing lightly. "No, I want to find the treasure and *then* trade the clue."

Most of her hair had come loose and trailed behind her in the wind. She looked back at me, and the whole scene hit me—her carefree and alarmingly mischievous grin, her flowing black hair cascading around her, and the vast, empty landscape sprawling behind her. Like she'd conquer the world if given half a chance.

"Devious. I like it." I jumped up next to Chiara. She shivered, but the cold wind felt like home. "Okay, so show me the clue."

Her lips twisted to one side.

"If you're dragging me to Riiga, I'd like to know everything, please."

She dug into her pocket and pulled out a small book. The book I'd given Jenna. When I first saw it in Chiara's hands back at the palace, it had hurt. My sister hadn't needed anything from me, not even a silly trinket to remember me by.

Chiara flipped through the pages to find a loose leaf.

"It's still empty," I said, nodding to the book. I wasn't sure how it had gotten to be empty, though. It'd had writing in it when I gave it to Jenna.

She snapped the book closed and tucked it away again, keeping her gaze down. "I'm . . . working on it."

I shoved my hands into my pockets to keep from tilting her chin up. Seeing her staring at the ground, like she was trying to hide from the world, didn't feel right.

Aleksa came back to us. "We must hurry if we want to make it into Riiga before the sun sets."

Into Riiga *today*? We were closer than I thought. Chiara unfolded the page, and the illustration of the Turian ring glared up at me. "I've seen this before," I said.

"Yes, but the clue is here, on the back." She flipped the paper over and held it for both Aleksa and me to read.

Three keys to find the library black:
one in snow, the heart of attack.
Another within the heart,
and surrounding it, too,
a ring of flax, of brown and blue.

"But the real clue," Chiara continued before I'd finished reading, "is here." She rotated the paper. In the margin, I could barely make out the words *vineyards that touch the sky*. "This is what made Yesilia think the . . . treasure is in Riiga."

Aleksa was nodding. "There are vineyards like this between Vera, the capital, and Elpa, to the northeast."

The Medallion warmed against me, a circle of heat against the windblown cold. Truth. It wasn't just a treasure, though. It had something to do with the Black Library. Which meant the mages, and possibly Janiis, could be *very* interested.

We'd have to be careful.

Chiara and I followed Aleksa east, trudging along with the moaning wind. When she stopped, I looked up from the animal holes I'd been dodging. Two huge pines rose in front of us, their trunks twisted against years of storms battering them.

Beyond, at the end of a field of tiny white wildflowers, lay the edge of the Plateau. Two piles of rocks, stacked neatly into peaks, marked the path. Twin pines, twin peaks.

Wind whipped straight through my skin here at the top of the cliff. It pressed against me, urging me to step back, to stay away, only to change directions and tug me closer to the edge.

As I approached the cliff, the vast water of the Many Seas stretched to the horizon. Between the rock piles, craggy steps descended. I leaned forward, trying to mark the path. The earth below bloomed in front of me, white waves crashing into the land. A tiny strip of beach was all that lay at the bottom of the cliff.

Beyond the flat land, the gray water stretched until I lost sight of its edge. A dark wall of clouds sat on the horizon, churning and blowing ever closer.

A snap of wind tugged at me, urging me even closer to the edge. A hand grabbed my tunic and pulled me back.

"Don't get so close," Chiara said, releasing me and stepping back.

"How did you know about this, again?" I asked Aleksa. I scanned our surroundings, wary of being so exposed. No road as an excuse for traveling, no trees to hide among. Only endless rocks. And hunger. My stomach grumbled, and Chiara's responded. She smirked at me, and I snorted. I never thought she'd be the type to joke around.

"Only a few Riigans knew about it. When the soldiers started arresting anyone who tried to leave, word spread among the enemies of Janiis and his advisor. But," Aleksa said slowly, "there may be another way for you to keep your treasure *and* find your father."

Chiara folded her arms, tucking her hands in her armpits to keep them warm. A strange instinct rose up—to take her hands in mine. Warm them. But she didn't want that from me. She needed my sword and my magic to help find her father. That was it.

"I have friends in Riiga," Aleksa said. "Friends who work in the palace, friends who work in noble houses. I could see if anyone has heard of Janiis taking a prisoner. He is vain enough to have boasted to *someone* about it, if he does have your father."

"So you'll help us?" Chiara asked, wind blowing tendrils of hair across her cheek. *Us.* Could we really do this? With Aleksa's help, and her friends' . . .

I paced away, then back again. "There are Turians loyal to Marko in Riiga. Could you find them?"

Chiara's mouth dropped open. "Luc! I'd forgotten—"

"Yes," Aleksa said. "I could find them." She spoke with such certainty. More certainty than I expected. "If we want to make it down the cliff before that storm arrives, we need to start now." Chiara bent to pull her cloak out of the bag she carried, but Aleksa stopped her. "No cloaks. Too easy to snag and lose your balance. If you fall, you fall for a very long time."

Chiara shoved her cloak back into her bag, which she strapped across her shoulder, the grim look of a soldier going into battle.

Only half my foot could fit on a stair. But another step, slightly larger, waited farther down. An old, frayed rope had been nailed into the face of the cliff, dark brown spikes sticking out every few feet.

"Go slow," Aleksa said quietly, reverently. "Sit down if you need to, and make sure your footing is solid before trusting your weight to it. The ropes on the wall might hold you, they might not. Trust your feet, not your hands."

Chiara and I nodded, and Aleksa crouched down, stepping onto the first step. Then the second.

Chiara looked up at me. "Me next?" she asked. "Or you?"

I didn't want her anywhere near this cliff. But I bit my tongue and said, "Me. If I fall, I won't take you down with me." And if she fell, there was a chance I could catch her.

She stepped to the side to let me by but then put a hand to my chest to stop me. A flurry swirled from her fingertips into me. She pulled her hand away. "Don't. Fall."

I smiled ruefully. Assassins had failed. Mercenaries had failed. But maybe the wind would succeed. "It might be better for Hálendi if I did," I muttered.

She shook her head. "I'm sorry, what?"

I'd said that louder than intended. "I won't fall." I shrugged like I'd been joking. Like it was nothing. But her stare drilled into me.

I stepped off carefully, calling on every lesson in balance Master Hafa had drilled into me. I made it to the third step down, then turned to help Chiara. She was right behind me, one hand holding her tattered, muddy skirt, the other pressing against the cliff.

And so we continued, the wind tugging, the steps crumbling, the rope at the side fraying. I stepped where Aleksa stepped, and I braced myself every time I heard Chiara's breath hitch.

Partway down, the path shifted directions, switching back. Rusted spikes stuck out of the face, but only threads remained of the rope. And this step was the longest yet. I eased down slowly, following Aleksa's directions, then turned to help Chiara. She slipped her ice-cold hand into mine and wedged herself next to me on the step, our backs pressed into the cliff.

"This marks a quarter of the way," Aleksa said from the step below as she continued on.

Next to me, Chiara blew out a long, slow breath. A quarter down. "Give me your other hand," I murmured. She stared at me like I had ice for brains, so I took her hand in mine, and pulled a thread of magic out, focusing on her hands to warm them.

She sucked in a breath and closed her eyes just as mine opened again. A tiny drop of rain landed on her cheek, and below us, Aleksa cursed.

"We must hurry. We cannot be on the cliff when the storm hits."

I released Chiara's hands after only a moment's hesitation, then crouched down, easing myself onto the lower step. Tiny pebbles came loose and bounced away, pinging down, down, down.

"Here," I said, reaching toward Chiara. "Let me help you down."

I was helping her to keep her safe. Warming her hands so they stayed strong as we climbed. But a tiny part of me just wanted to be near her. I wasn't quite sure why—she *was* beautiful, if quiet, but more than that, her fierce dedication in going after her father . . . I admired that. Would anyone traipse over the entire Plateau to find me?

She clutched me tighter as I eased her down the long step.

My other hand slipped around her waist. These steps were cut perpendicular to the face of the cliff, so I tucked her against the rock as she settled onto the step, pressed between me and the rock. I looked down at her for a long moment, our chests moving in rhythm with each other's.

She licked her lips and started to shrug, but stopped halfway like her tutors were still trying to break that habit. "At least if I fall, you can heal me, right?" she said, trying to lighten the moment.

It hit me—all of it. Our precarious position. The chances of succeeding *in* Riiga against King Janiis. How would I manage to protect her? Protect them both? "I . . . my magic isn't limitless," I said, my voice hushed. More raindrops splattered against the stone stairs. "If I'm too tired, or if the wound is too serious, there's nothing I can do."

It had happened before. Their faces were always with me—the ones I hadn't been able to save. Chiara's brother had almost been one. And Jenna wasn't with me now to lend her magic if something happened.

Chiara's brows furrowed and her fingers tightened around my arms. Like she could see the faces of those I'd lost right along with me.

"Ren?" Aleksa called out.

"Coming," I said, dragging my eyes from Chiara and taking the next step down.

The descent was agonizing, both in length and in the physical toll it exacted on us. I hadn't eaten enough, hadn't recovered from healing Ilma. Yet every time I cut a finger on a rock, my magic swirled to life. It seeped into my tired calves, into my back and shoulders. I wasn't sure how Aleksa and Chiara were faring, but neither complained.

When we stepped off the last stair—a small jump into long, soft grass—I fell to my hands and knees next to Aleksa. Completely spent. Chiara jumped down next to me. We rolled onto our backs and stared at the churning clouds as the wind whipped around us.

We lay there like that until Chiara chuckled.

"How is this funny?" Aleksa asked, one arm over her eyes.

More laughter bubbled up. "We did it," Chiara said. "We climbed down the *cliffs* and snuck into Riiga!" She snorted at the end.

Snorted. I tried to turn my laugh into a cough, but I don't think I succeeded. "We did do it, didn't we?"

A handful of rocks and dust bounced down the cliff, pinging against the stone and landing in the grass. The Medallion warmed a fraction. We all looked up, laughter forgotten. Black clouds pressed against the cliffs, and wind nearly flattened the grass. Rain pelted down, sharp, cold, fast.

"Let's go," Aleksa said, the lines on her face deeper than ever.

Chiara sprang up and I followed. I couldn't help but wish I felt a fraction of her excitement. While we were closer to finding her father, we were also in a kingdom whose fabric was fraying. Would we be caught in the chaos when everything snapped?

Three days until the wedding. Three days to find Marko, find whatever the clue Chiara had uncovered led to, and get out.

Enzo

I knocked on my mother's door like I had every day for the past twelve days. But my hands hadn't shaken like this before. I should have told her about Chiara leaving.

"Enter," she called. At least she sat by a window today, with the curtains drawn aside. One of my father's stockings lay on her lap, the needle and thread forgotten in her hand. "Enzo." A small smile lit her face, then faded when I didn't smile back.

The message in my fist crumpled. But I had to tell her. It had to be from me. I swallowed. "Mother." I swallowed again. Clasped my hands behind my back.

What little color she had in her cheeks drained. "Is it your father?" she whispered.

I shook my head and licked my lips, trying to find the words. "It's . . . it's Mari."

"Mari?" Her brows tipped down.

I knelt by her chair, slipping my hand into hers. Not because she needed my strength. But because I needed hers. "She's gone. Everyone has searched, but she's not in the palace. Not on the grounds. Jenna says"—I swallowed as my insides twisted around each other in knots—"Jenna says her tether is distant. That she's run away."

Mother's eyes closed and lines appeared on her forehead. I continued before she could speak.

"There's more. I've had a message from Yesilia. She's"—oh, how I wished I'd told Mother right when it was discovered they were missing—"she's in Cozzare. She and Chiara decided to try to recover Father on their own, and—"

"Mari *and* Chiara?" Mother whispered. "And Yesilia?"

I nodded. "Yesilia says the state of Riiga is worse than we feared. She says Ren caught up with them, and that they're safe. Mari hasn't been gone long, we don't think." I squeezed her hand. "Jenna will go after her."

Mother tilted her head. "Do you want her to?"

I pressed my lips together and studied the delicate skin of my mother's hands. How it had changed. Aged. "No. But she will go. I know she will. I can't force her to stay, yet the thought of her out there alone—"

"What does your heart tell you?" My mother's other hand covered mine.

I closed my eyes and pressed my forehead against her knee. "I know I can't fight mages and that Jenna can take care of herself. But I don't want her to have to do it alone. Not again. *I* should be the one going after Mari. After all of them. But I can't."

My mother brushed her hand through my hair like she had

when I was little. "You're grown now, Enzo. It's time to make your own decisions." I jerked my head up to see her smiling at me. She looked more peaceful than she'd been in days. "I can handle things here. Help Jenna find Mari."

I launched up and threw my arms around her. "Thank you," I whispered into her hair.

I wouldn't let a mage separate my family. Not again.

CHAPTER FOURTEEN

Chiara

Small alcoves pocked the cliff's face along the shore, some open to the wind and sea, others covered with vines and bushes. Aleksa had searched until she found us a very specific one to hide in. One with a box made of stone submerged in the white sand, which was filled with circular flat bread, dried fish, and water in a glass jug for anyone trying to escape.

Then she'd tucked Ren and me into the tiny cave and left.

I'd tried to talk her into waiting out the storm, but she'd said the weather would keep Janiis's guards off the streets so she could ask her questions in peace.

"There are still a few hours before the soldiers begin patrolling," she'd said, crouching under the low ceiling and looking out into the rain. "I will ask for news, see if your friend can help. Find out what new terror Janiis has unlocked. Vera is a half hour's walk from here around the bend. I'll be back before dawn."

Ren had nodded and settled back against the wall.

Aleksa gaped at him. "Just like that?"

Ren looked at me, then at Aleksa. "Just like what?"

I shook out the dried mud from my skirt the best I could. "She's surprised you accepted what she said."

Ren wrapped his coat tighter around him. "Why wouldn't I accept it? I've never been here; you're Riigan—you lived here." He paused. "And Chiara trusts you."

Which meant he trusted me. With the unexpected warmth that bloomed in my chest, like dawn's first rays or a warm blanket by the fire, came a sense of responsibility as well. Was I sure about Aleksa? She said she was helping us because we'd helped her sister. But was there more? Was I leading us into more trouble than we could handle?

"If I'm unable to return, meet my friend Edgars in Vera's main market. He can help you," Aleksa said. And then she'd ducked out into the storm.

I'd settled next to Ren—not too close, but close enough to feel the heat radiating from him and wishing he'd take my hands and warm them again. I swallowed back the memory of us on the cliffs. Of his rough hands gripping mine. The calluses had surprised me, though they shouldn't have. He was a man who wielded a sword more often than he danced. And though I'd danced with many men, most of them had soft hands, smooth skin.

And now we sat scrunched in a tiny cave in Riiga as the sun set behind the storm raging against the cliffs.

I'd never been this close to a man I wasn't dancing with before. I wasn't sure what to do with my hands, where to look, what to say without the music guiding me.

"Tell me more about the clue," Ren said.

I'd been staring at his hands. My eyes jumped up to his. There was barely enough light to see by. His usual smile was nowhere to be seen; he didn't laugh or joke or tease. He sat, his legs tucked up, arms resting on his knees. Head resting against the freezing rock behind us.

He looked . . . tired.

I grabbed my cloak out of my bag and huddled under it, glad it was still dry. "Three keys: 'one in snow, the heart of attack.' That's Hálendi's key." I stared at his chest. "You have it, don't you." It was a question, but it wasn't.

He tugged at the chain and pulled the Medallion out, cradling it in his hands and frowning at it. I leaned closer, asking silent permission to touch it. He held it out to me, and I ran my fingers over its surface. The runes were so intricate. It was strange to think how this piece of stone wasn't just stone.

"How does it work?" I asked. I looked up, and our faces were close. All the air solidified in my lungs. Ren pulled away, expression unreadable, tucking the Medallion back into his tunic.

"It resonates with the land's magic. Gives warnings, but not always. I'm still . . . I'm still figuring out how to use it."

He dug his heels into the sand and fiddled with a seam of his trousers. I didn't press him. The Medallion had led him to us. Had protected us from the riders on the road. It seemed like he was doing a good job of figuring it out.

"'Another within the heart, a ring of flax, of brown and blue,'" I continued. "That's Turia's artifact."

"That Brownlok has."

I nodded. "But it says *three* keys. I think there's a third key of some sort hidden near the terraced vineyards."

Ren let out a deep sigh and ran a hand through his hair, shaking out dust from the climb and exposing the white streak just above his temple.

Magic.

It was a concept as foreign as the Ice Deserts, yet also familiar. Grandmother Yesilia worked a kind of magic in her healing chambers. The people of Turia—young, old, poor, rich—worked their own magic every day as they lived their lives. In plowing their fields, taking seeds and nurturing them into plants and trees and *life*. In village healers who knew every use of every plant in the area.

And Jenna. Her magic had saved Mari and me. Had saved us all, really.

Even Enzo had magic of his own—the ability to see others' magic. But not me—I had nothing even close to resembling that kind of power.

A loud clap of thunder crashed and I shivered. The air here was filled with freezing water that clung to everything. Ren didn't have a cloak. No bag, either. He needed rest, but I was too exhilarated from making it into Riiga to sleep. We were *so close.*

"Did the men who attacked you take your supplies?" I asked. If he didn't respond with more than a yes or no, I wouldn't bother him.

He let out a rueful chuckle. "Yes. Shot me off my horse, then ran off with everything."

I blinked. "Shot you?"

He shrugged like it wasn't a huge deal that the king of Hálendi had almost met his demise. "I also might have met a mage."

"What?" I said too loud for the small cave.

"A man helped me when I was ambushed. I was injured, outnumbered, and he stepped in. After pulling the arrow out of my shoulder, he—"

I reached out to him—my hand holding his forearm before I could stop it. "An arrow?" I stared at his shoulder. An *arrow*?

Ren tipped my chin so I was looking at his left shoulder. "It was this one. And yes." Our eyes met. His fingers burned against my skin where he touched me. For a man from the frozen north, he had a lot of heat radiating off his body. My cheeks warmed and my heart beat faster and faster until I thought he'd hear it.

He dropped his hand, shaking it a bit. "He said the main road wasn't safe, and that I'd do better if I went to the twin pines and twin peaks."

I pursed my lips. "Was he Riigan?"

"He didn't sound Riigan." Ren winced and spit out the rest. "He didn't seem surprised when my arm healed on its own. Wouldn't say why he was helping me. Brown cloak."

"Ancient voice?" I asked. My ribs seemed to get tighter around my lungs when he nodded. "Brownlok," I whispered with a shiver.

It was so easy to forget about the mages when Janiis was the target. But I'd never forget Brownlok's voice as he and Koranth had plotted to find us when we'd been trapped in the palace.

"I don't know why he helped me, or if he recognized me. But he was heading north, away from Riiga."

I swallowed. "Toward Turiana." Brownlok had practically walked into the palace last time. The palace that was still under construction.

Ren's hand rested on my shoulder. "Jenna and Enzo will keep everyone safe."

They would. But that wouldn't stop me from worrying.

I leaned a bit closer. Should I ask if he was cold? I didn't want him to think I was like Cynthia or all the other girls I'm sure followed him around, finding excuses to get close to him. But he didn't have a cloak. It was freezing, Hálendian or no.

"Do you want to share?" I finally blurted out, lifting the edge of my cloak. We were packed in tight as it was, our knees almost touching. "If you're cold, I mean. Since you don't have a—"

"Yes," he said quickly, inching closer.

I undid the clasp with fumbling, mostly numb fingers. But when I tried to lay the cloak over both of us, I realized how big he was, and how small the cloak was. "Um . . ." I swallowed.

He leaned against the back of the cave and held one arm up. He tried to smile, to waggle his eyebrows. But it was half-hearted, at best.

"If you wink at me, I'll rescind my offer," I grumbled, and scooted closer, until his arm was around my shoulder and we touched from shoulder to hip to knee. Tiny fires erupted at every contact point—fires I tried to ignore. He didn't see me that way; he saw me as a sister.

"You're in luck, Princess," he murmured. "I'm too tired to wink tonight."

Being this close, the tension in his muscles bled into me. He was a warrior—he shouldn't be this tired. Even *I'd* made the journey.

"Did the jaunt down the cliff wear you down too much, Your Majesty?" I tried to tease.

"Between the cliff, Aleksa, Ilma, and this blasted cold seeping into my bones, I won't be much company tonight, I'm afraid." He swallowed and his arm tightened around my shoulder as he shifted to get comfortable. I tucked my chin toward my chest and leaned in. I couldn't help it—were all boys this warm?

"Can I tell you something?" he whispered. We were so close, his breath lifted wisps of my hair. Full dark had come, and still the storm raged. I nodded against his shoulder, not sure my voice would work.

"My magic? I pretend like it's limitless. That I'm invincible. But it's not. I just . . . I need you to know that. Before we go farther into Riiga."

He stopped, but I didn't want him to. I hadn't known him long, but he'd always been confident, like he had all the answers. And if he didn't, he could flirt until the right answer came.

"Will you tell me about it?" I asked. Hoping he would trust me. Hoping he felt the spark where we touched like I did.

His chest rose and fell next to me. "My body heals on its own. Which sounds useful, but not always."

"Why not?" I asked. Healing from bruises and cuts and sore muscles sounded wonderful to me at the moment.

He sighed and relaxed into me more. "I don't have a choice in which injuries my body heals, and which it doesn't. So if I'm exhausted and want to save magic, I can't until all my wounds are healed, no matter how small the bruise. If I desperately need rest, but am too cold, my body will spend magic all night to keep me warm."

Oh. I leaned a little closer. To help him.

"To heal someone else, I have to be touching them. All my magic does, really, is take something that's broken and urge it to fix itself. Or, in the case of sickness, to pull out the bad and replace it with good."

"Like Yesilia," I said.

"Exactly, just on a grander scale." His fingers tapped against my arm. I didn't think he was aware of the motion, but I felt the muscles in his arm moving along with it. "But it's not a bottomless well of power. If I'm tired, or worn out, or healing myself, that well is depleted. And if I try to heal someone and don't have enough magic for it, my own life force will be pulled out until there's nothing left."

I frowned. "What happens when you don't have any more life force?"

He exhaled, a quick puff of air. "I die."

"Couldn't you stop before you run out?"

He exhaled long and low, ruffling my hair again. "It's like . . . when you hold something tight for too long, and it's hard to let go?" I nodded. "When I start healing, a bond is formed, and it's hard to let go until the healing is complete.

"And also"—he took a deep breath—"I've never told anyone this, but when I'm healing, I'm not really aware of my surroundings."

Not aware? That's why he checked for the riders at the gulley before healing Aleksa. Why his eyes had fallen closed when he'd warmed my hands.

"I . . . Don't tell anyone, please. I just thought you should know—in case something happens."

"Thank you for telling me," I whispered. Ren was right—I *had* always thought him invincible. I still did, kind of—what he could do was amazing. But I understood him a little better now, his limits. And I couldn't help but feel a little more powerful myself, because he'd trusted me enough to share his burdens.

◆ ◆ ◆

I didn't remember falling asleep. Only the incessant rain and wind and icy splashes sneaking into the alcove every time I had almost drifted off. But now that my eyes were opening, slow blinks in the growing light, I realized what had woken me.

The storm had finally stopped. Tendrils of fog seeped in through the vines hanging over the cave's opening.

My body ached. From staying cramped in such a tight position, and from the stairway down the cliff. Then Ren shifted beside me.

I froze. The wall of fog in my mind evaporated in an instant. His arm still rested heavy around my shoulder. Apparently, I'd fallen asleep tucked up against his chest. What he'd said last night stayed with me—how tired he was, how his magic had serious consequences.

"Good morning," he whispered, and his voice, rough from sleep, made my stomach hollow out.

I eased away, out from under the cloak, which now held plenty of heat from the two of us. "Hi. Good morning." I snapped my mouth shut before I could say anything else inane.

I groaned and stretched. Every movement—muscles I didn't know existed—*hurt*.

Ren laughed. "Sore?"

I couldn't muster the energy to defend my lack of strength. "You seem rested," I muttered.

His smile wasn't the flirtatious one he used as a weapon; this one was softer. "I am. Thank you. For the cloak." I barely kept back a shiver—because shivering would hurt.

"I can heal the soreness, if you—"

"No," I said, maybe a little too quickly. "Save your magic, I mean. I'll be okay."

He nodded and busied himself with the box in the ground, handing me a small portion of the food we'd saved last night. "What do you want to do if Aleksa doesn't come back?"

I pulled Dora's remaining figs from my bag and gave him some. "She'll come back."

"But if she doesn't? The wedding is in three days. We need to be out of Riiga by then." He took a swig from the water jug, then held it out to me. "Promise me you'll leave Riiga before the wedding."

I took the water jug, but didn't drink. We were so close. I understood his concern, the wisdom of getting away before whatever event Janiis had planned on the chance it would affect Turia. I took a swig of the water and coughed at its staleness. "I agree, and I'll do my best. That's all I can offer."

Ren scrubbed his hands through this hair and over his face.

"I guess that's all I can ask, then." He had several days of a beard growing, blond stubble that made him look less charming prince—king—and more rough soldier. He scraped his hands through his hair again, combing the strands back. "Did you get much sleep?"

My cheeks heated, though I knew he'd never see the blush in the dim light. He seemed so casual about it all. Venturing into Riiga, cramming into a cave, me falling asleep on his chest.

"Yes," I said, and then I didn't know how or why, but the next words that slipped out of my mouth were "You make a good pillow."

He chuckled softly. "I'll keep that in mind when being king doesn't work out."

My brows dipped low. He'd said something similar on the cliff. "What—"

The vines covering the entrance pulled back, and Ren was on his feet, sword drawn, faster than I could follow.

Aleksa jumped, dropping her bundle and grabbing the vines like she could use them as a weapon.

"Sorry," Ren grunted.

Aleksa dropped the vines and slowly retrieved her things. "I-it's okay. Those skills will come in useful here. Even more so than when I left two months ago."

I sprang up and threw my arms around her. She went completely stiff, arms at her side. I didn't care if she returned the hug or not—she'd disproved the lingering fear I wouldn't acknowledge that maybe she wouldn't come back.

"It's dawn. You should have left already," Aleksa said.

I sat back. "Not without you."

Aleksa studied us both. Ren tipped his head toward me. "She didn't think I could get us through Riiga."

Aleksa snorted while I laughed in protest. "I never said that!"

Aleksa thrust a wrapped sandwich into my hands. "She was right. I have news. Eat first, then I'll explain."

We all sat facing the entrance to the cave, devouring the small breakfast. When we'd finished, Aleksa gathered the cloth wrappings and tucked them into the stone box.

"No one knew where your friend was," she started.

Ren folded his arms across his chest. "Wha—"

She glared at him. "Let me finish, please. He is in the city, but he moves often enough that no one knows where he's staying." She took a breath and continued. "I do not want to entrust my family's fate to an old poem." She held up her hand when I tried to interrupt. "My friend had heard of a single prisoner being held in the last cell of the palace's prison. Dark brown hair, Turian skin, and piercing green eyes."

My hand flew to my mouth. "My father," I whispered. In a dungeon, all this time. I ground my teeth together as Aleksa continued.

"The only way into the prison is from inside the palace, which is heavily guarded at the best of times, but with the wedding approaching, it is the worst time."

We had until the day after tomorrow to get into the palace and free my father. Or to find the key and trade the clue.

"So you don't want to follow the poem, but you don't think we can get to Marko," Ren said, standing up in the too-small space.

Aleksa clicked her tongue at him. "That is not what I said. I believe we *can* get to your father, *if* we can get into the palace. And that going after *him* instead of some clue will bring faster, better results, for my people and yours."

I stared at the fine grains of sand pooled in the folds of my skirt. We were so *close*. But how to retrieve him?

Ren couldn't pace, so he folded and unfolded his arms. "Is the palace hiring anyone to help with the extra wedding festivities? We could sneak in."

With Aleksa's network, it might be possible.

Aleksa shook her head. "They only hire Riigans for the grand parties and feasts held each night during the week of a royal wedding."

Grand parties? I stared at Ren, watching him fidget. Even stooping in a cave, his broad shoulders and fair hair marked him as different. "What if . . . ," I started, biting my lip. Ren caught me staring at him, and for once, I didn't look away. It might have been a trick of the sun burning off the morning fog, but his cheeks seemed to pink up. "What if we *don't* sneak in?"

"What do you mean?" Aleksa asked with a frown.

Ren stared at the vines, settling his hands at his waist. "I *am* a king. I guess I could knock on the doors and apologize for being late. I never sent a rejection to Janiis's invitation."

My lips tilted up in a half smile. "You didn't?"

He winced. "I forgot."

I chuckled. Why didn't that surprise me?

Aleksa shook her head. "No. Marko was taken before arriving in Riiga. There were men on the main roads looking for something. Someone. If they were waiting for *you*, there's a chance you could be captured, just like Marko."

Janiis would have major leverage against both kingdoms of the Plateau. I cupped a handful of sand and let it trickle between my fingers as I sifted through options. We'd need help to get into the palace with enough flair that Janiis couldn't sneak Ren away. More help than Aleksa's network of servants could probably give. Not when they were in such danger already.

"So what if we *don't* sneak in?" I said again. I let the rest of the sand fall through my fingers. We didn't have any other options, no matter how much I didn't want to call in this favor. "I know someone who could get you arrayed like a king. You could make a big entrance, splash it in front of everyone so you can't be taken quietly."

"Who?" Aleksa asked quietly.

"Sennor," I said, watching her carefully.

Her eyebrows shot up. "You cannot trust a Riigan nobleman."

"Has he supported Janiis in his new policies?"

Aleksa leaned to the side. "Not exactly, but he hasn't outright opposed him, either."

"You said anyone who opposes Janiis mysteriously reverts to supporting him, though. Maybe he's protecting himself." I straightened my back and clasped my hands gently in front of me. It was a tactic one of my tutors had employed—appear at peace, and lure your opponent into letting down their guard. "Just because some of the Riigan nobility choose to follow Janiis doesn't mean you have to distrust all of them. There are good people here. We can't lose hope."

Aleksa set both hands on her hips. "You would risk your father's fate on this?"

I resisted the impulse to fidget. "Can you think of another way?" She didn't respond. "He owes me a favor."

Ren's hand was wrapped around his sword, though I didn't know why.

"He can get us trunks of clothes to carry in, horses. Maybe even lend us his guards. He probably knows someone who could find me a decent dress, and I—"

"No," Ren cut in, glaring at me. "Absolutely not. Even if your *friend* is trustworthy, you are not going into the palace with me."

"What?" I stood, sand cascading from my dress. The stuff was beautiful, but it got everywhere. "I absolutely *am*."

"It's too dangerous."

"He's my father. I've come this far. I'm not about to sit back and wait around." I stared him down and that tired look came back into his eyes. The one that pulled his shoulders toward the ground. "What if I go in disguised?" I asked. "What if Aleksa and I both come disguised as servants?"

Both of Ren's eyebrows shot up. "I'm not the kind of king who brings two young women along with him to Riiga."

I held back a growl. He would *not* keep me from my father. "Then what if we go as boys?"

A laugh bubbled up from deep inside him. Tears ran out the corners of his eyes from his effort to stay quiet. I pressed the toe of my boot deep into the sand. But still he laughed.

Aleksa whacked his shoulder.

"Sorry," Ren said between chuckles. I stuffed my cloak into

my bag and looped the strap around my shoulder, across my chest. I bit my tongue—hard—to keep my eyes from welling with tears. I'd gotten all the way to Riiga. Come up with a plan to save my father. And he'd *laughed*.

"Sorry." He wiped tears from the corners of his eyes. "It's a good idea. It's just . . ."

"Just what?" I asked quietly, staring at his boots.

"Hey, no." He stepped toward me. I stepped away. "It's just, no disguise could hide the fact that you are . . . not a boy."

Not a boy? It wasn't a compliment, but it was better than his thinking my plan was bad. "That's your only concern?"

He lifted a shoulder. "Well, yes. Neither of you look like boys."

Aleksa and I shared a smirk. I'd crossed half of Turia and climbed down the cliffs to get to my father. I could endure wearing trousers for a day if it meant saving my father.

Ren groaned. "I have a feeling I am about to be proven wrong." He sighed and gestured to the opening of the cave. "All right. Lead the way. Let's see if your friend is willing to dress me up for a wedding."

CHAPTER FIFTEEN

Chiara

The wind never stopped blowing here. It pounded into us as we walked the strip of sand that led from the cave, around the bend, through the brush and attempts at cultivation in the wider land, and into the city that clung to the side of the cliff.

Each sinking step in the sand brought us closer to Vera—Janiis, Sennor, and my father. My plan was sound—*if* we could trust Sennor. I hadn't set foot in the maze garden for months. Could I face him? Ask him for help?

Beautiful old buildings leaned precariously against the cliffs. Oranges and pinks and reds and greens, splashes of color against the gray. White sand beaches spread along the base of the Plateau, deep blue waters crashing against them in a rhythm I could have watched all day.

The warm sun burned off the last of the fog and warred

with the salty wind. I could have stayed on the beach forever, but Aleksa led us on. Always on.

Vera's streets were lined with cobblestones, and twisted in ways I didn't expect, up, down, and around, flowing with the land.

It was only when you looked closer that you saw the cracks. The starving children peeking out from broken windows. Abandoned buildings. Ragged laundry strung up to dry between the narrow alleys. Signs of people barely surviving.

No one paid attention to anyone else as they walked through the streets with quick, purposeful strides. But on closer inspection, I found I was wrong. They *did* notice us. They noticed everyone. They just *looked* like they kept to themselves.

I brushed one of my braids over my shoulder, but the wind whipped it back. Aleksa had unwound my scarf from my head, braided my hair, and wrapped the scarf around my waist instead. She'd made Ren take off his vest and wear only his coat and tunic, and clasped my cloak over one shoulder instead of at my neck.

Every step into the city tightened my stomach until I couldn't draw a full breath. I didn't know how much longer until we arrived, didn't know how much longer I could take of not knowing.

"Does the wind ever stop blowing?" Ren grumbled as we darted into another alley behind Aleksa.

"Storm season is coming," Aleksa said. "The city is in a cove and stays fairly well protected, but out there"—she shook her head—"the wind eats boats whole out there."

"How do you know this man again?" Ren asked quietly as we passed empty barrels with rotted lids.

The words I'd buried months ago pressed up from my stomach. Could I say them? Ren held up a blanket from a laundry line so I could pass under, and I paused. He waited patiently, no sign of the flirting or charm or bravado I'd come to expect. He was just . . . Ren.

I could give him a different story. That Sennor and I had danced and he'd stepped on my foot. But Ren had told me about his magic—its limitations—things that he'd never told anyone.

I swallowed hard and wrapped the end of the scarf at my waist around and around my hand. "Lord Sennor attacked me back in Turia," I said as I passed under his arm.

I was four steps ahead when Ren caught up with me. "Sorry, did you say he attacked you?" His brows were furrowed so deep, a line creased between them.

My quick steps led me forward until he rested a hand on my arm so lightly, so gently, I immediately stopped. His normally bright features darkened like thunder about to roll. He opened his mouth, then closed it, like he was searching for words he couldn't find.

My insides quivered and my jaw trembled even though I wasn't close to tears.

"Can you . . . Do you want to talk about it?" he asked.

Aleksa coughed from up ahead. "Stay close," she called softly. I continued, and Ren fell into step beside me. All of this was for my father. I could do this.

"He—" I swallowed. Remembered Ren's confession. "He

tried to kiss me. Jenna somehow figured out he was planning something bad and got there before he could do anything else." I shook my head. The hand wrapped in my scarf was going numb. "She jumped over a hedge in the maze garden."

His eyebrows shot up. "Those walls are at least a foot taller than I am."

"I know," I said with a small smile. "She broke his arm and took out his guard. They found out afterward he'd been told I welcomed his advances, but . . ." I trailed off. Took a deep breath. Ren stayed silent. No jokes. His steps steady as we walked side by side. "He sent a letter two weeks ago."

Ren tucked his hands into his pockets. "What was in it?"

I bit my lip. "I didn't read it."

"You didn't . . ." His chin tipped down until it hit his chest. "We can find another way into the palace."

I unwound my hand from the scarf as we caught up to Aleksa. "The first sentence was an apology. Then I realized the letter was from him and tossed the rest. But he went out of his way to send the letter, and we need help. It's our best chance."

Aleksa pointed with her chin across the open square. "Sennor's villa."

Ren glared at the three-story building with yellowed vines trailing over half of it. "If it wasn't a sincere apology, I get to break his other arm?"

I swallowed my nerves and straightened my shoulders. "No. But I do."

We waited behind Aleksa as she watched the square.

"What are we waiting for?" I asked. I wasn't sure how much longer my courage would last.

"Patrolling soldiers," she answered. Ren watched the alley behind us. But then he slipped his hand around mine and held it.

"You're not alone," he whispered.

I wasn't alone. And I was tired of being afraid.

The orange door of Sennor's villa loomed ahead. If this wasn't the right choice, we'd have to change plans fast to keep the element of surprise. But I had to hope. It was all I had.

"Let's go," Aleksa whispered, and darted across the square.

Ren and I followed her through a tiny alley to a side door. Aleksa tapped a fast rhythm against the old, water-damaged wood. A woman cracked the door open, glaring at us with suspicion until she caught sight of Aleksa. "What are you doing here, *maza?*" she asked, frowning even harder at Ren and me. "And in such company?"

Aleksa touched her heart and bobbed her head. "We seek shelter for the afternoon. And an audience with the lord of the villa."

"I can offer you shelter," the woman whispered, then ushered us in, through the warm kitchen to a tiny room off the pantry with overturned wooden buckets to sit on. She handed each of us a cup of warm tea with a hint of honey. I caught several servants in the kitchen craning their necks to see us. The woman shut the door and stood in front of it, her arms folded. "I am Inga. It is an honor to house you, Lady Aleksa."

Lady Aleksa? I coughed and sputtered through my mouthful of tea. Ren patted my back and glared at Aleksa, who grimaced. The servants hadn't been itching for a glance at us but at *her.*

"Sorry," Ren interrupted with a smile meant to charm. "You two know each other?"

Why hadn't Aleksa said anything if she'd known Sennor's servants? I set the cup down and folded my arms.

"Oh no," Inga said, a slight blush showing under the influence of Ren's smile. "We've never met. But I know *of* her. We all do. . . ." Aleksa's head jerked back and forth, but Inga didn't pick up quick enough. "Janiis's heir?"

I blew out a hard breath and leaned over my knees. Janiis's *heir*?

"What?" Ren practically yelled, and both Inga and Aleksa shushed him.

Aleksa stood and touched Inga's shoulder. "Do you feel Lord Sennor could be trusted with a favor for me and my friends?"

I rubbed my forehead. At least she'd called us friends—she might be hard to read, but she didn't say things she didn't mean. Just layered them with hidden meanings.

"Yes," Inga replied, with a dark look for Ren and me. "He does not openly oppose Janiis to protect himself. He has cared for and protected all of his servants from Janiis's edicts. I believe he could be approached. But I thought you'd left Riiga to petition our case to Turia?" She stepped closer to Aleksa and lowered her voice as though Ren and I wouldn't be able to hear her. "Have these people forced you to return?"

I rolled my eyes. Ren caught me and snorted. I kicked his leg.

"No," Aleksa replied with a glare for us. "My friends will help us. You must trust me on this."

And Inga did. She led us through the bustling kitchen filled with the sounds of people so accustomed to their duties they could carry on deep discussions while performing them.

We went up a side stairway. The house didn't flow like in Turia; it twisted in unexpected ways. Inga led us into a small sitting room on the east side of the house. Harsh light slanted through the small windows crusted with salt. Two armchairs and a sofa faced each other. I sat in a chair, leaving the sofa for Ren and Aleksa.

"Who should I tell him is calling?" Inga asked once we were settled. She eyed my mud-stained dress and my posture and my ease in a sitting room. I regarded her right back, taking in her clothes and hair and the glint in her eye that wasn't unkind, but definitely calculating.

"Chiara," I said quietly, my voice running away now that the moment was almost come.

The house creaked and groaned as she left the room. My insides turned and flopped until they were a tangled mess. Sennor would come soon, and now Aleksa was Janiis's heir?

Ren glared at Aleksa. "Care to explain?"

She leaned on her knees, rubbing her hands together. "I never wanted his blood in my veins. Never wanted the responsibility of cleaning up his messes. But I can help my family—my people—who suffer greatly."

"Why didn't you tell us?" I asked, my voice a little stronger now. Maybe focusing on Aleksa would help me face the next conversation. "Is it safe for you to be here?"

Aleksa leaned back and crossed her arms tight as if she were an unraveling thread. "No safer than it is for you." Yet she'd come anyway. "Janiis loved his wife. But when she died eighteen years ago, he broke. My mother was a servant in the palace at the time. He vowed to share his life with her. Claimed to love her." She swallowed hard and glared at a bird stitched into the rug. "When she discovered how empty Janiis's promises were, my mother escaped and married my true father soon after she had me, and they had two children. Her husband loved me like his own."

Ren stared at the same bird in the rug, though not as angrily. "Is he—"

"He died last year. I didn't think the soldiers would come for us, but the law states that if the king should die with no heir, the council rules until the closest relative who shares the bloodline is found. Janiis never claimed me, but everyone knows I am his daughter." She shrugged and seemed to deflate a little. "So Janiis would, of course, remove any threat to his reign."

I studied my hands, rubbing my thumb over my knuckles again and again. Aleksa had taken a great risk coming back. "Thank you for helping us."

She nodded and pressed her hand to her shoulder. "Thank you for proving not all Turians had given up on us."

I *had* given up. But I'd never been so grateful to have been wrong about someone.

Ren cleared his throat. "Do you *want* to inherit the kingdom?" He tilted his head and studied Aleksa, his hair falling across his brow.

Her gaze fell to her hands again, clasped loosely in her lap. "I never wanted to"—she heaved a sigh—"but if it is the price I must pay for my family's safety, I will do it."

Ren pressed his fist to his shoulder with a half smile of understanding.

I waited to feel insignificant next to them, like I always did at home. But I didn't. I had come all the way to Riiga. I was lounging in the sitting room of the man who'd ruined the maze gardens. Maybe it was because Ren and Aleksa treated me as an equal.

One thing was certain—I was done being afraid. I didn't want to be invisible anymore. Didn't want to fit into someone's idea of a "perfect princess."

The door clicked open. Sennor stepped inside, his brows furrowed so low his eyes were mostly hidden. I exhaled long and slow. I could do this. I *would* do this. But not for my father. For me.

His gaze first landed on Ren, whose dark expression almost sent Sennor back into the hall. His eyes glanced over me and paused on Aleksa, before darting back to me. "Chiara?" he gasped. "I mean, Princess!" He sketched a short bow. Didn't approach. "What are you doing here?" he asked slowly, marking my companions again, this time lingering on Aleksa. "Excuse my manners," he tried again. "I meant, I hadn't heard you were in Riiga."

I kept my expression serene, pretending my throat wasn't half-closed and my heart wasn't trying to beat a hole in my ribs. "That's because you weren't supposed to hear I was in Riiga." I gestured to the chair next to me, proud when my hand trembled only a little. "Won't you have a seat?"

Sennor swallowed audibly, and a tiny part of me relished

making him feel like a guest in his own home. "Inga said you want to speak with me?"

He didn't leer or lean in like in my nightmares. Instead, he sat far back in the chair, legs crossed, hands clasped tight—too tight—on his knee.

"It's about the letter," I started, using everything my tutors had drilled into me to maintain my composure. It was the first time I was truly glad for the hours of etiquette lessons. "Did you mean what you wrote? That you're sorry?"

He shifted and gripped the armrest. His jaw flexed. "I was misled by several people as to what your motives were for meeting me in the garden, and the guard who accompanied us was not my normal man—he was there on Koranth's orders. Not mine." His top leg started bouncing, and he continued, quieter now. "When you protested my advances, I panicked." Ren growled, but I finally met Sennor's eyes. "I truly am sorry for hurting you. For trusting the wrong people." He rubbed his arm where Jenna had broken it. "It won't happen again."

I breathed in deeply, and something that had been festering inside me lightened and left. I hadn't realized the weight that I'd carried until it was gone. "Thank you for apologizing." It would take time before I *accepted* that apology.

Sennor stood with a nervous glance at Ren. "Now, if that's all—"

"Actually," I said with a curt smile, "there is one other tiny thing."

He shifted, eyeing the door with longing. "Yes?"

"We need to get into the palace tonight."

His eyebrows shot up. "You're a princess. They'd not deny you entrance."

I nodded. "I should have been more specific." I tipped my head toward Ren. "*He* needs to get into the palace, arrayed like a king worthy of Janiis's invitation."

Sennor's jaw snapped open, then closed. Studied Ren again. "*Is* he a king?"

Ren spread one arm along the back of the sofa. "Atháren, King of Hálendi, at your service." Only, he said *at your service* like a threat.

"Oh," Sennor said, then swallowed hard.

"I heard you met my sister," Ren said. "She's the nicer one."

Sennor paled, and I stepped in before Ren went too far. We needed Sennor's help, not his fear.

"Listen," I said, "I won't try to threaten you or demand any favors." Aleksa frowned at that. I didn't care. "We need your help. The fate of the Plateau hangs in the balance, and we need to get Ren into the palace safely, with enough fanfare to impress even Janiis's court. And, if you can manage it, help Aleksa and me with disguises." The house creaked in the never-ending wind. Sennor frowned at that same bird in the rug, but Ren was grinning at me like I'd returned his stolen horse. I ignored him and focused on Sennor. "Will you help us?"

Sennor clasped his hands behind his back. "You shouldn't go near the palace."

My shoulders fell a little. How could we—

"It isn't safe for any of you." His gaze darted to Aleksa repeatedly. "And you—are you who I think you are?" She sighed and shrugged, and Sennor rubbed a hand over his face. "None of you should go. There are strange things happening—people who get too close, who work with Janiis and his advisors, they do not come back the same. You are all too valuable—"

"We must go," I said firmly. "We *will* go. Will you help us, or not?" I stared at his knees. Silently begging.

Sennor rubbed his jaw. "By tonight?"

My eyes shot to his, but he was still staring at Aleksa. "As soon as possible."

He sighed, a great puff of air. "I will help. Let's see what we can do before Janiis's party starts at dusk."

◆ ◆ ◆

The clothes Sennor lent Ren didn't fit very well. Aleksa had braided my hair around my head and tucked it under a cap, and the paste Inga had used to thicken my eyebrows itched. But not as bad, I imagined, as the fake beard Aleksa now wore.

Ren had laughed for five minutes straight when Sennor brought out the cunningly devised contraption. But Sennor had been insistent that Aleksa wear the beard—she was most likely to be recognized in the palace by everyone she'd been running from.

My shoulders hunched at the thought of how ridiculous I looked in trousers, short boots, and the eyebrows. But Ren was the one all eyes would be on.

Sennor also couldn't lend a horse. He claimed he only paid for use of one when traveling on the Plateau. He offered a chair conveyance that servants carried on their shoulders—a tradition picked up from the Continent—but Ren had flatly refused.

For now, we traveled alone, but we'd meet a caravan of servants at the palace's walkway so that we couldn't be easily traced back to Sennor's.

We shuffled over the stonework, pressing against the wall as Riigans passed by with worried looks. "Be inside before nightfall," some whispered to us.

The closer we came to the palace, the more my collar itched. Would someone see through our patched-up efforts to get in? Ren's voice echoed in my mind, how one scream from me would have my father giving them anything they wanted.

Ren *was* the king, I reminded myself. He'd been invited. They'd let us in.

But would they let us out?

And if they did, would we be the same? Sennor's and Aleksa's warnings of people *changing* stayed at the front of my mind. We'd have to be careful.

We trudged along, Sennor's man ahead acting as guard, Ren behind him, Aleksa and me trailing in our disguises.

"We won't have much time," Aleksa murmured just loud enough for Ren and me to hear. "I'll get to the kitchens, see who can be trusted, find a way into the dungeon."

"I'm more worried about the way *out* of the dungeon," Ren muttered.

"You stay low," she said to me. "Keep your head down, and roll your shoulders forward. You need to look like a servant."

I wasn't sure how to roll my shoulders forward with this

bag, but I tried. If there was one thing I was good at, it was being invisible.

"And *you*," she said to Ren. "Janiis is all about flair. Swallow your doubt and act like a king."

I wasn't sure how anyone could mistake him for anything except a king, but his head jerked in an approximation of a nod.

We passed homes and shops nestled between the rocks jutting from the cliffs. Narrow stairs led us up and then down so many times I'd lost all sense of direction. Then we turned a corner onto a wide street, the first wide, straight road I'd seen in the city. Beyond that, the waters of the Many Seas stretched out before us.

The road was on top of a wall built of gray stone, bright torches lighting the way. On the right, a straight drop to a sandy beach. Rows and rows of military tents marched down the sand—neat lines, small fires nestled between them.

"What is this?" Ren muttered.

Aleksa hissed, "These are new."

Was her brother there? Would she stay with us, or go after him? I adjusted the bag on my shoulders. "I thought you said it was almost storm season." Aleksa nodded. "Won't all these tents be washed away?"

Ren cursed under his breath. "I'm guessing these soldiers won't be camped here much longer."

The sun was setting into the ocean, throwing orange and pink and purple across the sky, a dark line of clouds blowing in. On the left, the city rose up into the cliffs.

From here we could see three huge, jagged lines carved

into the rock from the top to the bottom. "What's *that*?" Ren asked.

As we watched, a huge platform was inched straight up by a set of pulleys and ropes that appeared tiny from where we stood, but had to be huge to hoist such a load.

"*That*," Aleksa said, "is what Janiis has been building with his forced labor."

Something about the scene was familiar, though I couldn't place— "My father had a drawing of this when he left." I closed my eyes and tried to remember. "Janiis had petitioned my father for land on the Plateau to construct the top of the pulley so that goods could be shipped faster and more cost-effectively."

Aleksa looked from the tents to the *three* platforms—not one, like my father had thought. "I don't think they are going to use those platforms to lift grain."

Ren rubbed the back of his neck. "So Janiis is planning to invade Turia after his wedding—a full-scale attack."

"One Turia isn't prepared for," I whispered. Even if we sent a message right now—and it wasn't held at the border—there wouldn't be time to get troops into position.

Ahead of us, the Riigan palace rose, separate from the city's chaos and colors, a gray edifice jutting up into the sky, tall, spindly spires making it appear taller than it really was. All the windows were lit, tiny squares of yellow against the cold stone.

Servants seemed to melt out of the alleys, congregating around us. Some even raised hastily made blue and silver banners.

Rows of guards lined the wall close to the palace. "Ready?" I asked.

Ren sucked in a shaky breath. "Ready or not."

"Here we come." Aleksa had fire in her eyes, a fire I hadn't seen since she'd been with her sister. We'd get in the palace, then we'd get my father out. And find some way to send word to Enzo that Riiga was coming for them.

Brownlok

Everyone in this kingdom was entirely too trusting, Brownlok decided. Two months ago, he'd taken the Turian king's palace by force, and now? Now he was sitting in an inn eating the best soup he'd had in over a hundred years.

But his hand shook as he dipped a spoon into the aromatic broth.

Koranth wanted the Black Library. But Brownlok *needed* it.

Ever since Graymere had used the forbidden magic to tie their life forces together so they could survive in the Ice Deserts until their release, food had become nothing more than a habit—nothing tasted better or worse, or really had much flavor at all.

He'd forgotten how much he enjoyed eating. Tasting. Experiencing moments, rather than passing through them.

His chest tightened until he bowed his head and clenched his eyes shut in pain. The spasms had been happening more frequently as time passed after Graymere's death. And Brownlok had a sinking suspicion his eternities were about to claim him.

"My parents are just outside." A little girl's voice pulled him from his thoughts. "I ran ahead, but they'll be along shortly. I'll just sit over there and get started. They're always complaining that I take too long when I eat anyway, and we've still a long journey ahead."

The girl spoke in circles around the kitchen boy serving dinner, who looked out the window, then shrugged as the little girl, her dark hair bouncing in tight curls, bobbed over to the table next to Brownlok's.

He forgot all about the pain in his chest, even the flavorful soup, when she sat. His magic, which had been draining away no matter how much he rested, bubbled up inside him again— not much, but more than he'd felt in weeks.

The kitchen boy brought a bowl to the table, and the girl slurped up the soup as fast as she could.

Brownlok smirked. Her parents weren't coming for her. But she was too well-dressed to be a street urchin. He tilted his head and studied her until she looked up and locked eyes with him. He'd seen her before—a portrait in a palace. A full grin bloomed.

"You'll burn your tongue if you don't wait," he said in a low voice. No one in the inn noticed them—the man in brown and the girl bouncing in her seat.

She shrugged and continued to slurp, a wary eye on the kitchen door. Brownlok reached into his cloak, pulled a few coins from his purse, and set them on her table. He chuckled at the fierce glare she sent him.

"Don't take offense, miss," he said. "You need the coin, so take it."

"Why are you helping me?" she asked between slurps.

A feeling that Brownlok hadn't encountered in recent memory—and his memory was long, indeed—crept into him. He swallowed, but the feeling didn't leave. "You remind me of my little sister," he said, the words slipping out.

She tilted her head, her curls dangerously close to dipping into the soup. "Where is she?"

Brownlok's smile slipped off his face. "She died long ago."

"Oh," the girl said. "I'm sorry."

"Can I help you get home?" he asked, fully aware how far from home she was.

The girl shook her head and leaned closer, her curls dragging through her bowl this time. "I'm going on a treasure hunt," she whispered. "No one thinks I can do it, but I'll show them." She sat back and nodded once, then tucked into her soup again.

Brownlok held in another laugh. He hadn't laughed in at least two hundred years. And he hadn't felt this strong in months. He studied her, the girl who once had eluded his search, and now sat across from him, free as a bird.

"Are you a friend of King Atháren?" he ventured to ask.

The girl went perfectly still. Then nodded slowly.

Brownlok leaned away, like her response didn't matter. "I saw him a few days ago. I could take you to him, if you like. He'd be sure to help you in your adventure. And maybe he'd send your family a note so they don't worry. Families do that, you know."

Another pang hit him with enough force to take his breath away. Longing. Regret. Feelings he hadn't touched in centuries. Feelings he didn't *want* to touch.

The girl pursed her lips and studied her now-empty bowl. Then she stood, came to him, and put out her tiny hand to shake. Brownlok's enveloped hers, and she shook with a hard grip. "Okay, let's find Ren," she said, and marched out of the inn.

Another laugh slipped out, though the farther she walked away from him, the wider the cracks in his magic stretched.

This tiny girl changed him somehow. Fixed whatever had broken when Graymere died. She waited by his horse, one foot tapping impatiently. He lifted her on, then climbed on behind her, turning south.

He hadn't killed the Hálendian boy because he thought an heir of Kais might be useful in their search for the library. Taking the girl south—going against Redalia's orders—was a risk, but this girl would be more useful than searching blindly for something he'd never find. Useful in more than one way.

Graymere had never let him have an artifact, and Brownlok paid the price for that now. But with this girl, he could change that.

"I'm Erron," he said, unsure why he'd started using a name he hadn't heard in centuries. It had been what his mother had called him. What his little sister had called him. Memories he preferred to keep distant.

"Nice to meet you," the girl said as she leaned forward, gripping the saddle tight and craning her neck to see everything she could as the horse walked down the road of the small village. "I'm Mari."

CHAPTER SIXTEEN

Ren

I understood now why Turia had never dealt with the inaccessibility of their southern agitators. With the sea on our right and the cliffs on the left, we were boxed in. Walking along the top of a wall that didn't have nearly enough exits, a crowd of servants around us carrying trunks that didn't belong to me.

The Medallion hummed a constant warning against my chest. Pulley mechanisms, troops lining the beach. A rescue attempt in the heart of Janiis's palace. And I couldn't get Sennor's mention of the odd happenings from my mind.

It reminded me of the strange reports we'd gotten from North Watch.

For now, I stayed in the center of the entourage Sennor had lent me. Eventually, I'd move to the front. Draw attention away from Chiara and Aleksa. If I could go in and get Marko on my own, I would.

My kingdom could survive without me. But the entire world might break if something happened to Chiara.

I still couldn't believe how Chiara had convinced Sennor to help us without using a single bribe or trade. She'd simply asked him to do the right thing—expected him to—and he had. She held more power than she realized.

A long line waited to enter the palace, inching forward as the sun sank to the horizon. We waited behind a family, a couple and their son and daughter, all arrayed in shimmering linens and shivering in the wind.

When we'd almost reached the palace, I moved closer to the front of our group and fiddled with the cuffs of my coat. It was longer than the traditional Hálendian coat, but had two lines of buttons marching down the front just like back home. I'd kept my trousers tucked into my tall boots. A blend of Turia and Hálendi, with a twist uniquely Riigan.

I'd shaved at Sennor's, and now ran my fingers through my hair, making sure the white was exposed. It was time to act like a king, as Aleksa had ordered.

The mother from the group ahead glanced back and caught sight of me. I winked, stifling a smile at how Chiara had threatened me if I winked at her.

The woman whispered to her husband, and then, slowly but surely, each person in line eventually snuck a peek at us.

"Well, we've been noticed," I murmured, but no one replied. I was alone here, at the front. As intended, but the weight I'd almost forgotten as I moved anonymously through Turia returned. The weight of a kingdom. The weight of *two* kingdoms, at the moment. Maybe three.

And then it was our turn at the gate.

"Name?" a woman in leather with a feathered helmet asked.

I cleared my throat. "Atháren, King of Hálendi," I said just loud enough to spark another bout of whispers. They spread like an avalanche through the courtyard and into the palace. I grinned like I hadn't a care in the world. "I'm a little later than expected, but I do believe King Janiis will allow me entrance."

Her jaw dropped. She took in the array of servants behind me. "If . . . you could come to this side door, Your Majesty, we can arrange your rooms, and—"

"No, thank you," I said. *Pretend this is fine.* "I've been starved for company too long." I pushed past her and through the ornate doors. I paused, giving time for my entourage to pile in behind me even as the guard protested.

Hundreds of pairs of eyes swiveled toward us. The sharp scent of too many perfumes, attempting—and failing—to mask the metallic tang of fish in the air, assaulted my nose.

Apparently Riigans didn't believe in foyers, because we had entered directly into a huge ballroom.

With all my servants.

Glaciers.

Well, we'd wanted a big entrance. We'd gotten one.

I pressed my hand to my shoulder and bowed, coming up with a wide grin and targeting the closest mothers and daughters. "I heard there was a party tonight not to be missed." I didn't speak loudly, but my words carried through the entire ballroom.

Guests turned to whisper among themselves, the prospect of

a young, unmarried king in their presence clearly too much to take in silently.

The grand ceiling arched overhead—an impressive feat—its painted mosaic tiles in swirling patterns reflecting the light from the sconces along the walls. Chiara, Aleksa, and Sennor's people shuffled along one side of the ornate room. They'd gotten me safely into the palace; now it was up to Aleksa to figure out a way into the dungeon. And back out.

The Medallion warmed until it scorched my skin. I scanned the room again, tracking Chiara's progress along the wall. She stared at the dais as if seeing a nightmare come to life.

I followed her gaze and froze. The woman seated next to Janiis rested one hand on his arm. Her deep blue-green dress draped her frame perfectly. Her sharp nails tapped against the throne's arm. Red hair curled and waved around her shoulders down to her waist.

The woman from my dream.

The one who'd killed my father.

A mage.

She stared back at me—through me. All the blood drained from her face until it was gray.

The Medallion went cold. Ice-cold.

My teeth ground together with the effort it took not to draw my sword on the dance floor.

"Your Majesty!" a high voice cried from my right.

I dragged my gaze away from the mage, faces swirling around me until one came into focus as she pushed her way to my side. She curtsied low, then latched onto my arm with a smile meant to entice, but all I could see was my sword in Janiis's bride.

"I'm so glad you decided to come," the girl said. She seemed familiar. My brow furrowed, and she laughed and hit my arm. "I have so many people to introduce you to."

"I . . ." My mind struggled to come up with a response, anything, but my eyes were drawn back to the dais. The woman still watched me. Her color had returned—cheeks flushed, eyes bright. Staring. Her plump red lips tilted up in a smile that raised shivers on my neck. Not the good kind. Janiis glared at her, then me.

A man in gray robes stood behind the couple, arms folded and surveying the scene playing out. I found Chiara's gaze again—this time on me. And the oddly familiar girl next to me. Chiara and Aleksa had no idea of the true danger lurking here. And I couldn't go to them. Couldn't warn them.

But I could draw attention away from them.

I put my hand over the girl's. "Of course, my lady. I am at your service, as always."

I glanced at Chiara from the corner of my eye. Willing her to get *out* of here. Her cheeks were flushed, and she stared, not at Janiis or his betrothed, but at me and . . . oh. The pieces clicked into place. Why the girl was familiar. Cynthia Hallen. The girl we'd sent into Riiga with men to look for King Marko.

Sweat dripped down my back. I'd brought Chiara into a palace with a *mage*.

The mage who had killed my father.

There'd been no traces where Marko disappeared. Because a mage *had* been involved. Marko and I had both received invitations. Had I just sprung the rest of the trap?

But perhaps Cynthia knew where Luc was. If I could get

Chiara and Aleksa to Luc, I could come back for the mage. For now, they needed to get *out* of the ballroom.

"Lead on, Miss Hallen," I said with a flourish. She stiffened when I left off her former title, but her face gave nothing away. She was like Isarr, then. A mask wearer. Safe in Janiis's court. One I'd have to be careful of.

We fluttered around the ballroom as she introduced me to influential families, most of which had daughters too old or young to be competition for her. We danced a few dances, and I even ventured to ask a few others to dance. All under the watchful eye of Janiis, the hungry eye of his betrothed, and the dark advisor behind them.

I would have to approach them, make them think I was here only for the wedding, accepting a gracious invitation. That I didn't know who Janiis's bride was. What they were planning.

I took my time approaching the dais, making sure I'd insinuated myself into several families' prospects. Moving closer, yet making them wait.

The trio stood and took careful steps down the dais—they were done observing the party from afar. I wouldn't make them come to me—wouldn't tip them off that anything was untoward.

"Your Majesties," I said, bowing with a fist to my shoulder once I'd stepped into their path.

"I expected you a week ago," Janiis said, staring up at me and puffing out his chest like he could make up for his lack of height by adding to his girth. The advisor stayed behind. No one introduced him to me. But why not?

I dipped my chin. "The duties of a king never end, as I'm

sure you know," I responded. My jaw ached from trying to stay relaxed. "I managed to slip away from my council. Convinced them that observing how you handle the business of your kingdom would help me as I transition into the role of king." Janiis's lips pursed and his nose rose into the air the more I flattered him. "And, of course, to congratulate you on your upcoming wedding."

Janiis looked at his betrothed with a worshipful gaze, and I wondered if he knew what she was. Who she was. A centuries-old murderer, wrapped in the appearance of youth and beauty.

"Atháren," Janiis said, his nose in the air, "I'd like to present my betrothed, Lady Redalia."

Redalia. The woman who'd killed my father had a name.

Her hand came up, the long sleeve of her dress trailing down, a long slit in the fabric revealing more and more soft skin. She touched my arm. Caressed it, really. A slow, seductive smile and dark, smoldering eyes washing over me, drenching me with her lust and making me wish for a thousand baths.

Something *other* slipped through my mind, and the Medallion flared hot, repelling whatever it had been. Soft and gentle; there, then gone.

"I am *so* glad you decided to come," she said, her voice pleasant and melodic. "Our celebration wouldn't be complete without you."

And then she winked at me. Winked. I vowed never to wink again.

The Medallion went so cold I was sure my skin had frozen to it. I bit into my cheek until I tasted blood. I couldn't react. Not here. Not now. I had to get Chiara out first. To safety.

My hand was moving toward my sword, so I changed its course to rest on my hip. The man lurking behind the couple stared at me, unblinking. It might have been the light, but his eyes appeared black.

"I wouldn't miss it," I bit out.

Redalia clung tighter to Janiis, stroking his chest but staring at me like she could drink me in. The lines around Janiis's mouth deepened and he tugged his bride-to-be away.

"Glaciers," I muttered. We needed to get out.

I caught sight of a servant ducking into the hall and strode after him. Cynthia attempted to catch my eye, but I'd made enough of an entrance. My lungs constricted, too tight for me to make conversation.

"Excuse me," I said as I exited the stifling heat of the ballroom. The servant jumped and spun to face me. "I would like to be shown to my rooms now. I—" I licked my lips and cursed my hesitation. Columns rose in the edges of my vision. Exactly like those in the crypt back home. *Focus.* "I'm King Atháren."

Would those words ever feel natural?

He bowed low. "This way, Your Majesty."

I paid close attention to every turn, marking the art and delicate vases. Glaciers, if he was supposed to lead me to my rooms but took me to the dungeon instead . . . I kept my hand on my sword. He moved agonizingly slow. I timed my breath with his steps and followed sedately. No reason for me to be in a hurry to get away. No reason for me to hurry to my rooms.

The Medallion didn't flash, didn't warm—no more than usual, here in Janiis's palace. But my hand squeezed my sword tighter and tighter.

Chiara would be in my rooms. She would be safe.

And I'd have to find some way to tell her she had to leave. Immediately. I'd stay and find Marko on my own. But she and Aleksa needed to get out. Before Redalia cornered me, before I gutted her in front of her betrothed, or before Janiis had me hung for the way his bride was looking at me.

The servant stopped at a room on the left, then bowed away. I slipped in and shut the door behind me. Locked it.

Chiara stood between a wardrobe and a chair piled high with clothes, folding shirts. The ordinariness of the task hit me, stopped me in my tracks. "Chiara?" I asked, a little out of breath. Torches burned in the sconces on the wall, then multiplied as I watched.

She didn't answer, didn't turn, just shook out another shirt with a *snap*. No Aleksa. I darted into the sleeping chamber, but she wasn't there, either.

"Where's Aleksa? She just left you here?" I moved until I was right behind her, put my hand on her shoulder to turn her toward me, but she jerked away.

"She went to the kitchens to bring us food and formulate a plan with the staff." Chiara's words bit into me, like I'd done something wrong. Like she knew what I was going to say. "I can handle myself. I don't need a nurse to keep me out of trouble. I may not be able to do much, but I can at least fold a *shirt*." She snapped another one out.

"You've got to get out. Leave. Tonight."

She lined up the seams. "That's not the plan." She went back to arranging Sennor's clothes. *Snap* and fold. *Snap* and fold.

Stone arches. Torches.

I slapped the shirt she'd just picked up, batting it out of her hand. "Find Aleksa," I rasped out. "Get out of the palace. Out of the kingdom. Enzo sent me to keep you safe. You *will* go."

She yanked another shirt from the pile. "Not without my father. You don't get to take my choices from me. You don't get to go to some fancy party, smile and laugh with all the nobles, with Cynthia, then tell me I can't stay."

"Miss Hallen?" *Tombs.* I shook the image away. I paced in front of Chiara, scrubbing my hands over my face. "Everyone wants something from me. Miss Hallen wants to be elevated above her family. Every mother wants a better title for their daughter, every father wants connections to the mysterious northern kingdom.

"But if they think they can get something from me, if there's a chance their family could rise in rank, they'll be less likely to help Janiis bury me. So yes, I played it up. I smiled and laughed and shook hands."

She pulled another shirt up, slowly this time, fingering the stiff material. "I—"

"And, oh yeah," I continued, my steps wider and faster now, "the woman standing next to Janiis on the dais? The bride-to-be? She looked at me like she knew me, like she wanted to cozy up to me in a dark hall. She's also the *mage* who killed my father. So Cynthia's claws in my arm kept me grounded enough not to attack her right then and there—"

Glass shattered.

I spun and drew my sword. No one. I stepped to the side. My steps crunched. Petals, orange petals drenched the ground.

"Ren?"

I spun again. Stopped my sword midswing. Not assassins. Chiara.

"Ren?" she said again. Her voice sounded so far away, like she'd called down to me from the top of the cliffs.

I flinched and dropped my sword. Stumbled. Orange bits of pottery scraped into my skin as I fell to my hands and knees.

I pressed my now-bleeding hand against my chest, trying to keep my heart inside my ribs. My lungs constricted, and every breath wheezed in and choked out.

Magic swirled to life inside me, reaching to my mind, my heart.

But the hand on my back, gently rubbing side to side, settled me more than the magic. I closed my eyes. Matched my breathing to hers.

"Can I tell you something?" I finally asked into the quiet stretching between us. Chiara didn't respond, but her hand continued its slow trek across my back. "Hálendi deserves better than me."

Her hand paused. I sat back on my heels, breaking the connection between us. I shouldn't have said anything, shouldn't—

"Why do you feel that way?" she asked, head tilted. She didn't dismiss my feelings or try to prove me wrong. A knot lodged in my chest loosened.

I picked up a tiny shard of orange. "People think being king means you have power. That you control the fate of an entire kingdom." I'd always thought that about my father. And it wasn't until he was gone that I realized how wrong I'd been.

"But the king is the *least* powerful person in the kingdom. You have no control over what happens. Even with magic, I couldn't help my mother—or my father."

I tossed the pottery shard away. "Even with the best training in the Plateau, I've been losing the battle with my own council and doing nothing but stanching wounds with patches and makeshift bandages to keep my people from bleeding out.

"There's always more. I don't think . . . I'm worried it will take more than I have to give." I paused, but Chiara didn't say anything, so I whispered, "I can't protect you *and* save your father. I can't do it all. And I can't bear to fail you."

She was silent so long I finally pulled my eyes up to meet hers. Those ridiculous eyebrows somehow made her more beautiful, with her cap off and braids pinned around her head like a crown.

"We'll do our best, Ren. We'll do all we can."

I wiped the blood from my now-healed hands onto my trousers. "I'm sorry."

She tipped her head. "For what?"

"If I'd come south earlier, if I'd trusted the Medallion, maybe your father wouldn't be here right now. None of us would."

She twisted the hem of her too-long tunic between her finger and thumb. "I'm glad you weren't there, Ren. You would have been in the same situation as my father." Silence stretched around us, pulling at all our cracks. She cleared her throat and dug her elbow gently into my side. "Besides, if you were captured, who would come rescue you?"

What was supposed to be a chuckle came out more like a sob. "Jenna?"

For some reason, she winced at that, but I wasn't sure what I'd said wrong. Jenna was all I had. Even if she'd found a new family, I hadn't.

I studied Chiara as she stared down at her hands. She'd come all this way for her father. Sat here and patiently listened to me panic. No one except Jenna had ever cared enough to dig deeper, past the carefree facade I showed to the world.

Maybe I *did* have more than Jenna.

"Admit it," I said, bumping her shoulder with mine. "You would have come for me." I hoped she would have, at least.

Her cheeks turned the most beautiful shade of rose pink I'd ever seen. She chuckled and I decided I could listen to that sound for the rest of forever. "Sure, Ren. I would definitely come to your rescue."

A knock came at the door, not loud, but I leapt between Chiara and the door, and she scrambled to jam her cap back on her head.

"Your Majesty," Cynthia whispered as she shut the door behind her. "I thought—"

She froze when she saw the broken vase. My sword on the floor. I picked it up and shoved it back in its sheath. I wouldn't last another hour in this cursed palace. There were too many threats.

"You're dismissed," Cynthia said, and it took a moment for me to realize she was addressing Chiara.

"She stays," I said gruffly.

"She . . ." Cynthia studied Chiara again, who glared at me like she wanted to burn a hole in me. "Was it *your* idea to pretend to be a boy servant to Atháren?" Cynthia sneered, one hand cocked on her hip. "You make an even worse boy than you do a princess."

I stalked closer, and she had the decency to step back from Chiara. "I don't remember inviting you to my chambers."

"An oversight I'm willing to overlook, for now," she said, and looked up at me through her lashes. Now I wanted *two* thousand baths. "We need time alone—so I can give you information." Her lips pursed and she looked Chiara up and down again. "Now that I think on it, you might look better in those trousers than you did at the last ball."

"Enough," I growled, pointing at the door. Chiara didn't need this, and I definitely didn't.

"Wait," Chiara said, pressing her hand against my chest. "What information?" she asked Cynthia. I had the crazy urge to hold her hand to my chest, to keep it there forever. But she snatched her hand back and folded her arms like I'd burned her.

Cynthia brushed her hair over her shoulder and widened her eyes dramatically. "I haven't seen any of the men Prince Enzo sent with me since arriving in Riiga."

Chiara frowned. "That's it? Your information is that you have no information?"

"No," Cynthia snapped. "Koranth is pulling Janiis's strings like a marionette—"

"Koranth?" I interrupted. "As in—"

"As in the former ambassador who helped Brownlok attack the palace and ran off with a shade blade. Who used me as a shield in the hall to escape." Chiara swallowed hard. Another threat I couldn't fight.

Koranth had a shade blade. Graymere's shade blade. So there were *two* mages in the palace.

"Koranth has control of the entire city. He uses Redalia like some sort of watchdog to enforce his decrees."

"Did Koranth see you?" I asked Chiara. We were in over our heads. If he knew she was here, we were probably already too late to ever escape the palace ourselves, let alone with Marko.

"No, he didn't see me. Everyone was looking at you." She set her hands on her hips and widened her stance like she was preparing for battle. "I don't think we should trust her."

Cynthia rolled her eyes. "I'm all you have."

"I'd rather have no help than yours—"

"Stop!" I said, rubbing my temples. My magic was still working in the background, keeping me from falling into another attack. But maybe this was why the Medallion had drawn me south—two mages controlling a kingdom would definitely disrupt the balance of the Plateau.

"I know, anyway," Cynthia said, looking at the floor. For once not taunting or gloating. "King Marko isn't here. I noticed that all on my own. And anyone—Turian *or* Riigan—who mentions anything about it disappears for a day, then returns . . . different."

"Different how?" I asked.

"They're themselves, except on certain topics, like someone scooped their ideas out and replaced them with what Janiis would have wanted."

Like when Redalia had spoken to me, the soft, gentle nudge from within that the Medallion had flared against?

"How did you escape that fate?" Chiara asked.

Cynthia huffed. "I play the fool. Here for a husband only." She adjusted a tendril of hair that had fallen loose. "And it's worked. So far."

"Can you prove it?" Chiara asked, and I wondered if there was anything Cynthia could say to ever prove herself. But it didn't matter—we needed to get out of the palace. A palace with a mage, a man with a shade blade, and an angry king was not where I wanted to sleep.

If the Medallion wanted me to defeat these mages, I'd find a way to do it without them having a key to my bedchamber.

"Luc had me hire a room above the abandoned tailor shop off the main market street. He's searching the city for any sign of Marko, but says Riigans aren't a trusting lot and he doesn't hold out much hope of finding anything." Cynthia stared at the floor again, a line deepening between her brows. "He's gotten a few notes to me here in the palace, saying he's still alive, still searching."

Chiara looked to me and I shrugged. "She's telling the truth." The Medallion hadn't warned of any lies. "Can you get a message back to Luc?"

Chiara shook her head, but if Cynthia had made an alliance with Janiis, we were never leaving the palace anyway.

"Can you?" I asked again. She nodded. I tore a scrap of paper from the desk near the fire, and wrote, *Beach will celebrate day after wedding, pull to the west, prepare at the top.* I hoped he'd be able to figure out the message. That he'd find a way to warn Enzo.

Cynthia took the paper without reading it, tucked it into

the front of her dress, and fluffed her hair. "I'll get this to him and let you know if I hear anything in return. Enzo said I'd be rewarded if I helped Turia."

She stood there, fiddling with the embroidery on her dress. I cleared my throat. "You can leave now."

Her head reared back. "How would it look to sneak into the Hálendian king's chambers and then leave right away? I should stay for . . . a while, at least."

Chiara seized one of Sennor's shirts off the pile like she'd use it as a weapon. I marched to the door, yanking it open. *"Out,"* I barked. "Now."

Cynthia spun with a huff, her dress flaring around her impressively, and swished back into the hallway.

I shut the door and pressed my forehead against it. What would Janiis do to the rest of the visiting Turians? They were trapped on the wrong side of border—they'd be powerful bargaining chips.

My shoulders dropped and my arms went lax at my sides. Chiara was back to meticulously hanging Sennor's shirts in the wardrobe. At least she wasn't snapping them anymore.

"Please," I whispered. "Please go. Find Luc, get out of Riiga."

She paused, turned back to the bag, took out a bundle, then held it out to me. "Your nightclothes."

I squeezed my eyes shut and shoved my hands in my pockets to keep from batting the clothing from her hands. "A mage my father couldn't defeat, a king your father couldn't defeat, and Koranth." I finally took the bundle, but held on to her hands. "Please. I can't protect you like this."

She swallowed but stood firm. "I want to hear what Aleksa says. If there's a chance to escape with my father, I won't leave him behind. This could be our only chance." Her voice hitched. "His only chance."

I set my jaw. "Fine." I marched toward the door.

"Where are you going?" she called out.

"To find Aleksa—"

Another short knock, and Aleksa slipped into the room. I stumbled back to keep from running her over. The tray she held tipped precariously, but she straightened it.

She glared at me, but then again, her usual expression was some form of a glare. The fake beard didn't help. I had a bad feeling she already had a plan—one I wouldn't like.

"Chiara and I can sneak into the dungeon tomorrow morning," she said. "My friend will create a distraction when they take trays to feed the prisoners. We'll get in, hide until the others leave, get Chiara's father, and take him out of the palace through the kitchens."

I folded my arms, trying not to think of everything that could go wrong, trying to think of something better. "How do you propose to break out of the dungeon?"

She held up two long straight pins. "I've picked that lock before."

I didn't want to know the story behind that—at least, not at the moment.

"We can trust most of the servants," she continued. "Janiis thinks himself so powerful he doesn't need to worry about the loyalty of the lowest. The advisor—Koranth—he's the one to watch."

I shook my head. "We have to watch Redalia, too—she's a mage."

Aleksa blinked three times. "Glaciers."

My lips tilted up. Glaciers, indeed. "And what about me? I sit back while you both go into the one place I'd rather you avoid?"

She pursed her lips. "You are the distraction. Go on a noisy tour of the palace that draws the eye of the king and his advisor—and bride—leaving the servant hallways free for us to sneak him out."

I pressed my eyes closed. "There are so many holes in that plan, I can't even begin—"

"Tomorrow morning is our only chance," Aleksa interrupted. "Then it's the party tomorrow night, the wedding, and the attack. We cannot be here when they attack. If we were discovered . . ."

She didn't have to finish. She'd be killed. Chiara and I would be tortured, used as collateral.

I wiped my hand down my face. The Medallion lay on my chest, the constant warning buzzing, but no more than usual for this cursed place. "I could be the one to sneak in and get Marko. You should both leave tonight." I knew they'd refuse, but I had to try one more time.

Chiara shook her head. "We're doing this. Tomorrow. I won't leave without my father. I wouldn't before, but now that Koranth and the mage are here, I definitely won't." She looked up at me, her hands clasped tight in front of her, and I knew I'd give in, I'd do anything she asked.

"Distraction? I can be a distraction." I didn't bother to ask how I'd get out of the palace once Janiis found his resident king-prisoner missing—it was clearly low on the priority list.

Chiara threw her arms around Aleksa. For one painful moment, I wished she'd jumped into my arms instead. Her eyes locked on mine. For her, I'd make it work. We'd free her father, then I'd find a way to stay in Riiga and defeat Redalia and Koranth.

CHAPTER SEVENTEEN

Chiara

Aleksa muttered something about how much her face itched and went into the other room, but I hardly noticed. I don't think Ren did, either.

Something was different in the way he looked at me.

I reached for Sennor's clothes again, anything to break Ren's stare that held me captive. The shirts really were unforgivably wrinkled.

When the door clicked shut behind Aleksa, Ren started pacing again. Pounding steps, one hand on his sword, the other rubbing his forehead.

I'd never seen anyone panic like that before. And yet, in those brief moments, I'd seen through his layers—the charm and bravado he protected himself with. The *real* Ren.

I'd folded and refolded the same set of trousers twice, so I tucked them away and went back for another shirt. But I'd lost track of Ren's pacing. He barreled into me, catching me before we both fell. We stood like that for a moment, his hands on my shoulders.

We'd been crammed in a cave all night, yet now, impossibly, even with space between us, we were closer than ever.

"We can do this," I said, trying to reassure him. "We'll all get out, including my father, and then you and Jenna and an army can come back for Koranth and the mage."

His hands tightened on my shoulders. "There's so much that could go wrong. We're penned in here, between the sea and the cliffs. I won't let her hurt you. I *won't*."

"I know." I tilted my head. "Why are you so desperate to protect me?" I was friends with his sister, and maybe Enzo had asked him to bring me home safely, but I was nothing to him. Of no importance to any kingdom or decision.

I wasn't like Jenna or Cynthia or even Mari. I didn't fill a room when I entered, hadn't mastered any particularly useful talent, didn't face life with excessive passion. I was . . . quiet.

We'd been getting closer. Become friends. Would he tell me why he cared? And did I want to know, when the answer would be something like *duty* or *responsibility*?

Ren dropped his hands. Swallowed. "I . . . I couldn't protect my parents. Jenna almost died, and your brother . . ."

My brows furrowed and I set aside the shirt crushed in my hand. He'd mentioned that last night, too. "Wasn't your mother traveling when she passed? You were very young, weren't you?"

"Five. I was five." He stared at some point behind my shoulder. "But I was also the future king. I had *magic*. It was my responsibility to take care of my family and kingdom. She asked me to come with her and Jenna. I told her I didn't want to go." He swallowed hard and met my gaze, and his dark blue eyes had never been deeper. "When my father told me my mother wasn't coming back, it . . ." He sucked in a shaky breath. "That was the moment everything fell apart. I've been trying to put it back together ever since."

"And your father," I said slowly, carefully. Wary of treading too hard in this tender space. "You were away. Not anywhere near him when the mage attacked."

His eyes dropped closed. "I should have known. Shouldn't have taken the Medallion with me. But I was so eager to prove myself, I didn't see anything beyond my own advancement."

He was both so right and so wrong. His pain—the pain of a five-year-old losing his mother, of a young king desperate to make the right choice, lay etched in every line of his face.

I wrapped my arms around him, pulling him close to me. He stiffened. Maybe I shouldn't have—

His long arms enveloped me, holding me tight. I squeezed my eyes shut and tucked my chin down, holding him up, letting him hold me up. Just being there, present, for a moment.

It had been weeks since anyone had hugged me. I imagined that as king, and without Jenna, it had been even longer for Ren.

I didn't want the hug to ever end, but eventually Ren sighed, and his strong arms fell away. I stepped back and swallowed. "Their deaths are not your fault," I said. "If something happens to me, that's on *me*. I understand that. You need to understand too—my choices aren't on your shoulders."

The barest beginning of a smirk tipped up one side of his mouth. "What if I want them to be?"

I wasn't exactly sure what he meant, or if he meant anything at all. "At home, no one ever let me make decisions. It took them *two* days to notice I was missing." I looked down to the pile of wrinkled shirts still waiting to be hung. "I like making my own choices. Taking my own risks. Please don't take that from me."

We stood close—close enough to almost touch. Did he lean toward me, just a little? "I'm sorry," he whispered. His hand flexed at his side. "Your choices are what have gotten us here." He lifted one shoulder. "I'm just the pretty face and the muscle."

I rolled my eyes and used every modicum of decorum I had not to lean into him. "Yes, leaving you in a ballroom full of drooling women—and Koranth—was not fun."

His blue eyes brightened. "Did you . . . Were you *worried* about me?" I wrinkled my nose and he laughed. "For the record, Miss Hallen wears too many masks for me to ever trust her." He leaned the tiniest bit closer and lowered his voice. "I want someone I can trust."

You can trust me was on the tip of my tongue, but I caught the words and held them back. Even though we no longer touched, the heat emanating from his body crackled in the space between us, weaving threads that pulled me toward him. His hand reached up slowly, almost brushing against my arm, hovering over my shoulder but still a breath away from contact. His eyes dipped to my lips, and my eyes immediately followed to his mouth.

I swallowed, my heartbeat pounding in my ears. Was he about to . . . Should I . . . Did I want him to?

And then his hand was gone. He took two steps back, glanced at my lips again, and took another big step back. He set his hands on his hips, then moved them to his sides, then behind his back. "I guess I'd better turn in for the night," he said, then winced.

I swallowed hard and nodded, trying to shake whatever threads still connected us. I grabbed his nightclothes, which had been set to the side, and held them out in an awkward, crumpled bundle. "Here," I said, my voice too high and too fast.

Ren licked his lips and leaned to take the bundle from me, as though he didn't want to get too close. He'd just been inches away from kissing me—or at least that's what I'd thought—and now he wouldn't come within arm's reach?

"Thank you," he said, frowning at the clothes. He sighed. "Sennor's clothes pinch in all the wrong places."

My eyes dropped to his chest and I couldn't help but agree— Ren and Sennor were in entirely different leagues.

"I—I, um," he stuttered. He wasn't moving away. His fingers rested against mine, just the bundle of cloth separating us.

"Have you still not eaten?" Aleksa's voice came from the other room. Ren and I jumped apart. "Best hurry. We'll need all the rest we can get." She bustled into the room, tossing the rest of Sennor's clothes into the wardrobe in a heap.

We moved to the tray—a small pot of stew with potatoes, peas, onions, and smoked meat. Ren kept his eyes down, avoiding mine. Had I misread what had happened?

Ren made me and Aleksa take the bed for the night. I protested—our disguise wouldn't hold up if we were sleeping there while our king took the sofa in the other room. He shrugged and said there was no way he'd let us sleep between him and the door, so it was either the sofa or he was joining us in the bed.

Not that I slept much, despite the arrangement.

Whatever that moment between Ren and me had been circled around in my head. My father was impossibly close. Koranth, too. Along with another mage. And the impending attack on Turia.

I fell asleep clutching Jenna's book.

When I woke, a lit candle flickered on a table, and Aleksa was gone. There were no windows to gauge what time it was, and for a moment, I thought maybe she and Ren had gone ahead without me.

I rubbed the grit from my eyes, grabbed my cap from the bedside table, refreshed my smeared eyebrows, and padded over the cold floor to the door separating the bedchamber from the sitting room. I listened at the door. Was Ren awake? I heard shuffling, so I opened the door and went in.

"Ren, have you seen—" The words caught in my throat, because Ren stood there, very much awake, and very much without his shirt on. My mind shut off. Blank.

His head snapped up, eyes wide, a shirt in his hands. "Uh, good morning," he said, voice rough from sleep. I clutched my cap to my chest like covering *me* up would somehow cover *him* up.

It took me a minute to look away from the expanse of his chest, from the lines and definition of a lifetime of sword work. "Do you . . . Aleksa?" I squeaked, unable to form a whole sentence.

"Food. She went to get food from the kitchens." Ren jammed

his tunic over his head and tugged it down, but it was one of Sennor's and pulled across his chest. He muttered something under his breath.

Then he winced and grabbed his chest. Where the Medallion lay.

He ran at me, pushing me back into the bedchamber as a knock came at the hall door.

The door didn't open. Aleksa would have let herself in right away. Ren pushed me toward the bed, hand going for his sword. But it wasn't there. He looked at me, horrified. He'd left it in the other room.

After another knock, the door clicked open, slowly, softly.

"King Atháren," a woman's low, melodic voice called from the sitting room. It should have been a pleasing voice—the tone and pitch were just right, but something about it made every muscle in me tense.

Ren muttered a word I'd never heard before, one that was all harsh consonants and guttural vowels, then pointed under the bed. "Do not come out—no matter what!" he hissed so quietly I barely heard him.

Footsteps approached. Heeled boots.

As his servant, I had every right to be here. But I muttered a curse of my own and slipped under the bed, scooting back until I was scrunched against the cold wall. Dust lifted into the air, settling around me as the woman entered the room.

"King Atháren, *there* you are."

I could barely see Ren's boots—he'd moved to the washstand—but they turned toward the woman. The hem of her elaborate dress—grapes on a vine embroidered with gold thread—swished against the stone floor. A sheer overlay shimmered against a deep red underdress, the quality of both the finest I'd ever seen.

"My lady," Ren said, his voice betraying no trace of the panic that had been on his face moments ago. He didn't ask why she was there. Or who she was.

She approached the bed, each step deliberate yet soft. She walked almost like Jenna. But where Jenna was a warrior, this woman was a predator.

"My young king, how fortunate you arrived in Riiga in time for my wedding." She sat on the bed and crossed one leg over the other. *Her* wedding? Janiis's betrothed was sitting on Ren's bed? A *mage* was within arm's reach?

No, *no*. We were so close to finding my father. I willed Ren not to do anything rash. Screamed at my nose not to itch. Prayed Redalia wasn't here to end our heist. Or us.

Ren walked to where I could no longer see his boots, maintaining distance between him and the future queen. "Fortunate, indeed," he said. His voice sounded odd. Flat.

Redalia stood and stalked toward him ever so slowly. "You remind me of someone, you know."

"Do I?" Ren asked, his voice pitching higher. His boots came into view as he backed away from her.

"You do," she said. They circled each other, step for step, Redalia tightening the gap. "He was a great king as well. He and I would have been powerful together." She'd gotten within a few feet of Ren. His legs were pressed up against the bed. My stomach clenched and I squinted, wanting to shut my eyes and ears to whatever was playing out, yet unable to. "You and I would be powerful as well," she purred. She took a step closer so her skirts brushed his boots.

This was the woman who'd killed Ren's father. Why wasn't he— Oh *no*. Sennor and Cynthia had both told tales of visits from Koranth's watchdog, that the people had been different after.

I couldn't let her get into Ren's head. I wanted to curse as I analyzed my options. But what could *I* do?

"You are about to wed a more powerful man than I will ever be," Ren said, though his voice sounded funny, like he was fighting his own words.

Redalia laughed, and I bit the inside of my cheek. "I like to keep my options open. That's why"—she stepped closer—"you have until dawn tomorrow to consider my offer. Come willingly, and you'll be rewarded. If you don't, well, I have ways to get what I want."

"That hardly seems like a choice," Ren said, breathing hard.

She backed toward the door, her skirts swirling around her ankles. "A willing servant is always more fun."

Her footsteps clicked through the sitting room and out into the hall, the door shutting behind her.

I couldn't move. She'd just . . . what had that been? Did she suspect we were here for my father? It didn't seem like she knew. Which meant—

Ren knelt, eyes finding mine in the darkness under the bed. He extended his hand, and I swallowed the dust coating my mouth and took it, letting him help me out.

I pressed my wrist against my forehead. "What just happened?" I asked. So many emotions jumbled up in my chest I thought I'd suffocate. "Who do you remind her of? What was she talking about?"

Ren sighed and sat on the bed, his head in his hands. "Kais, I think."

"The first king of Hálendi?" I asked.

He nodded. "I think so." He flopped back onto the bed and covered his eyes with his arm. "Something dark in me responded to her, to her power. Her offer." He shuddered. "I only barely resisted her, and only because the Medallion was burning against my chest and I knew you were hiding under the bed. I can't . . . I don't think—" He broke off with another curse I didn't recognize.

I slowly approached Ren. Sat next to him. Took his hand and moved his arm so it no longer covered his face. His blue eyes latched onto mine desperately.

Redalia's sharp floral scent lingered in the room. I held on to his hand, clasping it between us—to give support, and to keep mine from trembling. "But you did resist."

He swallowed, the muscles in his jaw and throat flexing, his eyes studying mine like he'd find his answers in them. "But I almost didn't. It was like her voice was clawing through my mind, working my tongue for me." He shuddered violently. "Even now, her voice is echoing in my head."

I brought my other hand up and clasped his in both of mine. "I believe in you, Ren," I whispered. I cleared my throat and squeezed his hand. "But let's find my father and get out of here, just in case."

His stomach tightened in a laugh, and he sat up next to me, holding tight to my hands. "Sounds like my kind of plan."

The hall door opened again, and we both jumped. "I'm getting my sword," Ren muttered, and marched into the sitting room.

I pressed my hand against my stomach and followed slowly, peeking into the room first to see who had entered.

Aleksa set a breakfast tray on the table while Ren buckled on his sword. She handed him a note, then took a bite of round bread from the platter. "Your friend Hallen gave this to a servant who gave it to me to give to you. But I don't know what it means."

"You read it?" Ren asked with a frown, unfolding the scrap of paper.

Aleksa took another bite. "Of course I read it. I don't trust that girl."

Ren's brows furrowed as he read. "I don't know what this is supposed to mean. It's from Luc, but I don't think it's a response from the note I sent." He handed it to me.

The paper was small and dirty, and revealed a single word, *smarito,* with Luc's signature.

I opened my mouth, then shut it again. "It's an old Turian word. But he spelled it wrong."

Ren leaned closer. "If it's in code, every detail is important. What letter—"

But I didn't hear the rest of what he said. *Smarrito* was the correct spelling of the old Turian word that meant *missing.* Luc had spelled it wrong intentionally.

Loud rushing filled my ears, and my knees buckled. Ren caught me by one elbow, and Aleksa caught the other. They helped me stumble to the sofa.

"Chiara?" Aleksa said, from so far away. "Chiara!" She snapped her fingers in front of my face. "What does it mean?"

I clenched and unclenched my teeth, and Ren forced the paper from between my fingers. "I think . . . I think it means Mari is missing." I looked at Aleksa. "My little sister."

As I explained how I'd decoded the message, Ren cursed and reached for the back of the sofa, then eased himself down next to me.

A knot twisted in my stomach. Every potential scenario whipped through my mind, lashing out with each possibility worse than the last.

It wasn't possible. Mari had to be safe at home, hiding away.

"Breathe, Chiara," Ren murmured next to me. "Come on, you need to breathe."

The world spun around me. I shut my eyes against it, but my head kept spinning. Ren pushed my shoulders forward until my head rested on my knees.

Aleksa sat on my other side and stroked my back. "You need to breathe. In and out. Come on, Chiara."

In, out. The world didn't spin quite as much. But I couldn't lift my head from my lap. What could have happened to Mari? Was she out in the world somewhere—lost? Hurt? My mind marched down a path paved with all the terrible things that could happen to my joyful, exuberant sister.

Had she tried to follow me? I *knew* how she hated being left behind. Yet I'd left without her. She was only eight—I couldn't have asked her to accompany us. Maybe I shouldn't have come to Riiga. But we were *so close* to freeing my father. I could feel it.

"We'll find her," Ren murmured, brushing his hand against my arm. "We'll get your father today, and then find Mari."

I nodded and swallowed back the sobs aching to get out.

A soft knock came, and a boy stuck his head in. "Aleksa? I'm ready."

She nodded to him. "Wait in the hall. He'll be right out for his tour."

I brushed at the tears on my cheeks, then marched into the bedchamber and splashed water on my face, careful not to muss the eyebrows. I leaned on the table, fingers splayed wide. Get my father, find Mari.

Ren leaned against the doorframe, hands in his pockets.

He stopped me when I tried to walk by him, and wrapped his arms around me. I pressed my forehead into his chest, willed myself not to break apart.

"Focus on the next step," he whispered into my hair. "Only the next step. Get your father out of the dungeon. Out of the palace. Out of Riiga. Then we find Mari."

I nodded, but didn't let go. Couldn't yet.

"Thank you," I said, and my voice came out strangled and whispery. I pulled away and straightened my cap. A tiny line marked his brow as he studied me, head tilted to the side. What did he see when he looked at me? A useless princess? A girl who looked better in disguise than as herself?

He licked his lips. Hesitated. "Chiara, I—"

"It's time," Aleksa said. "We need to get into position."

Ren nodded, never looking away from me. "How will you get Marko out of the palace?" he asked Aleksa.

"Disguised in a group of servants going to market. We can get him to your friend hiding in the city."

Ren nodded. Straightened his shoulders.

I grabbed his arm. "How will you get out?"

His mask fell into place, the one with the perpetual smile and twinkling eyes. I hated that mask. "I'll come up with something. You worry about getting your father out. I'll meet you at the cliff cave before dawn tomorrow."

He tipped his head for me to step into the hall first. "Rescue your father."

"Get out of Riiga." Aleksa tapped the doorframe.

I straightened my shoulders. "Find Mari."

CHAPTER EIGHTEEN

Ren

"And this is where the royal families' commissioned portraits hang," the boy said in his nasal voice, which I'd been listening to for the past half hour. He and I had covered all the main parts of the palace, and now walked the gallery.

Though they tried to hide, we'd been followed by a bevy of courtiers. Which was fine by me—with all eyes on me, no one would see Chiara, Aleksa, and Marko sneaking out.

I'd never experienced anything close to what I had with Chiara yesterday. All my life, I'd always been the strong one for everyone else. But talking with her was . . . freeing. I could just be me.

More courtiers and servants in the halls bowed or curtsied as we passed, marking my barely concealed boredom and the young man's overly proud recounting of the history of the palace and Riiga.

But the boy had also taken me by almost every exit the palace had, using the main rooms to orient me to each.

Echoes of Redalia's voice still swam in my head. She would have been beautiful, if her eyes weren't black caverns. I'd never heard of anyone manipulating someone's will as she did; it was imperative we leave. *Soon.*

The plan was ridiculous. Walk in, get Marko, and walk out. In a palace full of enemies and mages, trapped between the sea and the cliffs. But it was so ridiculous it might actually work.

A throat cleared ahead of us, and the boy stopped, his shoulders tight, his stance a fighting one.

"Excuse me, Your Majesty," the guard said with the slightest nod to my rank. "King Janiis requests your presence in his chambers."

Three courtiers and two of their servants roamed the gallery with us. All of them stopped to listen to our interaction. If I refused or offered some excuse, what kind of repercussions would it cause? If I accepted, I'd be walking straight into trouble. Had Janiis found out about Redalia's predawn visit? Or perhaps it was Redalia herself summoning me. My hands went cold. I wasn't sure I could resist her again.

Or it could be Koranth, with his unsettling black eyes and shade blade.

Or maybe all three.

The odds were not in my favor.

"We are almost finished with our tour. We have only the grand foyer, which is just up those stairs," the boy said, pointing at the narrow staircase across from us, his nasal tone conde-scending. I'd have to tell Aleksa she'd made a fine choice in the guide—he was perfect.

The guard, however, folded his arms over his broad chest. What he lacked in height, he made up for in width. "You, boy, have other duties to attend to. I will escort His Majesty to the king's chambers. You're dismissed."

The boy shrugged one shoulder and meandered to the stairs while the guard took me in the opposite direction from the king's chambers. We went down two short sets of stairs, toward the black door of the dungeon, where the tour had started. The boy had explained that because of the sand, an underground dungeon was impossible. So Janiis kept prisoners in the wall we'd ridden over to the main entrance of the palace.

We'd ridden right over Marko's cell without realizing it.

The guard led me past the dungeon and around two corners, to a small door I'd have to crouch down to enter. A door that had been carved out of rock, exactly like the dungeon's. The guard knocked, then opened the door, waiting for me to enter first.

A dark cell of a room waited beyond, with Janiis sitting behind a desk, and three guttering candles fighting against the shadows. Though there had been other people mere steps ago, no one roamed this passage. The guard put his hand on his sword. The Medallion beat a steady warning against my chest, but what could I do? If I refused to walk into this room, Janiis could have me imprisoned under a false charge or tossed out of the palace. Chiara and Aleksa would be left on their own or dragged out with me, with no hope of finding Marko.

But it was only Janiis. I could handle him.

My boots scraped against the uneven stone floor. The guard put his hand out. "You shall not speak with our sovereign armed thus."

It was a bad idea, but I unbuckled my sword and handed it to the guard. "Don't lose that," I told him. "I'll be wanting it back." He smirked, and again, I considered bolting for one of the exits I'd just learned about. But Chiara was right—this was our one shot.

My steps echoed as I entered, each sounding like a failing heartbeat.

Janiis studied me, the candlelight casting deep shadows on his face. The door shut softly, and the guard took his place in front of it. Before I could utter a greeting, two men came out of the shadows behind me and grabbed my arms, yanking them back until I could barely breathe. Two more men emerged from the shadows behind Janiis, both larger than any Riigan I'd ever seen. But they weren't mages.

I didn't fight them—especially since fighting them would have pulled my shoulders out of their sockets.

One of the big ones in front of me slammed his fist into my stomach hard enough to empty my lungs but not hard enough that I passed out. I groaned and dropped my chin to my chest. These were professionals, then. I swallowed back bile and coughed until my lungs filled properly. My magic responded, so I breathed slow; there were surely more wounds to come.

Janiis stood, the chair legs scraping against stone. He lifted a wickedly curved dagger from the bejeweled sheath at his waist and studied it in the candlelight.

I sighed. It was a knife that would not leave a neat scar.

"You are not supposed to be here," Janiis said, eyes still on the dagger.

My shoulders ached and my stomach throbbed. "I'd be more than happy to leave, Your Majesty. The guard was quite insistent I follow him. But if he's made a mistake—"

One of the hirelings—I wasn't sure which—punched my jaw, snapping my head to the side. Blood coated my tongue and trickled from my lips.

"Not *here* here, you fool," Janiis sneered. His inability to sense my sarcasm filled me with the insane urge to laugh. "You were supposed to be taken care of before arriving."

I lifted an eyebrow. "Like King Marko?"

Janiis's eyes turned to glittering slits. "Something similar, yes." He paced closer and pressed the tip of the dagger to my cheek. "Don't think I didn't see how you looked at my bride last night."

With revulsion? "I wouldn't dream of interfering with your happiness," I said, tipping my head as though we were in a ball-room. *Don't die. Keep Janiis occupied while Chiara and Aleksa retrieve Marko.*

He growled and pressed the dagger's edge to my throat. His hirelings pulled my shoulders tighter, pressing me into the blade.

"She's using you, you know," I said breathlessly, rising onto my tiptoes to ease the strain on my shoulders. "She wants your kingdom for herself."

Janiis scoffed. His eyes moved to my exposed neck. The blade shifted and its point pressed into my skin, lifting the chain of the Medallion. Curse after curse ran through my head. Janiis pulled it free and held it close, inspecting both sides.

He returned the blade to my throat, the Medallion's chain clutched in his fist. "Just because *you* can't manage your kingdom, boy, doesn't mean I can't manage mine. You probably can't even give me one good reason not to gut you right now. You have nothing to offer, nothing I couldn't take for myself."

His grin chilled me to my core. I couldn't heal from every wound. And I couldn't let him leave with the Medallion, even if he didn't recognize its worth.

I swallowed the last of the blood in my mouth—my lip had healed. "One reason? Okay, here's one: I named my sister, Jennesara, as my heir should anything befall me on my travels."

The blade eased off my throat enough for me to swallow, and Janiis's brows furrowed until he looked like some sort of furry rodent. "But," he started, piecing everything together far slower than I expected, "she's betrothed to—"

"To the Turian heir, yes," I finished for him with a grin. "And with Marko *missing,* they'll have a spring wedding *and* coronation. Which means if anything happens to me, Turia's queen will become Hálendi's queen. A force you could never dream to stand against. A combined empire so mighty, it would swallow your pitiful cities clinging to life on the fringes of the Plateau until Riiga is only a forgotten memory."

Janiis spun on his heel and shoved his dagger into its sheath. He let out a guttural yell and slammed the Medallion onto the desk. Then he turned and swung his fist into my gut. Harder than I expected from a man who had someone else do everything for him.

My breath left my lungs in a huff, and one of my shoulders popped, spreading fire down to my fingertips and ribs. "W-wow, Janiis," I stuttered through the pain. "I didn't know you had it in you. Who taught you to punch?"

Janiis grabbed my face in his hands, pinching my cheeks. The door opened behind me, casting garish light over the Riigans. Glaciers, if a mage had come—

"Lord Koranth requests your presence, My King," a boy said, his voice quivering and squeaking.

Janiis released me and straightened his robes, then walked to the door. He paused and spoke to his guards. "Make sure he's still alive when you're done with him."

Something heavy smashed into the side of my head, scattering lights across my vision. My cheek slammed into the stone floor and someone's boot connected with my ribs. There was a knife in my boot, but I couldn't take my arms away from protecting my head, couldn't think through the blazing pain. I'd heal, but one thought rang clear through the haze: Chiara. I had to make sure Chiara was safe.

Then everything faded to black and the pain finally, blissfully, floated away.

CHAPTER NINETEEN

Chiara

Windowless rooms shouldn't be allowed when building any structure. We'd been waiting in a dark room ever since Ren had started his tour at the dungeon's door. I didn't know how much time had passed, or how much longer it would be until the kitchen staff brought trays for the prisoners.

"Stay at the edge of the corridor when we get in—there are grates in the center you could trip on," Aleksa said quietly. She'd been doing this since we arrived. Giving tips, details, anything to smooth out our plan.

"Grates in the middle, don't cough at the stench, ground will be slippery," I repeated back. I wanted to ask her why she'd been in the dungeon before, but everything in me focused on *now*, on executing the plan. "Your friend causing the distraction will be okay? Not get in too much trouble?"

"He's quick—he knows the risks and agreed to them. He'll be okay." More endless waiting in darkness. More time to think of everything that could go wrong. "When we go into the hall, don't look at anyone, but also don't look at the ground. Don't fidget."

I checked that my hair was tucked tightly beneath the cap. "Be invisible. I can do that."

A series of shuffling steps passed by the room. Aleksa froze, and so did I. It was time. Now or never.

"Let's go," I whispered.

Aleksa cracked the door open and checked that no one marked our entrance into the hall. We followed behind the row of children who held one tray each—one for each prisoner.

"Wait," Aleksa murmured, catching my coat sleeve and slowing me down. "Wait for the signal."

I breathed out slowly. Didn't jump when Aleksa's friend— her cousin, she'd said—stumbled into the guard who'd just opened the black door.

The tray of slop dripped down his uniform and he lashed out. The boy ducked, but that only enraged the guard more. The other children had frozen, completely focused on the scene playing out.

"I'm sorry, sir, I didn't mean—"

Aleksa and I slipped through the open door, then raced as fast as we could—dodging the grates, my tunic pulled up over my nose. The long corridor had only one torch, next to the door. Barely enough light to illuminate the rivers of sludge dripping from the doors to the grates.

We ducked into an alcove near the middle of the corridor where the torchlight couldn't reach.

My lungs seized with the need to cough. The scent of human waste mingled with wet stone and dead fish reached in and stole the breath from my lungs.

But no one made a fuss or raised a cry. We'd made it in.

The children slid the trays through a small opening at the bottom of each door, then hurried back.

The guard started closing the door with a taunting call, and the boys sprinted toward the exit, barely slipping through before the door slammed tight. From the other side, the guard guffawed loudly, then all was quiet.

I plugged my nose, unable to bear the stench any longer.

"Last door," Aleksa said, nodding at it.

My footsteps sounded loud above the constant dripping of water and waste. Finally, I stood before the last black door, shorter than all the rest.

How could I both hope my father was behind the door and pray he was anywhere else? The thought of him locked in this tiny cell broke something fundamental inside me.

Aleksa stood shoulder to shoulder with me. I'd come so far—crossed my kingdom, climbed down the cliffs, confronted Sennor. And yet, "I don't think I can—"

She reached for the latch, lifting the metal knob and sliding it to unbolt the door. The wood stuck against the rock frame. She tugged hard, and the door came open with a loud *pop*.

What if it *wasn't* my father? What if it was some awful murderer who would kill us right here and now? What if—

"Who's there?" a deep, scratchy voice whispered from the black hole in front of us.

It was . . . Could it be my father's voice? I squinted and caught the outline of a figure huddled in the middle of the cell.

"Father?" I whispered around the oily air coating my tongue. I held my hand up to block the meager light from the end of the hall, squinting into the hole. "Is that you?"

The man crawled to the opening warily, holding his hand up to shield his eyes. It was him. My father. More haggard than I'd ever seen him before. His beard and hair were a tangled mess, dark smudges hollowed out his eyes, and he crouched like a cornered mouse. Like we were the cats. He studied me with brows pulled into a V, then Aleksa, then me again.

"Who are you?" he whispered. His eyes never left my face.

He . . . didn't recognize me? He wouldn't forget me. He *wouldn't*.

I reached toward him and he flinched. "I-it's me, your daughter."

His head tilted and he gave me the look he'd given me a thousand times—when he'd seen right through me, right into my soul. But then his eyes clouded and he put a hand to his head. Was he ill? Perhaps it was the lack of food and water.

"You must come quickly, sire," Aleksa murmured, gesturing him into the hall with us.

"I have a daughter?" he muttered to himself, shaking his head. "I have a daughter." He inched his way out of the cell, squinting and hunched and jumpy all at once.

I swallowed back the lump that had grown in my throat and held my hand out to assist him. "Father, what happened to you?"

He grabbed my wrist in a sudden move, holding me tight and staring at me again. "What is your name?"

I glanced at Aleksa, who watched us with a worried frown. Then I rested my hand over my father's. "Chiara. My name is Chiara." A tear rolled down my cheek, and my heart and stomach and lungs all rearranged themselves until I couldn't tell up from down, in from out.

Something had happened. Something was *wrong*. And it wouldn't be fixed by food and water. Getting out of the palace, instead of being the last step, would now be the first.

My father muttered something under his breath, shook his head, muttered some more. Aleksa shut the cell door with another screech, and moved toward the main doorway, but my father kept staring at me, ducking his head down to look into my eyes.

"Chiara. Yes, I had a daughter named Chiara. I remember how proud I was of you." Something clicked into place, a tiny spark of clarity in the cloudiness. "How proud I *am* of you."

I threw my arms around him with a sob and he staggered back a step. I pulled away, but he gripped my arms to keep me close. He reeked of death and mold, but I didn't care. His hand came up to touch my cheek, then stopped when he realized how filthy he was.

"I'm sorry I didn't say goodbye, Father. I'm sorry I didn't tell you I loved you. I was angry, and—"

"We've got to go *now*," Aleksa whispered to us. She was halfway to the main door, so I slipped my arm under my father's.

"Come on," I said as we took the first unsteady steps around the grates.

We limped along so slowly. How would we get him out of the palace? Tight bands wrapped around my lungs. I'd find a way. There was no possibility of me leaving him or losing him now that I'd found him.

"I don't remember," he said quietly into my ear as we inched toward the light. "I don't remember anything."

Anything? I nodded and bit my tongue to keep more tears from forming. What had they done to him?

Aleksa crouched, straight pins in hand, listening at the tiny crack at the bottom of the door. She waited longer, like a statue. I helped my father lean against the wall and caught my breath from supporting him. Heavy boots marched by, more than one set. When they'd passed, Aleksa wiggled the pins into the lock, pressing one down and moving the other back and forth.

Sweat rolled down my spine. Should it take this long? Had they changed the locking mechanism?

The latch clicked.

Aleksa eased the door open and held it for us. I took my father's arm, and we crossed the empty hall in a limping rush. Aleksa slipped her arm around my father's waist, and we squeezed our way down the short stairway toward the kitchens.

Every step left my father gasping for breath. I kept my eyes focused on the uneven stairs. How would we get him out? He'd never make the long walk along the wall into the city. He wouldn't last long wading through the deep sand even if we could somehow get him down to the beach.

"Do you know me?" he asked Aleksa. "Do I know you?"

"We've never met," she said, out of breath.

We reached the top of the stairs and turned the corner, but

someone stood in our way. I pushed my father back around the corner, keeping an arm behind me to hold him up.

"I knew you were up to something." Cynthia's hissing voice had me snapping my head up so fast I almost pulled a muscle in my neck. She stood in the middle of the hall like she'd been waiting for us.

Aleksa stood with me in an effort to conceal my father behind us. She didn't speak, only watched Cynthia warily, like she'd strike at any moment.

"I demand to know what you're doing," Cynthia said, arms folded and her nose in the air. "You shouldn't go behind Athárens back. And," she added with a smirk, "you reek of fish."

The echo of a door shutting somewhere in the palace combining with the sting of her words snapped something within me, and the dam I'd always held tight broke open.

"This has nothing to do with you," I said, pointing my finger in her face. "Stop bullying everyone around you and own up to your actions."

Cynthia's face turned a dangerous shade of scarlet and she stepped closer, hands fisted at her sides. "*My* actions? Everything was taken from me by *my father's* choices. I have no prospects, no friends, nothing. I have to *earn back* my inheritance. Everyone turned their backs on me. So don't you *dare* lecture me about *my* actions. *You're* the one with every opportunity, every advantage, yet you squander everything you've been given."

I studied her then, cheeks flushed, eyes livid and tinged with desperation, elbows locked straight. The air around us no longer reeked of dead fish, and I took a deep, cleansing breath. She was desperate and afraid. Not dishonest. My father had trusted her.

The kitchens—and the help Aleksa had recruited—lay beyond her. We'd either go through her, or . . . I winced, then swallowed my pride.

"You want to restore your name? Earn your inheritance?" I heard myself asking. "This is how you can do it." I turned my shoulder and brought my father to stand before her. It took a moment of confused staring before she realized who he was. She immediately dropped into a deep curtsy, eyes fixed on our shoes. "You can either help us, or get out of the way."

Cynthia's head snapped up, her mouth gaping open. She stood and took a step back. Swallowed. Closed her mouth. Footsteps passed in the hall at the bottom of the stairs.

I shook my head. Maybe I'd been wrong about her. "Time's up."

Cynthia put her hands out. "Wait, wait. I'll help. Of course I'll help." She blinked rapidly and pursed her lips. "What's the plan?"

Aleksa nodded toward the short hallway behind her. "I've got friends in the kitchens. We can hide him in the pantry, then they can sneak him out at the end of their shift."

Cynthia's perfectly arched eyebrows shot up and the familiar sneer was back. "And, what, he'll just walk through the gates and across Riiga?"

I rolled my eyes and slipped my arm back around my father's waist. He leaned so heavily against me, I wasn't sure how much longer he could stay standing. "You have a better idea?" I grumbled, pushing past her. I scowled at the ground—she was right.

Cynthia folded her arms and nodded. "It just so happens I do. He can rest here." She peeked into a nook that held a bench and a tapestry on an easel. I helped my father sit. Aleksa watched the hallway. Were the halls always this empty? Ren's distraction must be working. A twinge of worry shivered through me, but he could handle himself.

"Do you know me?" my father asked Cynthia.

Her head reared back and she nodded slowly. "Yes, sire, of course I do." She frowned at me and I shook my head a little.

He exhaled and rested his arms on his knees, head dropping.

"He'll be okay—he just needs food and water," I lied. I arched my back, stretching it. "Well? What's this 'better idea'?"

Cynthia pushed her shoulders back and puffed her chest out. "It just so happens I'm scheduled for an outing into the city. I wanted a tour and was granted a carriage that will take me to the main market square. The carriage leaves from the kitchen entrance in half an hour. We can hide your father in a trunk on the back and drive him right to Luc's, as long as your friend"—she nodded to Aleksa—"has a driver we can trust."

My mouth dropped open and I snapped it shut. Of course she'd be granted a carriage even though there was probably only one road that was wide enough and straight enough for it to go on.

Aleksa nodded, eyes widening. "He won't have to go in a trunk. We can dress him in livery, and he can ride in the carriage into the city with you as escort!" She looked at me, wide smile on her face, and though I hated that Cynthia would be the one to save the day, I shoved down my petty jealousy and slipped my arm under my father to help him stand again.

"Okay, we'll get him into servants' clothing. You arrange the carriage."

She nodded imperiously. "I'll go get ready."

I clenched my teeth. "Really? A fancy dress isn't the top priority right now, Cynthia."

She arched an eyebrow. "But if I don't look and act the part, their suspicions will be raised."

I kept the phrase *acting the part of a petty, spoiled brat* to myself and turned away, focusing on getting my father to the kitchens. He hadn't spoken during our exchange, only watched us warily, and with every moment of silence, I worried more.

What could they have done to make him forget? It was like . . . like magic. Koranth had hated my father, worked tirelessly against him when he'd been ambassador. I swallowed hard. If Koranth had done something, how could my father ever recover?

Ren. Ren was a healer. He would help.

If he could.

CHAPTER TWENTY

Chiara

The cook was yelling at someone in the kitchens, his back to the door, so Aleksa and I snuck into the pantry and settled my father onto a huge sack of grain in the corner. He leaned his head back against the wall, eyes shut. The gray in his hair and the lines at his eyes and mouth had never been so pronounced. His skin had never been so sallow.

Would his strength last until we could get him into a carriage? Would Luc be equipped to help him?

A small girl slipped into the pantry and handed Aleksa a cap and a heavy purplish coat. We helped him into the coat, which hung to his knees, and wiped his face clean of the muck of prison as best we could. There wasn't much we could do about the smell.

"You'll have to stand up straight, sire," Aleksa told him.

"But keep your eyes on everyone's shoes and your arms straight at your sides. Don't help Cynthia into the carriage, only open the door for her, then sit right next to the driver."

He nodded, then shook his head. "You keep calling me sire. And that girl curtsied to me. Who . . . Am I someone important? Can you tell me my name?"

I blinked, and time stopped for a moment. The shouts from the kitchens dimmed, and specks of dust that floated up from the purple coat were caught in the murky light from the slit window at the top of the pantry.

He didn't remember his name? Who he was? I bit my lip to hold back a sob. He'd been watching us this whole time, waiting for some clue as to his identity.

Ren had told me himself, his magic had limits. Is this . . . was this something my father would ever recover from?

"Your name is Marko," I whispered, and held his hand. "You're the king of Turia."

He settled the cap on his head and straightened his shoulders as best he could. "Am I a good king?" he asked quietly. "Did I deserve to be in that dungeon?"

I shook my head, dislodging a few more tears. "You are the most kind and understanding and fair king in the history of Turia. And no one deserves to be in that dungeon, least of all you."

He swallowed and swayed, then sat back down. "I wish I could remember," he muttered, rubbing his forehead.

Aleksa rummaged through the shelves and pulled out a handful of dried apples and raisins. My father grabbed for them, but she held them back.

"Wait, sire. Eat slowly, or you'll retch them back up. One at a time. Keep the rest in your pocket and eat when no one is looking."

"Water?" he asked. Begged.

Aleksa bit her lip, then darted into the main kitchen and was back before I could voice a protest. She held out a wooden cup, and Father slurped its contents down in three gulps.

He ate two apple slices, pocketing the rest like each was a gold coin. A fiery hatred built up inside me. I was half ready to burst out of the kitchen and find Janiis in whatever corner he hid in and make him pay for what he'd done to my father. Koranth, too.

A rumbling sound passed by outside. A tiny seed of doubt sprouted. Was this all too easy?

"Come on," Aleksa said as she took my father by the elbow and helped him stand. "The carriage pulled up. You'll go out and stand by the door and wait for Cynthia. You remember what I told you?"

He nodded and touched her shoulder. "Thank you for helping us." He dipped his hand in his pocket and put a few raisins in his mouth. He frowned at me, eyeing my dirty clothes. "What about you? Are you coming as well?"

I shook my head and gestured for him to leave. "I'll find a way out and meet up with you. Don't worry about us."

"But—" he started.

"You've got to go now, Your Majesty," Aleksa whispered, peeking through the door she'd cracked open.

My father leaned in and kissed my cheek, then sidestepped

along the edge of the kitchen and outside. The door stayed open just long enough for me to catch a glimpse of the fine carriage.

Aleksa put her hand on my arm. "You find Ren. I'll keep watch over your father."

If it hadn't been for her, we never would have made it this far. Too easy or not, my father might have been suffering in that prison for weeks longer, might have even—

I took her hand and squeezed it. "Thank you," I choked out.

Aleksa exhaled. "Don't thank me yet. Go."

I snuck back into the hallway, my footsteps echoing. No one else was out—they were all tucked into their rooms to prepare for the party tonight, the last celebration before the wedding.

Would Koranth find me here, alone in a hall? A door flew open. I jumped away and squeaked. Cynthia stuck her head out and grabbed my arm, pulling me into her room.

"What are you doing?" she demanded.

"I'm finding Ren and getting out of here while we can," I responded, moving toward the door. "The carriage is ready for you."

"Wait," she said, holding one hand out. And for once, all bravado, all snobbery was gone from her expression. She bit a fingernail between her teeth, a habit I'd never once seen her indulge in. "Ren isn't in his rooms. I asked my servants to keep an eye on him for me so I'd know his whereabouts—"

I opened my mouth to interrupt, but she held her hand out again with a wince.

"I know how that sounds, but I'm telling you, he's not in his rooms and they don't know where he is. Last they saw him, he'd been summoned to see Janiis. I told them to each find an errand and get out of the palace one by one so they wouldn't suffer the consequences when we aren't at the wedding tomorrow."

That twist of worry grew into a snake, coiled, ready to strike. Ren said he would go directly back to his rooms and wait for us once he was done with the tour.

"All right," I said in a voice much braver than I felt. "Aleksa is in the kitchens watching over my father. Take her with you, as a tour guide or something. She'll help you find Luc's hiding spot." I swallowed and tucked my hands into my pockets. "Get my father to Luc. When I find Ren, we'll get out and meet you in the market."

Cynthia put her hands on her hips and frowned, though her expression lacked its usual bitterness. "I don't think you should stay."

I set my hand on the door latch. "We must get my father to safety before the wedding. Turia will need him." Would he be any help in his current state, though, or would adding that pressure only harm him further? "No one suspects Ren yet. We'll be okay."

Cynthia finally nodded, and followed me into the hall.

"Thank you," I whispered.

She didn't sneer or preen, only nodded, a quick bob of her head. She turned toward the kitchens. I went the other direction, farther into the guest wing.

The door to Ren's rooms creaked a little as I opened it. No fire in the grate. No note on the table. A tiny sound came from the bedroom—like leather rubbing against leather, or a shoe sliding across wood.

I pursed my lips. Something heavy and oppressive in the room kept me from calling Ren's name. I passed into the bedroom. Empty. Bed made, full water pitcher on the bedside table. As I turned toward the bathing room, two arms grabbed me from behind, wrapping me so tight all the air left my lungs in a whoosh.

I reacted on instinct—lunged to the side, hooked my arm behind his knees, and tossed him onto his back.

But it wasn't one man. It was four. Swords out, countenances grim. What would Jenna do? She'd fight. But if I tried to, I'd lose. Instead, I put my arms out to my sides, rounded my shoulders. "I'm only looking for my king," I said in an extra-low voice. Was it too low? Would they see through my disguise?

The man I had tossed got up and grabbed one of my arms, jerking it behind me so tight that tears pricked the corners of my eyes. "Let's go," he said.

"Where are you taking me?" I demanded.

One of the men marching ahead must have heard the wobble in my voice. He sneered at me. "We have orders to round up all the Hálendian's servants. His punishment is your punishment."

Punishment for what? My heart tripped and raced, and my lungs wouldn't fill properly as they marched me out of the room and down the side hallways the servants used. Down endless stairs until I finally recognized the long hallway. The black door of the dungeon loomed ahead on the right. *No.* I dug my heels into the stone floor, but my shoulder wrenched when one of my feet caught on the uneven stones, stealing my breath.

The men continued past the dungeon and around one corner, then another, to a door set deep in the rock, and so low most of them had to duck to enter it. One of my escorts un-locked the door, revealing a black room—no window, no light, nothing. I dug my heels in again, but I was no match for the burly men holding my arms, and they tossed me into the room as if I were nothing more than a down-filled pillow.

I slammed against something that jammed into my stomach and then toppled over, tumbling me with it. My shoulder and then the side of my head hit the stone floor. I rolled once more, then came to a stop. My chest heaved. My ribs ached. The dark world spun around me and a sharp pain twisted in my head.

I lay there, unmoving. A slit of light from under the door cast an arc that didn't extend far.

I reached out to see what I'd hit and touched a long, flat surface. Wood. A splinter dug into my fingertip. I sucked in a breath and snatched my hand away. A table of some sort, maybe a chair. I rolled onto my hands and knees, feeling my way closer to the light. If only half of my plan had gone right, I was glad it was the part where my father got out of that wretched cell. Whatever came next, I'd hold on to that.

"Who's there?" a strained voice said from my left.

I startled and fell to the side, scrambling back and reaching for anything I could use as a weapon.

Then the accent registered in my fuzzy mind. I sat a little taller. "Ren?"

A groan, then, "Glaciers." Another groan and shifting, like he was sliding across stone. "Where are you?"

I swallowed and blinked, trying to find him in the darkness. "By a chair?" I crawled closer to the light and saw a shape moving toward me, like he was using his arms to drag his body behind him. "Ren?" I whispered, my voice coming out hoarse and low. Something trickled down my temple and I wiped at it, then crawled to him.

He groaned and collapsed into me, knocking me back, his head in my lap. "Easy," he murmured. "Give me a bit; I'll be good as new."

He didn't sound like he was close to good or new. My shaking hands felt his hair, traced a huge bump on his scalp and fingered his face, or what should have been his face. It was puffy, and a gash along his forehead bled freely.

I took the edge of my coat and pressed it to his forehead. "What happened to you?"

He coughed, a wet rattling from deep in his lungs that sent my heart pounding harder than when the men had dragged me toward the dungeon. "Janiis got jealous of my dashing good looks. I'll be fine."

I pulled at his coat, tracing along his ribs. Two, three, four broken. I cursed and cursed again. Ren chuckled, then groaned. "I've never heard you curse. Don't make me laugh."

"You're going to be fine," I muttered to him, pulling off my jacket and putting it under his head.

He snagged my hand and held it tight, his breath ragged. "Let . . . let me lay here for a moment," he said, and tilted his head, still in my lap. "I'm a . . . healer, remember? I just need more time. Then we'll find a way out."

I closed my eyes against the blackness surrounding us. Focused on the feel of his hand holding mine. I ran the fingers of my other hand through his long hair. "These are serious injuries, Ren. You can't just—"

"Watch," he rasped. "Well, feel, I guess." He placed my hand against his cheek. Under my fingertips, the swelling started to go down. I realized it wasn't his cheek but his eye that had swollen shut. Next was an unsettling shift under the skin below his eye, like the bones of his face were clicking and popping back into place. He moved my fingers to his forehead, where the gash had healed. Then to his lips. The split had come together, and my mind stopped on how soft his lips were, how tiny sparks danced over my fingertips at their touch.

"See?" Ren whispered, his warm breath sending shivers up to my shoulders. "Just let me lie here a moment." He took my hand again and placed it over his heart, and I scooted back until I rested more comfortably against the wall. He sighed and relaxed into me, his head growing heavy. But he didn't release my hand, even as it rose and fell with his jerky, rattling breaths.

I stroked his hair, and sure enough, the lump had mostly disappeared. His breathing evened out. I leaned my aching head against the wall, my stomach starting to turn uncomfortably.

I'd heard that happened with head injuries, but it was more than that. No matter how I tried, I couldn't think up a solution to our predicament. Ren injured, his magic drained. I couldn't do anything with a sword even if we had had one.

My father was out of the castle—I hoped—but had no memory. Turia needed him, especially if Janiis attacked. The Plateau would crumble without him to help fight the mages. We needed to find Mari.

And, cavolo, Ren was the *king of Hálendi*. What would they do if—? No. I would find a way out.

The book, the tiny book Jenna had given me so long ago, dug into my leg. I wished I'd written something in it.

Wait. The book. The clue! The thought of using it to bargain for our lives passed briefly through my mind, but I dismissed it—Janiis would take the clue and kill us. If the mages needed the clue, they'd kill Janiis and take it. Either way, the Plateau would be worse off if Janiis got it.

"How bad are your injuries now?" I asked. I needed Ren with me. I couldn't get my father *and* Ren out on my own.

He sighed. "A few ribs. My leg. Shoulders. My head is mostly better."

"How long until you're healed?"

His chest rose as he shifted, and I heard a bone snap into place. "A little longer," he grunted.

"How long have you been here already?" I whispered.

He didn't answer for a while. "I'm not sure. I was stopped on my tour of the palace and escorted in here. Janiis said I'd been making eyes at his bride."

"And he didn't kill you on the spot?" I asked.

"He wanted to, but when I told him Jenna was my heir, and that with a missing King Marko, Turia and Hálendi would unite as a single kingdom if he killed me, he got mad and had me beat up instead."

I chuckled low. "That's quite the twist."

He squeezed my hand. "I take it you were caught before you found your father?"

I licked my dry lips. "No, actually."

His face turned up to mine, though I couldn't tell if he could see me in the dim light from under the door. "You found him?"

"We got him out. Cynthia, of all people, took him in a carriage to the market to meet up with Luc."

He brought my hand to his lips, kissing my palm. Warmth zinged up to my elbow. "You did it, then. You saved your father."

A tear ran down my cheek. "He's safe, but . . ." If I told Ren, he'd immediately offer to help. Give my father whatever magic he had left.

"But what?" he asked, holding my hand tighter.

He needed to know. If we miraculously escaped, we'd have to find a way to get my father up the cliffs. "Something's wrong with him. He didn't recognize me. Couldn't remember anything—who he was, why he was here. Nothing. I'm afraid Koranth had something to do with it."

Ren exhaled, and his breathing sounded much better. "But he's out. Luc will take care of him."

I stared into the dark room. "Koranth hated my father. I'm worried he won't ever regain his memory."

Ren didn't move, didn't say anything for a long while. "We'll handle that when we have to. First, we escape."

I checked his ribs. My fingers skimmed along his tunic, and I realized what was missing. "He took the Medallion?"

Ren sighed. "No. They took my sword, though."

One side of my mouth quirked up. "You really need to figure out your priorities."

He shrugged. "It was my favorite sword. The Medallion is on the table, I think. Janiis doesn't recognize worth unless it's plated in something shiny." He shifted like he would try to get it himself. I held him down.

"Let me." I scooted out from underneath him and felt my way to the table, knocking over a candle before I found the chain of the Medallion. I crawled back and slid the chain around Ren's neck, then tucked the Medallion under his tunic. "So what do we do now?"

"We rest. We wait." He laced his fingers through mine. My heart beat a little faster, and I was glad to not be alone in this. But it was more than that. I was glad *Ren* was with me. No one else could have made me smile in this hole of a room. No one else could make me believe that we stood a chance at escape.

I exhaled long and slow. I'd sit in a dark room for however long it took, as long as my father made it to freedom, back home, where he could heal from whatever Janiis and Koranth had done to him. And then Ren and I would find a way out.

CHAPTER TWENTY-ONE

Ren

Time behaved strangely, stuck in the dark as we were, my head and body aching, my magic draining my energy even as it mended the broken bits of my body. The only constant was Chiara. How she cradled my head and brushed my hair back, her warm hands and soothing murmurs.

I'd need to think on the problem of Marko's memory soon—not only the political ramifications but also figuring out whether there was a way for me to heal him. I wasn't sure if I could heal someone from an injury of the mind like that. And if I couldn't . . . could I handle Chiara's disappointment?

"Ren?" she asked quietly.

"Mmm?" was the only answer I could muster up. My body didn't hurt so much anymore, only the exhaustion that came after healing. Plus, her hand stroking my hair felt amazing.

"What do you think will happen once that door opens again?"

Her hand trembled. If Janiis found out his prized prisoner had escaped, there was nothing I could do to protect Chiara from his wrath. From Redalia. From Koranth. I took a deep breath to settle my heart rate and keep from using any more energy. I'd need it soon. All of it.

"Well," I started, but Chiara's hand slipped over my mouth. My mind emptied at her touch. Then I heard what she must have heard—scratching by the door.

Not against stone. Metal on metal. A tiny *click,* and the door popped open. It wasn't much brighter in the hall than it was in the room, but I caught the silhouette of a woman—dress, hair pulled up, hands in front of her holding something.

I rolled up and crouched in front of Chiara. Redalia would have to go through me first.

"Chiara?" a high voice whispered. "Ugh, I can't see anything, so if you're here, speak up."

"Cynthia?" Chiara said from behind me, her hand on my shoulder.

Cynthia let out a nervous breath. "Oh, good. I wasn't sure I'd find you before the end of the party. It's only pure luck I did. If the kitchen servants hadn't been whining about their extra storage room being occupied, I'd never have—"

"You came back?" Chiara asked. Her hand went under my elbow, and I realized she was trying to help me stand.

Cynthia dragged her foot against the ground, the loose gravel catching at her slippers. "Of course I came back. I am not my father. Besides, no one would suspect *me* of anything."

She wasn't wrong there. She played her part perfectly.

"Now," she continued as Chiara and I limped toward her, "we just have to find Atháren, and then—"

"You already did," I said, my voice scratchy. Cynthia jumped a little and leaned forward—squinting into the dark maybe?

"Oh. Well. How nice." She backed into the hall as Chiara and I made it to the door. My leg wasn't fully healed, but it would have to do.

"Do you have a plan to get out?" I asked, mentally going through the exits from my tour this morning.

"This way," Cynthia said, checking the hall again. "Everyone is at the last party before the wedding. Aleksa said the carriage I took this afternoon would be returned to the stables outside the city tonight. They haven't had time to return it yet because of the wedding preparations. We can hide in the carriage, and find our way from the stables to the market, where Luc and the king are hiding."

"My father is safe, then?" Chiara asked, hope lifting her voice as we slipped into another hall.

"Yes," Cynthia whispered. "He was when I left him. But . . ." She paused, a long silence I filled with one bad scenario after another. "He kept holding his head. He's in pain."

"Your servants," I said. "Will they suffer in our places?" Janiis was ruthless, Redalia even more so. I wouldn't leave anyone here if I could help it.

She shook her head. "They're all out of the palace. They should be hiding with friends of Aleksa."

And she still came back? Perhaps I'd misjudged her.

We approached the first set of stairs. Chiara's hand found

my forearm in the dark and she leaned close. "Can you make it up?"

I swallowed down my first reply—that I definitely needed her assistance. "I'll make it. Let's get out of here as fast as we can."

But Cynthia was leading us toward the kitchens, where a roar of noise accompanied the last-minute preparations. Too many eyes.

"Wait," I said, and they stopped. "This way." I led us down a different hall, then up two steps to a narrow door that opened on the side of the palace facing the ocean. The roar of pounding waves masked the creaking of the salt-crusted door.

We backtracked along the outer wall to the lone carriage tucked out of the way. It was positioned perfectly for us to slip into unnoticed by the servants still bustling in the light cast by the stars and torches.

But the carriage was different from what I had expected. Smaller. Only one harness for one horse—would all of us fit into the tiny contraption?

We snuck along in the shadows of the palace. I unlatched the carriage door, and helped Cynthia in, then Chiara.

"Get this carriage out of the way!" a man yelled from a few paces away. "We've got the queen's flowers coming in next."

I crammed myself inside and latched the door as a wagon filled with flowers rolled to a stop ahead. A whole *wagon* of flowers?

Considering Redalia's proposition this morning, the marriage clearly wasn't a love match. I'd been so focused on getting Marko out and keeping Chiara and Aleksa safe, I'd missed a key question: Why would Redalia marry Janiis? She had enough power to take what she wanted—enough power to sway the minds of men. My head fell against the seat back as a wave of exhaustion rushed over me, though my leg ached a little less.

Maybe Redalia's magic ran out, like mine. It would take longer because of her experience and her artifact, but still. Why Riiga? Why Janiis?

And what was Koranth's role in all this? Was the wedding Redalia's idea? What could Janiis possibly have to offer her? But if Koranth hadn't been destroyed when Jenna killed Graymere, and he held Graymere's shade blade, did that mean . . . Graymere was still alive in a way? *In* Koranth?

It was the only thing that made sense, the only reason Redalia would be getting married to the king of the smallest kingdom on the Plateau when the Continent had always been the mages' goal. Why Janiis would listen to Koranth, would come when Koranth summoned him.

Which also meant the mage who'd tried to kill my entire family was still alive. And had sent Brownlok north. Toward Jenna.

Glaciers.

The carriage jostled, and another servant strode by, grumbling about bringing a horse up *again*. Cynthia and her dress occupied most of the carriage, with Chiara and me squished together on the other bench. I didn't mind the close quarters. Especially when the beginnings of panic bubbled up.

The carriage lurched forward suddenly, and we pressed back against the seat, away from the tiny window. "Will the driver check inside once it's at the stables?" I whispered as we swayed along. If there was only one location to keep animals, it would probably be guarded. And I still didn't have a sword.

Cynthia paused. "I . . . I hadn't thought of that."

I rubbed my leg and leaned closer to the window. We'd passed from the wall onto the city streets. "We should jump out." Neither of them made a sound, just stared at me. "I don't have a weapon, and it will be harder to fight our way out of the stables. We're in the city *now*. I say we jump."

"We can't jump from a moving carriage," Cynthia said, one hand on her heart.

The carriage slowed to take a tight turn. "See?" I said. "Wait for the turns. I'll help you down."

I unlatched the door and eased myself onto the step, pressing into the side of the carriage. I held my hand out. "Cynthia, come on," I whispered.

She shook her head and pressed farther into the corner. Chiara put her hand in mine instead. I held her close, one foot in the carriage, one foot out. "On the next turn, I'll lower you to the ground. Go immediately to the wall of the nearest building and wait for me to come to you."

She nodded against my chest. "Just . . . don't drop me," she whispered. The carriage slowed. I held her wrist, and she held mine, and I lowered her carefully down. She hit the ground running and ducked into the shadows.

I stepped back in and held out my hand to Cynthia. "See? Not so hard. I'll come with you." She cowered away. Every second took us farther from Chiara. So I grasped Cynthia's arm, wrapped it around my shoulder, and forced her to stand.

"Don't let go," she said over and over. Her nails dug into my skin.

I eased onto the step again, the wind whipping into us. There weren't any turns coming. We were already too far from Chiara, so I jumped onto the street. Cynthia didn't run when we hit. Her feet dragged and caught, and we both tumbled to the cobblestones. I rolled with her into the shadows and held my breath. Had the driver seen us?

But the carriage rumbled away, the door still hanging open. I should've shut it.

"Comfortable?" Chiara asked from above us, a note of annoyance in her voice.

I pushed Cynthia off me, though she clung to my shirt until a seam ripped. "You were supposed to wait for us."

Chiara helped Cynthia up. "You were getting farther and farther away. I didn't want to lose you."

"You won't," I coughed, wishing my magic wouldn't heal these new bruises. I needed a store of magic more than I needed pristine ribs. "You won't lose me." I pulled myself up off the ground, hands on my knees, body aching. Leaned against the wall.

Get to Luc, and then get everyone out of Riiga. Find Mari.

Then I'd deal with the mages.

✦ ✦ ✦

"Not that way," Cynthia hissed, tugging on my already ripped sleeve. "We need to go *this* way."

An icy wind slithered against my skin, raising chills along

my neck and arms. The cold here was different from back home. Here, it soaked into your bones until you dissolved.

Everything looked the same—narrow, rocky roads, buildings that loomed on either side. And the silence.

There were no people out. Not even a stray cat. All the windows shuttered.

Chiara scooted a step closer to me.

Heat flared at my chest, sudden and painful. I gasped, and Chiara wrapped her hand around my elbow.

"Keep searching!" a voice echoed, followed by boots running along cobblestone. We pressed ourselves flat against the cold building. Two soldiers marched past the alley we hid in.

After two more turns, the looming buildings hid more and more twilight as night stole through the city on the heels of the wind. Cynthia stopped. Three paths opened to us—one leading up a steep set of stairs and curving around the building in front of us, another to the right, another to the left.

"Which way?" Chiara whispered.

Cynthia shook her head and bit her lip, studying each path. Her shoulders rounded and she squeezed her eyes shut. "I can't remember."

A dog barked close by. I pressed the Medallion into my chest. *Which way?* But it felt the same as it always did—a gentle heat buzzing a warning into me.

Cynthia wrung her hands. "The market is off the main square in the middle of the city. Luc's hiding on the cliff side of the square, one street over, two stories up," she repeated from memory.

Raucous laughter broke the night, approaching from the left.

"Come on," I whispered, pressing the Medallion harder. The path up could keep us away from searching guards, but it could lead to a dead end, and there wouldn't be anywhere for Chiara and Cynthia to run if there was a confrontation.

Chiara snatched my hand from my chest. "*You*, Ren. I trust you. Not some relic." She put her hand in mine. "Which way should we go?"

My instincts said turn right. But nothing here was like Hálendi.

I grabbed Cynthia's elbow and tugged Chiara's hand, pulling them into the street to the left. Their steps padded behind me, light and quick. More laughter approached. I kept running, then darted to the left again, into a tiny alley.

We pressed against the walls, chests heaving, as four men strutted by, swords at their sides, bellies hanging over their belts.

"Don't know why he's making such a fuss. How are we supposed to find a single man and his servant in a city full of mangy beggars?"

He, meaning Janiis—or Koranth?

Chiara and I locked eyes. They'd discovered us missing. Had they discovered Marko's absence yet?

"Doesn't matter," another guard continued as they passed out of sight. "I don't want to give *her* any reason to summon us—she gives me the shivers."

The men continued on, never once looking our way. We followed the alley, and when we came to the end of it, Cynthia put her hand out.

"It's there!" she whispered, pointing toward the alley on the left. "On the corner!"

We crept along, following Cynthia through a doorway with nothing more than a ragged strip of cloth covering it. We paused, getting our bearings in the dark interior. Broken furniture piled in the corner, barely illuminated by the moonlight through a gaping window. Dust and cobwebs swirled in the wind, but the floor was swept clean.

Cynthia took off, running toward the stairs.

"Wait!" I hissed, and snatched for her hand, her dress, anything, but she raced up the stairs. I pushed Chiara behind me and followed Cynthia, trying to keep my boots quiet on the creaking stairs. She ran right to the top and burst into a dark room.

A sword swooped down at her. I shoved Cynthia to the side and jumped out of the way.

"Easy, Luc!" I growled.

Something smashed against my shoulder and I spun to find Aleksa, wide-eyed, the neck of a ceramic vase clutched tight in her hands. "Sorry," she whispered.

I winced and rolled my shoulder back. "Good arm." Heat from my magic traveled from my middle up to my shoulder to ease the ache. I already wanted to curl up in a corner and sleep for a day. I could handle an ache. But the magic sensed the need and slithered through my shoulder until it had been repaired.

I leaned against the doorframe. Chiara brushed by me to Cynthia, who lay sprawled on the ground. Had she fainted? I shut the door, shaking my head to stay awake. Now wasn't the time to pass out.

Luc kept his sword raised and peeked out the window, but

all remained quiet below. "Are you insane or just stupid?" he growled at Cynthia, his rough beard and slitted eyes making him look more bear than man.

She scooted so her back was against the wall, her dress sweeping a path through the dust and dirt. "I'm sorry," Cynthia murmured, hand over her heart. "I . . . I didn't think."

"Use your head, girl, or there won't be a next time," Luc muttered, and sat on a rickety stool by the window to keep watch.

"Ease up," Chiara said to him as she knelt by a bed tucked in the corner. "She didn't understand the risk, and now she does. She'll do better next time."

Chiara defending Cynthia. Huh.

Aleksa went to the bed and sat, wiping a man's brow. Marko's. The blankets moved up and down with his breathing.

Moonlight alone lit the room, shafts of soft light filtering through the tattered rags at the windows. Wind blew freely through the cracks in the walls and through the broken windows.

I studied Luc again. Deep grooves were etched around his eyes that I didn't remember. He looked like he hadn't slept in weeks. His clothes, once a clean, pressed uniform, were wrinkled, dirty, and had some suspicious-looking tears, like he'd come too close to a blade. He snatched up a blanket at his feet and wrapped it around himself.

I rested my hand on his shoulder, my eyes drawn back to the mound on the bed by Chiara. "Are you hurt, Luc?" I asked quietly.

He shook his head, still focused outside. "No, Your Majesty." He darted a glance at the bed, then back to the window. "Never better." A muscle ticked in his jaw as he studied the rips and stains in my shirt and trousers. "You?"

"Good as new." I swallowed, not wanting to ask, but needing to know. "And the king?" I asked even quieter.

Luc sighed, a long breath that rustled the threadbare curtain next to him. "He's . . ." His mouth opened and shut a few times, and he swallowed hard. "I've given him everything I can think of to ease the pain. But his mind—I don't know how to fix that."

"Did you get the message out about the attack?" I asked. Enzo would need all the advance warning he could get.

Luc maintained his watch out the window. "Yes. It was a clever riddle. I haven't made many contacts I can trust here, but one had a boat. I sent the message up the coast with him. Not sure Enzo will get it in time, but it was a better option than the pass."

"Do you have an extra sword?" I asked, painfully aware of the lack of one at my side.

Luc rubbed his forehead. "I had to sell my spare—these Riigans trust me less than I trust them. They won't sell me anything, and swords are a precious commodity at the moment."

I squeezed his shoulder, then made my way to Chiara. I'd find another way.

Chiara held her father's hand as he rested. His beard and hair had been trimmed, though not expertly, and he'd had a bath. Lines of pain were carved around his mouth and eyes, even in sleep.

I brought a chair closer so Chiara could sit and still hold her father's hand, then helped her into it. She never took her eyes off him, and I wished I could use magic to somehow transport all of us back up the cliffs and into safe territory.

Maybe I should have let Jenna come—she could hide everyone, or use her magic to fight our way out. At the moment, all I could do was heal a few bruises. I didn't even have a sword.

"What do we do now?" Chiara asked, careful to keep her voice low.

Luc responded first. "We must get King Marko out of Riiga, but I don't know how to get him past all the guards Riiga's paranoid king has posted."

I sat in the middle of the floor, too tired to pace. "It's not just Janiis. Koranth is alive and controlling everything from the shadows. I think . . . I think, because he has Graymere's shade blade, that Graymere's magic, or maybe even Graymere himself, could be *inside* Koranth."

Chiara took off her cap and unpinned her braids. "His eyes are black now. He doesn't posture like Koranth always postured."

"And," I added, piling on the gloom, "Janiis's betrothed is another mage. Redalia. The one who killed my father."

"Cavolo," Luc muttered.

I lay flat on the floor, too tired to even sit. "There's another way into Turia—a way we came down. A set of stairs and ropes set in the cliff farther east. Is he strong enough to make it up?"

Aleksa wiped the king's brow and dipped the rag back into a basin of water. "The ascent is harder than the descent. You need your wits about you—" She cut off with a sharp glance at Chiara, who put her face in her hand.

My eyes closed and I pinched my leg to stay awake. "I could try healing him—"

"No," Chiara said. "You don't have the strength."

I rubbed my palms into my eyes. She was right. I hated that she was right.

"Can we smuggle him out by boat?" Chiara asked.

Luc grunted. "Storm season is here, and the seas get bad the farther north you try to go. But maybe. We'd have to find someone we can trust. And a place to hide, away from the city, in the meantime."

Cynthia spoke up hesitantly. "I overheard most of the guards will be pulled into the palace tomorrow for the wedding ceremony and that citizens are required to attend."

I put my hands under my head, adjusting my shoulders as Sennor's shirt stretched too tight across my chest despite the rips. "You could get Marko to the cave while the mages and guards are busy with the wedding. Hide while Aleksa finds a boat."

"What about you?" Chiara asked, whipping around to face me.

The rags at the window above Marko swayed in the moonlight. "I'm not leaving Riiga until I've dealt with Koranth and Redalia."

"No." She stood, her chair scraping along the wood floor. "They're in a heavily defended palace, with an entire kingdom of soldiers at their disposal. You are not staying here to confront them on your own."

I lifted up onto my elbows. "I got Redalia alone once; I can do it again. I'll figure out a way to get to Koranth, too."

Chiara wrinkled her nose and crossed her arms. "If we all go back to Turia, we can regroup and come back with our own army. And"—she swallowed hard—"we need to find Mari."

I lay back down. Mari. "What do you know about her disappearance?" I asked Luc.

He grunted. "Only that she's missing from the palace."

Not enough to make a plan, even if we were in a position to help her. For now I'd have to trust that Jenna and Enzo would find her.

"There isn't time to leave and come back," I said. "Riiga can't be invaded with enough troops to stand against the mages. Storm season prevents a sea attack, and they control the passage at the cliffs. I'm here now. The Medallion has been guiding me south for *this*. So I can—"

"We can lure them to us." Chiara's hand went to her pocket, and she started pacing. It made me dizzy, so I closed my eyes. "What if we follow the clue, get the third key *now*, then lure them to wherever we want to confront them? A wide-open space with our armies."

"That might work," Luc said, tossing a threadbare blanket to Cynthia, who shivered in the corner. "I'm assuming this third key is in Riiga?"

I sighed and squeezed my eyes shut tighter. Too tired to think.

"What is the key to?" Aleksa asked from her spot by Marko.

I cracked an eye open—Chiara pulled the book with the illustration of the Turian key from her pocket. The one I'd given Jenna as a birthday present, and then she'd given away.

"It's to the Black Library—the ancient store where the first king of Hálendi hid all of the mages' learning and artifacts," Chiara said, pacing faster as she warmed to the topic. "The mage Brownlok stole the Turian key, Hálendi has the second key, but there's a third key."

"You think," I muttered.

"*Three* mages?" Aleksa groaned.

An idea came to me. A memory long forgotten. I scrubbed my hands through my hair and forced myself to sit up. "There might be an artifact in the Black Library that can heal your father. I learned about it long ago, and remember thinking it would be easier to have an artifact to heal others so I didn't have to get so tired. I don't know its limitations, but—"

"We find the key, find Mari, defeat the mages, get the artifact from the Black Library, and heal my father!" Chiara said, loud enough for Luc to shush her.

Marko had been kidnapped and imprisoned. He'd lost all memory of his family, his home, his self. Because of Koranth and Redalia. Because I hadn't acted soon enough when the Medallion urged me south. Because I'd left my father alone in the castle when I knew there was a traitor in our midst.

I shook my head. "That's a massive oversimplification, but yes. You all need to get to Turia safely before Riiga attacks. I'll find the key and meet you—"

"Not alone, you won't," Chiara said.

I lay back down. "It's too dangerous. There are too many things that could go wrong."

She stood so regally, despite the trousers and dirt and her

hair in two crumpled braids. "Do you trust me?" she asked quietly.

"Yes." I didn't even need to think on it.

She swallowed. "Then I'm coming. Luc and Cynthia and Aleksa can get my father to the cliffs. They can hide in the cave while they find passage to Turia. You're still healing. You can't do this alone. And I have the clue." She tapped the book, which was back in her pocket.

The Medallion warmed against my chest, not in warning but in confirmation. I almost sighed with relief. I didn't want her to get hurt, but I was so *tired* of carrying everything on my own. So tired.

"The ancient vineyards are west of the city," Aleksa said slowly. "You follow the cliffs along the shore. You won't miss them." She shrugged and tucked her chin down. "I can show Luc to the cave."

Luc studied us, then gave me a slight nod. "We can let King Marko rest through the morning, then get him to the cliffs during the ceremony, then find passage. You get the key, and come back to the cliffs. If we're not there, we'll meet you in Turia—"

"At Lessia's inn, at the western crossing," Chiara said. It was a good choice—Dora and her sister would protect Marko's identity until soldiers could be summoned to escort him home. And maybe, by some miracle, Yesilia would still be there and be able to help him.

I exhaled and slowly sat up enough to hold out my hand to Chiara to shake in their custom. "Okay, then. We'll leave early tomorrow, before dawn. We're going to find the last key to the Black Library."

A small smile bloomed on her dirty face and she put her hand in mine, shaking it once. If something happened to her, I wasn't sure I'd survive the aftermath.

I'd just make sure nothing happened to her.

Redalia

Redalia had dreamed of him last night, of Kais and all that could have been.

The young Hálendian king had more fortitude than she'd expected. Atháren's time was up. She'd take his loyalty—willingly or not. And then she'd control Riiga *and* Hálendi. Turia would fall next.

"Excuse me, Your Highness."

The girl whispered so softly that Redalia almost missed what she said as the servant behind her brushed her hair again and again until it shone.

She'd awoken in a foul mood—she always did when she dreamed of Kais. "What is it?" she asked with a yawn.

"Um, there's been a development that Lord Koranth would like to speak with you about." The girl's eyes stayed fixed on the floor, her hands clasped tight.

Redalia stood, ignoring the fluttering maid who stepped forward with a long silk robe. "What sort of disturbance would require my attention on my wedding day?"

The girl swallowed, looked to the other maid for help, then plunged ahead. "I was told to tell you that Lord Koranth has an early wedding present for you, and that it would be worth your time, even today."

Redalia batted away the robe and held out her hand. "I will need to be dressed to meet Koranth," she said, a slight frown marring her perfect face. The servant brought forward a beautiful green dress with a train and gold embroidery. But Redalia shook her head. "No, I will wear red today."

CHAPTER TWENTY-TWO

Chiara

The words of the poem had been burned into my memory since I found the clue ten days ago. I replayed them as Ren and I crept through the city toward its northeastern border. The only things moving on the streets this early were cats foraging for food.

The wind chased after us and tugged at my cap. My scalp itched and I wished I could pull my hair down from under it. Soon I'd get to leave off the wretched disguise. I hadn't painted on my eyebrows today, but I'd kept the trousers.

"I expected more . . . life out here," Ren whispered, leaning around the corner.

We'd slept only a few hours under threadbare blankets. I'd shivered until drifting off—had Ren been able to rest and heal? I'd thought about scooting closer, but hadn't dared.

Aleksa had kept watch over my father so Luc could sleep. They'd make it to the cave. They'd be okay.

I swallowed and glanced behind us, but no one was there. "Do you feel like we're being watched?"

Ren started across the street and I scurried after him. "Yes," he whispered as we climbed the path, which led us around a shop. "I think we are definitely being watched. But I don't know if those watching are allies or foe."

In my pocket, the book Jenna had given me so long ago pressed against my leg. Silly as it was, it helped me feel safe. Redalia was in the palace getting ready for her wedding, Koranth with her. Brownlok was last seen in Turia. We could do this. Find the key, get out.

The main buildings of the city ended, and scrubby trees marked a path out of the city. We passed the cave we'd hidden in, and the meadow with the stairway I could barely make out, even knowing it was there. Then the path turned upward. The land dropped away on our right, a sheer drop into the ocean crashing against the rocks below, the steep hillside to the left the only path forward.

Short trees flanked the path, their leaves edged in orange and turning brown. The dirt trail turned sharply, and we had to scramble to keep our footing. Soon, the trees ended, and we were exposed on a hillside so steep only tall yellow grass could survive.

All my focus centered on getting enough air in my lungs for the sudden ascent and stepping carefully so I didn't slip off the narrow trail. Ahead of me, Ren stopped.

"Look," he said, and pointed. I arched my back, clicks and

pops running down my spine. What I saw made me forget my aches.

Water, so deeply blue it was almost green, stretched out across a space far more vast than I'd ever seen. The sun hadn't crested the water's edge yet, but it flung purple and orange and pinks across the sky. My fingers itched to paint the scene, to capture the beauty—the endless sea and sky, the force of the crashing waves so powerful I could hear the roar even up here.

I leaned closer to Ren's shoulder, and our breaths matched up for a brief moment as we watched the first curve of the sun step into the sky. Salt hung in the air and tasted like life and freedom and power rolled into one. The wind beat against us, flattening the long grass and pulling my cap free from my head.

"Oh no!" I yelped, reaching out.

Ren's arm went around my waist and pulled me from the sharp drop. I stood with my back against his chest, watching my cap tumble out of sight. "It's just a cap," he said, and slowly released me. "Please don't go near the edge."

I'd said something similar to him at the top of the cliffs. Did he remember? It seemed like it'd been months ago. We'd come so far. And we still had so far to go.

I twisted and found my face closer to his than I expected. The heat from his back soaked into me, clashing with the biting wind. "I'll be careful." My voice came out hoarse and breathy at the same time. The wind tossed his hair around until I itched to smooth it back.

He leaned closer and the wind snatched my breath away. And then the view behind him caught my eye.

"Ren, look!" I gasped. He spun around, hand going for the sword that wasn't on his belt anymore. I stepped around him and scrambled uphill to get a better vantage.

Before us, paths crisscrossed the cliff face, each a few feet above the last. And between the paths, thick, gnarled vines grew from the ground and stretched along fences, wide golden leaves catching the morning light. The grapes had all been harvested, but the vineyard rose up into the sky.

" 'Vineyards that touch the sky,' " I said, repeating the line from the clue.

"Let's walk while we talk," Ren said. "Tell me the poem again?"

" 'Three keys to find the library black,' " I started.

"We have that figured out—the Medallion, the ring, and the third key." He breathed heavily—he wasn't as healed as he let on.

I slowed my pace and nodded. " 'One in snow, the heart of attack'—the Medallion. 'Another within the heart, and surrounding it, too, a ring of flax, of brown and blue'—the ring Brownlok stole."

He climbed over an outcropping of rocks and turned to help me up. "Within the heart," he muttered.

"Turia." A rock slipped out from under my foot, and I stumbled under Ren's scrutiny. "Because Turia is the heart of the Plateau?"

"What else have you already figured out?" he asked, tilting his head.

"Maybe the brown and blue is a symbol of the keys uniting the kingdoms?"

A slow smile spread across his lips. I swallowed and continued on, brushing by him. Focus on the key. Focus on getting my father out of Riiga, finding Mari. There'd be time later to think about whatever was happening between Ren and me.

The path began winding down again, and I went slowly, keeping to the heels of my too-big boots.

"And then there's 'the final key, not a key at all: behind the falling door, that gives life, but takes it more.'" Those lines weren't part of the clue in my book—they had been in the book about the vineyards. And I'd forgotten until now: it had also mentioned blood.

I didn't look back at Ren, but his footsteps followed mine. Whenever I could, I glanced over at the ocean, at the orange sun burning its way through the horizon. "I don't like the sound of a falling door," I said, wavering.

"And 'where neither snow nor heart can find.' That could mean it's not in Hálendi or Turia?"

I held on to a branch to keep from sliding down the steep trail. "Riiga wasn't a kingdom yet. And while the land here technically belonged to Turia, it was never claimed. Too hard to travel and communicate." We walked a little longer, my calves burning, until the trees had risen tall enough to obscure our view of everything except the vineyards on the cliffside ahead.

But eventually even the vineyards were obscured. Until a bend in the path, when the trees dropped away, when everything dropped away.

A tiny stream of water cascaded from the top of the cliff all the way down to a pool of water below, where waves crashed against the rocks. The waterfall created a tiny bay, and a rope bridge with wood planks lining the bottom stretched from our side of the path to the far side of the bay, where the trail continued.

The bridge looked sturdy enough, and Ren started to continue on, but I held his arm. "Wait," I said, unable to look away from the water. "What if . . . 'Behind the falling door, that gives life—' "

" 'But takes it more'?" He stared at the waterfall, then at me. "You think . . . this?"

I shrugged and waved my hand. "If there's a cave behind it, it could be a falling door."

"And water gives life."

I stared at the waterfall with a shiver, thinking of how wet we'd get, how cold. "We should at least look."

Ren stepped off the path, beating a new trail in the yellowed grass. We had to backtrack when we came across rocks too large to climb and brush too thick to pass through. But eventually we made it to the edge of the pool and the little rock shelf that circled it.

Morning light touched the boulders below the surface of the clear blue water, the bottom fading the deeper it went. We edged along the rock shelf, getting wet with spray the closer we came to the thin falls.

I'd imagined us passing through the water to find the cave, but once we'd made our way to it, there were several feet of space behind the fall. Even so, we might as well have gone directly under. Ren's shirt clung to him and his hair was plastered against his scalp. The outline of the Medallion stood out against his chest. I forced my eyes away.

My shirt wasn't as finely made or as transparent as his, but I had never been more glad for the strips binding my chest than I was now.

Ren glanced down at his shirt, then at mine, then immediately away, his cheeks turning pink despite the freezing water.

But there was nothing here except solid wet rock.

I pushed against it, digging my fingers into the cracks. "Maybe if we—"

My foot slipped on a patch of moss. My heart stopped, but Ren grabbed me, steadied me. "If you fall in, the waterfall will trap you at the bottom of the pool."

I nodded. A door that gives life but also takes it.

We crossed through the other side of the waterfall and made for the trail, into the sunshine.

"Keep looking?" Ren asked as he stared at the path ahead.

"Keep looking."

✦ ✦ ✦

We searched every fall we came to as the sun rose higher. Doubts marched through my head as we hiked. Had my father made it to the cave? Maybe I should have stayed with him instead of chasing some clue deeper into Riiga.

Ren stopped in a patch of shade. His shoulders drooped—he should be resting, not traipsing along the coast. And I'd never been closer to so much water, yet unable to drink any of it. He wouldn't say we had to go back. Just like he wouldn't tell me how truly exhausted he was.

"Maybe we should turn around," I said.

He started walking again. "We haven't found—"

"There's too much coast to search." I stayed, and Ren faced me. "We shouldn't have come. Let's go get my father out of Riiga. Find Mari."

He studied me, his hair whipping around him, blue eyes matching the sky and sea. "One more. Let's find one more waterfall. If it's not there, we turn back."

I licked my dry lips. "One."

He led, me trudging several paces behind. The sun rose until it hung in the center of the sky, but still we marched on, the vineyards to the left, sea on the right. Slowly, so gradually I hardly noticed, a loud rushing overtook the crashing waves. But what—

We'd reached the bottom of the trail. Ahead of us, huge cliffs rose straight into the sky, too straight and steep for even vineyards to grow on. The cliffs jutted up, forming an alcove sheltered from the buffeting wind, and a massive waterfall cascaded from the top all the way to the bay below. The roar was louder than anything I'd ever heard, and white foam billowed up from where the water hit the waiting pool beneath.

Droplets of water caught on the wind and speckled my face like tiny pricks of ice.

"Whoa," Ren whispered.

"Yeah," I whispered back, our shoulders touching. The pool rippled outward from the falls, and the water flowed into the ocean, churning where tides collided.

One more.

Ren held his hand out to me. "This will be slippery."

I put my hand in his, but not because I was worried I'd fall.

The closer we got to the falls, the clearer it became: there was nothing hidden behind the water. And with the amount of water covering us—and every surface—if there were a key, it would have been destroyed from the water by now.

But Ren led me along anyway, taking each step carefully. And when we were completely behind the fall, a fissure in the rock appeared, wide enough to edge through. We stared at it for a moment.

"Do we go in?" Ren shouted to be heard over the water.

I stared at the black crack and shrugged. The chances of finding a key to the Black Library that had been hidden for so long were infinitesimal.

Ren went first, and I followed, glad he kept my hand in his. Rock scraped against my back and chest, pulling at my hair and wet clothes. It felt like we'd been sliding through the rock for ages, but then it was over. We spilled into a tiny cave, my feet sinking up to my ankles in sand.

Light filtered in from higher up in the crack, casting an eerie glow that waved and danced like the falling water beyond. The roar of the falls was lost in here, and it felt like we were somehow breathing underwater.

But the cave was empty.

I edged around the walls, where the sand didn't seem quite as deep, looking for markings or anything that might hint we were in the right place. Ren started from the other side, bending low and searching high. This was our last chance. The longer we were in Riiga, the greater the likelihood of being caught and thrown in the cell that my father had occupied for too long. Or worse, that my father wouldn't make it.

I ran my fingers along the walls, searching every groove and edge and plane, but when we met in the middle, I couldn't help resting my forehead against the rock.

"It's not here," I whispered. I slammed my palm against the rock with a grunt. "I need it to be here."

Ren's arm slipped around my shoulders. "Hey," he said, turning me to face him. He touched his chest and adjusted the chain at his neck. "Let's look again. Maybe we missed—"

"We don't have time. We don't know if we're reading the clue right. Or if it's even important. What if it was some old scholar making random notes?" A tear leaked from the corner of my eye and I marched through the center of the cave.

My first step away from Ren, my foot sank into the sand. But not just to my ankle—my whole leg. I let out a strangled gasp as I lost my balance and fell forward, my other leg and one hand also sinking in.

"Ren!" I called as the sand pulled at me and rose to my chest and neck as though it were swallowing me. How was this possible? How—

"Don't move!" Ren scrambled along the side of the cave, staying at the edge and reaching out for me. I reached with the hand that hadn't been submerged toward him, but our fingertips didn't even brush. Too far away. Still sinking. I lifted my chin. Sucked in as much air as I could.

Ren jumped in after me.

"No!" I yelled, but he didn't sink. His boots stayed on top of the sand, even as the granules tickled my cheeks. Some force pulled me deeper, squeezing around me. I closed my eyes as sand filled my ears and covered my head.

Ren grasped my wrist.

The moment he touched me, the sand changed and solidified. The force was no longer pulling me down, but I was still buried. My lungs screamed for air. I couldn't move.

Ren pulled on my wrist—it was barely enough to get my face out of the sand.

I coughed and sputtered, moving my head, neck, anything I could. The rest of me was stuck.

"Wait," Ren said with a deep frown. "Let me dig you out."

I spat out the grit as he knelt next to me, but as soon as he released me, I started sinking again. "Don't let go!" I said. He grabbed my wrist again. "What is this place?"

He dug with his other hand until my elbow was free and I could hold on to his ankle. "If I had to guess," he said, scooping sand away, "I'd say we were in the right place. Kais was a land mage. The enchantment doesn't work on me—maybe it recognizes my magic."

Land mage. The sand. I wriggled my legs slowly, trying to create space, even if it was just the illusion of it. "Get me out," I muttered over and over, helping him dig once my other arm was free.

My toe hit something as I yanked my leg up and scrambled out of the Chiara-sized hole. I fell forward, next to Ren, clinging to him. "There's something down there," I said, panting and moving all my limbs, shaking away as much sand as I could.

"What—"

"A rock, or something. Maybe—"

He transferred my hands back to his ankle and knelt, scooping sand away. He reached into the hole and came up grinning, holding a box made of stone. Grains of sand fell away, catching in the intricate etchings that covered the surface.

"You . . . you found it," I said, brushing my fingers over the etchings.

"Technically, *you* found it," he said, holding it out for me to take. He helped me up, and we crouched by the entrance, where the ground didn't try to eat me.

"But you knew to keep going. The Medallion?" I asked.

He shrugged. "I think, because Kais created them both, they're connected. Something drew me on." He shrugged again. I sighed—what a wonder to feel that, to have *magic*. To *not* die in a pit of sand.

"Open it," he said.

A tiny clasp held the top closed. I unlatched it, then dug my fingertip in and lifted. The stone lid grated as it opened. Inside, a rolled parchment lay on black velvet, perfectly preserved.

I unrolled it carefully, and the supple material bent like it was made yesterday, not hundreds of years ago. Lines of ink twisted and connected together, small words marking locations, a path.

" 'The final key, not a key at all.' "

"A map," Ren said, his voice full of wonder.

An intricate, old map of the Plateau, traced in bold and thin lines. In the corner . . . I leaned closer and gasped. "The poem! It's here, but there's more:

> *Three keys to find the library black:*
> *one in snow, the heart of attack.*
> *Another within the heart,*
> *and surrounding it, too,*
> *a ring of flax, of brown and blue.*
> *Two make up one, the key to the door.*
> *Two kingdoms to hide, to be found nevermore.*
> *The final key, not a key at all,*
> *marks the journey's end,*
> *its start at the wall.*
> *Hidden both deep and high*
> *Where neither snow nor heart can find*
> *Where waves ne'er reach*
> *and vineyards touch the sky.*
> *You will find what you seek*
> *behind the falling door,*
> *that gives life, but takes it more.*

Ren and I stared at each other in the rollicking light. "We found it," I said, a laugh bubbling up. He laughed with me.

We'd found it. The map the mages needed. That the mages would do anything to get.

Ren traced a line that went from Turiana to Riiga, then along the western coast and up through an inlet into the Wastelands. From there, what looked like random dots filled the space between the inlet and a tiny dot marked with the words *Black Library.*

Ren rolled the parchment back up and set it in the box. "Let's get out of Riiga."

I swallowed. "Agreed."

Marko

Vague snatches of memory came to Marko in the night and morning since he'd been freed. Usually when he wasn't paying attention, when he wasn't trying to remember. Faces. Voices.

The girl—Chiara, his daughter—had said he was a king. He didn't feel like a king. He was just . . . Marko. He didn't understand how he could have so much knowledge of life and the mechanics of living, without any of the details associated with *his* life. Where had it gone? Would it come back?

Everyone treated him like he might break if they spoke too loud. With how his head ached, they might be right.

When he'd woken that morning, a new boy and girl—both on the cusp of adulthood—watched him. They knew him. Cynthia had taken pity on him first and introduced them as Enzo, his son, and Jenna, his son's betrothed.

No one would tell Marko why they were here.

Soon, Aleksa had said, people would flood the streets to attend a wedding. She'd given Marko and the others directions, made them repeat the directions until memorized in case they got separated. North until they met the cliffs, east until the meadow, vines covered the entrance.

A memory flashed before him, swinging a little girl with a mess of black curls into the air and laughing. Then it was gone. But the feeling behind it, the love, was not.

"Mari," Marko whispered. Everyone stopped what they were doing and saying. He found a chair and sat. His legs hurt. Everything hurt. "Little Mari."

"You remember?" Luc asked.

"I—"

But he didn't get to finish. The door burst open, slamming against the wall hard enough to shatter bits off the edge of the door. A woman wearing red stormed in and the air in the room solidified. This was the woman who had come to Marko in his cell.

The man with black eyes came in behind her, the man who had taken everything.

Marko couldn't breathe, couldn't move. No one else could, either, except the fair-haired girl. She whirled into action, her sword an arc of destruction.

The woman in red drew a gold dagger and deflected her blow, fighting effortlessly.

"Get everyone out!" the girl shouted over her shoulder. She attacked and attacked until the woman's concentration was fully on her and they were released from whatever spell had held them bound.

Luc and Enzo grabbed Marko.

"This way," Luc grunted. Instead of passing the dueling women for the stairs, he turned them toward a window in the back. He stepped out onto a narrow ledge, pulling Marko with him, and slid down a wooden awning into the alley behind the shop.

"Jenna, come on!" Enzo yelled, but she yelled back, "Go! I'll catch up."

Aleksa and Cynthia slid next, followed by Enzo. They raced along as fast as they could, but Marko couldn't run like they needed him to. Couldn't lighten his heavy, painful steps.

They burst onto the road as a stream of Riigans took to the streets and bells sounded from somewhere beyond. The call to the wedding had come.

A shout rose up—guards circling the front of the shop spotted them and gave chase. Enzo drew his sword, and Luc started to as well, but Enzo shook his head. "Take my father far from here. I'll hold them off, give Jenna time—"

The first soldiers had reached him.

Chaos erupted in the street—shouting, metal on metal, the scrape of boots on stone. Marko's stomach turned and the pounding in his head thrashed harder and harder.

Luc drew his sword like he would help Enzo anyway, but Marko stumbled again as Aleksa and Cynthia dragged him away, and Luc turned to Marko with a curse.

"This way," Aleksa murmured. "Hurry."

Right before Marko turned the corner, the soldiers overran Enzo, swallowing him in their midst. Enzo. His son. His chest constricted and he stumbled again, but Cynthia held him up, tugging her torn dress out of the way.

"Come on, Your Majesty," she said, eyes and mouth pinched. "He'll be okay. They both will be."

And although Marko couldn't remember much of anything, he knew without a doubt that Cynthia was lying.

CHAPTER TWENTY-THREE

Ren

Chiara carried the stone box. Neither of us had a bag or any convenient way to convey it. And not only was it smarter to keep the Medallion and map as separate as we could at this point, but I trusted her.

I trusted her.

And even soaked, dressed as a boy, she was *radiant*.

Focus. We'd gathered all the pieces we needed—Marko, the map. Getting *out* of Riiga would be a whole new challenge.

This tiny trail that connected cities clinging to the cliffs in the kingdom amazed me—that a kingdom could stay united despite such a tenuous connection.

Getting back up the path kept me plenty warm despite the storm brewing. But when we reached the first waterfall, the clouds that had been building all morning opened, sending a cool mist down.

The path turned to mud, so we walked to the side of it, climbing over rocks and vines. I took Chiara's hand as often as I could, wishing I could take the time to use my magic to warm her, but it would be pointless. I couldn't keep my magic from working on my own body, though I was more accustomed to the cold.

We were close—so close to the cave where the others should be hiding by now. At the next turn, two figures blocked the trail, a huge brown horse grazing beside them. One tall and wearing a long cloak, the other a child. *Danger,* the Medallion seemed to whisper. *Traitor.*

I eased Chiara behind me. I really needed to find a sword. The knife in my boot pressed against my ankle, but I wanted to see if we could get around these travelers without a confrontation before drawing it.

They stood, not running at us, not calling out. Was I just being paranoid? No. The Medallion warmed the closer we came. My father had trusted the Medallion; I would, too.

A swift punch of grief knocked into me, stealing the air from my lungs as I tried to focus on the approaching threat, on keeping Chiara safe.

I missed my father. Missed all the lost opportunities, all the wisdom I hadn't asked for, the time we no longer had. I wished I had taken the time to properly care for his tomb before I left.

"Chiara," I whispered. "I don't think—"

"Mari?" she choked out.

And then the child's stance became familiar. Her brown-and-gold cloak. My heart stopped for at least three beats when I caught sight of wild curls tucked into the hood of her cloak.

Chiara tried to move past me, to go to her sister, but I held her back. The Medallion screamed to run, but what could I do? I couldn't leave Mari here.

Chiara pushed against me with her icy hands. "Ren, what are you—"

"Good afternoon, Princess Chiara," said a voice that was both ancient and youthful. My magic shivered in response to the sound. *Mage.*

The bottomless brown eyes, sharp jaw, features shaded by his cloak. The man from the woods, who had fought off mercenaries. Erron. And he had his hand on Mari's shoulder.

Mari.

Her gaze was shuttered, seeing yet unseeing, and she stood frozen. Not recognizing us, breathing calmly, hands tucked into her cloak. She seemed unharmed, other than this unnatural stillness that had come over her.

"What do you want, Brownlok?" I asked, my stance wide and ready. Chiara's breathing hitched behind me. I pulled all my focus forward. On Brownlok. On the exact moves I would use to break the hand touching Mari.

"Now, now, young king," Brownlok said, keeping his hand on Mari's shoulder. "No need for violence. We each have something the other wants, I believe." The Medallion's chain itched at my neck. The map in Chiara's hand. I swallowed. I'd never faced a mage before. Didn't have a sword. If I failed . . . I cut the thought off, but it circled in the back of my mind, taunting me at all I stood to lose. All *everyone* stood to lose if I failed.

Brownlok reached into his cloak and drew out a disk about the size of his hand, a hole through the middle forming a ring.

The Turian key.

Then he tossed it at my feet.

No one moved. He wouldn't just give it to us. And if he thought I cared about some stupid ring when his filthy hand was on little Mari, he was about to learn otherwise.

"You know what that is, young king?" he asked.

"Yes, but I'm more concerned with your hostage."

Brownlok smiled, and it wasn't as fearsome as I expected from the man who'd had the guts to take over a palace in the middle of a fortified city and managed to escape again.

"I wouldn't call Mari a hostage," he said. "But I can see you won't be distracted. So here's the arrangement. I need to find the Black Library. Not for whatever dire purpose you're thinking of." He smirked like he could read my mind, and I narrowed my eyes at him. "The simple fact is, my life force was tied to Graymere's. So when your sister ended his existence, the threads keeping me here began to snap."

"You seem healthy enough," Chiara spoke from behind me. Her hand grasped my shirt and she moved closer.

Brownlok still didn't take his hand from Mari's shoulder. "Appearances can be deceiving, Princess. Your sister reminded me of something I'd forgotten: a pure heart is the strongest magic of all. Mine is far from pure, and without the artifacts in the Black Library, I will die. I find I'm not quite ready for that."

"So you want us to take you there?" I asked, pushing false

bravado into my voice. I couldn't reveal that his words had any effect on me. "What, because you asked nicely?" Chiara dug her fingers into my back. I knew I was provoking him, but so far, he hadn't made anything clear—what would happen if we refused? Would he really hurt a child? He'd helped me on the road. "You haven't hurt Mari yet. Why would you now?"

Brownlok's head tilted and he studied me. "Mari has not yet outlived her usefulness."

Mari remained at his side, unseeing. Frozen. No matter how much I'd trained, even if I had a weapon, I wouldn't be fast enough to keep her from harm if I attacked now.

Brownlok glanced at Chiara. "You have the map?" How did he even know about it? Then I remembered—he'd infiltrated Turia's palace, possibly read the same books Chiara had.

"We need time," Chiara said, stepping next to me. "We can get to the library if we work together, but we need a ship. I know people who can get us one."

My lips pursed as Chiara continued. I would *not* be working with a mage. Other than the bow on his horse's saddle, he carried no weapon I could see. Except magic—and I didn't know what kind of mage he was, what his magic could do. I could heal, but Mari and Chiara couldn't. If something did happen to me, I couldn't risk leaving them defenseless.

Brownlok gestured for us to go ahead of him. I picked up the ring at my feet and tucked it into my pocket.

"I will trade Mari's life for one artifact from the library. You can do whatever you want with the rest." He stepped back, and Mari mirrored him. The deal was good—*if* he kept his word. "But we go to the docks now."

"N-now?" Chiara stuttered. "Our friends are hiding on the way to the docks. They can help us get a boat. Save time before this storm hits."

Brownlok studied her. I fought the urge to step between them. There was no way he'd allow us to meet with friends. The chances of overpowering him would be too great. "I will allow you one stop."

Which meant his magic was more powerful than a group of people united against him. I put my hand on Chiara's arm and nodded to Brownlok.

I didn't like the way he kept ahold of Mari. But Chiara had won us a chance. Luc had a sword. Between the two of us, we could find a way to get Mari away from Brownlok, magic or no.

"One stop is all I need." Chiara pointed a finger at him. "But if you hurt her, I will personally make sure you regret it."

I blinked at the venom in her voice. She glared at Brownlok, then focused on Mari, like she could break whatever magic held her sister captive through the sheer force of her will.

Brownlok settled Mari onto the horse and rode behind her, pressing his knees into the horse's sides and keeping it at a walk behind us as we left the cliffside trail and sank into the deep sand of the narrow strip of beach near the hideaway.

A meadow to our right signaled the secret stairs—the ones Brownlok already knew about. Did he know about the secret cave? Did the other mages?

Vines grew down the cliff face. Chiara brushed her fingers against them, searching for the opening. I focused on the sounds of Brownlok and Mari. Each hoofbeat. The Medallion stayed hot.

Chiara darted inside the cave when we reached its entrance. I slowed to give her more time to explain to the others. But she came out again straight off.

"There's no one there."

I yanked back the vines. Sure enough—empty.

"This was your one stop," Brownlok said. His horse flicked its tail and tossed its head, impatient to be on its way. "I've kept my bargain. Now we go to the docks."

But . . . they were supposed to be here. To wait.

Chiara leaned against me, looping her hand around my arm. She squeezed tight, but I couldn't look at her. She'd see my worry—that maybe Marko and the others hadn't ever made it to the cave.

◆ ◆ ◆

Brownlok didn't go near the palace as we traveled the empty streets of Vera—in fact, if my sense of direction was correct, he avoided it. Did Redalia and Koranth know of his plans, or was he playing us all for fools?

And did it matter if he was? He had Mari.

The closer we got to the docks, the more the metallic scent of fish saturated the air. Even the drizzling rain couldn't dispel it. Brownlok slowed as the docks came into view, tying his horse to a post and walking next to us, Mari on his other side. He studied the boats rocking in the turbulent sea—most too small to hold all of us. Even if we found a boat large enough and a captain who would take us, would we survive the storm?

"Well, well, well, Brownlok. What have you brought for me?"

My gaze snapped forward, and I tucked Chiara behind my shoulder.

Koranth stood in front of us around the bend in the docks, his black eyes as bottomless as the sea behind him, his skin as gray as the sky, black blade at his hip. Redalia stood beside him, black cloak rustling in the wind coming off the sea, slits of red flashing underneath.

The scene beyond the mages was worse.

Jenna lay still in the bed of a cart—too still—her hair tangled behind her. Enzo slumped against a wheel, purple bruises stark against sallow skin. Cris stood guard over them both.

The Medallion switched from hot to ice-cold so fast it pulled the air from my lungs.

Years—we'd been the best of friends for *years*. Cris had helped me scare Jenna's untrustworthy suitors away. Snuck into the kitchens with me. We'd rescued each other from punishments countless times. And now he preened with these mages, standing over my sister as if he'd won some prize.

He'd betrayed me once, and I'd let him get away. He wouldn't escape again.

My hands clenched so tight that Chiara gasped, and I loosened my hold on her. But only a little. I needed her here, grounding me. Keeping my head in the present, and not focused on gutting Cris with whatever mildly sharp instrument I could find.

Jenna was supposed to be safe in Turia with Enzo. Her magic was like nothing I'd ever seen—how had Redalia captured them?

"I thought I told you to find the Black Library," Koranth

said to Brownlok, his voice scraping like a rusty spoon against stone.

Brownlok set a hand on his hip as though he hadn't a care in the world. "And that's what I'm about to do. I told you I needed more pieces to find it. I've got the pieces now. You have a boat?"

Koranth gestured to a medium-sized ship at the docks. A small crew of rough men stomped between the dock and deck, preparing for departure despite the waves coming in.

"I don't think we should get on that boat," Chiara whispered.

"I don't think we have much of a choice," I muttered.

Chiara couldn't stop staring at Enzo and Jenna. "Is she . . . ?"

"No," I whispered. "She's breathing." Though I didn't know what ailed her. Had they stolen her memory, like they'd stolen Marko's?

"Everything is prepared for our journey," Koranth said, raising his hands like he addressed a crowd. "Lord Cris will relieve you of your weapons and artifacts, and then we'll be on our way." He gave us a terrifying smile. "It's thanks to his keen tracking skills we are having this delightful reunion."

I wanted to kick myself. Getting Marko out of the palace *had* been too easy. We were the targets all along.

I stared down Cris as he approached with coarse rope looped over his shoulder. His features hadn't changed, yet I barely recognized him. Darkness had settled into his eyes, into the shadows of his face. He flicked my empty belt. "What, no sword?"

My jaw stayed clenched tight. He didn't deserve an answer.

A man—huge and rough—grabbed Chiara from behind, wrapping a thick, meaty arm around her neck. I lurched for her, but Cris drew his sword, stopping me.

Chiara shook her head at me, like that would get me to stand down. Too many threats, from too many angles. How could I possibly keep everyone safe?

"Your crest," Cris grunted, ready to attack. Crest? Oh.

I ripped the chain with the Medallion off and thrust it into Cris's hands. Then swung hard, my fist ramming into his jaw. Cris fell back two steps. He swung his sword. It arched toward me. Mari screamed. But the mages needed me. And Cris knew it.

At the last second, Cris changed the angle, and the blade sliced through my shoulder, the cut deep and long. I flinched, but uttered no sound or cry of distress. Cris didn't deserve the satisfaction.

"What are you doing?" Redalia spat. "We need him whole."

The man holding Chiara shoved her forward and joined his crewmates.

"If he had a weapon, he would have used it. He'll be good as new soon, won't you?" Cris glared at me, then shoved his sword back into its sheath. He might as well have been shoving it into my chest. I'd confided in him. He put the Medallion over his head and tucked it into his tunic. I'd *trusted* him. "You are king no longer."

And from the heat in his glare, I didn't think I'd be alive much longer, either.

No one protested that he'd taken the Medallion. One of the keys. Did they . . . Was it possible they didn't know its importance?

Koranth pulled his hood forward, leaving only his glittering eyes visible. "While it is kind of you to join us, Princess," he said, dipping his hood toward Chiara, "you do not have the blood of Kais in your veins, nor do you have magic that could assist our journey."

My mouth dried out. No. No no no no—

"You are therefore of no value." Koranth nodded to Redalia. "Kill her."

CHAPTER TWENTY-FOUR

Chiara

Redalia held her hand up, and searing pain like I'd never felt before stabbed through my chest. Like she had my heart in her hand and was pulling it out through my skin. My face tilted to the sky. My thoughts fragmented. I couldn't even scream. Raindrops that tasted of fish and salt dripped into my open mouth.

Then something changed. Her power released me. I collapsed in a heap on the dock. Phantom echoes of pain lanced through my bones.

Ren stood in front of me, arms out, one sleeve dark red with his blood. He shook his head, as though shaking away Redalia's tentacles. "We need her if you want to find the Black Library," he growled at Koranth. "She's your best chance at interpreting the map."

I lay unmoving, afraid the pain in my chest would return. What was Ren talking about? I had no clue how to interpret the map, and he knew it. I groaned. My hand wouldn't unclench from the stone box that no one had bothered to take from me.

"What do you mean?" Koranth asked. Redalia's hand stayed on her golden dagger.

Ren's stance never changed. He stood over me like he'd fight anyone who came near, even without a weapon. "We found the map to the Black Library. She can interpret the poem written with it."

Koranth glared. "Search her."

"She has no weapon—" Ren started, but Redalia held her hand out and he froze in place.

Cris gently pried the box from my grip. "No," I muttered, too weak to push him away. He flinched when he met my eyes, but he dug into my pocket and pulled out Jenna's book.

The book still had the clue in it.

"Only these." He handed them to Koranth.

Koranth lifted the latch on the box with shaking fingers, and the wind tugged his hood back. The black caverns of his eyes seemed to glow, and his lips twisted up in a fearsome grin. "I've searched for hundreds of years," he muttered. "Finally!"

Hundreds of years? How ingrained was Graymere in Koranth?

Redalia took the book and began to flip through it. "It's blank," she said with a sneer. "Nothing worth writing about?" She hadn't seen the loose page. My legs trembled too much to stand, but I propped myself up to sitting.

Ren glared at her, still standing over me. Blood dripped from his fingers. "There was another part to the poem. Chiara memorized it."

Koranth's teeth ground together as he thought, and his eyes twitched. "Fine. She'll live. For now."

A dangerous glint appeared in Redalia's eyes as she considered me, and Ren's words from before came back—how I could be used for leverage against my father. Now, I'd be leverage against Ren, Enzo, and Jenna.

Redalia tapped the book against her hand once, waited until I followed the motion with my eyes, then tossed it into the sea.

My heart—my hope—sunk along with it.

Then Mari was by my side, and Ren, too, each with a hand under my arms to help me up. Brownlok hovered next to Mari, arms folded, glaring at us.

"Chiara?" Mari asked, her eyes huge brown pools in her face. "What happened? When did you get here?"

I hugged her close, unable to speak yet.

Ren held his hands in front of him to be tied. No fresh blood dripped over the knots Cris jerked tight around his wrists.

It had been *Cris* I'd seen at Lessia's inn. The rocks that had loosened from the cliffs in the fog—had he descended after us?

One of Koranth's men picked up Enzo and began dragging him toward the ship. Another hefted Jenna over his shoulder like a sack of grain and followed.

Ren's chest rumbled in the start of a growl, and I slipped my hand into the crook of his elbow and leaned against him, still weak from whatever Redalia had done to me. "Not yet," I whispered hoarsely. "Not yet."

Koranth turned to us and held out his arm like he was welcoming honored guests onto the ship. "This way, if you would. I'd hate to see anything happen to your family."

I tucked Mari to my side and followed Ren over the narrow gangway and onto the vessel. Brownlok stayed right on our heels, then Redalia and Cris. One of the ship's crew pulled the board onto the ship and tucked it against the railing. The deck swayed and bobbed with the waves below, and my vision spun along with my stomach.

Koranth pointed to where the mast rose from the deck. "You'll enjoy the journey much more from right here where I can keep my eye on you," he said. His voice sounded funny— deeper and more slurred than when he'd been ambassador in our palace.

Crew members came behind us with clubs, herding us to the center of the deck. Enzo was already settled against the mast, and Mari and I sat quickly, huddled against the rough wood at our backs. I hoped that if we complied, they wouldn't tie us up. They didn't. Not that Mari or I were a threat to anyone here.

Jenna wasn't with Enzo. The man holding her must have taken her elsewhere on the ship.

A man with a dark beard—the one who had grabbed me earlier—shoved Ren back so he fell next to me. With his hands tied in front of him, he couldn't catch himself and his head smacked against the mast. Mari flinched into me. I helped Ren sit up as he shook the pain away.

Mari put her hands on Enzo's face, gently prodding his bruises. "He's so cold, Chiara." Her tiny voice wavered. Her curls fell into her eyes when she turned to me and Ren. "He needs Yesilia. And Jenna, she's . . ." She choked up and couldn't speak. I wouldn't tell her about Father. She didn't need more troubles.

Ren swallowed and his lips tipped into a smile. He leaned over me and Mari, grabbed Enzo's arm with his bound hands, and closed his eyes. Only Brownlok paid us any mind, and he didn't object.

Ren leaned into me more and more the longer he held on to Enzo. His skin took on a grayish hue. The words from the cave in Riiga came back, how he had to be touching a person to heal them, how if he gave too much magic, he'd—

I wrapped my arms around him and pushed. He didn't budge. I pressed my back against the mast and shoved with all my strength. Ren tumbled onto the deck, away from Enzo.

He lay still for two long seconds, then pulled himself up with a groan.

"Don't you *ever* do something like that again." I kept myself from yelling, but only barely. His brows furrowed like he didn't understand me. "We need you," I whispered, my words choked and broken.

His normally sparkling eyes were bleak, dull. "I don't have a sword. Don't have the Medallion."

I took his face in my hands. "I don't care. Be. Careful."

Enzo began to shift and groan, and my attention snapped to him. My bottom lip trembled as his eyes opened slowly, then fell closed again. The crew bustled around the deck, unconcerned with us now that the docks faded in the distance.

I wrapped my arm through Ren's and helped him sit. "His face still looks like it's been smashed," I whispered.

Ren nodded. "He was more broken than I expected. It's good he still has bruises. I don't want them to think he needs to be tied up." He leaned against me, heavy again. "Thank you. For stopping me."

I breathed out slowly, tamping down my jumping thoughts and stomach. My mind shifted, looking for opportunities. Mari and I weren't tied up. Ren had the ring. Maybe we could leverage that for Jenna. "I don't like this," I whispered, tears mingling with rain on my cheeks.

"I don't, either." His head dropped, and he blinked slowly. "I . . . I may have overdone it."

My fingers dug into the muscles in his arms. "What? What do you need?"

He leaned into me. "Sleep."

Jenna's energy had been drained when she used her magic to help us escape Brownlok's men during the palace invasion. It seemed so long ago, yet it had been only a few months. And now we were on a ship off the coast of Riiga with Koranth and his mages. Jenna wouldn't be able to help us now. Ren's head fell onto my shoulder, heavy with sleep.

I studied the men around us. Each was barefoot and kept his balance easily on the waves. Each had a knife in his belt, sometimes a sword or club as well. Five in total, all busy with their tasks—raising the sail, tightening ropes. The waves here were even bigger, though we stayed within sight of the Plateau's cliffs rising from the foaming sea.

I couldn't tell how fast we traveled as we rode the waves, only that we headed west. Toward the Wastelands.

My stomach turned and rolled with the waves. I didn't want to move and disturb Ren, though I wasn't sure he *could* be roused after using so much magic.

Helpless.

Alone.

Useless.

So tired. Hungry. What Redalia had done to me, the pain had been like she'd taken a knife to every part of me at once. But I hadn't forgotten like my father.

"He hasn't stopped watching us," Enzo muttered. My eyes shot open. Had I fallen asleep? Enzo stretched his back and neck.

Full night had descended, and with the clouds blocking the stars, we may as well have been in that windowless room in Janiis's palace. I had no idea what time it was, how long we'd been at sea. But at least Enzo was awake. Alive. I leaned over Mari and hugged him. He squeezed back gently.

"Who's watching us?" Mari asked loudly. A couple of men looked over at us, like they'd forgotten we were there. One glared at Enzo, then ducked into a door at the other end of the deck.

Brownlok stood on the one raised portion of the boat—the captain's quarters. A crewman steered the ship with a great wooden wheel, making small adjustments and calling out to the men at the sail. Brownlok silently watched us from under the hood of his cloak, which he held tight against him in the wind.

"Up on the bow," I whispered to Mari. "The others are in the captain's quarters, but he's still here."

"Where?" she craned her head around. Brownlok was smirking by now, so I just pointed him out. No use being subtle with Mari around.

"How do you know so much about boats?" Ren asked. He still rested against me, but his hands were in his lap, working at the knots. He needed more rest—he shouldn't be awake yet.

I shrugged. "There's a whole shelf of books with pirate stories in the library." I pointed to the rope. "Do you want help?"

"No," he said. "I don't want you getting in trouble if someone catches you."

"Well," Mari said, shifting next to me on the hard deck, "I'd rather have Brownlok watching us than anyone else. He's the only nice one."

My brow furrowed. "Mari, what happened at home? And what do you mean, he's nice? He kidnapped you!"

She shook her head and frowned. "He didn't kidnap me. I ran away. You got to come on the adventure, and I wanted to help Father, too." Her shoulders dropped and she tucked her hands under her arms. "Everyone always leaves me behind," she finished in a whisper.

I pulled on one of my braids that had fallen over my shoulder to keep from screaming. She was *eight*. She really thought she could run away and there wouldn't be consequences? My head and stomach ached, and I rubbed my forehead. Hadn't I done the same thing?

"What about you?" Ren asked Enzo. "Did you get my message? Do you think Janiis will attack even though the mages are here?"

Enzo rubbed his forehead, prodding his bruises. "What message? What do you mean, attack?"

Oh no. What would all those villagers do when Riigans overran them?

Ren sighed. "Janiis is amassing troops. He built three gigantic pulley systems to raise an army onto the Plateau and invade Turia."

"Cavolo," Enzo muttered, holding his head tighter. "If you sent a message, my mother would have received it. She'll . . . she'll know what to do."

Would she?

"How were you and Jenna captured?" I asked. Maybe it would help me piece together a solution. A way out. I pulled Ren's hands into my lap so I could pick at the knots. I didn't care if someone caught me. I needed to *do* something.

Enzo sighed long and low. "Jenna was going to go after Mari. I knew she was—she'd never let anything happen to her. But I didn't want her to go alone, not when she faced everything alone last time. So we chased after Mari for days, following her trail into Riiga."

He didn't say it, but I could see Mari connect the pieces on her own—*she* was the reason Jenna and Enzo had been captured and were in danger, which put all of Turia in danger.

Hálendi's king and heir. Turia's future king.

There would be no one left to rule.

I jerked at the cursed rope around Ren's wrists. "You shouldn't have left the palace," I snapped at her.

Mari folded her arms over her chest. "I can take care of myself."

I pushed the rope away. "No you *can't*," I hissed at her.

Two tears tracked down her cheeks. Enzo and Ren were silent on either side of us. I shut my eyes even as my throat closed.

"I'm sorry," I whispered. Mari leaned into me, her chin quivering. If I hadn't left, Mari wouldn't have, either. Ren, Enzo, and Jenna wouldn't be here.

My father was free, but at the cost of everyone else.

She hadn't done this. *I* had.

I put my arm around her shoulder and held her hand. "I'm sorry. It's not you I'm angry with. I'm angry with myself." Mari sniffed and wiped her hand on the back of her sleeve. "I'm sorry I left you behind."

"And what about Brownlok?" Ren asked, distracting Mari. "He was nice to you?"

Mari's head bobbed. "He let me ride his horse and we ate all the sweetbreads we wanted, and he always made sure I got the warm blanket at night. He said he was taking me to see you and Ren," she said to me. She frowned. "But he hasn't been very nice to anyone else now that we're with the mean lady and Koranth."

Ren winced as the rope scraped against his wrists. "Mari, Brownlok is a mage. You can't trust him."

Her head jerked back. "He said he would bring me to you, and he did! It's those other mages who tied you up." She wrapped a curl around her finger. "I'm scared," she whispered.

Enzo took her hand in his. "We'll be safe if we stay together."

She bit her lip. "What about Jenna?"

Mari's words hit Enzo hard. Because I'd laid the blame at

her feet, when really it belonged at mine. I squeezed her shoulder. "Jenna will be okay. We'll make sure she's okay."

"Does anyone else think Brownlok's fascination with Mari is odd?" Ren asked quietly.

I nodded, as did Enzo. Mari folded her arms and slumped against the mast. "He's my friend."

"Just stay close to us, okay?" I whispered to her. "We won't leave you again."

The waves pressed against our ship, making the deck roll and tilt until I had to squeeze my eyes shut. The remains of Graymere in Koranth, Redalia, and Brownlok, all together. Jenna unconscious, Enzo injured, Ren drained. Perhaps if we could get Cris on our side . . . Sennor had needed another chance. Same with Cynthia.

"What if we try to convince the crew, or Cris, to help us?" Ren flinched, but I continued. "Surely we can bribe them with more than what the mages have offered."

Enzo grunted. "The mages offered the men *magic,* so I don't think they'll listen."

"Magic?" Ren asked. "How is that possible?"

Enzo leaned a little more against the mast, weakening. "I have no idea."

I shivered. "What about Cris?"

Ren was silent for a long time. "He's chosen his path. He won't deviate from it."

That's what I'd thought about Cynthia. About Sennor. "Would he if you let him?" I asked gently.

Ren didn't answer me, but said, "At any cost, we need to maintain our usefulness to the mages."

Or we'd die. He didn't say it, but we all heard it.

Ren had thought quickly when he'd said I was necessary to finding the library. The words of the poem ran through my head again and again until they lost all meaning. My life would depend on figuring it out. Everyone's lives would depend on it. My father—had Janiis recaptured him? And Aleksa, Luc, and Cynthia . . .

I sniffed, and Mari slipped her hand into mine, her other hand in Enzo's.

"I don't think I like this adventure as much as our last one," Mari muttered, glaring at a crew member watching us. He spit something over the side of the ship and grinned at her with black teeth. She stuck her tongue out at him.

"I don't, either, Mari," I said.

The wind worsened as we traveled farther from Vera. Storm season was coming. Did these men intend to risk everything for the mage's reward? A single, swaying lamp hung near us, casting a sickly glow. There were no stars to guide us, just endless black as we churned through impossibly huge waves. One crewman dropped a rope as thick as my arm on our laps, looping it around the mast so we didn't tumble from the deck as the ship tilted.

We sailed on through the night, my head bobbing as I fell asleep only to be jerked awake by a wave. I wasn't sure how long it had been when someone nudged my foot. I blinked slowly awake, taking too long to shake off the fog of not enough sleep.

Cris stood in front of me, arms folded, scowl in place. "We need our course."

Ren laughed, dry and wheezing. "We've been traveling for ages. *Now* you need a course?"

Cris wrapped his hand around my arm just below my shoulder and lifted. I stood awkwardly, stumbling forward from under the heavy rope. Cris pointed his sword at Ren's stomach. A wound he wouldn't heal from.

I put my hands out to keep my balance. "It's okay. I'll look at the map and get the course." No problem. I'd studied plenty of maps before. This one . . . would be no different. Except my life would depend on it.

Cris sheathed his weapon. "If you try anything, one word from me and Jenna won't wake."

They had all the power. For now.

I shook my head, and Ren leaned back. "Just . . . be careful," he said to me.

Cris dragged me off before I could reply. We stumbled along the swaying deck, toward the square of light visible from the captain's quarters. I tripped up the steps.

Cris's grip tightened. "Don't try to escape."

"I'm not that good of a swimmer," I muttered back.

The door opened, and Cris shoved me in, then left. My first, traitorous thought was how *warm* the room was.

Then I caught the glares from Koranth, Redalia, and Brownlok.

"Oh yes," Redalia purred, polishing her dagger in the corner next to Brownlok. "I'm sure *she* will be able to do what we could not."

My skin prickled, remembering what Redalia had done to me before.

Confidence. Make them believe it. Just like every time I faced down an arrogant noble.

"The young king said you could interpret the map." Koranth swept his hand over a table bolted to the wall. Maps scattered its surface. "Interpret."

CHAPTER TWENTY-FIVE

Ren

When Cris had turned his back on me, guiding Chiara toward the captain's quarters, I wanted to follow and toss him overboard. But Mari was sniffling in her sleep, huddled against Enzo, who looked like he could use a warm fire and a soft bed. For a week.

"Sleep," I told him. "You'll need it."

He shook his head, staring into the night that had swallowed us. "How can I? They have her, Ren. I can't . . . I can't let anything happen to her."

I raised an eyebrow and leaned my head against the mast. "And I can?"

"Of course not, I just—"

"Relax," I sighed. "I only meant we're in agreement. We'll find a way to keep her safe. To keep everyone safe."

My body screamed for sleep, for food and water. My magic had healed the wound on my shoulder, though slower than usual. Enzo's body had been damaged far more than I expected. Once I'd started letting magic flow into him, his body pulled more and more for the hidden injuries I couldn't see. Bruises and cracked bones and his head . . . I shuddered against how much magic it had needed to heal.

Chiara had saved my life.

And Jenna? I still didn't know how badly she was injured. Her magic would work to heal her physical injuries, but what else had Koranth and Redalia done? Marko's body had been healthy enough, yet he'd remembered nothing of his life. Had they done the same to Jenna?

I ran my tongue along the dry roof of my mouth. I'd had nothing to eat in way too long. Nothing to drink. Water sloshing against the boat, the gentle swaying, kept my thirst at the forefront.

Never before had I been so out of control of a situation. The knife in my boot may as well have been a soup spoon. I couldn't take out five crewmen, three mages, and my traitorous best friend on my own.

I wasn't strong enough to save everyone.

"If something does happen to me," I said quietly to Enzo, "or if you have the chance to save everyone else, promise me you'll get them away?"

Enzo was silent for so long I thought he'd fallen asleep. "Same," he whispered finally. "I'll make the promise as long as you promise me as well."

Jenna would never forgive me if something happened to Enzo. It had to be me. I'd make sure it was. "I promise."

Enzo shifted so Mari was more comfortable, then rested his head back against the mast. Soon his breathing was deep and even. I envied his ability to sleep, though the head injury and healing probably had something to do with it.

Different situations ran through my head, possible strategies to outmaneuver the mages. Despite their magic, Koranth's shade blade, and Redalia's gold dagger, they remained massively ignorant: they'd left the ring in my pocket, and Cris had the Medallion.

Brownlok knew the value of the artifacts. The others didn't. Perhaps they assumed Brownlok still held the Turian ring. Or perhaps they knew their power outweighed everything else.

In every scenario I came up with, someone fell by the wayside—I couldn't save everyone. Couldn't even think up a scenario where everyone except me made it out.

The black boots were back.

I groaned—softly, so I wouldn't wake Enzo and Mari. "Miss me already? Or did the grown-ups kick you out of their important meeting?"

Cris scoffed and leaned against the railing, arms folded, sneer in place. "Even now, your arrogance makes you assume you'll remain unharmed. That those you love will remain unharmed."

Not strong enough. I held tight to the rope around us, fighting the urge to push Cris overboard. "What happened to Jenna?"

He lifted his chin. "Mage Koranth is keeping her poisoned. Just enough of a dose to keep her asleep and alive."

Poison. Not an injury, then. Wouldn't take as much magic to heal her, if I ever got the chance. "Why?"

"To keep you in line," he said, like it was the most obvious thing. "And so Redalia can have her revenge after they've found the library."

I rolled my eyes, but tucked the information away. Redalia needed the library first. "Not that, ice head. Why *you*? What do you get from of this alliance? You really think *mages* will keep *you* around after they've gotten what they want?" I swallowed and stared at his boots, forcing the words out, though I didn't want to. But for Chiara—for all of them—I'd try. "We were friends."

Cris crossed one leg over the other, casual as ever. "Is it really friendship when you're set to be the next ruler and I couldn't even get my own father to acknowledge me?"

I hadn't known Leland was Cris's father until they'd both betrayed me—how long had he known? How long had he been seeking Leland's approval, and keeping it from me?

We'd been close. But Cris had always been aware of our differing statuses—little things, like who entered a room first, how he'd fade into the background in certain situations. I never cared about any of that; I thought he hadn't minded.

I rubbed my aching forehead. "*Yes*. To me, we were friends. They'll kill us, Cris. You're going to watch that happen and do nothing?" He didn't have an answer to that. No snarky comeback. "Why do you persist in this path?"

He turned away, a silhouette against the nothingness beyond. "There was no going back. You'd never have forgiven me."

He said the words so quietly I had to strain to hear them.

Was he right? Was Chiara? My anger still boiled hot—too hot to touch—but *never*? "I might have," I finally said.

He laughed. "We both know that isn't true."

My jaw was so tight it ached, but I had to continue. "I hope I would have forgiven you. Cris, this is insanity. These are *ancient mages*. They won't share their power with you once you've served your purpose."

He finally turned around, bleakness streaking from his eyes down his shoulders and into the tips of his fingers and boots. "Then I'll need to maintain my value."

He stalked away, up the short stairs next to the wheel, and didn't look at me again.

I wasn't sure whether I wanted to hit something or curl up and sleep. How could he claim to be my friend, yet turn from me so quickly, so completely? How had I missed the mask my *best friend* wore?

I tucked my legs up and wrapped my arms around them, settling my head on my knees so I could watch the door that hid Chiara. I touched my chest where the Medallion had been. I'd come to rely on it, and now my dependence hobbled me.

I didn't know what to do, which path to choose. When to fight, when to wait. But I guess its magic wouldn't have worked on the sea, anyway.

Chiara was powerless in there. Her key to survival was an old poem committed to memory, one we'd already solved to find the map.

Mari jerked awake, like she'd had a nightmare. "Hey, it's okay," I told her. She wiped tears from the corner of her eyes. "Here," I said, holding out my hand.

She slipped hers into mine. "You can keep holding my hand," she said, even as her eyes drifted closed again. "Brownlok said I helped keep him from fading away."

Her voice drifted off and she settled back into sleep. She was right. She *did* help me feel like I wasn't fading away.

The boat continued to roll and heave as we tried to stay ahead of the storm. A line of bright light seared my eyes, startling me from the half sleep I'd fallen into.

The door opened, and I caught a glimpse of two people—Koranth and Brownlok?—before a man escorted Chiara back to the mast. I didn't want to release Mari, but I wanted her and Chiara between Enzo and me, so I slid over to make room. She settled next to me with the same grace she'd use while wearing a fancy dress in a ballroom, tucking the rope back around her like she'd place a napkin on her lap at dinner.

But as soon as the man walked away, her shoulders rolled in and she tucked her knees up. I wished I could put my arm around her, and tugged at the knots at my wrists again. The rope only rubbed against my skin, which in turn drained another grain of magic to heal the burns forming.

"Are you okay?" I whispered. Mari and Enzo hadn't stirred.

She nodded, brows furrowed.

Why wasn't she saying more? What had they done to her? I touched her arm. My hand shook, and the edges of panic snuck under my guard. "Did anyone hurt you?"

Chiara blinked. "Oh. No. Just . . . thinking."

My eyebrows shot up. "Thinking? You go into a room alone with three mages and a captain of dubious origins, and you come out pondering life?" She laughed, and the sound loosened the panic's hold on my lungs. "What happened in there? What's got you thinking?"

She stared at the blackness beyond the ship's railing. "I did it. At least, I think I did."

I tilted my head. "Did what?"

"I figured out the map."

A slow smile grew. She glowed with pride—a little green cast to her skin, but still glowing. "How did you do it? Another pirate story?"

She chuckled. "I studied old maps with Yesilia. They're different—not based on the compass directions we use, so you have to know how to orient them. I matched up one of the captain's maps with the one we found using the inlet, where the random lines start." She paused and leaned closer. "Do you still have the ring Brownlok threw down?"

I nodded. "Brownlok didn't mention it?"

She shook her head. "Maybe Mari is right. He was willing to trade with us—"

"That doesn't mean we can trust him. It just means he has his own agenda." Something about what he said, that he'd trade Mari for one artifact, didn't sit right. Maybe he wanted the same artifact we needed for Marko. I didn't know what it looked like, only that it existed, so I wasn't much help there.

I flexed my fingers, trying to keep the numbness at bay. "Did you see Jenna?"

Chiara set her chin on her knees. "No. There was a small closet, though. Maybe she was in there? Or she could be in the hold under the deck."

Torches. Arches. I closed my eyes and breathed the fresh,

cold sea air. Jenna was alive. Cris had said Redalia wanted her alive.

"We'll find her, Ren," Chiara said, leaning forward to catch my eye. "She's strong. She'll be okay. We'll get out of this."

Chiara had more faith than I did. She shifted and tugged at her trousers, adjusting her too-big boots. "The *one time* I'm not wearing a skirt is the time we get kidnapped."

A chuckle rose in me at her unexpected comment. "You *want* to wear a skirt?" Jenna had moaned for *years* about being forced to wear dresses around the castle.

Chiara shrugged and tugged at her trousers again. "Of course! Layers means it's warmer, and men don't stare at my legs as much."

I immediately moved my gaze from her legs to her eyes, which were laughing at me. I bumped my shoulder against hers, and the panic loosened. I'd expected her to wilt under the pressure. We were on a boat with mages, probably sailing to our deaths, which would also mean the deaths of our families and our kingdoms. "You aren't . . . scared right now?"

She sighed, leaned closer. "I'm terrified. But that won't help us survive. And we *are* going to survive. I'm just not sure how yet."

If she hadn't lost her spark, neither would I. I tilted my head, grinning at her. "Well, tell me when you figure it out."

She frowned in concentration. "I will."

I swallowed and eased my hands between us, reaching for her hand.

She jerked away. "No! Don't waste your magic."

I almost teased her about sounding like Jenna. But the

words stuck. I cleared my throat. "It wouldn't be a waste, but no magic. I promise. I just . . . I just want to hold your hand." *Because the panic is threatening to choke me and last time your touch helped calm me.* But I couldn't say those words. "If that's okay?"

"Oh," she said on a sigh. She slipped her hand into my bound ones, and though her fingers were ice, heat flared in my chest. I'd find a way, somehow, to keep them all safe.

✦ ✦ ✦

The storm caught up to us in the night. Huge waves crashed into the boat, tipping and tilting us one way, then the other. Rain and waves soaked us in icy water, and it was all we could do to hold on to the rope around the mast to keep from being washed away.

The tempest finally eased as morning neared, and the crew found bits of canvas to wrap themselves in, content to sleep in their corners. I'd expected a crew like this to be loud, boisterous. But these men stayed quiet—because of the uncharted waters, or the mages?

Mari slept on Chiara's lap, her hand resting on mine. I still held Chiara's hand when we woke as the sun burst over the horizon. Mari's touch slowly regenerated my magic, somehow, despite my exhaustion. But my magic was still dangerously low.

When the sun rose behind us, there was little relief—the wind pulled its rays away. The cliffs loomed over us, a constant presence to our right.

We awoke before the sailors.

"We need to figure out a plan," I whispered. Brownlok steered the boat but wouldn't hear us from this distance. The others leaned closer. "We cannot let the mages find the Black Library." If they did, they'd be unbeatable, even against all the armies of the Plateau combined.

Enzo kept his arms folded, a permanent scowl etched on his face. "There are too many of them to fight off, even if we had weapons."

Chiara held Mari's hand. "Ren has the Turian key still. Could that be used to trade?"

I sighed and tilted my head from side to side. "All anyone has to do is threaten Jenna, and it's over. But once they stop giving her poison—"

Enzo looked at me sharply.

"Cris told me when he was threatening to kill us." I shrugged. "You needed sleep more than you needed to hear him spouting his garbage. But Jenna can't climb sedated. She can access my magic through her tethers. She lent me her magic so I could heal you back when Leland . . ." I could barely say the old man's name. I cursed my weakness and cleared my throat. "Maybe it goes both ways. Maybe I can lend her *my* magic, and she can use it to fight."

"She can't climb sedated," Enzo echoed.

"Could we take away Koranth's shade blade?" Chiara asked. "Then he'd be just a man, right?"

I nodded slowly. "That could take care of him. But Redalia still has her dagger. And we'd have Brownlok, as well."

Mari tucked her hands under her arms and leaned over for warmth. "I'm telling you, he's not mean like the others."

I sighed. "He may not be mean, but he has his own motives, Mari. He wants what he wants, and I don't know what he'd do to achieve his goals." Especially since it meant life or death for him. Survival or extinction.

Wait. Redalia was more or less fine without Graymere because she had her artifact. What if Brownlok wanted to *create* an artifact? What had Jenna said about the mages' artifacts? That they had to perform some sort of sacrifice involving a lot of blood . . .

He hadn't hurt Mari. Kept her whole and happy. She amplified magic.

Oh no. No no no no.

Brownlok wanted to *sacrifice* Mari and use something in the Black Library to create his artifact. Trade her life for his artifact.

Glaciers.

"We take them out one at a time, then," Chiara was saying. "We worry about Koranth first. Then Redalia. Then Brownlok. Then the crew."

Mari bobbed her head, unaware. Excited to be included. I bit the inside of my cheek. Hard. I'd have to warn the others. But I didn't want to scare Mari. Not if we didn't have to.

I nodded at Enzo. "One at a time. We see a chance, we take it." He nodded back, remembering our pact. I'd let Jenna take every last drop of my magic if it meant she could save the rest of them. Because I couldn't live with anything less.

CHAPTER TWENTY-SIX

Chiara

The thick canvas sail snapped in the wind, and silver-tipped seabirds darted overhead, splashing into the water in terrifying dives. We were given dry crusts of bread and a ladle of water midmorning, but nothing else.

No matter how I wished it, the wind never ceased, blowing us toward the mages' destination.

Take them out one by one. That was the plan. A plan that didn't involve me—I had no fighting skills. No magic.

As the sun rose in the sky, not quite at its apex, the cliffs loomed closer. We'd shifted directions until we skimmed alongside the solid face of rock jutting into the sky. The closer we came to the cliffs, the more the energy began to change on the ship. The captain called out more directions, and if the men didn't respond quick enough, he swore up a storm that made even Ren blush.

The fourth time Mari asked what a word meant, I covered her ears.

And then a massive inlet appeared. The sea flowed into what looked like a crack in the Plateau. The sun beat down, illuminating the jagged walls, the stripes in the different kinds of rock.

Two men lifted a huge anchor and dumped it overboard, and two others pulled at the ropes attached to the sail until it was neatly stowed away. Slowly, we came to a halt, the waves lapping against the ship, last night's storm a distant memory.

The captain's door creaked open, and Koranth emerged, then Brownlok and Redalia, followed by Cris, who carried Jenna. Her hair had mostly come out of her braid and draped over Cris's shoulder. She was pale. So pale. But her hand, fallen to her side, revealed a small ring on her middle finger—her artifact, which protected her from magic. My brows furrowed. Did they not know? Why had they let her keep it? The chain of the Medallion was still around Cris's neck. Did any of them realize what he held?

Next to me, Enzo tensed, and I prayed that Mari by his side would keep him from lashing out. We couldn't. Not yet.

They forced us all into a dinghy, and two crewmen who would stay with the boat lowered the dinghy into the sea.

Brownlok stayed by Mari's side. Redalia watched Ren with a smirk that gave me chills. Koranth kept caressing the bag at his side and muttering to himself.

It took the rest of the day to row to the inlet. The walls loomed on either side of us, and led us through a twisting canyon that darkened as the sun set, like we'd entered the heart of the Plateau. Koranth kept his nose pressed against the map, then squinted at the cliff walls around us, the brush on the shore on either side. Eventually, he called for us to land, even though the inlet continued.

When we lurched onto sand, Cris took Jenna off the dinghy first, then the others followed, each of the crewmen pulling a pack from under his bench. Ren and I were last, and the ground tilted under me until I got used to being on solid earth again.

The crewmen started making camp—one set the fire, another laid out bedrolls. Not enough for us, but enough for the captain and his men. Though from the way Redalia was eyeing the bedrolls, I figured she'd end up with one by the end of the night.

"You four, over there," Koranth said, pointing to a patch of dirt away from the fire. It'd be another long, cold night, but at least we'd be together.

Except Jenna. Cris had laid her near the mages.

We watched the crewmen prepare their dinner, our stomachs growling. One of the men brought us fish and raisins.

"Eat what you can," Koranth said from his spot by the fire. "Tomorrow, we climb."

I glanced at Enzo, and he and Ren had the same look. We might climb tomorrow, or tomorrow might be the day we escape. I wished there was some way I could help in the fight, but the most I could do was keep Mari out of the way. I only hoped it would be enough.

❖ ❖ ❖

A hand came around my mouth after I'd been asleep for what felt like seconds, and I startled awake. The hand was big and rough, but gentle. I sat up groggily with help. Stood. Then I saw Enzo and Ren asleep on the ground.

If it wasn't Ren . . . I scraped at the hand, but it clamped down tight on my face and another hand wrapped around my waist. I slammed my boots into his feet, kicked back against his shins, but he lifted me and staggered toward the base of the cliffs. I screamed against his hand, thrashed against his hold with everything I had.

"Quiet," he hissed. Cris. We were trapped between the Plateau and the water—what was his goal?

I twisted hard in his arms and was finally able to get away from his hand covering my mouth. But I didn't yell. "Cris, wait," I said quietly. I stopped thrashing, stopped struggling. It surprised him enough to loosen his hold. "If we join together, we can defeat the mages—"

"What do you think you're doing?" Ren's voice growled behind us.

Cris's arm wrapped around my throat and the sharp ring of metal cut through the night as he drew his sword. "I'm maintaining my value," he hissed. The others hadn't woken. It was just Ren, matching Cris's steps, hands bound in front of him.

I raised my chin, trying to get enough air to speak. "Cris, no one's awake. Let's get out of here. We get Jenna, take the boat, go home."

"I have no home," he snarled, and his arm squeezed my neck. Sennor and Cynthia had needed another chance, had taken it when offered. Why wouldn't he take this chance?

"Cris—" Ren started.

"I'm not stupid. I know the mages will kill me when they're done with me. I have to do this. I have to take her."

Ren took a step closer. Bound hands, no weapon. What was he doing?

"Why her?" Ren asked, fury edging his words.

Cris scoffed. "She can read the map. She can interpret it. I have her, I have the knowledge."

Ren didn't say anything to that—only stalked closer.

"Cris." I stood on my tiptoes trying to find air. My voice was nothing more than a sandy whisper. "We're your friends—"

"I have no friends!" His voice boomed in my ear, followed by pressure on my neck and a *pop* that reverberated so loud every other sound, every other sensation faded. Then the pain came as its echo. Blinding, raging pain.

My lungs heaved, but there was no air to take in, like my . . . like my throat had collapsed.

A crunch came from the side, a dark figure nothing more than a blur. It slammed into us, and I hit the ground in a heap. The muffled sounds of a fistfight, the glint of a sword in the grass out of my reach. I didn't care. I writhed on the ground, scratching at my neck as my vision faded.

Cold hands rested featherlight on my neck, warming more and more until their heat consumed me. The *pop* repeated, but no pain followed. Just air. Beautiful, crisp air that tasted like dirt and the sea and the night. I pushed Ren's hands away, breaking his contact with my skin.

Someone stepped in the grass near my arm. The glint of metal caught the edge of my vision. Cris bent, dragged the sword out of the grass. A dark stain spread from his nose.

"Look out!" I gasped. Ren crouched on one knee over me, as if to shield me from the sword.

Cris's blade came down at Ren.

"No!" I wanted to scream, to rage and leap to his aid. But all that came out was a whisper.

Then Ren's bound hands came up, a big rock within his grasp. He used it to deflect Cris's blade just enough to miss his shoulder. Ren grabbed Cris's arm, forcing the blade of the sword deep into the ground, then wrenched a dagger from its sheath at Cris's waist. Ren spun fast and tripped Cris, sending him sprawling into the grass. He held the dagger between his knees and cut the rope binding his wrists.

By that time, Cris was up again, several steps away, watching Ren warily.

"We're not friends," Ren said.

Laughter rang through the camp. Both men froze, though Ren never took his eyes off Cris. Everyone was awake now, watching the two Hálendians fight. Enzo held Mari tight, keeping her from running to help and getting in the way of their blades.

Redalia stood on the shore, robes draped around her. "Oh no, by all means continue," she said with a melodious chuckle. "I'd love to see who wins in this little battle of wills."

Koranth stood next to her, arms folded over his chest like he was watching a bit of sport.

No. Each breath stung. My knee throbbed. I dragged myself backward as fast as I could, out of their path, but they stood between me and camp.

"Isn't this what you wanted?" Ren taunted Cris, spinning

his blade as he stalked closer, a dark tone in his voice I'd never heard before. "Or did you only want to fight if I was weaponless?"

Cris spit blood from his mouth to the side. "Always so arrogant. Pretending to know what's best for others, what everyone else wants."

"Yet you can never figure out what *you* want. So don't—"

Cris interrupted with a lunge. I don't know how Ren did it—the move was too fast for me to see—but his dagger slid along Cris's sword, tangling with the hilt, and suddenly the sword was flying through the air. Cris punched Ren's arm, and he dropped the dagger but snagged the sword.

They circled each other once again. Cris tilted his head. "Just like old times. Except Jenna won't save you now. No one will."

He sidestepped Ren. I didn't realize he was coming for me until he was too close. I tried to scramble up, to run. He grabbed me. "*I* am valuable. *She* isn't!" he screamed, the words ringing in my ears.

How could I be *so useless* that he could use me against Ren twice?

Ren went still. Everyone did. The air around Ren changed. Darkened. His hand raised slowly, palm forward. He stalked closer, picking his way through the brush.

"Let her go," he said, his voice flat and hard. "You want to fight? Fine, let's fight." He closed his hand into a fist, and I gasped as Cris released me. Not because the pressure was gone, but because I'd felt it—whatever Ren had done. Like a thick rope had slithered by me and wrapped around Cris.

Cris fell to his knees, mouth open in a silent scream, arms at his sides. In the background somewhere, Redalia clapped.

"No!" I yelled, and ran at Ren. I hit him full force, but he didn't break focus, didn't release Cris from the torture. Ren's eyes grew darker until they were almost black. "No, Ren," I said softly, brushing my hand against his arm. "Not like this. This isn't who you are."

His face twitched, and his hand wavered. "It's who I could be."

"No. Nothing is worth the cost of becoming like them." He still didn't move, and Cris was turning an alarming shade of gray. "Ren," I whispered right in his ear. "Please. Don't make this choice."

Ren's eyes met mine, and for one brief moment, I thought I'd lost him. But then Cris slumped to the ground. Ren's face crumpled, and his hand dropped to his side.

"I didn't mean . . . I almost . . ." He trailed off, shaking, staring over my shoulder where Cris lay. He fell to one knee, and I steadied him.

"Excellently done," Redalia purred from her spot by the coals. "I'm not sure even I could have picked out his life force when he was so close to—"

"Look out!" Enzo called.

I turned in time to see Cris lurch up, knife in hand. He pulled back and released it, and I watched, horrified, as it came at me, flying end over end.

Ren was there, sword in hand, and batted the knife out of the air as though it were a leaf. His sword shook in his hand and he left the point in the dirt. His chest heaved. My heart tripped and sped against my ribs, painful and too fast.

"Stand down, Cris," Ren said hoarsely. "It's done. I don't want to fight you. This isn't who you are."

Cris picked up a rock and threw it at us. Ren put his hand out, and the rock smacked into his palm. What was Cris *doing*?

Cris picked up another rock. "It's *done* when I say it's done," he snarled. He threw the rock, but it went wide. He took another lurching step toward us. "You don't get to command me in this. You don't get to tell me how I feel or what I deserve or *who I am*."

I stayed behind Ren as Cris advanced, backing us toward the river.

"What are you talking about?" Ren growled. He held his sword in front of him.

"You can't *save* me. I could have stopped my father, and saved yours. But I didn't. Nothing can change that." His voice wavered. "It's my fault you're all here—"

One of my feet landed in icy water. I gasped, sharp pinpricks shooting up my leg.

Ren's focus turned to me, to see what had happened. Just for a moment. A breath. A heartbeat.

So he didn't see what I saw. How Cris lunged forward, impaling himself on Ren's blade.

Ren's eyes widened and his lips parted. His head snapped forward and he released the hilt like it was on fire. But it was too late.

Cris fell to his knees, the sword deep in his chest, blood spreading over his shirt. He looked up at Ren, and in a gurgling whisper, said, "I'm sorry."

He'd . . . he'd . . . I'd offered him another chance. Why didn't he take it? Why . . .

He fell to one side, eyes open. Unseeing. Ren stood frozen, staring at his now-lifeless friend. I reached my hand out to him as if moving through molasses. As soon as it touched his arm, he flinched away from it, from me. He fell to his knees, hands outstretched to his friend, his face almost as gray as Cris's.

No. He didn't have enough magic. Not after healing me. Not after everything. It would kill him.

"Do not waste your magic on him," Koranth said from across the camp. "If you touch him, you won't be able to wake your sister." His black sword was at Jenna's neck. "And if you so much as touch that sword or knife, she dies."

Ren stopped, hands hovering over his friend as the last of his blood seeped out. His shoulders rounded. His eyes shut and he released a deep, long breath. "Don't hurt her," he whispered in a broken voice.

Water lapped at the shore. Someone in camp shuffled their feet. I thought my heart had maybe stopped. I would give anything to take back that cursed gasp. It was only cold water in my shoe. Such a small thing shouldn't carry such a price.

Koranth sheathed his sword and brushed off his hands like he'd been hard at work all morning. "Well, since we're all awake, we might as well get climbing."

We were so close to the Black Library. Too close. Not enough time, not with Ren broken, Jenna poisoned, Enzo still healing.

The crew started gathering their packs and supplies. Ren pressed his hands into the ground to force himself to stand. I didn't reach to help him. He wouldn't want my help. It was my fault he'd turned away. My fault he hadn't seen what Cris intended.

No one muttered about skipping breakfast. Not when Cris lay still next to the bank and Ren stared at the cliffs, unmoving, in the exact spot he'd tackled Cris. He lowered himself to his knees, using one hand, then the other, as though he were an old man with a bent and broken back. He wiped his hands in the grass. There was still blood on them when he stood.

When they were ready to start searching for a path up the cliffs, Koranth went to Cris and pulled the blade free from his chest and cleaned it. "It's a Hálendian blade. Worth too much to leave here." He tossed it to one of the crew, who reluctantly caught it. Then he dug the toe of his boot under Cris, and rolled him over once, twice, until the water carried him away.

I swallowed and turned my eyes away. Enzo's arm came around me; Mari's hand slipped into mine. But Ren stood apart from us. Just a step, but still apart.

CHAPTER TWENTY-SEVEN

Ren

I'd killed him.

"Keep up," the man behind me said, kicking my leg.

I sidestepped away from him and shook my foot. The Medallion settled lower in my boot, by my ankle. When Cris and I had fought, I'd pulled at the chain. I'd found it lying there in the grass after . . . after . . .

Glaciers.

Long grass brushed against my knees as we trudged along the base of the cliffs. If the mages wanted to get up so badly, they could find the passage without my help. Kais had been a land mage—he could have formed a stairway up, then erased its presence just as easily.

"What if there *is* no way up?" Mari grumbled from her spot in line. They'd left my hands untied. Perhaps they were optimistic to find a way up the cliffs. Or maybe they could see how useless I was in my current state. Either way, crewmen separated all of us. Jenna was still slumped over a crewman's shoulder at the back of the line. Enzo barely kept up, limping.

Koranth heard Mari's question from his place at the front. "Then your sister dies."

Chiara didn't react to the bait. She'd been the only thing stopping me when my rage at Cris had taken over. Cris's life force had been bright and powerful; I'd wanted it for myself, on some deep level. But Chiara had been there, had stopped me.

If I'd been wearing the Medallion, it would have gone the coldest it'd ever been.

My magic had never felt like that before. Dark. Heady. I'd almost done to Cris what Redalia had done to my father.

And while there had been a time I'd wanted to kill Cris, I realized how wrong I'd been. I wanted him to be held accountable for his actions, but not like this.

Bile rose in my throat as the vision of Cris lying half in the water, half out hit me again. The horror in Chiara's eyes, the weight on my sword.

His death didn't fix anything. My father was still dead. Our friendship was still destroyed. I was still alone. And I'd almost become like Redalia.

Cris hadn't been wearing a mask as my friend. He'd worn the mask when he turned away from me.

I stumbled to the nearest bush and retched behind it.

"Stay in line," the gruff voice behind me commanded.

I wiped my face on the hem of my shirt and stumbled back.

We'd been walking for at least two hours, and the sun had just barely risen.

But a sliver of an opportunity had arisen with the artifact scraping against my calf.

Chiara had studied the map, and I had the two keys. If I could keep the mages from realizing that, we could sneak away tonight after everyone slept—find the Black Library first. Destroy it before they realized what we'd done.

"Here!" Brownlok called from ahead. "I've found a stairway!"

We all trudged forward, and sure enough, around a slight bend in the cliff wall, long, narrow stones marked a path upward, one that switched back and forth and looked like it had been preserved perfectly despite the ages it had been there.

How close was the Mages' Library to the top of the cliff? How much time did we have?

Koranth's eyes lit from within, a black fire behind them. Redalia grinned her most terrifying grin, and Brownlok had found a place next to Mari once again.

Glaciers, I needed to find a way to keep him away from her, needed to warn the others of his plan.

"All right," Koranth said, turning his glare on me. "Wake your sister."

The crewman who had been carrying Jenna over his shoulder dumped her on the ground next to me.

Before anyone could react, Brownlok whispered something in Mari's ear, then put a knife at her throat. "Don't try anything heroic," he said to me. "Just wake her."

Enzo lunged at Brownlok despite Chiara trying to hold him back. Redalia drew her golden dagger and stepped between them.

Koranth's chin lifted. "Well? What are you waiting for?"

I went to where the crewman had dumped Jenna and gently rolled her onto her back. A bruise was growing on her forehead, probably from being carted around like a sack of grain. But other than that, she appeared whole, if thin.

"Have you been giving her food and water?" I asked, brushing her hair out of her face. "Because she won't be able to climb if she's weakened from hunger."

Koranth gestured to one of the crewmen carrying a huge pack, and he tossed me a bag with dried fruit, meat, and a waterskin. "Then it's your responsibility to make sure she can make it."

Redalia's eyes flashed, and she folded her arms tight. "We shouldn't waste food on someone who will die soon anyway," she muttered, but loud enough that everyone heard. Chiara's hand wrapped through Enzo's arm, keeping him from lunging at Redalia.

Chiara hadn't looked at me since I'd killed Cris.

I shook away the thought. Heal Jenna. I slipped one hand into hers, then rested my other palm against her cheek. Everyone watched. Would they be able to tell I'd lost awareness? Would I even have enough energy within me to heal her? Or would she wake and I . . . not?

My eyes fell closed and I released the magic within me. Sparks prickled against my palms. A pocket of cold, of darkness, lay in her middle, and while most everything else was whole and healthy, the poison kept sucking and sucking at my magic.

She gasped and startled awake, breaking the connection between us.

"Ren?" she asked. The world tilted under me, and she steadied me. She took in the cliffs rising above us, the cold wind whistling in the canyon. "Where are we?"

"Don't do anything stupid," I whispered, pressing a hand to my head to stop the spinning.

"Welcome back, Princess," Koranth sneered. Jenna tensed. I squeezed her arm. Redalia's smile had faded and Brownlok still held Mari apart from the others.

"Don't do anything stupid," I whispered again, nodding toward Mari and Brownlok. Her eyes found Enzo and stayed there. Everything in her gaze softened, and if she'd been able to walk, she probably would have jumped up and run to him. "Drink," I told her. "Then food. Then we climb."

She gulped down water, then pushed the waterskin away with a groan. "Climb?"

I nodded up the cliffs, my stomach sour and hands clammy. "We get to see the Black Library. Do you think the treasure hunters back home will be impressed?"

She ignored me, her eyes still on her betrothed. She took my arm and I helped her stand and hobble over to the others. Enzo wrapped his arms around her and buried his face in her neck.

"Your men first, Captain," Koranth growled. The captain didn't look happy about it, but he and his men complied, taking careful steps on the smooth stones. "Now you four. We'll be keeping Mari with us."

Brownlok tucked Mari to his side, and though her brows were furrowed, she wasn't scared. She wasn't, but I was.

Enzo led the way, with Jenna next, then me, then Chiara. I didn't like her behind me, where I couldn't help if something happened, but Jenna needed both Enzo and me. Her legs were shaking by the first switchback.

"Here, drink more," I told her, pulling the waterskin up and helping her drink while Enzo steadied her. "Maybe we can get to the library first," I muttered. "Destroy the artifacts before they get them."

"Maybe," she whispered. But she was too weak to outdistance any of Koranth's men. And we couldn't leave her behind.

"Keep moving!" Koranth barked from below us.

"You should have gone ahead of us if you didn't want to wait," I snapped back. "Or you should have let me wake Jenna sooner."

I closed the waterskin and we started moving again. As we rose, the rocks and dirt turned a shade of red I'd never seen before. By the time the sun burned directly overhead, a shout rose from the crewmen ahead of us.

Enzo had his arm wrapped around Jenna and was supporting most of her weight. My legs burned, and I both wanted to stop climbing and to never reach the top. If we reached the library before nightfall, we'd need another plan.

My eyes were glued to the next step, my lungs focused on taking the next breath, when the stairs evened out. The land opened before us, a wash of crimson sand blowing over packed dirt. Black rock peeked out from scrubby brush like patches of diseased skin. The entire earth appeared to list to the side, sloping to the left, all the way to the looming red rock mountains on the horizon. They rose in peaks, shadows, and harsh lines like the rock had been thrust out of the ground recently.

On either side of the stairway, huge red rock formations rose from the ground like statues carved by the wind itself, a strange, twisted mimicry of the twin peaks at Riiga's border.

"Whoa," I whispered. Up here, the wind carried the day's heat, and the sun beat off the ground in shimmering waves.

But . . . there was nothing. No library, black or otherwise. No trail marked. A tiny drop of relief cooled my fear: we had more time.

Chiara climbed up behind me, and her mouth dropped open at the view. Dark circles marked her eyes, and exhaustion stooped her shoulders.

Brownlok came next with Mari, guiding her away from us. Chiara and I moved closer to Enzo and Jenna as Redalia and Koranth crested the final stairs.

The three mages stood in a line, taking in the expanse before us, and some insane voice in my head whispered to push them off the cliff. Redalia blew me a kiss, as if she could read my thoughts and dared me to try.

Koranth's maniacal grin melted away. "Where is it?" He pointed a long, bony finger at Chiara. "You said it would be at the top of the cliffs!"

"No, I showed you how to find the inlet," she said with a big swallow. "It's up here somewhere—check the map."

He pulled the map out of his bag, almost ripping it in his haste. He, Redalia, and Brownlok studied it, while the captain and his crew drank from their waterskins.

But the mages didn't ask Chiara to advise. She bit her bottom lip, brows furrowed. I shook my head and whispered, "Let them try to figure it out on their own first." Then she'd appear even more useful if—when—she figured it out.

I sat on the rocks to wait by the red monoliths guarding the stairs, and the others followed. How was it so cursedly hot up here this close to winter?

The waterskin I still carried didn't have much left, but I passed it to the others anyway. They each drank, and then Chiara handed it back, her fingers brushing mine. I flinched. How could she stand to touch me? Not when I'd—

I lifted the opening to my mouth and took one swallow. It wouldn't be enough. Not for this desert wasteland.

"I have an idea," I started quietly. I stretched out my legs and kept watch on our captors. No one paid us any attention. "I have the Medallion and the ring. Chiara, do you remember the map well enough to guide us?"

She bit her lip and dug the toe of her boot into the dirt. "I think so, but how—"

"It was in the grass," I said, cutting her off. Jenna studied me carefully. I cleared my throat. "The mages don't know I have it, don't know its worth. Tonight, we can sneak away after everyone is asleep. If we get to the library first—"

"What if we reach it today?" Jenna asked, resting her elbows on her knees.

Enzo handed her more food from the almost-empty pouch. "Are we close?"

Chiara shrugged. "The map didn't show a clear path from the top of the cliffs to the library. I'm not sure."

I ran my hand through my hair to dislodge the dirt and sand. "So we keep to our first plan if an opening arises. Jenna, you can access my magic through the tethers, right?" She nodded, rubbing her hand against her leg. "What if you use my magic to shield yourself, knock Koranth's sword away, and take Redalia's blade?"

Enzo scratched his jaw. "Ren and I can get the crew's weapons. Chiara and Mari would have to stay close so they couldn't be used against us."

Chiara winced a little, but nodded.

Jenna scrubbed her hands over her face, like she was trying to wake up fully. "Brownlok has been sticking too close to Mari."

I wiped the sweat from my forehead, the sand gritty against my skin. "Mari said something to me earlier, when we were on the ship. Brownlok told her she helped him feel like he wasn't fading away. I felt the same way when she touched my hand, like she amplified what magic I had left."

Chiara frowned. "So Brownlok needs her to keep his magic strong? *Mari* has magic?"

"I can see magic," Enzo said with a shrug.

"And magic usually runs in families," Jenna added. "When that shade attacked me in the dungeon, there's no way I could have made it, not with my wounds. But Mari was there the whole time. Holding my hand, helping me along."

Chiara dug the toe of one boot into the dirt and muttered something I couldn't hear. But the mages would need Chiara to interpret the map soon, so I had to spit it out now. Had to warn them.

"It's not just that." I leaned my elbows on my knees. "When

Brownlok first approached Chiara and me, he offered us a trade—he gave me the Turian ring and said he'd trade Mari's life for one artifact if we helped him find the Black Library." I swallowed and rubbed my hands together. "But I think he meant literally—that he wanted to use Mari's life and something in the Black Library to *create* an artifact for himself, like Redalia's dagger."

Jenna turned a little green. "To create an artifact like that you need—"

"Blood," I finished. "A lot of blood."

Chiara put her head in her hands. "But Koranth and Redalia don't know," she whispered. We leaned closer. "Brownlok has kept Mari away from them this whole time. I think Brownlok knows Mari amplifies magic, and the others don't."

The closer we got to the Black Library, the more I had to face the reality that I might have to choose between them all. Choose who to save. Jenna or Chiara? Enzo or Mari?

A wave of chills skittered down my back despite the heat. "We can't let Korenth and Redalia figure it out. Can't let Brownlok hurt Mari."

"This way!" Koranth finally yelled, bunching up the map, eyes darting around like maybe if he looked hard enough the Black Library would appear.

They hadn't consulted Chiara. She stood and brushed the dirt from her trousers and tried to smile. We'd need to find our chance to escape soon. Before our usefulness expired. Before we escorted the mages to the Black Library. Before I had to choose between them.

We followed, the crewmen in the rear. The four of us stayed close, Brownlok and Mari walking behind.

My first steps into the red sand had me stumbling to a halt. My magic trickled down, leeching into the ground.

This wasn't regular sand—it was a demon version of the sand in the cave behind the waterfall where we'd found the map.

Jenna paused, too. Enzo and Mari didn't seem to notice any change.

I lifted a shoulder, and Jenna shrugged in response.

"What is it?" Chiara asked softly.

I frowned. "It feels like the earth is trying to swallow me. Do you feel it?"

Her eyebrows pinched together. "It's hard to walk in the sand and with the tilt, but not bad. Not like before, when—" She shuddered, then studied me, squinting. "Do you feel okay? You look tired."

I rubbed my hand along my face, the rough stubble scratching against my palm, grains of sand trickling down. "I'll be okay," I said, though I *was* tired. I hadn't had time to recover from healing Jenna, and whatever new trick this was made it worse. Moving my legs turned into a chore, like rocks had been tied to my ankles.

Brownlok and Koranth both sagged as they stepped into the sand, and Redalia let out a hiss. At least it affected us all.

We walked. And walked. *And walked.* Yet the mountains remained firmly out of reach. Worse, the sun was stuck in the sky, hovering nearly overhead. Every breath stung, and my tongue was a dry scrap in my mouth.

Finally, when at *least* another hour had passed and nothing had changed, I stopped and put my hands on my knees, inhaling more sand than air. "We aren't *going* anywhere!" I yelled at the ground. I didn't want to anger the mages, but if we didn't get out of this heat soon, we'd all die anyway.

Koranth screamed in frustration and stalked toward Chiara. "Why didn't you say we were going the wrong way?"

She backed away, step by step while I eased between them. "I'd need to look at the map to know which way to go! You didn't ask me!"

Koranth stopped. Shook his head hard enough that a few chunks of hair fell out and drifted to the red sand. Turned to Redalia. "I *knew* we needed a better path to the gorge. I told you, Redalia. You never listen to me!"

My head jerked back at his wild accusation, at his body's decay. Enzo, Jenna, Chiara, and I scooted a little closer. Mari wasn't close enough to grab from Brownlok, but this might be our only chance. Could we risk it? Brownlok wouldn't hurt Mari. Not yet.

But if it was kill the mages or lose Mari . . . could I make that choice? I couldn't swallow, and my empty stomach rolled.

Redalia didn't draw her weapon. She tilted her head. "I used to listen to you." The crewmen clustered tighter, muttering.

Koranth shook his head again, more hair coming loose. "We shouldn't even be here. We should be in Turia. Expanding Riiga onto the Plateau."

I looked over at Enzo, and he frowned back. What was Koranth talking about? He'd been driven like a madman toward the Mages' Library, and now, all of a sudden, he wanted to be in Turia?

Brownlok strode past us and spoke low to Koranth. But Koranth jerked away and spun so he faced open desert instead of his comrades. "No!" he yelled . . . to himself? "No. This is the way to solidify Riiga's status."

Redalia glared at Koranth, her arms folded tight across her chest.

"Get Mari," I whispered to Chiara. My eyes locked with Jenna's and Enzo's. I gave Jenna a tight nod, and she winked out of existence.

Enzo and I leapt at the crewmen, who shouted alarm when Jenna disappeared. A hole opened within me, like someone had pulled out the plug and my magic was draining away. I threw my fist at the nearest man, taking his club from his belt and hitting his temple with it. A sword would be better, but I'd make do.

I swung the club as fast and hard as I could, keeping one eye on Enzo and one on Chiara, who'd dashed to Mari and kept us between them and the mages. Someone got a kick in to my back, and I grunted and fell to one knee, then swung the club behind me, connecting with something solid.

Koranth had drawn his blade, but it was knocked away into the red sand by Jenna's invisible hand. Or maybe foot. I didn't know, or care, as long as she could get to Redalia before I had nothing left.

The black blade fizzled to nothing in the red sand. Koranth screamed.

A flash of gold, and Redalia's dagger was in her hand. She

raised it slowly, lazily, and flicked her wrist. Jenna winked back into existence and flew backward, rolling into sagebrush. The connection between us dissolved. I cursed—she was too drained from the poison, too weak to carry a fight like this.

A fist connected with my jaw. My head jerked to the side and I stumbled over someone's leg, landing hard in the red dust.

"You cannot win," Redalia snarled, and lifted her hand as though she'd kill Jenna right here.

"Wait!" Chiara yelled, and jumped in front of Jenna's prone form. "You need her."

Someone kicked my ribs and the club was ripped out of my hands.

Almost within reach, Enzo lay on the ground, too, weaponless. Overpowered.

Redalia held her gold dagger ready; Brownlok wielded Jenna's sword. Koranth hadn't disintegrated like his shade blade. Pity.

Chiara stood before the three mages, her trousers dirty beyond belief, her tunic even dirtier, and her hair a snarled mess. Yet her posture was perfect. Proud.

Koranth dragged his hand down and formed a *new* black blade out of the air and sheathed it. "How do we reach those mountains?" he asked Chiara, his voice deadly low.

Sweat dripped down my back and red dust covered me, seeping into my skin like poison. I was so far away. So tired and drained. I wouldn't have enough magic if they hurt her.

"If you read the poem in the corner, it explains." She hesitated a long moment. Winced. "There's . . . a key. You need the key."

I clenched my teeth to keep from correcting her. She'd lied to keep the Medallion in my boot. But if they found out . . .

Koranth had frozen, his left eye twitching. "The key," he muttered. "Where is the ring?" he bellowed, his voice echoing strangely despite the open desert.

He pulled his black sword. I leaned forward, ready to run to Chiara. A crewman pressed his club to my temple.

Koranth marched toward Brownlok. "You had it. You're hiding it from me. I *knew* you were a traitor!"

Brownlok raised a hand. "You are mistaken, I—"

Mari jumped between them. "No! Don't hurt Erron!"

Jenna, Enzo, Chiara, and I, and even Brownlok, all lunged for Mari. Koranth grabbed her, holding his sword to her throat. "Give me the ring!" he screeched, spit foaming at his mouth. The longer Koranth stood there, the more he came into focus. Like his edges had been blurred into the air, but now they sharpened. "I'll kill this one first. And then your precious Jennesara, then—"

I'd been so focused on Koranth and Mari that I'd forgotten Redalia was even there. But now she stood behind Koranth, a scowl on her face. A gold tip poked through Koranth's chest. Her dagger. She'd— His eyes disintegrated as we watched, turning to nothing but dust in his head.

Mari darted out from under Koranth's limp form and ran to Enzo. He turned her away so she wouldn't see Koranth's sightless eyes.

Redalia pulled her blade free with a jerk, and Koranth fell to the side. His black blade disintegrated. Brownlok stumbled to his knees.

Chiara put a hand over her mouth like she'd be sick. I was too thirsty to throw up.

"Now," Redalia said, her voice dangerously low. "Where is the ring?"

Brownlok sheathed Jenna's sword, which I didn't think wise, given how Redalia glared at him. "Atháren has it."

Redalia turned her venom on me. Better me than anyone else. I held up my hands, and the man holding his club to my temple backed off. "I have it here." I dropped to one knee. My hand slid past my pocket where the ring nestled and into my boot. "But we'll still need the map."

Redalia took the bait and looked at Koranth's body, at his bag. My fingers wrapped around the knife in my boot. I stood, stepped forward, and threw in one solid motion.

It should have hit her right in the heart, or where a normal person's heart would have been. But she caught the blade in her bare hand, a hair's width from her chest. A smile bloomed on her face like a bruise spreading under the skin. Then she laughed, a small chuckle growing until black tears streamed from the outside corners of her eyes and trailed down her cheeks.

She took my knife, turned it, and thrust it directly into the boulder next to her. As though the solid rock were nothing more than soft bread. She raised her hand, which dripped blood from the deep gouge, and licked her palm.

A sharp gust of wind blew razor bits of sand into my skin, and even with Koranth dead, I couldn't help but feel our situation had gotten infinitely worse.

"You see, young king?" she said, turning her palm toward us. "We are more alike than you know."

Her palm was perfect once again, not a scratch or scar marring it. My hands fell limp to my sides and my legs threatened to give out.

Redalia was a healer.

Enzo helped Jenna stand, and she took Chiara's and Mari's hands until we were huddled together again.

I'd almost pulled out Cris's energy—exactly like Redalia had done to my father. That's what Brownlok had meant when he'd said that anything could be twisted.

Her dagger glinted in the never-ending sun. It would be nearly impossible to kill a healer as powerful as she. And *with* an artifact?

We didn't stand a chance.

"You like this, young king?" she asked, smirking and lifting the dagger higher. "Don't touch it if you want to live. There's a reason Kais didn't steal my artifact. I enchanted this little beauty so it could only be wielded by one stronger than I am." She twirled the dagger one final time and slipped it into its sheath. "And since I absorb the life force of everyone I kill, I'm *very* powerful."

I eased down to my knees in the sand. We wouldn't win this fight. *Couldn't.*

CHAPTER TWENTY-EIGHT

Chiara

Redalia shook her long cloak out and sat demurely on a red boulder, its edges worn down by wind. "Now," she said, turning her burning gaze on me as Brownlok moved to stand at her shoulder, "the key."

I rubbed my aching throat.

If we gave up the keys, we gave up our last hope. Time to prove my worth. "There's a problem," I said softly.

"Yes, what?" Redalia snapped. "Speak up."

I clenched my hands at my sides. "One of the keys is—" I started, but Ren reached into his boot and pulled out the Medallion before I could finish. He handed it to me, along with the ring, and closed my fingers around them.

His gaze burned into me, even as he spoke to Redalia. "There's no problem."

Redalia tilted her head. "I suggest you find us a way through this desert, because I do not like being here." She pointed the tip of her dagger at me. "You will be the first to die if you delay."

She turned to speak with the captain, demanding more water. Brownlok stayed by her side, watching Mari carefully.

"She still wants to find the library?" I crouched, setting the keys in the dirt.

Ren knelt next to me. "She's always been after it—"

"No, *Graymere* has always been searching for it. And now Koranth," Jenna said.

"She has her dagger," I continued, studying the artifacts closely, trying to see with new eyes. "So why bother with all of this?"

Intricate runes covered the Medallion's face, once-deep etchings now soft and smooth with time and countless kings running their fingers over them. The ring was flat on both sides, unadorned save for one tiny mark, a chip on the edge.

Jenna turned each of the artifacts, flipped them over and back. "The Black Mage's crystal staff is in the library. And Graymere's sword."

I wiped the sweat trickling down my temples. Redalia was already unbeatable. Why would she need *more* power?

"Three keys," I muttered. "The map." Ren addressed Redalia and Brownlok. "We need the map."

Redalia smiled. "Then come and get it." She gestured to Koranth's body, which stared at the sun with sightless eyes. I swallowed down my rising stomach. The map was still in his bag at his side.

Ren pressed his hand against the ground to stand, but Redalia shook her head. "The girl—or no one."

"It's okay," I whispered.

It wasn't. I didn't want to go anywhere near that man. I could still feel the phantom pressure of his arms around me when he'd used me as a shield against Jenna before Graymere attacked the palace. It had been at *his* urging that Sennor cornered me in the garden.

But it was also my fault we were all here. Ren had followed me, and so had Mari, Enzo, and Jenna. *I* had been the one to figure out the clue. To find the map.

It was *my* fault Cris was dead. My fault the mages would soon find the Black Library.

The first step was the longest, and then I was at Koranth's body. Already, his skin flaked away as though he'd been dead for months, not minutes.

I knelt in front of his corpse. Held my breath. Carefully lifted the flap of his bag and reached inside. Koranth's weight shifted, almost like he flinched.

I jumped away with a scream, but the map stayed clenched in my hand.

Redalia's gaze drilled a hole in my back as I returned to the others, but I'd done it. Now we'd have to figure out a puzzle no one had solved in hundreds of years. Or we'd all die.

No pressure.

"The solution is in the poem," I muttered. "I'm sure of it."

Three keys to find the library black:
one in snow, the heart of attack.

Another within the heart,
and surrounding it, too,
a ring of flax, of brown and blue.
Two make up one, the key to the door.
Two kingdoms to hide, to be found nevermore.
The final key, not a key at all,
marks the journey's end,
its start at the wall.
Hidden both deep and high
Where neither snow nor heart can find
Where waves ne'er reach
and vineyards touch the sky.
You will find what you seek
behind the falling door,
that gives life, but takes it more.

It would take me *days* to decipher this. Days we didn't have. I turned to Jenna. "You do it. You defeated Graymere; you can figure this out."

She frowned and studied the map, then shook her head slowly. "I didn't even realize the words on the back of the drawing were important." She leaned closer and pointed at two lines. "These, though. I saw this written in the margins of a book when I was researching Graymere. 'Two make up one, the key to the door. Two kingdoms to hide, to be found nevermore.'"

Two make up one. What if— I snatched the two artifacts and placed the ring around the outside of the Medallion. I twisted the ring one way, then the other until the ring and the Medallion clicked together. "'Another within the heart, *and surrounding it, too,* a ring of flax, of brown and blue.'"

Ren's smile was the only one I could focus on, the only one that hit me. "And flaxen fibers woven together become very strong."

Enzo cleared his throat. "But that still doesn't help us find our way," he said, glancing to where Redalia smirked at us and Brownlok remained hidden under the hood of his cloak. Behind them, the crewmen were sprawled out taking sips from their waterskins.

Ren leaned in, brushing against my shoulder. He didn't move away. I needed him there, needed someone to help me carry the burden of responsibility.

Enzo moved the combined artifact over the map, trying to get the random markings on the Medallion to make sense. Turned it. Turned it again. He even tried twisting the artifacts so they'd separate again, but they wouldn't budge.

But that should have done something. *Two make up one, the key to the door.* Maybe this was just the key to the door. Maybe—I swallowed. Maybe the artifacts had nothing to do with the map.

"There has to be something else," Jenna said, glaring at Redalia and Brownlok. "Something we're missing. I am not letting those monsters spill one more drop of blood—"

Blood. "In the first book, the first clue Yesilia helped me find, it mentioned blood. Maybe . . . maybe the artifact needs blood to work or to show the path—"

Ren scooped up the artifacts and cradled them in his hands. "Redalia said I reminded her of Kais. Maybe someone with Kais's blood has to be the one to do it."

It was as good a guess as any, and our time was running out. I took his hand. "But just a little."

He pursed his lips in an attempt at a smile and ran his smallest finger against the edge. The chip in the ring cut his skin— just a nick, but a drop of blood splashed onto the Medallion, then another.

But the cut wasn't healing. A cut that tiny should have barely bled one drop. Ren was more drained than he let on.

"Chiara," Enzo whispered. "Look!"

I changed my focus from Ren's hand to the artifact. The ring shifted, turning around the Medallion. On its own. The chip Ren had cut his hand on stopped, pointing to the right.

I put one hand over my mouth. Redalia stood over us, a strange glint in her eyes.

"Very good," she murmured to me. "Maybe it was a good thing I didn't kill you after all." She gestured toward the maze of rocks and dust. "Lead the way, young king."

Brownlok stood and brushed sand off his cloak, his shoulders slumped. The crewmen grumbled, but hefted their huge packs once again. We'd figured out the clue, but that would only bring us closer to death. For us, and for everyone we loved.

✦ ✦ ✦

The mountains that had stayed perpetually in the distance finally grew larger as we approached. Ren held the keys, and as the chip in the ring moved, he moved with it, zigzagging across the desert, keeping the notch pointing forward like some sort of magical compass.

Time skipped ahead, making up for the hours we'd been trapped in the endless noon.

Hot wind blew against us, with giant dust clouds rising from the desert like monsters reaching for the sun. Patches of puffy clouds sped across the blue sky, yet their shade never reached us. In the distance, a whirlwind of red dust twisted from the ground up into the sky. The crewmen watched it uneasily, but I kept my eyes on the artifact. On Ren.

He was weakening. Something about the desert was pulling the magic from him and Jenna.

"Mari," I whispered. "Go hold Ren's hand while he walks. He needs your help."

Mari tipped her head, her tangled mess of curls falling to the side, but skipped ahead and slipped her hand into Ren's. He grinned down at her, almost like he used to. Before I'd plunged him into this mess.

I swallowed and kicked at the sand. The one time I'd tried to do something big, to be seen, I'd dragged everyone I loved into a death trap.

Redalia, Brownlok, and the crew walked behind us, an ever-present threat. The Black Library loomed somewhere ahead.

By the time we reached the mountains, the setting sun washed the landscape in an extra rinse of shimmering orange.

"We continue on," Redalia said in her calm, smooth voice. The crewmen shifted their packs, but not one uttered a word of dissent.

Huge chunks of rocks protruded from the earth like a hastily erected wall, a dry streambed the only narrow opening at their base. Ren and Mari led us into the gorge, a massive canyon through impossibly steep mountains. The land around us churned, the layers of exposed rock tilting at strange angles. They were different colors—reds and yellows, grays and browns, and even a little green, like they'd been mixed and tossed by a cook—and faded like they'd been blasted by the sun.

Pyramids of sand and rubble from fallen rock acted as buttresses to the sheer walls. The entire place was crumbling bit by bit, and we were walking straight into it.

When the sun fully set, a chill seeped into the landscape faster than I'd thought possible. My breath fogged in the night.

"I can't see the direction any longer," Ren called out. His voice sounded stronger than it had earlier.

"We must halt here!" the captain called from the back. Redalia snarled something at him, but the man actually showed some backbone and responded—something about the heavy packs and his men needing rest.

We stopped, circling close together in a wide part of the path. As we settled in, my stomach tight from hunger and my throat aching with thirst, I kept my head down, hoping the mages wouldn't change the situation. We had the key; we had Mari.

Ren brushed his hand against my arm. "You okay?"

The rasp of a sword being drawn silenced any reply. Brownlok held the blade at Enzo's neck. "I will hold the key for safekeeping," he said to Ren.

I tugged Mari closer as Ren tossed him the key. Brownlok shoved Enzo to the ground and stalked back to Redalia.

We were together, safe for now. But how long would that

last? The mages would kill us now, or kill us later. A tiny part of me hoped they took me first, because I didn't think I could watch anyone else die.

Ren knelt, slowly, achingly, and sprawled on the ground, too tired to even smooth out a patch of sand to sleep on.

Jenna, Enzo, Mari, and I curled up close. Mari chattered with Jenna until Redalia snarled at her to cease. I didn't know exactly why, but Redalia needed the Black Library. She wouldn't take these risks, otherwise.

I tried to stay awake, to figure out *something*, anything, to get us away, to keep us from the fate we were marching toward. But any way I tried to spin it, I didn't have the skills we'd need to make it out alive. I wasn't strong enough.

I was only good at helping the mages get what they wanted.

Stars shone bright against the black walls of rock jutting into the sky's domain. Ren shifted closer to me. Was he asleep? Or had he moved closer intentionally?

Jenna curled into Enzo's side. It was so cold, but I couldn't reach out to any of them. It was my fault we were all here. I should never have left the palace.

CHAPTER TWENTY-NINE

Ren

I'd never particularly liked sand, but whatever this red dust was, was atrocious. Last night, I'd tried to stay awake and think of a way to get the keys back from Brownlok. Sleep had claimed me too soon. When I woke, I felt more tired, more drained than when I'd gone to sleep. Jenna looked marginally better than I felt. Even Redalia and Brownlok looked worse for wear.

Chiara had been distant yesterday, and while I was grateful to Mari for lending me her strength—and that she wasn't anywhere near Brownlok—I kind of wished it had been Chiara who had taken my hand, magic or no.

Mari had woken before us and was already next to Brownlok, chatting as he pulled food from a pack for her.

I rubbed my hands over my face, brushing as much sand

away as I could. Barely any magic, no knife, no way to protect any of them. And what Chiara said had stuck in my head—why would Redalia be so insistent about finding the Black Library?

Brownlok had said his life force had been tied to Graymere's. Maybe Redalia's had been, too. She'd managed to ensnare an entire kingdom within a few months; I shuddered to think of the damage she could do at full strength.

We continued our march, me at the front, Brownlok by Mari's side, Redalia watching us all from behind. I imagined the point of her blade digging into my back with every step.

And then, subtly, the landscape shifted. Instead of crumbling ledges and lines, everything softened. Rounded. The blood on the key dried, and I nicked the side of my finger again. A small cut, yet it didn't heal. Not for a long time.

Chiara stayed at the back of our group of four, with Enzo. She'd gotten quiet again. Like she'd been at the palace. And I didn't know how to fix it.

"What is this place?" I whispered to Jenna, who trudged a step behind me. More red stone giants rose around us, like those by the stairs at the cliff, with bulbous heads and misshapen rocks stacked one on top of the other. No life grew here. No scurrying animals. The hard layer of earth underneath the red sand was cracked like a loaf baking too long. The key shifted to the left, and I followed it up a narrow incline, two huge stone formations on either side.

Jenna glanced at the mages behind us. "I don't know. But it's only affecting those with magic. Chiara and the crew don't seem to feel it."

I licked my lips and pulled myself up the last bit of rock, the sand staining my fingertips red. "But you feel it, too, right?"

She laughed mirthlessly. "I feel it, though less than you probably." Her finger with the ring fluttered.

My brow furrowed. "It's magic that's draining our magic?"

She shrugged. "I don't know, but you look awful, and I know I don't feel as bad as you look."

I chuckled. "Aw, thanks."

"Hafa taught me about a balance in the land," she continued. "That the Wild was created inadvertently because of the magic Kais used to enchant the borders of the Ice Deserts. Perhaps this place is to balance out *both* those lands—a land of *no* magic, a land that drains it."

Balance.

The Medallion, connected to the ring as it was, didn't work like it used to. Or maybe it couldn't work like that here—maybe all it could do was point, and only with the strength of my blood to aid it.

Either way, I really hated this place.

"Any idea why Redalia would be so insistent on finding the Black Library?" Jenna asked, brushing her hair over her shoulder.

"A few. But I hope I'm wrong."

She rubbed her temple. "What are you thinking?"

I sighed and kicked a small rock out of our path. "Brownlok told me his life force had been tied to Graymere's, and that his threads of existence started snapping when you killed Graymere."

She spun her ring around her finger. "So you think Redalia's not at full power? That some of her magic left with Graymere?"

"Yes." I turned slightly right, following the key's arrow

through two bushes too small to offer any shade. "If Graymere's artifact carries *his* power, and *he* had a piece of *her* power, she'd want it back. But it's more than that. If Graymere tied their lives together . . . what if the Black Mage did as well? What if, by obtaining the crystal staff, Redalia would not only regain her *full* power but also that of the Black *and* Gray Mages?"

"Glaciers," she muttered. "We can't let her get that staff."

"Or the sword," I muttered back.

The land sloped down, then back up in the distance, like a huge bowl. A bowl filled with twisting red monsters turned to stone. If I looked at them straight on, they didn't move, but from the corner of my eye, as we walked the path the key marked, they seemed to shift and turn.

"Look!" one of the crewmen shouted. "Water!" A clear pond shimmered to the right of the path. The man broke off from the group.

"Wait!" his captain called, but the man didn't heed him.

He sprinted behind one of the formations. I froze. He didn't appear again. He should have been *right there,* but he was just . . . gone.

"Stay on the path," Jenna murmured, rubbing her stomach. We edged a little closer to each other.

"We need food," the captain said to Redalia. What he didn't say—our need for water—screamed loud in the silence. "We've followed you through this forsaken land long enough. You promised us magic."

"Your reward is coming," she said. She looked like she'd rather send us each down a different path to see which of us didn't die. "We may rest for a moment."

The crew grumbled, but I didn't catch more than the occasional *magic, treasure, worth it.*

Redalia studied Brownlok and Mari much too closely.

Brownlok wouldn't be able to hide Mari's ability much longer. He looked half-dead as it was. When Redalia found out about what Mari could do, would she kill Brownlok and use Mari to amplify her magic? Or help Brownlok create his artifact?

Assuming we weren't all already dead, maybe we could make a move if the mages fought with each other.

The crewmen opened their packs and pulled out their rations, passing some to the mages. My stomach cramped, and my fingers could barely grip the artifact.

"Oy," I called. "We can't march with nothing but red dust in our bellies."

The captain threw us a few strips of jerky, which landed in the dirt. Chiara's hand on my arm kept me from retaliating. She picked up the jerky and blew the dirt off them, then handed one to Jenna and Enzo to share. She tore our strip in two and handed me a portion.

As she tore off a chunk of her meat with her teeth, Chiara said, "We need more time. A plan. Something."

I ate the gamy strip of what I suspected was actually salted leather, not meat. I coughed—too salty.

Jenna spit sand from her mouth. "We can't leave the path. Can't go on a fake path."

Enzo tapped his fingers against his leg. "Could we overpower them?"

I shook my head. "Tried that."

"We can't just let them into the library," Enzo said with a frown.

I shook my head again, harder. Redalia would win, even if she wasn't at full power.

"Enough," Redalia said, her arms folded under her cloak despite the heat. Didn't she feel it? Wasn't her magic draining into the cracks in the earth like mine?

"Once we get to the library, find a way to get Mari away from Brownlok, and keep her away," I said, standing.

"And don't let them get Graymere's sword or the Black Mage's crystal staff," Jenna whispered.

She whispered to Enzo and Chiara what she and I had talked about as we started forward again, winding around the red, twisted soldiers guarding the invisible path, all the way up the other edge of the bowl.

I kept my eyes down, my mind empty. An empty mind meant no panic. No arches, no tombs.

This couldn't be the end.

Jenna grabbed my arm. "What are you—" I started, but the sight before me cut off what little air I had to spare.

A massive mountain of red rock stood before us, its top flat as though it'd been lopped off with a sword. Massive, intricately carved doors nestled in the mountain's face stood at least ten times as tall as me. Two rows of sand monsters in two straight lines guarded the path to the doors, sentinels long forgotten, their faces and limbs washed away with time.

The Black Library.

For centuries, the legend had grown and shifted among my people. And now, here I was, standing in front of it. A desert stretched between us and the doors, empty of life, of tree or bush or animal, preserved perfectly in its barrenness.

We wouldn't win this. There wouldn't be a last-minute escape. No way to charm or cheat our way out, no way to avoid the crash at the bottom of the free fall.

Chiara climbed up next to me. "You're doing it again," she whispered.

"Doing what?" I asked, dragging my gaze from the doors to her.

"Taking responsibility for other peoples' actions. Stop it." She stared straight ahead, shoulder to shoulder with me. "Chin up," she whispered.

Hearing her echo my own words, words I'd never said to her but I'd said to Jenna countless times, hit me hard. We were close, but not dead yet.

I grinned. It was fake. She knew it. I knew it. But if she needed me to smile, I would. And if there was any way to keep her alive, to keep them all alive, I would.

The captain pulled his sword and pointed it at Redalia. Like he meant to attack her with it. His men set down their packs and pulled their weapons.

Surely . . . surely they weren't *that* ice-headed to think *they* stood a chance against Redalia and Brownlok?

The captain sneered at her. "You stay here. I don't trust you not to knife us in the back while we collect our treasure."

Redalia held her hands out in submission. "You may take whatever you want. Just remember—the staff is mine."

Jenna and I exchanged a glace. She *did* want the staff.

Brownlok rolled his eyes at her show, and I was inclined to

follow his lead. But the captain, blinded by thirst or the heat or a massive amount of stupidity, shouted, "We've made it! Come on, men, our reward awaits!"

And with that, he and his men, all covered in a thin layer of red dust that stuck to their sweaty faces, took off running toward the massive doors.

"Wait!" Enzo bellowed, but the men kept running. "Come back!"

Redalia folded her arms, her eyes gleaming under her cowl. Brownlok watched her, not the men, and my stomach sank. I racked my mind, but couldn't figure out why Redalia would be pleased these ruffians were about to invade—

Chiara grabbed my arm and squeezed, muttering a line from the poem. "'You will find what you seek behind the falling door.'"

The waterfall but also—

Oh, glaciers.

A loud rumble shook the earth, and a great crack rent the air. The two massive red doors, with all their intricate details, tipped forward as if a giant invisible hand had flicked them. The crewmen skidded to a halt. They tried to scramble away, but the rows of red rocks *moved*, blocking their path to the sides.

I wanted to divert my gaze but couldn't. Chiara pressed her face into my shoulder. I wrapped my arms around her.

Their screams were cut off. Silenced with the crash of the doors onto the desert. A great gust of wind, with biting grains of sand, whirled into us, knocking me back a step.

I coughed and wiped the sand from my face as the dust settled. My stomach rolled and churned. I wished I'd closed my eyes.

"I didn't realize it was magic," Enzo muttered. "I've never

seen so much of it before. I thought"—he coughed and wiped at the sand coating his face—"I thought it was the heat shimmering in the air."

Jenna held his arm. "They wouldn't have listened to your warning anyway."

No wonder the mages had kept the crew with us—to carry supplies and test the enchantments around the library.

"Excellent," Redalia said gleefully. "We are weeding out the weak and useless quite a bit today, then, aren't we?" She looked us over. "Who's next, I wonder?"

Where the doors had been, smooth rock now mocked us. At the base, a smaller door was cut into the rock. Normal-sized, with no adornment or etchings, from what I could tell from this distance.

"He can see magic." Brownlok nodded toward Enzo. Mari trembled next to him, her hands over her eyes.

I glared at Brownlok, and he stared back at me. He'd helped when I was outnumbered. Been kind to Mari. His lips twisted to the side, and he rested a hand on Mari's shoulder. She immediately threw her arms around him and pressed her face into his side.

Brownlok startled at the contact, frowning at Mari, but patted her back gently.

Redalia raised one perfectly shaped brow and studied Enzo like the next specimen she was about to gut. "Then perhaps he can get through the enchantments."

My voice stuck in my throat. I couldn't watch Enzo fall victim to whatever traps had been laid centuries ago. Chiara had nearly drowned in *sand*.

Jenna stepped forward. "I can get through the enchant-ments," she said with a frown, her fists pressed against her legs. She swallowed. "The artifact my father gave me—the sword—protects me from magic because I'm an heir of Hálendi."

My eyes fell to the ground and I held Chiara closer. Jenna was lying. It was the ring that protected her. Redalia studied her, and the air seemed to solidify as we waited. Would she believe Jenna? Would she give her back her sword?

Finally, with a great exhale, she nodded to Brownlok, who unsheathed Jenna's sword and handed it to her.

"Wait," Redalia said. "Are there more enchantments be-tween the door and here?" she asked Enzo.

"Yes." He studied the land, hands on his hips. "Surrounding the rock towers."

Redalia adjusted her cloak. "Then we all go to the door."

I went to squeeze between Jenna and the mages, but she shook her head and tapped the finger with the ring against her leg. I stepped up to the front instead, letting her stay between us and the mages, and held my hand out for Chiara.

As Brownlok moved to follow, Redalia snatched Mari from him, her fingers digging into Mari's upper arm. Mari yelled and tried to pull away. Redalia jerked her sharply.

"Be still," she commanded. Mari whimpered in her grip. "You're an amplifier, aren't you?" she said with a scary, slow smile.

"Mari, no!" Chiara held her hand out. I held her back, hat-ing myself. But Chiara couldn't do anything—none of us could.

Brownlok glared at Redalia, but gave a tight nod. "Her power has kept me from fading like Graymere within Koranth."

Redalia trailed a finger down her golden dagger. "Do not keep secrets, Brownlok. It doesn't become you."

He bowed his head, his face now a mask of indifference. He hadn't told her about making the artifact. What was his endgame?

Mari stopped fighting, though tears ran down her cheeks in muddy tracks. Chiara sagged against me, shaking. My feet moved like tree trunks had been chained to them. I couldn't do this. Couldn't watch as the mages hurt and killed us, one by one.

"Let's hope you can get us safely through," Redalia sneered to Jenna and Enzo, and Mari whimpered again.

Jenna nodded to me, and I swallowed and took my first careful step into the expanse leading to the door.

"Any clues in the poem about what happens after the falling doors?" I whispered to Chiara, partly to distract her, partly in hopes that she'd think up some way to keep us from marching to our demise. "Say it for me again?"

She repeated it loud enough for Jenna and Enzo to hear as well, but nothing came to mind that would be helpful against rock monsters.

The remains of the huge doors loomed in front of us, edges crumbled from the impact. We climbed up the broken pieces and continued over the cracked surface.

The sun beat against us mercilessly, and the ground shimmered as though we were walking on a cook fire, amplifying and rebounding against us.

The red monoliths stayed in their places. Whether because of Jenna's ring, or the key, or our relationship to Kais, I didn't know.

The next door we'd have to cross had only two markings. There was a circular indentation in the rock, and a slit right next to it, a few inches in length. And even though I faced my imminent demise, a tiny spark started in me.

This was it. The *Mages' Library*—the ultimate treasure. A place of legends and bedtime stories. Stories my mother told often because I'd begged her to.

I caught Chiara watching me, and I lifted my chin—no wink, but I grinned. A real one. This was a place my ancestors had made with Turia's ancient queen. A place no one had found since its creation.

If we were going to die, it might as well be here, and it might as well be big. I'd make sure I took out as much as I could when it was my turn.

Chiara's lips trembled, and she lifted her chin, too.

Jenna's hand paused over the markings. "Any magic?"

Enzo shook his head. There was no handle, no lever, no discernible entry point in the door, just the barest slit forming a rectangle in the wall of rock.

But the circle was about the correct size for the ring and Medallion.

"I think . . ." I swallowed against the sand coating my throat as Brownlok and Redalia pressed closer. "Shall we try the Medallion and ring?"

Redalia's focus barely wavered from the door, but she gave a tight nod.

I rubbed my hand against my trousers, then took the key from around my neck and rested it in the indentation. The chip in the ring aligned with a marking, and what I'd thought were maker marks on the back fit snugly into the rock. Just like a key.

A hiss emanated from the rock, and as I pressed, the key sank deeper into the rock, as if it were clay and not stone.

I held my breath, but nothing happened. At least the door hadn't fallen on us.

"Well?" Redalia snapped, jerking Mari's arm.

I pushed against the wall. That should have worked. The marks on the Medallion . . .

Brownlok stood with folded arms, staring at Jenna.

"She knows," he said.

Jenna bit her lip and closed her eyes. "It's Kais's sword," she murmured.

Redalia drew her dagger and had it at Mari's throat before I'd even blinked. "Do not say his name," she hissed at Jenna.

We all stood frozen, unwilling to move and endanger Mari any further. Jenna went completely rigid, staring at Mari with the knife at her throat.

I raised my hands, palms out. "She didn't know." Though I should have guessed. Redalia had thought I looked like Kais, but never said his name. She'd wanted me, because he'd rejected her.

Redalia lowered her knife, but didn't sheath it.

Jenna shook her head a little, as if shaking away a memory, and slid her sword into the slit in the door.

Nothing happened.

Her shoulders dropped. "I thought surely . . ."

I pulled the sword out and inserted it again. Enzo tried, with the same result: nothing. When Chiara stepped up to it, she gripped the handle and attempted to turn it.

It grated, but she was able to twist the sword all the way around. As she did, the artifacts next to it turned, a small clicking noise marking its progress.

"Glaciers," Jenna murmured, and I nodded in agreement.

When the sword had gone a full circle, the door slid backward, dust and dirt cascading down as stone grated against stone. A whoosh of cool air blasted into my face.

"Mortals first," Redalia said, her dagger resting on Mari's shoulder.

We'd failed.

CHAPTER THIRTY

Chiara

Enzo went through first to scout for more enchantments, then Ren. My heart stopped when they stepped through the doorway into the shadows beyond. Jenna motioned for me to go next.

The wall was at least two feet thick, and perfectly smooth. A cavern opened ahead of us, lit by tiny holes in the ceiling, like stars mimicking the night sky. The cavern floor was smooth, gray rock. In the very center stood a palace with a circular foundation, unconnected to any other part of the cavern. Its walls, carved intricately from the foundation to the top of the domed roof, shone like black glass.

The Black Library.

I'd done it. I'd gotten us to the Black Library. It would have been a thrilling achievement if it didn't also mean our deaths.

We'd almost reached the end of our usefulness.

Ren's hand slipped into mine. The others filed in behind us. A tiny shaft of light illuminated a door in the shiny black rock.

"There are more enchantments between here and the next door. Step where I step, and be careful," Enzo said.

"What are you waiting for?" Redalia asked, delighted. "Go."

We made our way carefully to the door of the library, matching Enzo step for step. This door had only one indentation, small and circular. Jenna pressed her ring into it, but kept the ring on her finger. The door opened with a gentle rasp. We crowded in, the mages right behind us.

Inside was like no library I'd ever seen. One great, circular room rose around us with a huge firepit in the middle. And, odd though it was, a bright fire crackled merrily from the center of the low stone wall containing it. The room was mostly bare of furniture, only a small table near the fire, with two chairs tucked neatly into it.

The walls were made up of shelves. *Filled* shelves. Carved from the same black rock as the edifice, the shelves scaled all the way to the domed ceiling. Scrolls filled one entire section, leather-bound books another, and across the cavernous room, yet another section had been devoted to jars of all heights and widths, colors and clarity, stoppers still in place, as though time hadn't touched this place.

Redalia and Brownlok focused to the left of the fire, on a section holding objects of all types and sizes, everything from a mace to clay pottery to necklaces and jewels. Even a shovel rested against one shelf. And not a speck of dust on any of it.

Should I try to beat them to the shelves? Stay and escape through the door?

Redalia brushed by us, still holding tight to Mari, and the door option fizzled away.

Ren took a few more steps into the room, following the mages, frantically searching for the artifacts that they wanted.

"Where is it?" Redalia muttered. She moved objects on the shelves, starting at the ground and moving upward, growing more and more frustrated. She uttered a word I'd never heard before, and swept her arm across a shelf, scattering its contents onto the floor. A large plate shattered into tiny pieces.

She held Mari tight, her dagger at Mari's neck again. "Come away from the door," she commanded without looking at us, and my feet moved of their own accord, step after step, until I stood a pace away from the fire. The others followed, even Jenna, though I had no idea whether the magic affected them the same way.

My throat ached for water. Everyone scanned the shelves for the staff and sword. I was the only one in the room with no magic. What had I been thinking?

The heat from the fire singed my clothes and hair. Once I realized the magic had released me, I stepped away from it. I caught sight of something—two somethings—resting against the table, leaning against it like someone had left them there but was planning to return.

A long silver sword, and an even longer black staff.

My mouth dried out and my heart beat painfully against my ribs.

Redalia squinted at me, then followed my gaze. I couldn't

even shout a warning, couldn't move. She saw what I'd seen, and glided to the table. She sheathed her knife, picked up Graymere's blade and tossed it to Brownlok, then took the black staff with the hand that wasn't holding Mari.

There was no magical wind, no bright light, but when Redalia laughed in delight, the tiny flicker of hope I hadn't realized I'd been clinging to so desperately went out.

Redalia and Brownlok held more power in their hands than the entire Plateau combined.

"I've done it, Brownlok!" She lifted her face toward the ceiling and inhaled deeply, then faced the rest of us. "Now you will pay for what Kais did to me, to all of us," she said quietly, though one eye twitched when she said his name. Her hair flowed down her back and she glowed with life. "I will kill all of you, and then I'll kill your families. The world will be *mine*."

Mari whimpered at her side, and Redalia grabbed her by the hair. "You want an artifact?" she said to Brownlok. "Go ahead. Kill her with Graymere's sword and take both their powers for your own. We'll be unstoppable."

No.

I tried to leap toward Mari, but my feet wouldn't move. Couldn't. Redalia's eyes found mine, and she smirked.

Mari's brows tipped down, and she grabbed her hair, trying to ease Redalia's grip. Her tears had stopped. She didn't speak to Redalia, but to Brownlok. "Erron . . . you're my friend," she said, her voice hoarse. "You said I was your friend."

He gripped the sword tighter, jaw set. As he held it, he sharpened into focus just like Koranth had.

Redalia laughed. "You know nothing, child. He's waited for this as long as I have." She grinned at him, feral and lust-filled. "You can have *everything* you desire."

"Erron," Mari pled with him as he stalked closer to Redalia. "Wait. Please—"

Redalia muttered a word under her breath, and Mari's voice stopped, though her mouth continued to plead. Brownlok ignored her, studying the long silver blade in his hand instead.

Something flew at him from the side of the library, but it evaporated into nothing with a flick of Redalia's staff. Enzo's hand dropped. He'd thrown something from a shelf.

There was nothing we could do against such power, yet I couldn't let this happen. Not to Mari.

I fell to my knees. "Please, Brownlok—Erron," I cried. "Please, not my sister."

He flinched.

Please.

I couldn't watch. Couldn't turn away from the impending horror. I should never have come. Should have stayed home. I'd be useless, but alive. Everyone would be.

Mari reached out and grabbed the shovel that rested against the shelf, then swung it. Redalia, more stunned at the sudden impact than injured by it, shoved Mari away so hard she slid across the ground and slammed into a shelf.

Mari's chest rose and fell, her wild curls tumbling around her. Brownlok stared at her, impassive, but didn't go after her.

Redalia pressed the staff into the floor, and a crystal embedded in the top—so black I hadn't noticed it at first—began to glow. Rivulets of light trickled down the walls, through the floor, and up into her staff as if she were drawing power from the very stone.

Jenna stared at Enzo, hard, then at Ren. A muscle in Ren's jaw twitched, and he gave a nod. I wished I were against the wall with Mari, somewhere I wouldn't be in the way of whatever they were planning. Because they *were* communicating something, I just didn't know what.

Useless.

My knees shook, and I wished I was wearing a skirt to hide them, to give any semblance of normalcy to these last moments. I wished I had one more minute alone with my friends, my family. But as I scrambled to think of what I would tell them, a small comfort came: they knew I loved them. There was nothing to say that they didn't already know.

Jenna made her move, so fast it took me a moment to realize what had happened. She blinked out of sight as Enzo wrapped his arms around me and pulled me back, diving behind the fire. My skin slicked with sweat almost instantly.

"I lied about the enchantments in the cave," he whispered. "If you have the chance to run and warn the Plateau, take it."

He'd *lied* about—

Jenna blinked back in at the wall, tossing a knife from the shelf to Ren with one hand and swinging the mace at Brownlok—at his sword. Brownlok dodged the blow, twisted, and cut clean through the mace's handle, sending the spiked ball scraping against the floor straight at Enzo and me. I dove one way, Enzo dove the other. A deep trail of gouges marred the floor in the mace's wake.

Jenna went low and drove her shoulder into Brownlok's stomach. Shoved him back, right where Ren was waiting. Ren slammed the hilt of his knife into Brownlok's wrist. The sword clattered to the ground, and Ren grabbed Brownlok, holding his blade against the mage's neck.

Redalia only smirked and pointed her staff at Jenna. Jenna squeezed her eyes shut and held up her ring. Redalia frowned and took the staff in both hands. Jenna's arms shook, and she began to scream.

"You forget that Graymere didn't have his artifact. I have two," Redalia snarled. "You are no match for me. None of you are!"

"Stop!" Ren shouted. "Or I'll kill him!"

Redalia shrugged. "More artifacts for me." She prowled closer to Jenna. But Jenna flickered out of sight. Redalia's face twisted into a scowl. She angled the staff toward me, but then Jenna was there, right next to her, lifting Redalia's gold dagger away.

Jenna twisted the dagger, gripping its hilt, moving to strike. But then she froze. Her eyes widened, and she stumbled away, hand still clenched around the dagger.

Redalia's laugh echoed through the chamber. She lowered the staff so it rested by her side, giving her full attention to Jenna, who was now writhing on the ground, alternating between screaming and moaning.

Enzo lunged toward Jenna. He kicked the dagger out of her hand, and dragged her farther from Redalia, who watched it all gleefully.

"You think you have any hope of survival?" She raised her

hand to the shelves with jars and clenched it into a fist. The jars exploded, filling the air with a thousand scents. The heat of the fire evaporated any liquid before it reached me. "*You* cannot wield *my* dagger."

I inched around the fire. Mari sat up against the shelf, groggy but alive. Enzo held Jenna against his chest. There was nowhere to run. Redalia was willing to sacrifice Brownlok. We had no leverage.

She was right.

In all the stories I'd ever read, good triumphed over evil. But real life wasn't a story. My ending wouldn't be a happy one. And there was nothing I could do about it—I didn't stand a chance against a mage.

I'd lived my whole life being invisible. Fearing to be seen and rejected.

I wouldn't die hiding. Wouldn't run away.

So I stood.

Ren drew my gaze. He always had. He still held Brownlok at knifepoint, despite Redalia's nonchalance. But he stared at the gold dagger on the ground near his feet.

"Oh yes, young king," Redalia purred. "Take the dagger. Now is *your chance.*" She laughed again. "You are always trying to save everyone else, but who, dear Atháren, will save *you?*"

Ren would take the dagger, try to wield it. But he would fail, just as Jenna had. Redalia would kill all of us—if we were lucky—and then she'd leave this cavern and unleash her power on the world.

My father would die without remembering any of us.

Ren stared at the dagger, but Brownlok stared at *me*. His chin tipped down, an infinitesimal nod.

Mari had trusted him. He had to be a powerful mage to have survived so long without Graymere's power keeping him here. More powerful than Redalia?

We had no more options. No more chances.

I willed Ren to look at me, to *see* me. One heartbeat, two, then, miraculously, his eyes found mine. Everything in me said this was the right course, our only hope. And if it was incorrect, well, it wasn't like they could kill us twice. I didn't think.

Let go, I mouthed.

Ren didn't move, though the gold dagger lay so close, taunting him as much as Redalia.

I swallowed and resisted the urge to wipe the sweat running from my hair down my temples. *Trust me,* I mouthed.

Trust yourself, I added silently. He didn't need the Medallion to make the right choice, or any magic to aid him. He was enough, with or without it. I knew it, I only hoped *he* knew it as well.

Then his arms came away from Brownlok, and he stepped back.

Brownlok didn't reach for the gold dagger. He didn't wield it *or* give it to Ren. Instead, he kicked it.

It spun in two full circles as it slid toward me as if on ice, the gold catching and throwing reflected light from the fire. I stopped it with my boot. The details etched into it were more exquisite than any I'd seen, the blade sharpened to the finest point.

Redalia trembled, her face white as she glared at Brownlok. "You would choose these *children* over me?"

Brownlok's impassive face cracked, and his eyes narrowed. "I thought you didn't care."

Ren let out a laugh. "Oh, she cares. She doesn't take rejection well. Isn't that right, Red?"

She slammed the staff into the ground and Brownlok and Ren flew backward, hitting the shelves and landing with a *crack*.

Then Redalia turned to me.

Her eyes were lit with black fire. A slow smile spread across her face and she chuckled, one hand on her hip, the other using the staff to lean on.

"Oh yes, this will be a fair match, I'm sure." She bobbed her head toward me and I flinched, but nothing happened. "Look at yourself. You have no skill to speak of; you're trembling. You are *useless*."

I didn't speak. I couldn't force air into my lungs or unclamp my jaw. Ren pushed himself up—healing, though slowly. Jenna still clutched her arm, Mari crouched next to her, and Enzo stood over them. Weaponless.

Redalia shrugged. "Well? What are you going to do now?"

I took a gasping breath. I wasn't useless—at the very least, I could be a distraction. My hands shook, but I did the only thing I could. I reached down and grabbed Redalia's dagger by the hilt, and held it in front of me.

No one moved. Not Ren or Jenna or Enzo or Brownlok.

The dagger trembled, but not because my hands were trembling—well, not completely. It was *power*. Redalia's power.

And . . . and it didn't hurt.

Redalia growled and wielded the black staff in front of her with both hands.

I pulled my shoulders back to the exact position they'd taken every day of my life. I had no skirt to swish, so I raised my chin instead. "I am *not* useless."

Redalia twirled the staff once, sizing me up again now that I held her dagger.

I swallowed. The dagger didn't tremble anymore. "Believing in goodness and caring about others isn't a weakness. I *choose* to see the good in the world." Redalia advanced toward me. "But you? It doesn't matter how much power you wield, how many artifacts you collect. No one will ever love you. You will always be alone."

Redalia's eyes turned to slits and her nostrils flared. She brought the staff forward and inhaled.

I didn't raise the dagger in defense. I tossed it into the fire behind me.

If Redalia was going to take over the Plateau, she could do it *without* her precious dagger.

The flames licked at the gold plating, and the meticulous designs melted away.

A shock wave exploded out of the fire, but not one of flame or ash or anything tangible. The only one hit by it was Redalia. She held the staff in front of her, but even with its protection, she was blown back three steps.

Ren kicked Graymere's sword at me, and I tossed that in, too.

"No!" Redalia screamed. She lunged at me. I dove out of her way. Ren ran at her from behind, pushing her into the fire, staff and all.

Another explosion tore through the library, and this one knocked me into the shelves. My ribs ached. Everything went black. I blinked, but it wasn't my vision. The fire had gone out.

Then Enzo was there, lifting me, dragging me and Mari toward the door, Jenna limping behind. I coughed. "Wait! Where's Ren?"

Enzo frowned. Didn't stop. "Ren's coming. We've got to get out."

I found my feet and took Mari's hand in mine. The ground shook. The entire library shook. Scrolls, books, and trinkets crashed from their shelves. A dim light shone from the rock itself, getting brighter as cracks formed in the floor like a vase about to crack.

A great chunk fell from the domed ceiling and smashed to the ground, spraying us with tiny shards.

The rock around us dimmed, and even when we made it into the cavern beyond, the ground shook and bits of wall and ceiling tumbled all around us.

"Hurry, Mari." I looked over my shoulder. Enzo scooped Jenna up into his arms and dodged another chunk of fallen rock.

But Ren wasn't behind us.

"Wait, we have to get—"

Enzo pushed me along and Mari pulled, her hand clamped over mine.

A small white rectangle, the door, the only shaft of light, grew as they forced me toward escape.

"Wait!"

Enzo pushed Mari and me through first, then followed with Jenna. He set her down, and Mari helped her while Enzo grabbed me and dragged me from the opening as I fought to go back in.

No. *NO.*

The mountain groaned and shrieked, the ground rumbled. A huge crash rent the air, and then a gust of debris blew out of the entrance, sending me sprawling onto my back. Dust rained down on us, smothering and final.

Ren.

Marko

Marko had been cramped in the tiny cave with Luc and Cynthia for two days while a storm raged. They'd hid in a cellar after the attack on the street, then snuck to the cave later that night.

And while the accommodations were tight, at least Luc and Cynthia had finally stopped bickering. Silence reigned, but that was probably for the best. Marko's head was ready to split open at the slightest sound. No one had to tell him something was wrong. His head hadn't gotten better with the food Aleksa had been bringing them.

And now, Aleksa was late.

Marko stared at the ceiling, as though the entire cliff would swallow them soon.

Finally, light footsteps sounded outside, and a hand rustled the vines covering the mouth of the cave—the signal of a friend entering so that Luc didn't gut them.

Aleksa ducked inside the next moment, an unfamiliar, broad smile lighting her features. "It's safe to come out!" she whispered.

Marko rubbed his aching leg. He was too old to sleep on cold rock, and Enzo still hadn't returned for him. So why was this girl retrieving them, and not his kin?

Cynthia sat up, all traces of sullenness gone. "Really?" she squealed. Marko winced at the sound, but he couldn't begrudge her hope—sitting under solid rock for so long took its toll. But the cave smelled better than the dungeon.

Aleksa darted a glance at Marko, then leaned close to Luc, whispering something in his ear. Luc's eyebrows shot up. "You're sure?"

She nodded and held the vines open. "This way, Your Majesty."

Marko grunted as Cynthia put her hand under his arm to help him stand. The king's first step outside the cave, into the soft yellowing grasses at the base of the cliffs, suffused into him. The sun beat against him, warming him despite the chill wind blowing off the ocean. The sky arched overhead. He'd missed that sky.

"This way," Aleksa said, bobbing her head toward a faint path through the brush.

Luc took Marko under one arm, Cynthia took his other. They walked for a long time, and though stretching his legs felt wonderful, Marko tired quickly and leaned more and more on his friends. Eventually, they entered a city—the same city they'd escaped from, he presumed, though nothing looked familiar.

Only stray animals wandered the streets. Luc kept his hand on his weapon.

"Shouldn't we be on a boat?" Marko finally asked. "The plan was to get to Turia." To safety. But the girl was leading them deeper into Vera. A sound rose then, almost like the waves they could hear from their tiny cave crashing against the shore.

Aleksa looked back with a grin. "That *was* the plan, but as it turns out . . ." She paused as they turned a corner. The little lane fed into a square filled with people, a large wooden stand took up the middle, and a group of soldiers in brown and gold stood atop it. "As it turns out," Aleksa continued, "Turia came to *us*."

Marko's eyes snapped back to the soldiers. Dark hair, olive skin. An old woman with silver hair and deep wrinkles pointed her finger at one of the soldiers like she was chastising him. Something about her felt familiar.

Then the soldiers on the platform shifted, and a woman appeared, deep in conversation with a tall man, pointing out something on a large unrolled parchment.

Dark hair twisted behind her head, a gold scarf wrapped into it. Marko's brows furrowed. That hair—it should be hanging down her back, long and wavy. And instead of a dress, she wore leather trousers and . . . was that armor?

He shook his head, trying to reconcile what his mind was telling him with what he saw. A sharp pain split his skull. The woman turned her head, almost as if she were drawn by his gaze. Locked eyes with him.

Any pain wisped away on the wind. Her features were plain. Average. And yet, she was his *heart*.

She gasped and started toward Marko, and for a terrifying moment, he thought she'd fall right off the edge of the platform, but a soldier took her hand and helped her down. The crowd parted for her, and she ran, stopping just shy of him.

Her brows dipped down and she watched him carefully, a trembling hand reaching partway to him, but hesitant, as though she were afraid to touch him. But he wasn't afraid.

He slipped his hand around hers and drew her hand to his heart. He closed his eyes and inhaled, catching her faint scent, another forgotten memory. When he opened his eyes again, her face was there, like a ghost from his past. He didn't remember their life together, but he knew. He was home.

CHAPTER THIRTY-ONE

Ren

A huge chunk of the cavern ceiling crashed onto the Black Library's domed roof. A crack reverberated through my bones, and the next moment, the entire library collapsed.

Black shards exploded toward us, but Brownlok—Erron—covered us with his cloak, protected us from the worst of the debris.

Five steps from freedom, and the stupid sword was stuck.

Rock screeched against rock, cracking like a spiderweb above us. Like ice over a lake about to break.

"I thought you *didn't* want to die," Erron muttered with a cough, leaning heavily against the wall.

I jiggled the sword and tugged again. *Finally,* it came loose. I jammed it into its sheath on Erron's belt, tucked my arm under his shoulder. "I don't."

I pushed him through the door first, muttering curses about promises and rocks and swords. And then sunlight seared my eyes, and we were out.

A blurry shape flew toward us, a brown smudge in the wash of red. I blinked. Chiara plowed into me, almost knocking us all over, and wrapped her arms around me.

Enzo came and helped me with Brownlok. With Erron. We stumbled away from the mountain as it fell in on itself, piece by piece, until the only thing remaining of the Black Library was a pile of rubble.

We collapsed in a heap, coughing and breathing and letting the sun roast us as the ground shuddered beneath us.

We'd done it. Well, Chiara had.

Jenna hit my shoulder, but her punch lacked strength. She held her right arm close to her stomach. "What took you so long?" she asked, her words a shadow of the shout she probably meant them to be.

Erron lay still, a hand over his eyes. He tried to unclasp the buckle of the sheath, but couldn't manage with his shaking fingers. I carefully unhooked Jenna's sheath from his belt, then handed it to her. "Stupid thing was stuck." The key—the Medallion and ring—rested heavy in my pocket.

Jenna gasped and wrapped her good hand around it. "Thank you, Ren."

Chiara groaned next to me, face ashen. "I didn't get it," she muttered. "I didn't find the artifact for my father."

"You were a little busy saving everyone, so—" I reached into my pocket and pulled out the key, then a white scarf, its pearlescent fibers shimmering. Erron had assured me the small square of cloth was the right artifact. I handed it to Chiara, its power crackling under my fingers. "Erron helped me find it. That's what took so long."

She held the artifact in her hands and tears streaked tracks through the reddish mud on her cheeks. Then she clenched it in her fist and threw her arms around me. I buried my face in her neck and squeezed my eyes shut. She smelled like dirt and sweat and something distinctly *her*. She smelled like *life*.

She sniffed loudly and wiped her nose along her filthy tunic, but her face was already smudged. I laughed and brushed my thumb against the dirt.

She shook herself, then turned to Erron. Mari sat next to him, holding his hand. His skin had lost all color, and his breath rattled in his chest.

"What does it do?" Mari asked, staring at the cloth.

"Heals," Erron said.

Mari squeezed his hand and smiled up at us. "Erron saved us—now we can save him!"

She didn't know about her father. None of us had told her.

Chiara held the artifact to her chest, hesitating. But then she held it out to Brownlok. "She's right."

I swallowed hard. I'd never known someone like her, hadn't known people like her existed.

There were no birds to make sounds, no critters scratching against rock. No wind, even.

Brownlok folded Chiara's hands back over the scarf. "Thank you, but no. It would take all of its powers to heal me. You have a greater need awaiting you."

Mari sniffled. "Well, what about wintergrain root? Yesilia says that will heal anything."

Brownlok chuckled, ending in a dry cough. "It's not poison that's killing me, little one. It's my past." He patted her hand. "I've lived a long time. It's okay."

Chiara folded the scarf gently and put it in her pocket. "Thank you," she whispered to him.

Mari sniffed, wiping her nose with the back of her hand. "Stay close to me, then. Maybe it won't hurt as much."

I stood, then helped Enzo up. "Thank you for getting them out."

"You're thanking him for leaving you behind?" Chiara said with a dark look at her brother.

Enzo rubbed the back of his neck. I held my hand out to him. "I asked him to take care of all of you. And he did." Enzo took my hand and we shook. I wouldn't worry about Jenna in Turia anymore.

Enzo and I helped Erron up, and Chiara and Mari helped Jenna. We were a ragged bunch, but we were alive.

We finished off the food and water in the packs the crewmen had dropped, then trudged through the endless red sand, retracing our steps long into the night. The key didn't work anymore. Jenna said she felt the difference too—the artifacts and magic felt *quieter*.

The red sand still drained my energy, but not as much as before. I wasn't sure whether it was because I had reason now to hope or whether destroying the Black Library had something to do with it, but either way, I'd take it.

We followed Chiara's map through the gorge and faced the moonlit expanse of desert between the mountains and cliffs.

"If the key doesn't work, the enchantments shouldn't, either," I said.

Enzo nodded. "I don't see anything."

So we walked straight through, stumbling over sagebrush and snake holes. Jenna was weak, but not worsening. Brownlok staggered next to me, my arm under his shoulder, Mari on his other side. I wasn't sure if he appreciated me dragging him out of the cavern—his face was frozen in a grimace.

A hand slipped into mine.

"I know it's not as good as Mari's, but you look like you're going to fall over."

I grinned down at Chiara as best I could. "You're wrong," I said to her. "Your hand is every bit as good as Mari's."

She'd stood against a mage with nothing but her courage and her kindness. She believed in me. She trusted me.

I wasn't sure how I'd be able to leave her when the time came to return to Hálendi.

Chiara walked the smallest fraction closer to me and I leaned into her. I couldn't help myself. She studied the map in the faint light. "We should reach the cliffs soon. We can camp for the night, climb down in the morning, and rest again, if we need it."

My lips tipped up. I could get used to this new, commanding Chiara.

Behind us, Jenna muttered a curse.

Her hand appeared normal, yet she said it felt as though it were on fire. And there was nothing I could do. Not yet, anyway, not when I was so empty myself. But I knew my sister well enough to know she didn't need an apology or explanation.

"If you'd just let me heal you," I told her in a singsong voice, "you could stop cursing like a blacksmith."

She grunted and cursed again. "You can heal me once your skin isn't so gray."

I shrugged, though she knew I knew she was right. I had no idea how much magic she'd need from me, and especially now with Chiara's hand so snugly in mine, I didn't really want to die.

We reached the cliffs with a few hours of night left, so we curled up in a pile of limbs, too exhausted to care that the ground was hard and oddly cold. I never thought I'd miss the suffocating heat.

The sun rose eventually, as it always does, and we slowly— ever so slowly—made our way down the stairs. We drank our fill from a spring that bubbled out of the cliff and rifled through the packs the crewmen had left because they hadn't wanted to carry them up. There wasn't much, but we gathered what we could.

When we rowed out of the inlet to where waves crashed against our tiny boat, the only thing that met us was an endless horizon. The boat we'd sailed here in was long gone.

So we did the only thing we could. We stayed near the cliffs and rowed.

And rowed.

And

rowed.

We took turns sleeping and rowing through the night and the next day as well.

"We all know you're faking it, Erron," I said to break the silence and to take my mind off the aching muscles in my back and arms and legs. "So how about you take a turn rowing?"

He didn't think I was funny, and Mari glared at me for a solid hour afterward. But Chiara pursed her lips to keep a smile at bay and stared at the coast. Always at the coast.

Dros, the westernmost city of Riiga, came into sight, but we voted to continue on—we needed a way up the cliffs.

Clouds blacker than I'd ever seen tumbled toward us from the horizon. If we didn't make it back before the clouds reached us, there was a good chance we'd end up smashed against the cliffs.

And I really looked forward to telling Edda I *had* gone to Riiga . . . and destroyed the Black Library.

Instead of more teasing, I asked Erron to tell us about his life, about his home before the Black Mage had changed everything. A distraction—for him and for me.

And he did. He spoke of his family, of his sister. How close they'd all been but also how poor. Redalia had been the one to find him, to recognize his abilities, and he'd been so taken with her beauty and power and confidence, he'd followed her on promises of a better life for his family.

But then his family died while he was away training. Casualties in a war he was supposed to protect them from.

Erron stopped talking, and I didn't prod. Mari took up the narrative then, of things she'd overheard in the palace, of what such and such noble had said when they thought she wasn't paying attention or couldn't understand. She had all of us in stitches, laughing so hard I thought we'd tip right into the ocean.

My hands were the only ones not blistered, so I took more than my fair share of turns at the oars. By the time the first signs of Vera came, I was ready to never set foot in a boat ever again.

We tied off at the first dock we came to, Chiara guiding us. I asked her where she'd learned about the coast of Riiga, and she just shrugged and said it had come up in her studies. I vowed to shake the hands of each of her tutors.

"We get to the cliffs and climb to Turia, yes?" Enzo asked. The thought of climbing yet another cliff made me want to vomit.

"What about King Marko and the others?" Jenna asked.

I helped everyone off the boat one by one, then scrambled up. "Aleksa knows how to keep them safe. And the sooner we get to Turia, the sooner we can recruit help."

Chiara and Mari nodded their agreement, and we started toward the city. The docks were mostly empty, which was good since we really couldn't hide our presence anyway.

"What are you doing?" Jenna asked with a nod to the oar I still held. She leaned heavily against Enzo, one hand cradled against her stomach, though her coloring had improved.

I shrugged and pointed the oar toward the city rising before us. "I'm not about to walk into that city without *some* kind of weapon."

Jenna opened her mouth, then closed it and shrugged. "Yeah, good idea."

As we walked the main path from the dock into the city, everything was . . . different. The streets were cleaner, there were actually people out and they looked . . . happier. As we passed, they stopped whatever task they were about—laundry or cleaning or crafting something—to stare at us. But not in fear. In awe.

"Are you seeing this?" I whispered to Chiara as we passed yet another family sitting outside mending clothing despite the incoming clouds.

She nodded. "What could have changed?"

The death of Redalia, for one.

But this, this was like a blanket of fog had been lifted from the city.

Pattering feet approached from around the corner. Someone running. I stopped and held the oar in both hands. But it was Aleksa who sped around the corner, dressed like a princess, of all things. She caught sight of us and barreled past me, throwing her arms around Chiara.

"Oh! I'm so glad you're back! And alive!" she said, her face buried in Chiara's shoulder.

I was glad about that as well, though maybe not in that order.

"I wasn't sure what to tell your mother, and she's been so worried—we all have, but—"

Chiara's head jerked back and she held Aleksa at arm's length. "My mother? What does she have to do with—"

Aleksa's eyes widened and she grabbed Chiara's wrist, dragging her down the alley she'd come from. "Your mother. She came."

"Our mother is *here*?" Enzo asked from behind them.

Aleksa grinned. *Grinned.* At a stranger. "Brought her whole army. Hálendians, too," she said with a nod toward me. "Janiis *didn't* get married—he couldn't find Redalia and drank himself into a stupor for days. Queen Cora overwhelmed the guards at Rialzo and marched her whole army down the cliffs. Swept right in and surrounded the palace, and penned in the soldiers on the beach. There was nothing Janiis could do but submit."

We turned another corner, and the palace rose in front of us, the long road to the doors edged with white tents and soldiers milling about. But not many.

"Where are all the soldiers, then?" I whispered as we started down the road. "This isn't enough to lay siege."

Aleksa beamed. "That's just it. Queen Cora swept the city, offering aid to anyone who would stand with her. And most every single Riigan stood with her, including most of Janiis's army. Even his own court defected when they saw the people support her. I was standing right next to her when she approached Janiis. She said, 'One thing my husband always says: When you don't take care of your people, your people don't take care of you.'"

"Way to go, Cora," I muttered. I flicked Aleksa's very fancy cloak, which was fastened over one shoulder. "Dressing to your new station?"

She sucked in a long, shaky breath and smoothed her hands over her dress. "I've asked Cora to assist, for a little while. But . . . they want me to take over in Janiis's place. Those who'd been under Redalia's spell said he was no longer fit to rule after welcoming a threat like that into the palace."

Chiara hugged her. "You'll be wonderful."

She would. "Building a kingdom from the ground up isn't easy." I stared at the sea. I'd have to go back and face my kingdom again. Face my father's tomb.

"I'll send you advice when I figure it out," Aleksa said with a shrug.

I bit my tongue to keep from laughing out loud. "You do that."

A few soldiers rose to stand when we passed. Whispers rippled ahead of us, and soon every soldier stood at attention.

We marched to the palace, the only sound the endless waves crashing against the shore as black clouds swirled over the city. The wide doors opened onto the grand ballroom-turned-foyer as the first raindrops fell, and Aleksa told the maid who greeted us to run and fetch the queen.

"But my father," Chiara whispered to Aleksa, "is he well? Did he make it into Turia?"

Aleksa shook her head. "There was a storm, and then your mother arrived. He's here, resting. Yesilia and your mother are taking care of him. Of everyone. Your mother sent all the mercenaries home, started projects in every part of the city—to feed those without food, to clothe those who need extra help before the worst storms arrive, crews to repair buildings. Everything."

Mari glowed with pride. "Our mother is the best."

I chuckled as servants rushed around, all busy with some task that I was sure wasn't for the luxury of the nobility. "She really is."

A door banged open at the other end of the massive room, and Queen Cora, her cream-colored gown flowing behind her, sprinted across the polished floor. Chiara, Enzo, and Mari took off to meet her, and she tackled her children in a hug, all of them falling to their knees in a tight embrace.

Jenna leaned against me and threaded her hand through my

elbow. A sense of peace washed over me, one I hadn't felt in a long time. Not since Jenna and Father and I had been together at home.

Even though our parents were gone, and even though Hálendi and her troubles awaited me, everything would work out. Not because I would take care of it all myself, but because there were good people in the world, people who cared about others and lifted each other up. People who trusted and loved.

Chiara turned her head and our gazes tangled. Her eyes glistened with unshed tears, a smile I hadn't ever seen before lighting her face. A smile without worry, without self-doubt.

Erron sighed next to me. I extended my arm to him. "Well, come on, Erron. I still owe you for helping me out against those mercenaries. Let's find you a bed to die in."

He grunted and rolled his eyes. "If I'd known how annoyingly cheerful you are, I would have let them kill you."

I smirked. "No, you wouldn't have."

He paused, and his eyes found Mari. He gave a slight nod. "No, I wouldn't have."

The queen and her children finally pulled themselves together and approached us. "Thank you for returning to us whole," the queen said, and pulled Jenna into a tight hug.

When she released my sister, she grabbed my shoulders. "Edda said I could borrow some of your soldiers. I hope you don't mind."

I choked out a laugh, a shaky feeling passing through me that felt suspiciously like relief. It was over. It was really over. "No, Your Majesty, I don't mind at all."

Then she pulled me into a fierce hug. I squeezed my eyes

shut at the unfamiliar, unexpected contact. She didn't let go. I didn't know if she sensed how badly I needed a mother's hug, but she held on for a long time. Tears tracked down my cheeks and I squeezed her right back.

When she released me, I wiped my cheeks with the back of my hand, and she nodded once. "Thank you," she whispered.

"And who are you?" she asked Erron.

He shifted under the weight of her gaze, like a boy in trouble. I put my arm under his shoulder to support him again, then said, "This is Erron. A friend."

Cora nodded to him, and Mari wrapped her hand in Erron's, though her shoulders slumped alarmingly and dark circles left grooves under her eyes.

"You need to rest," Erron murmured to her.

She shook her head, and her curls didn't bounce like they usually did. "You need me."

He smiled a little. "I'll be okay while you rest."

She frowned. "You won't be okay if you die."

Erron's lips pursed in a smile. "Death comes to everyone. It's my turn."

Mari shook her head harder. "Yesilia will be able to help you. Mother says she's looking after Father. She can look after you, too. Promise me," she said, her fierce eyes trained on his. "Promise me you'll stay alive until she can help you."

He held her gaze and gave a solemn nod. "I will do my best."

Chiara took Mari's and Enzo's hands. "Can we see Father? Is he . . . is he any better?"

Cora put her arm around Mari and guided them toward

the door she'd come from. "Will you come as well?" she asked Jenna, Erron, and me.

There was so much I wanted to say to Chiara, but now wasn't the time. My legs shook, and I was still holding the ridiculous oar. Erron leaned heavier against me.

"You go," I said to Jenna, nodding her on. "I'll look after Erron."

The others hurried across the ballroom, while a boy came and led us down a nearby hall to a chamber for Erron. I helped him lie down, then slouched into a chair by the bed, stretching my legs out in front of me.

"You don't have to stay," Erron said. His voice had turned paper thin.

I tipped my head against the back of the soft chair. Riigans knew the value of a good chair. I'd have to commission one to take home with me. "I don't mind staying. As long as you stop yapping. I'm tired."

Erron coughed out a laugh, and his eyes fell closed. I hoped he would keep his promise to Mari. But if he couldn't, I didn't want him to be alone. Not after what he'd done for us, for the entire Plateau.

I kicked my boots off and settled in as best I could, the oar on the floor beside me, not a rock or speck of red sand in sight. I'd find a bed and sleep. Soon.

CHAPTER THIRTY-TWO

Chiara

"Father, you must accept," I said again, holding out the silvery-white scarf.

Yesilia sat by his side, silent. Everyone else, besides Ren, stood behind me. I sat at the edge of my father's bed holding his hand. His coloring had improved, and his grip was strong.

Everything I'd done—sneaking out of the palace, putting myself and everyone else at risk, the crewmen's deaths, Cris—all of it had been for him.

He . . . he *had* to let it heal him.

"My heart remembers what my mind does not, carina," he said. "I am not in pain, and Yesilia is helping me." He squeezed my hand. "Perhaps this Erron Brownlok needs another chance."

Another chance. I couldn't force my father to accept the gift. And yet, his decision felt right, no matter how much it hurt.

I kissed his cheek. "Are you sure?"

He nodded. "I'm sure."

Mari and I left and went to Erron's room. It was small and unadorned, but boasted a large window overlooking the ocean. The rains had come, pounding against the cliffs and against the palace.

Erron stared out the window as his chest rose slowly with each gasping breath. When we entered, Ren sat up in the chair near the bed, oar by his feet. Mari sat by Erron and took his hand.

Erron had seen me more clearly than anyone ever had. And it was as though he'd wiped mud from my mirror, allowing me to see myself as well.

"Do you want a second chance, Erron?" I asked when I reached his bedside.

He frowned at the scarf I held out. "Your father?" he whispered.

I pressed the scarf into his hand. "He said you deserved a second chance. He's healing. He'll be all right." Erron coughed, dry and rattling. "I think you deserve another chance, too."

"How . . . how does it work?" Mari asked.

Erron's fingers could barely grip the delicate fabric. "Need . . . healer. . . ."

"Me?" Ren asked, scooting forward.

Erron's eyes fell closed. "Transfer its power into me."

Ren frowned, but sat on the edge of the bed next to Mari. "I'll try."

I didn't have magic; I wasn't needed here. But Erron shook his head at me. "Stay." I went to the other side of his bed so I wouldn't be in the way, and took his other hand. "Pure heart is the strongest magic of all. You helped me remember something I never thought I'd forget."

His hand was so cold in mine, so insubstantial. Would the artifact be enough? "What's that?" I asked quietly.

He sighed. "That I don't want to disappoint my little sister."

I squeezed his hand gently and swallowed hard. "She'd be proud of you right now."

Ren placed the scarf on Erron's chest, then put his hands over it. Mari put her other hand on top of his.

They closed their eyes, and for a while, nothing happened. Then, ever so slowly, like a flower blossoming in spring, life flowed back into Erron. His skin returned to its normal hue, his breathing evened out. Even his eyes were less sunken.

I watched Ren carefully for any sign of fading, but he remained healthy, whole, until he blinked his eyes open. I set Erron's hand on his stomach. The scarf had turned from pearly white to gray.

Ren stood and adjusted the blanket over Erron. "He'll probably need to rest," he told Mari. She nodded silently. "I'll find you some scones, shall I? They dip them in sugar here."

Mari perked up. "Yes, please."

He leaned close as he passed me, holding the now-gray artifact. "If there's anything left in this, I'd like to see if I can use it to heal Jenna's hand." I nodded, and he left for the kitchens, squeezing my shoulder on his way out.

"You're going to stay?" I asked Mari.

"Yes. I don't want him to be alone if he wakes."

I stood. "How did you know he could be trusted?"

She set her chin in her hand, her elbow resting on the bed. "He didn't dismiss me because I'm little. He listened to me."

"Well, you're a good judge of character," I said, and hugged her tight.

"We all are," she said. "We get it from Father."

My lips trembled, but I twisted them into a smile. She was right.

I wound my way to my room and fell into bed, intending to take a short nap. I slept through the night and into the next morning. Exhaustion still laced through my bones, but my mind was awake, so I dressed.

I spent time with my father, holding his hand, answering any questions he had for me. He asked about what I liked and disliked, what my favorite books were, anything and everything to get to know me once again.

I also spent time with Aleksa and my mother in the throne room. My mother had transformed it into a command center worthy of any general's tent. Tables had been set up along the walls, with a Riigan and a soldier seated at each. Runners came and went all day, and my mother and Aleksa made decisions on how best to support and help the people with what they needed.

At home, my mother had always stayed busy, but I'd never seen her with such fire in her. Aleksa told me she'd never seen a more fearsome sight than the queen of Turia marching into the city, a banner of gold behind her catching the last rays of the sun, calling for vengeance on anyone who'd harmed her family.

She'd arrested the council, tossed Janiis into his own dungeon to await trial for when a new council had been formed, and razed the labor camps within a *day* of arriving. And though it had taken time to amass her troops at the base of the cliffs, there were so many Riigans willing to help, it was an easy matter to capture those few who remained loyal to Janiis.

I watched the whole process in the throne room, taking notes in a new book. Writing thoughts, ideas, plans for the future.

Every now and then my mother or Aleksa would ask my opinion. And I was surprised to find I always had one.

One thing I knew, *this* is what I wanted. I wanted to help people, to find the good and support it.

"Ahem." A tall, blond man knelt in front of me, white streak prominently displayed. "Her most illustrious princessness wouldn't happen to have time to walk with a lowly servant, would she?"

"What?" I laughed. It had been less than a day since I'd seen Ren, yet I'd *missed* him.

"It was what Mari suggested I call you." He shrugged.

Why had he been talking to Mari about me? I took Ren's hand and waved to my mother, who watched us carefully with a look only a mother can give.

"Hurry," I whispered to Ren. "Or she'll start questioning *us*."

He laughed and pulled me out of the throne room, down stairs, all the way to a familiar hallway near the bottom of the palace. We passed the dark doorway and the guard stationed in front. Janiis was behind it somewhere, getting a taste of his own dungeon. I couldn't believe my mother had sentenced him to wait there until things could be sorted out, but she'd said, with a cold fury burning in her eyes, that he deserved the time—to consider all he'd done, and, more importantly, all he hadn't done.

Ren didn't stop until we reached the wide windows at the far end. The ocean stretched out in front of us, a bank of dark clouds swirling over the shore. It had stopped raining for the moment, but it would come again soon.

We stood side by side, watching the ebb and flow of the ocean, the constant motion permeating the silence with peace.

"Your mother is terrifying," he finally said.

I snorted. "You have no idea." He focused on the waves, and I focused on him. "I'm sorry about Cris," I whispered.

He turned to me. I wasn't sure if it was the clouds outside or something else, but his eyes had never been so blue.

"Why are you sorry? He almost killed you."

I lifted a shoulder. "I'm sorry you lost your friend. I'm sorry I distracted you when he . . . when he—" I couldn't finish. My adventure, my impetuous decision to go after my father had come at a heavy cost—more than just Cris's life.

Ren's fingers brushed down my arm and tangled with mine. That spark I'd first felt from him so long ago reappeared with a vengeance.

"I tried to give him a chance to change. Twice. Because of you." He brushed his thumb along mine, sending trails of shivers up my arm. "I lost my friend long ago. But someone once told me I shouldn't take responsibility for other people's choices."

I squeezed his hand. "That person sounds wise."

His smile, which had been growing, dropped away. "I want

to—" he started, then licked his lips and swallowed hard. My heart started beating faster. He was nervous. We'd survived so much in the past few days, what could he be nervous about? But his unease triggered my own. "Listen, I have to put my kingdom back together." He looked at the ground and dug the toe of his boot into it. "And I didn't want to leave without . . ."

Oh. I only kept from slumping out of habit. He was leaving.

"I . . . of course," I said, unsure what else to say. We hadn't come to any agreement. Hadn't expected to *have* a future, let alone spoken of it. He had his kingdom to take care of.

Disappointment draped over me like a wet cloak. But I'd watched my mother single-handedly put Riiga back together; I would accept whatever he had to say with grace, and I would find a way to help others, to find the good and encourage it.

But, glaciers, would I miss him.

Ren shook his head. Gripped my hand tighter. "No, what I meant to say is, I have to put my kingdom back together, but"—he swallowed again, and my heart leapt at that three-letter word—"would you consider coming with me? As ambassador for Turia?" He rubbed the back of his neck with his free hand. "There's so much to be done, and I could really use your help."

The spark was back, lighting a fire in my veins. "Me?" I asked. "You want *me* to serve as Turia's ambassador?"

He stepped closer, taking my other hand as well, our fingertips brushing, igniting the space between us. "I want you," he said, his midnight-blue eyes deeper than the ocean and brighter than the moon. "Only you. I trust you."

He leaned in slowly, asking permission. I tilted my chin up, my eyes falling closed, and his lips brushed mine. Once, twice. A kiss that said we had time. That we'd figure things out.

"Are you sure you should be kissing your ambassador?" I asked, breathless. He rested one hand on my cheek and ran his gaze over my features like a caress.

"Yes, I'm absolutely sure I should."

I bit my lip. "As long as you don't kiss *all* your ambassadors."

His laugh echoed down the hall. I'd need to write about that sound later. Because that was a sound worth remembering.

ACKNOWLEDGMENTS

Drafting and revising this book as a pandemic ravaged the world wasn't ideal. But as I spent more time with my family, without running from one thing to the next, I got to experience the best parts of life and remember that together, we can do anything. That it's because of our relationships and the people around us that life is beautiful and joyous and sometimes hard—but also worth it.

This sophomore book tested and stretched me. I hope it was an escape for you, a reminder that you are more incredible than you give yourself credit for. Also, start giving yourself credit. It's okay. I give you permission, if you need it.

My agent, Laura Crockett, has proved time and again that I am the luckiest author ever to be her client. Thank you for your guidance and support. And thank you to Dr. Uwe Stender and TriadaUS for your tireless efforts on behalf of this tired author.

I was lucky enough to have two fantastic editors championing this book. Thank you, Monica Jean, for helping me dig deeper into the heart of this story, and Hannah Hill, for your editorial genius and support in getting this book into the hands of readers.

The team at Delacorte Press is phenomenal at what they do: Beverly Horowitz, Tamar Schwartz, Cathy Bobak, Nathan

Kinney, Drew Fulton, Kris Kam, Megan Mitchell, Megan Williams, and Jenn Inzetta. I maintain that copy editors are actual wizards, so thank you to Heather Lockwood-Hughes for transforming my words into magic.

Thank you to Alex Dos Diaz, who managed to outdo himself with this cover art (a feat I didn't think possible), and Regina Flath, for designing another stunner.

My writing groups have supported me through everything and deserve all my thanks: Becca Funk, Camille Smithson, and Spring Rain; Adelaide Thorne, Amy Wilson, Brittany Rainsdon, Kelly Hamilton, Marla Buttars, Rebekah Wells, Sarah John, and Amber Goodson.

A special thanks to Lisa Johnson for designing the coolest website ever and Diane Thompson for having all the best ideas and enough talent to pull them off; and to the Clawson Family for the research trip and a much-needed escape from the weight of real life.

To all the friends and family and readers who reached out to say *Shielded* made a difference in your life, thank you for taking a chance on me. I wouldn't be here without you.

My extended family need an extra heaping of credit: Dan, Kathryn, Claire, Oscar, Ivy, Lisa, Jacob, Ruby, Violet, Pearl, Mike, Amy, Jack, Holly, Diane, Mark, Dianne, Breanne, Kevin, Luke, Sam, Emma, Kyle, Aaron, Rowan, Alder, Collin, Berlyn, Christian.

My mom and dad always believed in me, and I wouldn't be anywhere close to where I am without them.

To Cameron, thank you for proving the dedication in

Shielded right again and again. Cason, Siena, Milo, and Bex: I didn't think I could love you more, but I do. Every day.

To you, dear reader, you are strong enough. You are enough right now, and you'll be enough in the future. Keep trying. Keep believing. Keep making a difference that only you can make. I believe in you.

ABOUT THE AUTHOR

KayLynn Flanders is a graduate of Brigham Young University with a degree in English Language and a minor in editing. When she's not writing, she spends her time playing volleyball, reading, and traveling. She lives in Utah with her family and thinks there's nothing better than a spur-of-the-moment road trip. She is the author of *Shielded* and its sequel, *Untethered*.

KAYLYNNFLANDERS.COM
@KAYLYNNFLANDERS